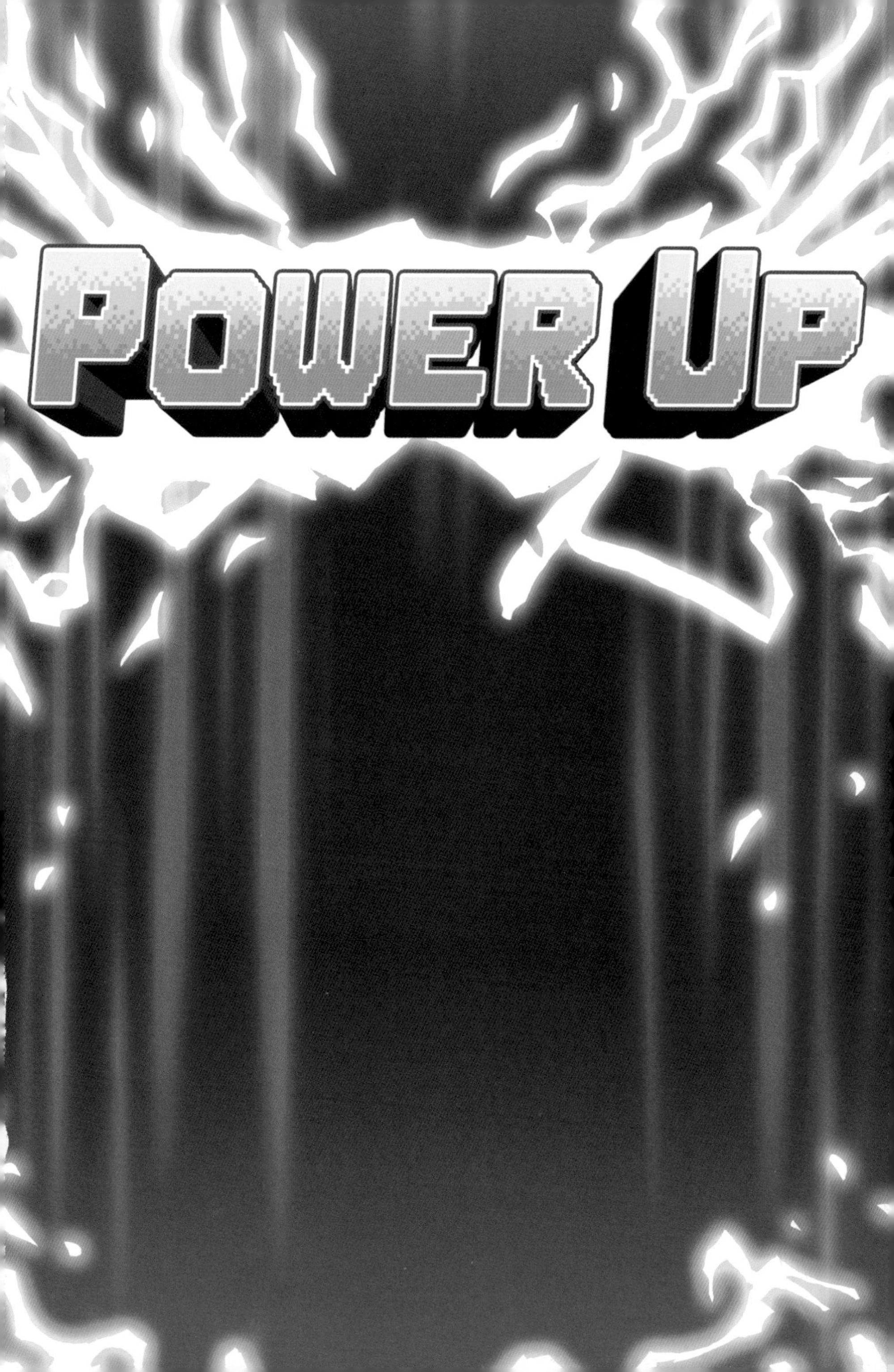
POWER UP

ETCH IS AN IMPRINT OF
HOUGHTON MIFFLIN HARCOURT PUBLISHING COMPANY.

HMHBOOKS.COM

THE ILLUSTRATIONS IN THIS BOOK WERE CREATED DIGITALLY.
THE TEXT WAS SET IN A FONT BASED ON DARNELL JOHNSON'S HANDWRITING.

COVER DESIGN BY PHIL CAMINITI
INTERIOR DESIGN BY PHIL CAMINITI
COMPOSITION BY LIZ CASAL

ISBN: 978-0-358-32571-0 HARDCOVER
ISBN: 978-0-358-32565-9 PAPERBACK

MANUFACTURED IN CHINA
SCP 10 9 8 7 6 5 4 3 2 1
4500813726

FOR ROY, NORA, AND THOMAS—THREE KIDS RAISED TO BE GAMERS —S.N.

TO ALL THE YOUNG ARTISTS, DON'T BE AFRAID TO GROW IN FRONT OF THE WORLD. —D.J.

POWER UP

WRITTEN BY
SAM NISSON

ILLUSTRATED BY
DARNELL JOHNSON

HOUGHTON MIFFLIN HARCOURT
BOSTON   NEW YORK

CONTENTS

PUSH

CHAPTER 1

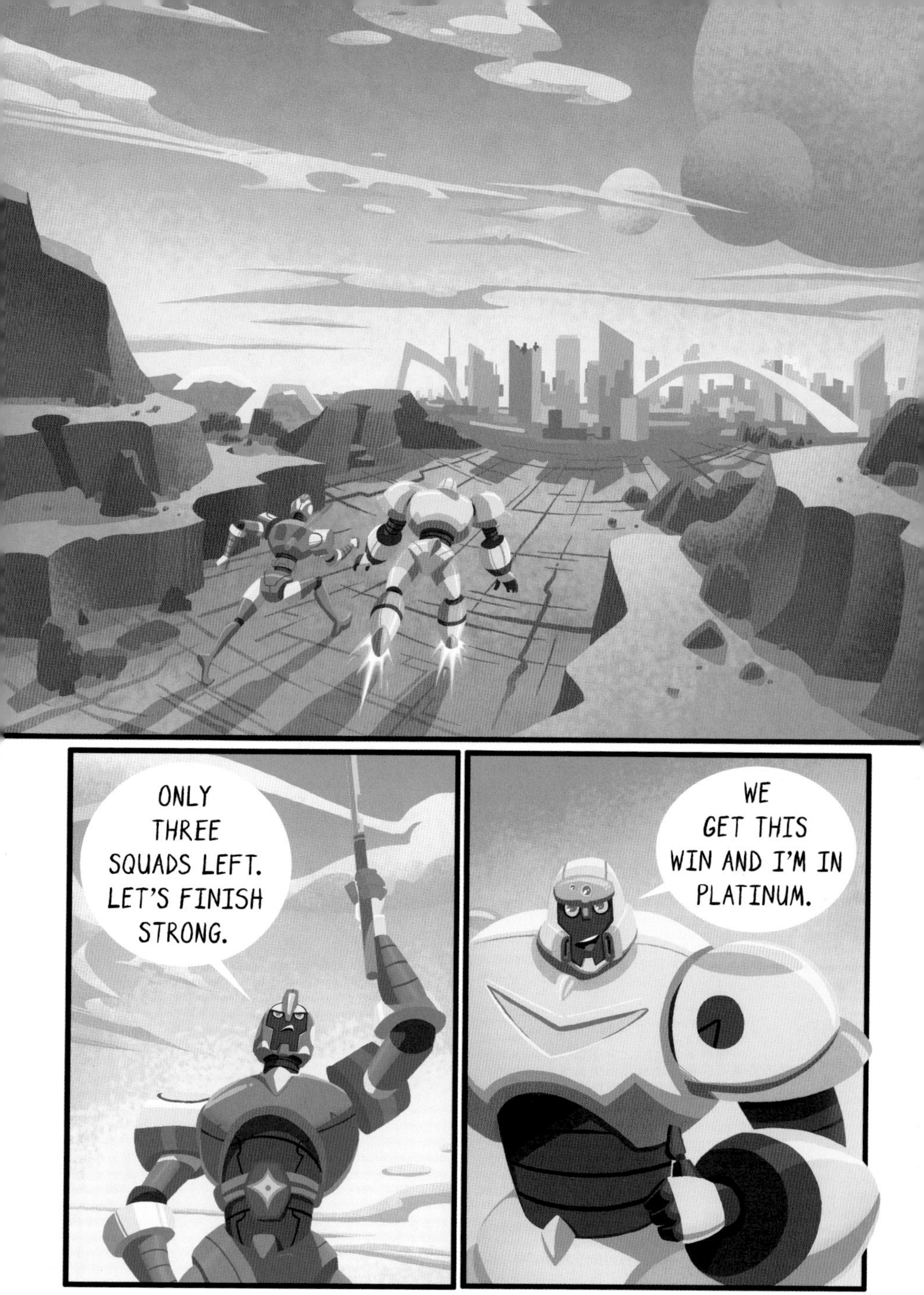
ONLY THREE SQUADS LEFT. LET'S FINISH STRONG.
WE GET THIS WIN AND I'M IN PLATINUM.

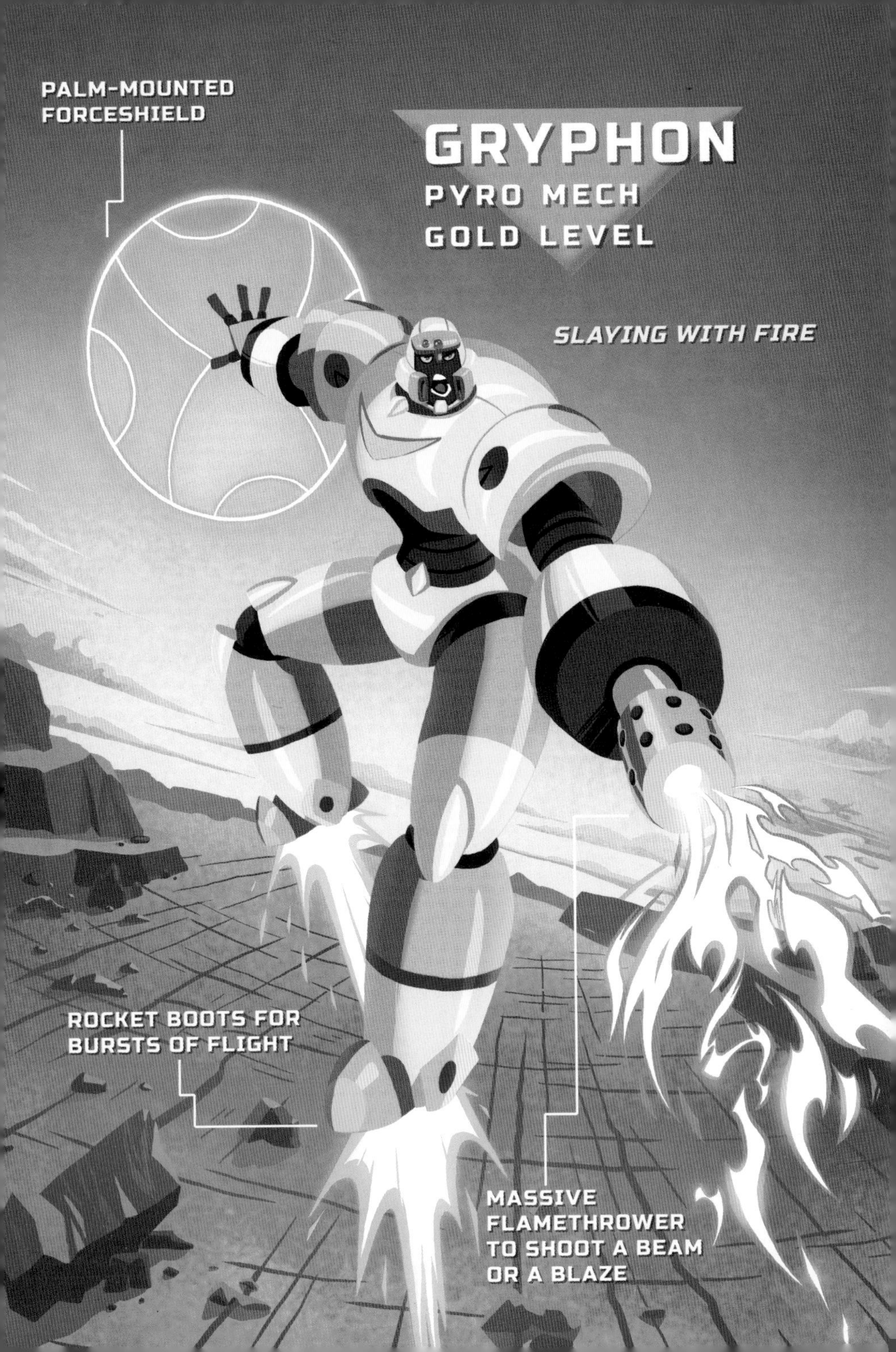
PALM-MOUNTED FORCESHIELD
GRYPHON
PYRO MECH
GOLD LEVEL
SLAYING WITH FIRE
ROCKET BOOTS FOR BURSTS OF FLIGHT
MASSIVE FLAMETHROWER TO SHOOT A BEAM OR A BLAZE

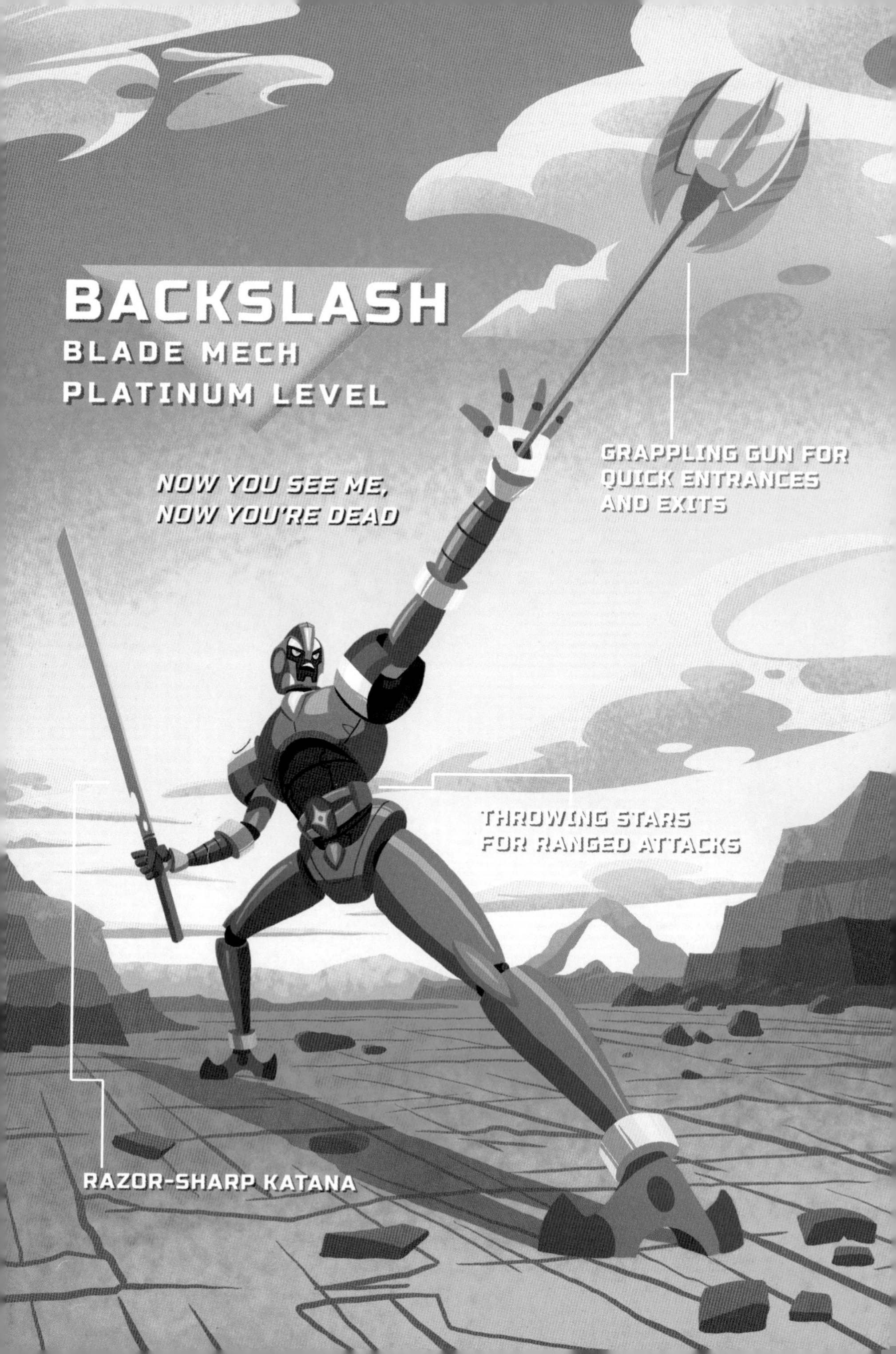
BACKSLASH
BLADE MECH
PLATINUM LEVEL
NOW YOU SEE ME,
NOW YOU'RE DEAD
GRAPPLING GUN FOR
QUICK ENTRANCES
AND EXITS
THROWING STARS
FOR RANGED ATTACKS
RAZOR-SHARP KATANA

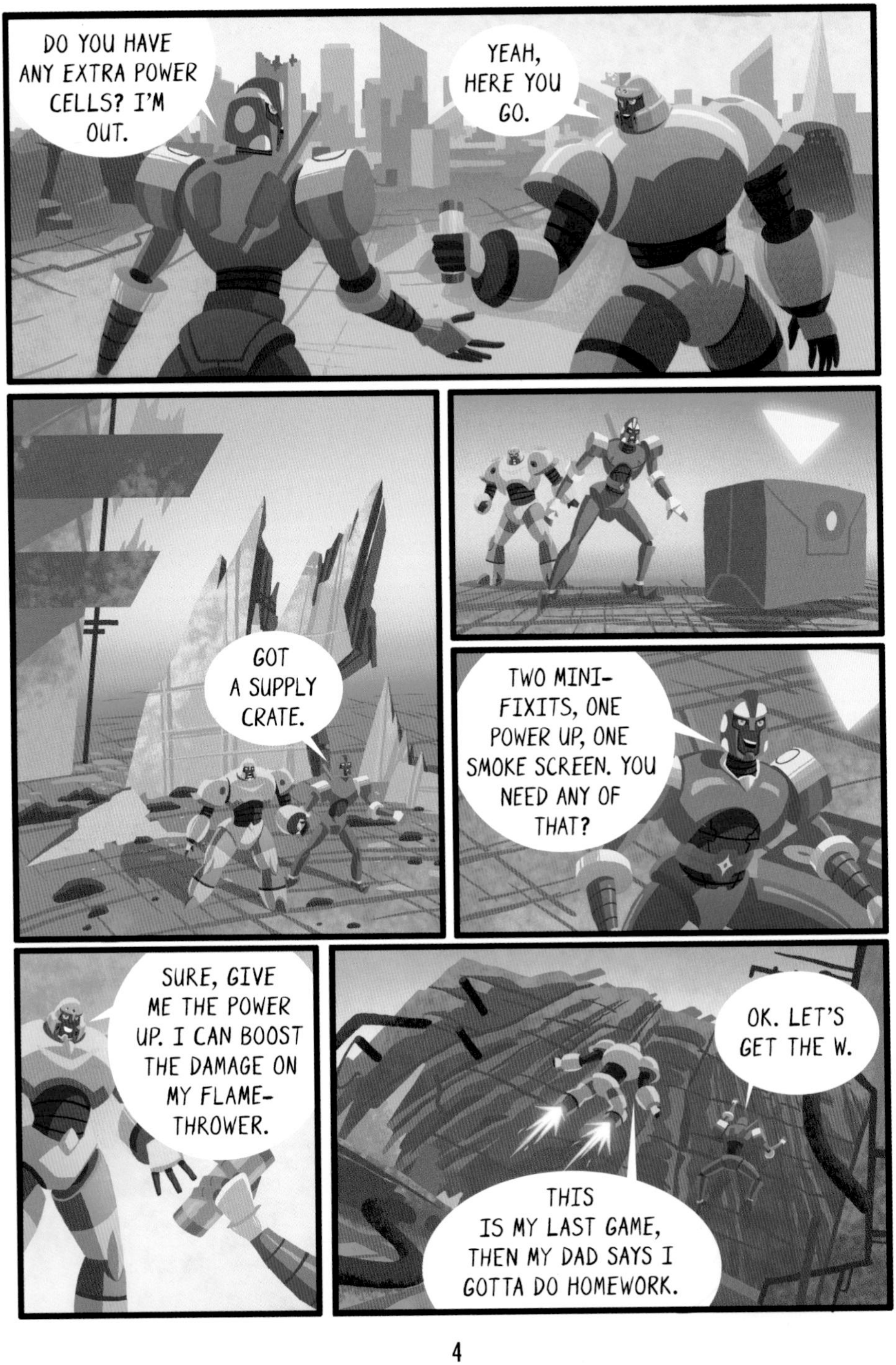
DO YOU HAVE ANY EXTRA POWER CELLS? I'M OUT.
YEAH, HERE YOU GO.
GOT A SUPPLY CRATE.
TWO MINI-FIXITS, ONE POWER UP, ONE SMOKE SCREEN. YOU NEED ANY OF THAT?
SURE, GIVE ME THE POWER UP. I CAN BOOST THE DAMAGE ON MY FLAME-THROWER.
OK. LET'S GET THE W.
THIS IS MY LAST GAME, THEN MY DAD SAYS I GOTTA DO HOMEWORK.

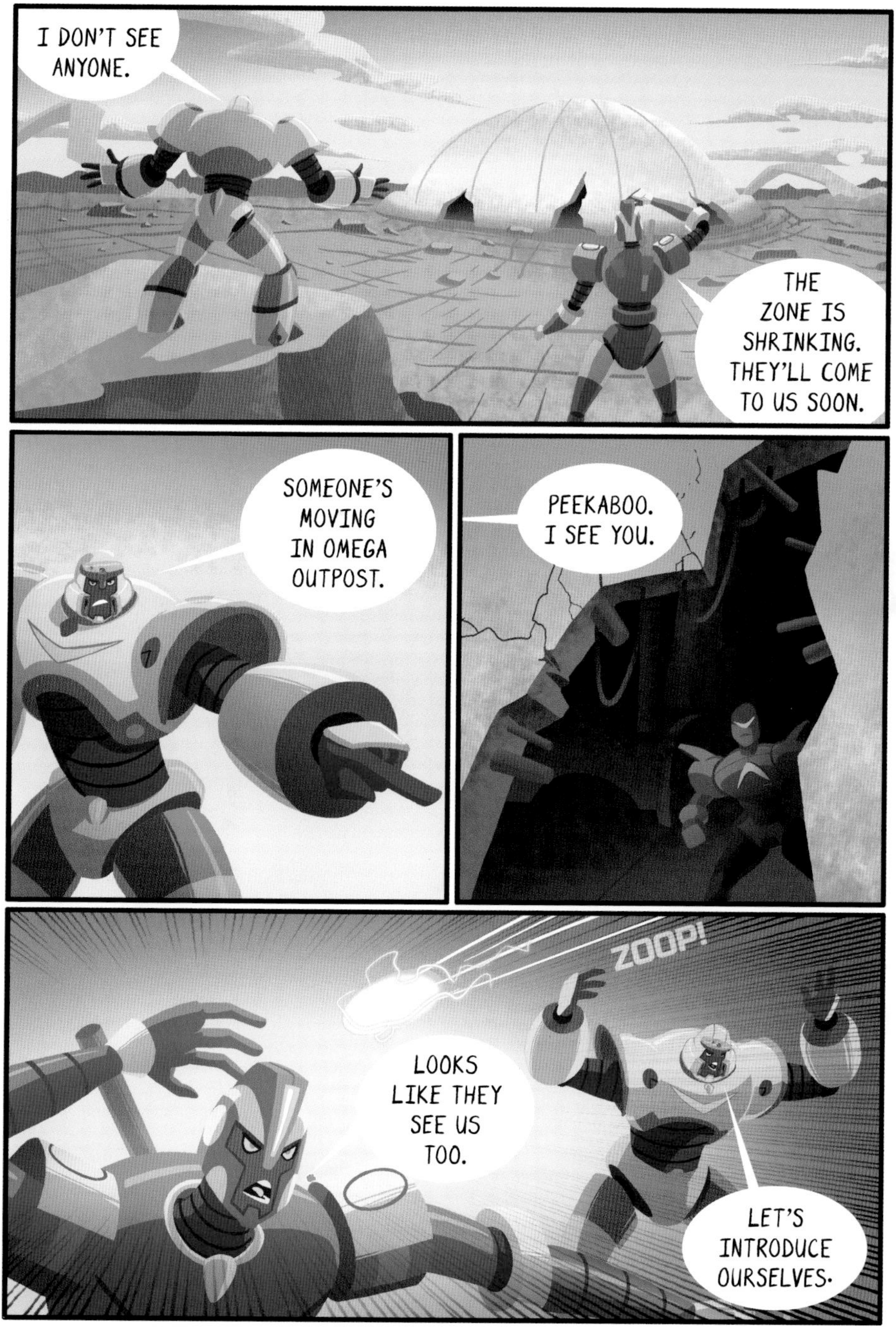
I DON'T SEE ANYONE.
THE ZONE IS SHRINKING. THEY'LL COME TO US SOON.
SOMEONE'S MOVING IN OMEGA OUTPOST.
PEEKABOO. I SEE YOU.
ZOOP!
LOOKS LIKE THEY SEE US TOO.
LET'S INTRODUCE OURSELVES.

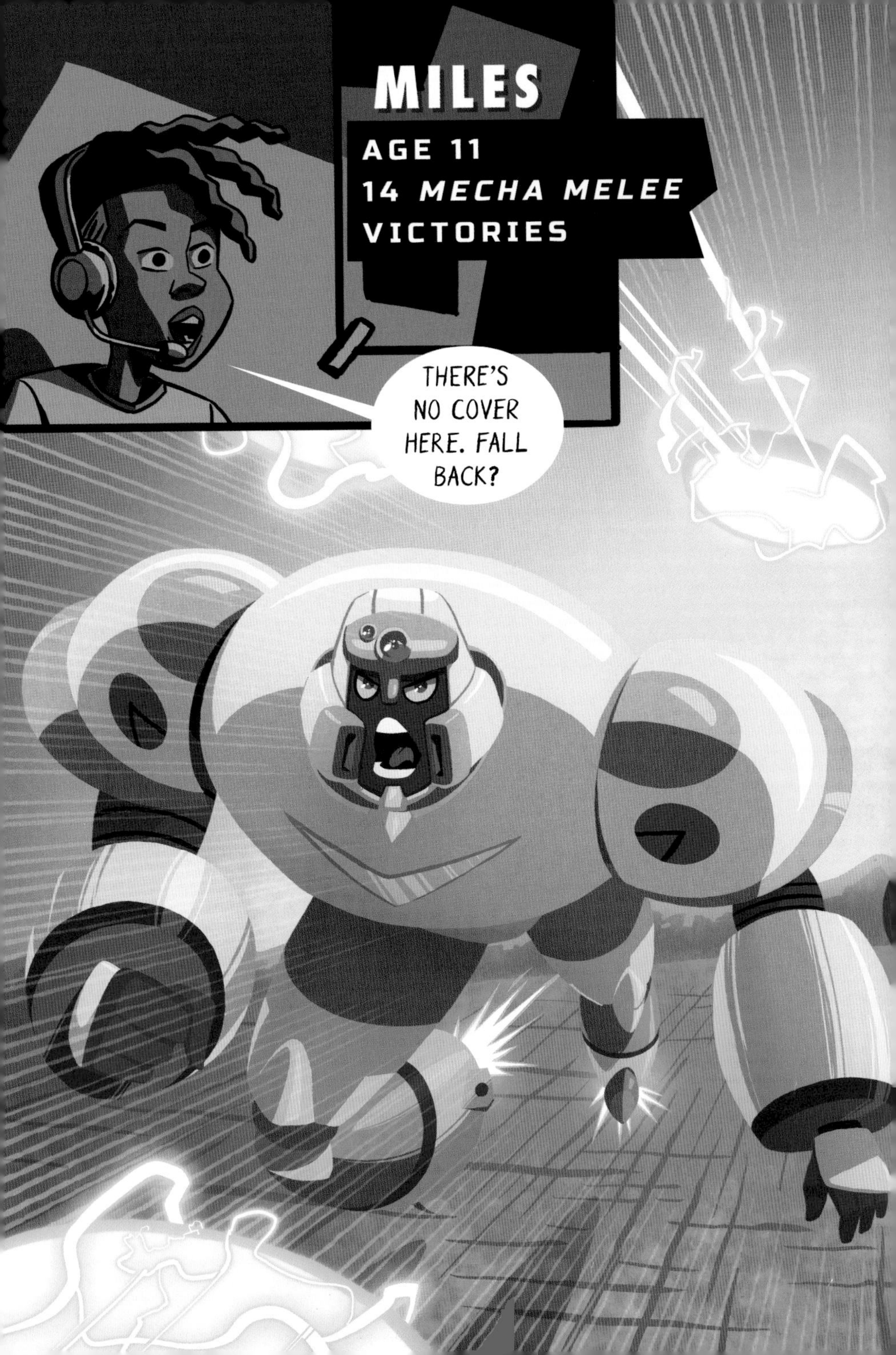
MILES
AGE 11
14 *MECHA MELEE*
VICTORIES
THERE'S NO COVER HERE. FALL BACK?

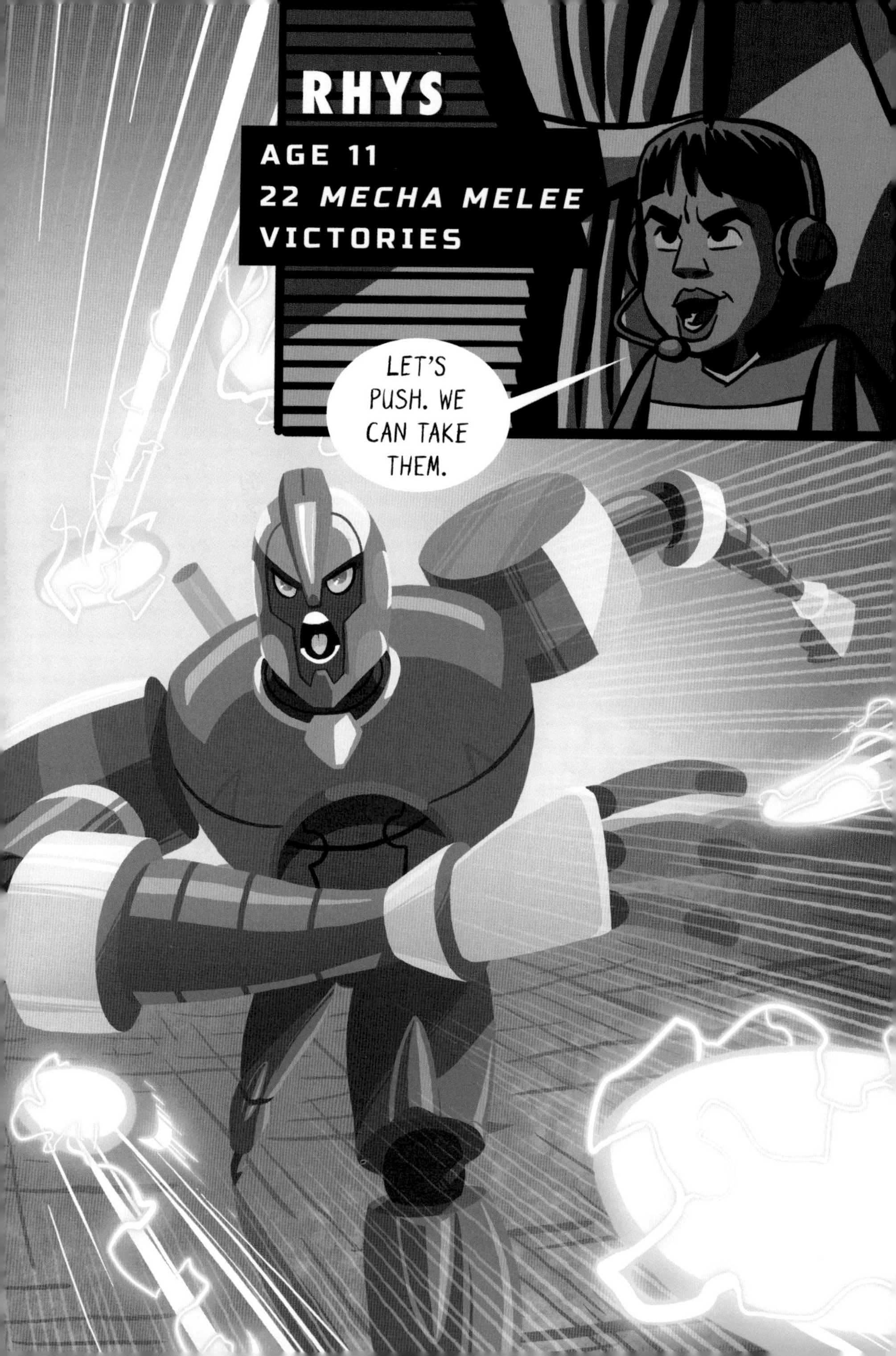
RHYS
AGE 11
22 *MECHA MELEE* VICTORIES
LET'S PUSH. WE CAN TAKE THEM.

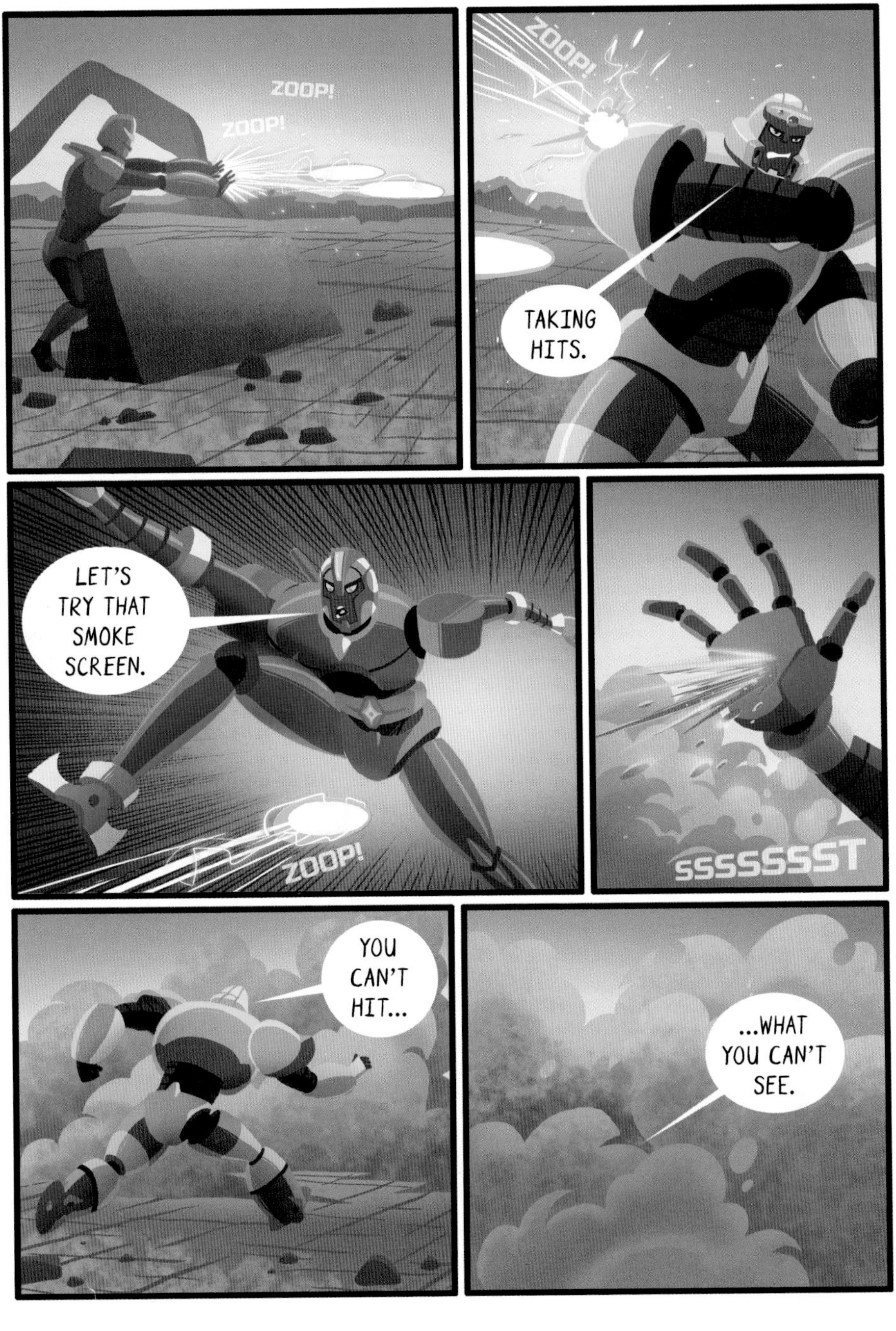
ZOOP!
ZOOP!
ZOOP!
TAKING HITS.
LET'S TRY THAT SMOKE SCREEN.
ZOOP!
SSSSSSST
YOU CAN'T HIT...
...WHAT YOU CAN'T SEE.

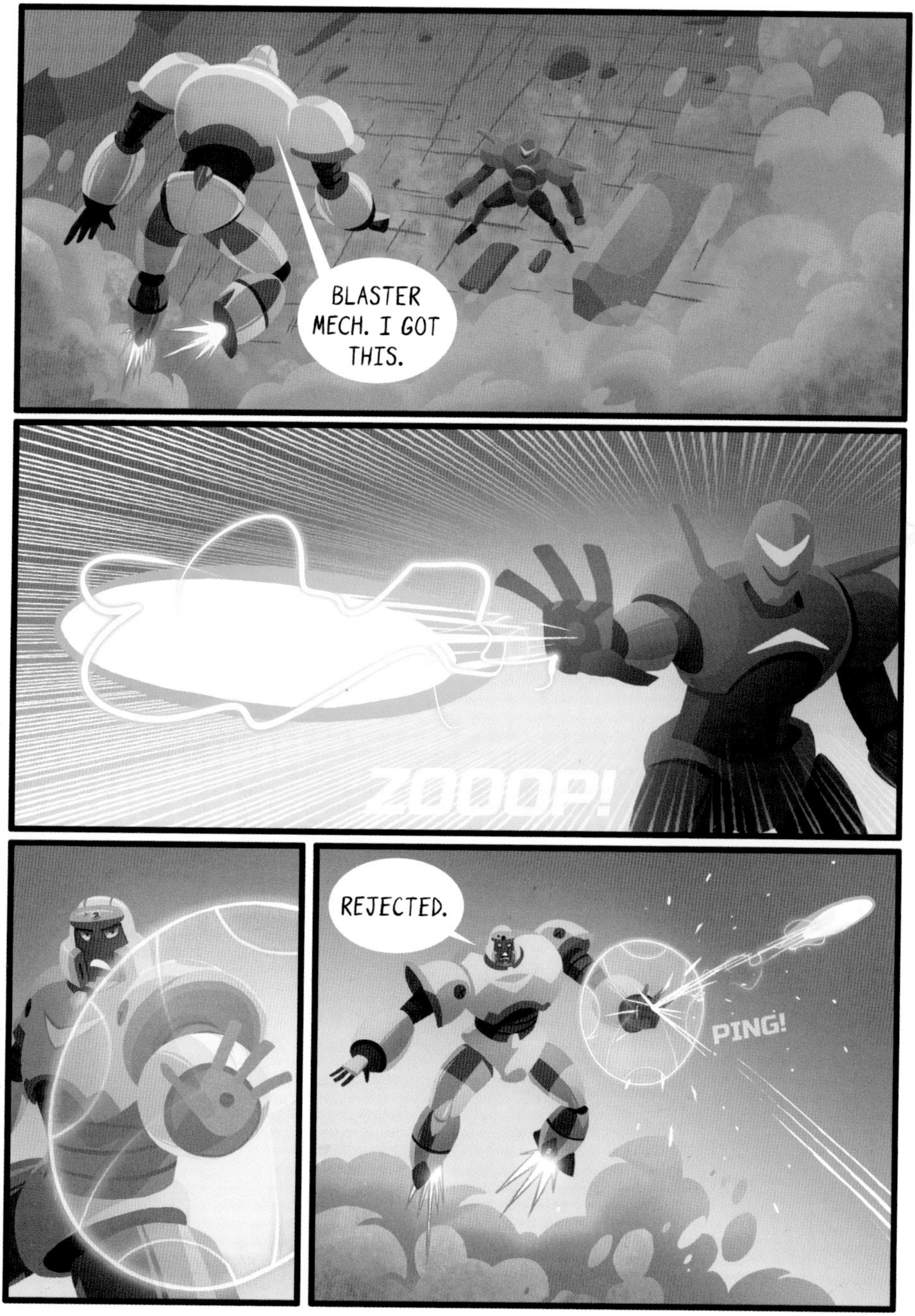
BLASTER MECH. I GOT THIS.
ZOOOP!
REJECTED.
PING!

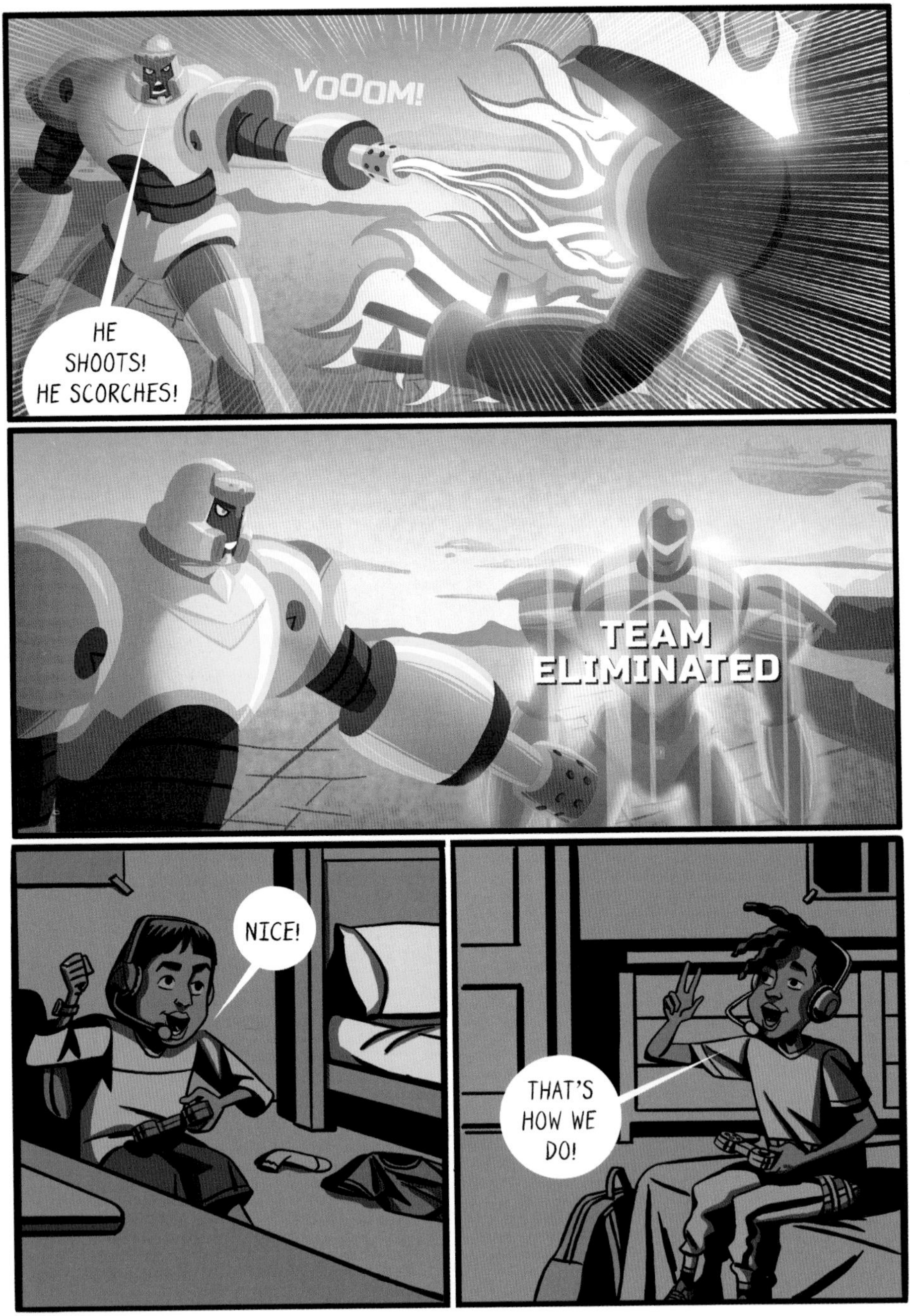
VOOOM!
HE SHOOTS! HE SCORCHES!
TEAM ELIMINATED
NICE!
THAT'S HOW WE DO!

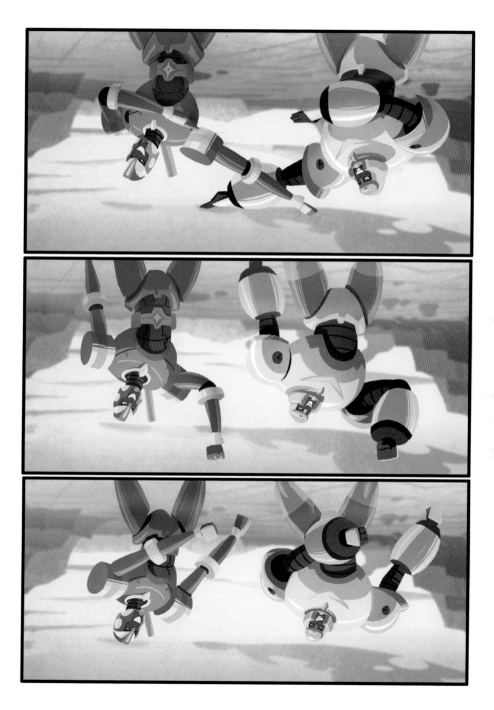

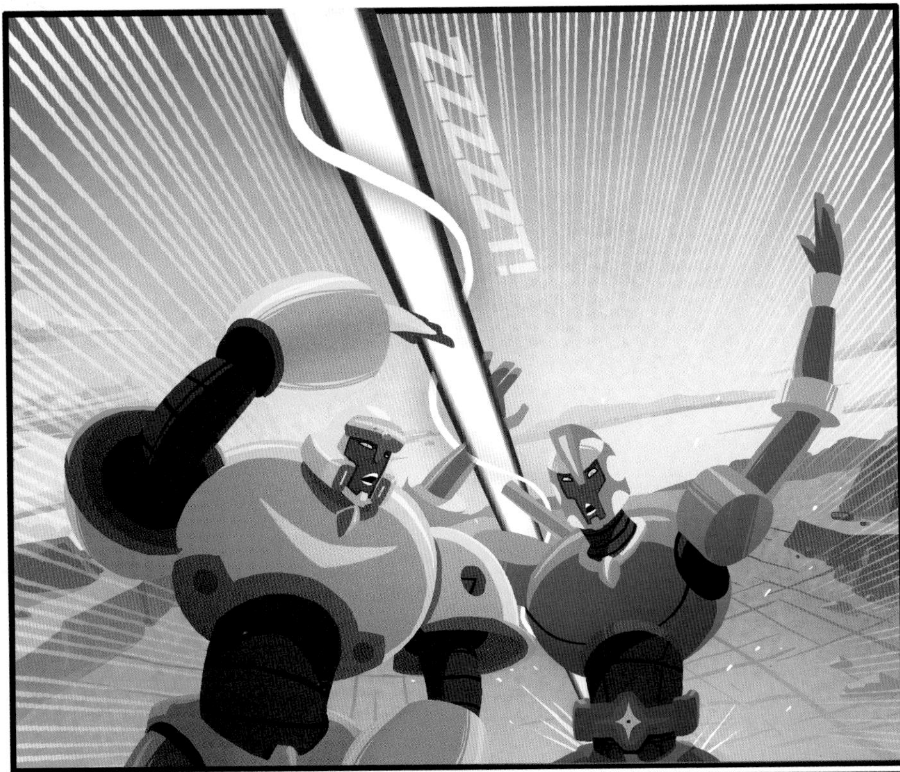
ZZZZZT!

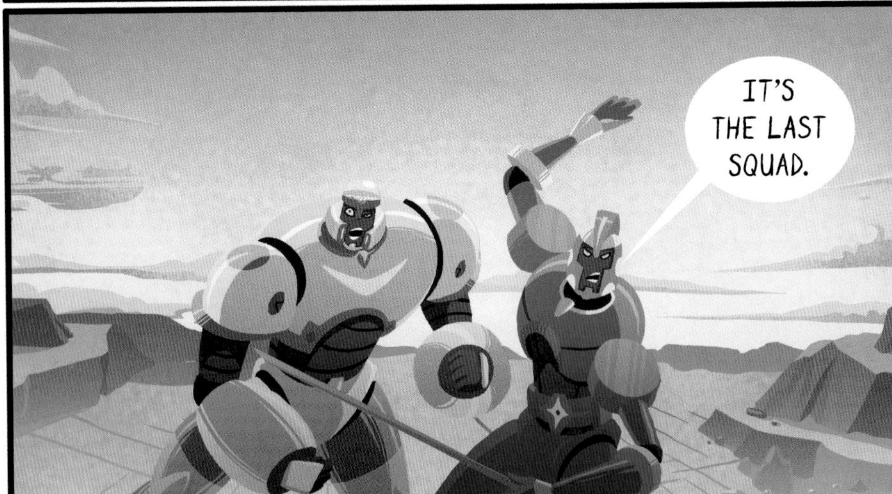
IT'S THE LAST SQUAD.

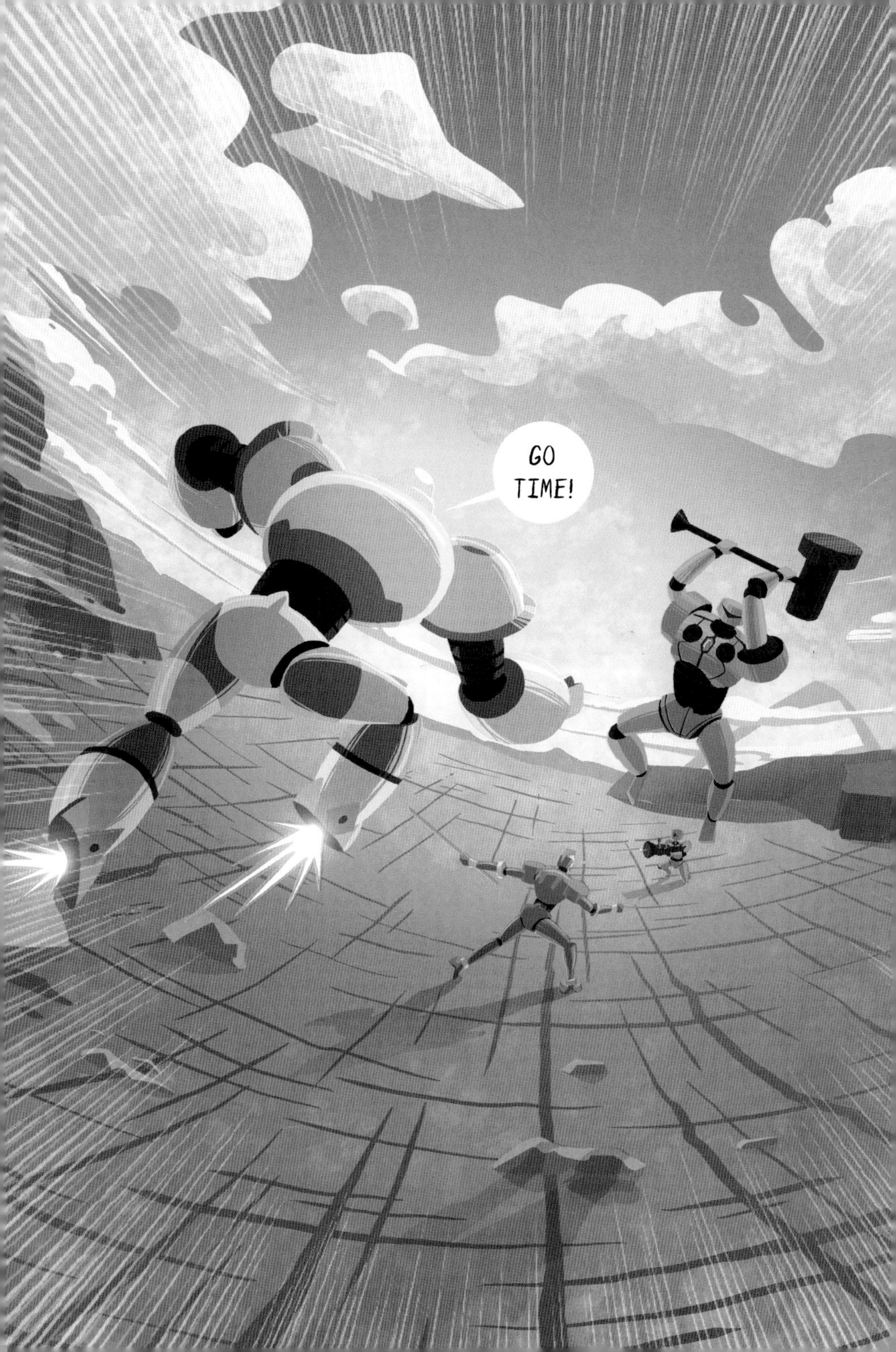
GO TIME!

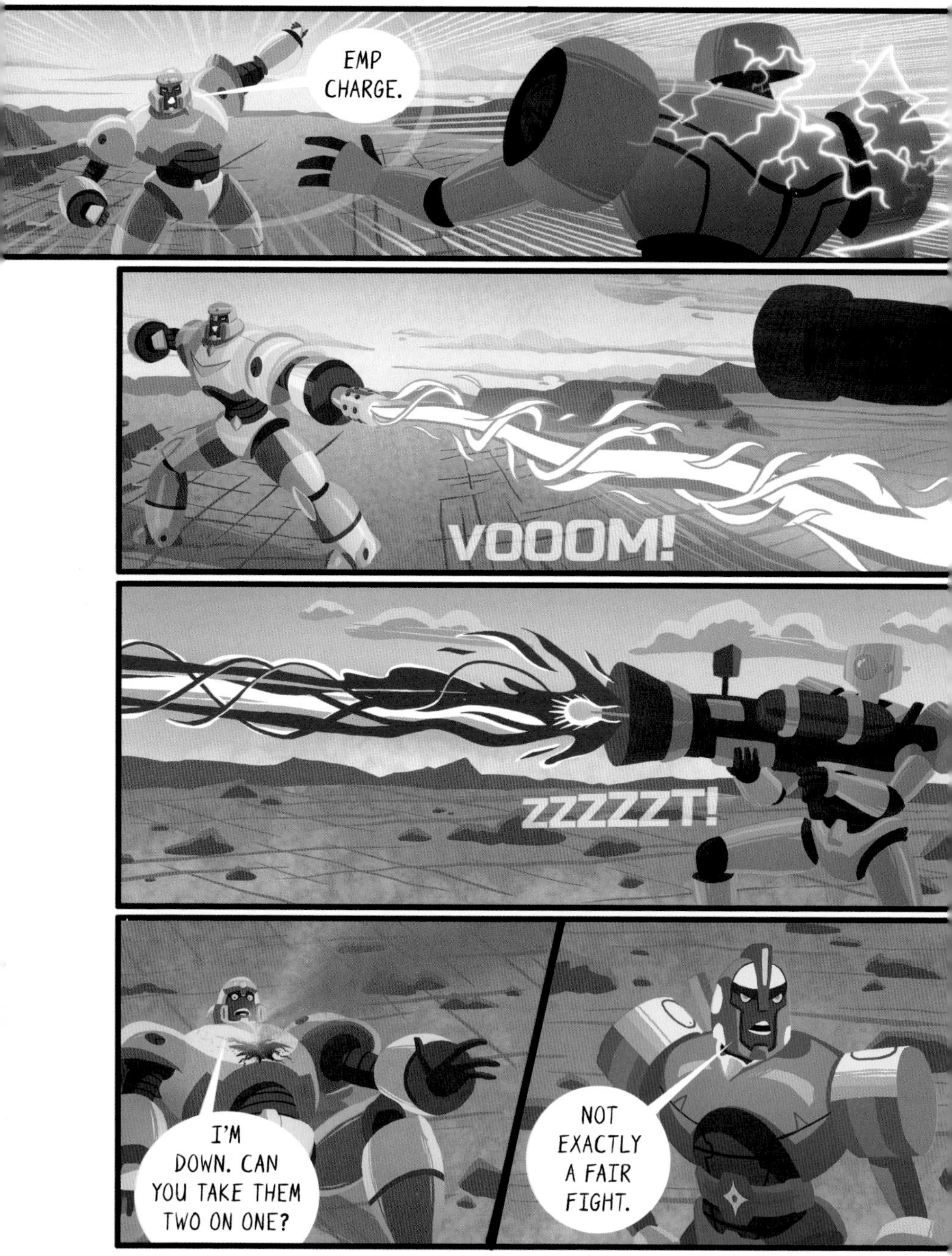
EMP CHARGE.
VOOOM!
ZZZZZT!
I'M DOWN. CAN YOU TAKE THEM TWO ON ONE?
NOT EXACTLY A FAIR FIGHT.

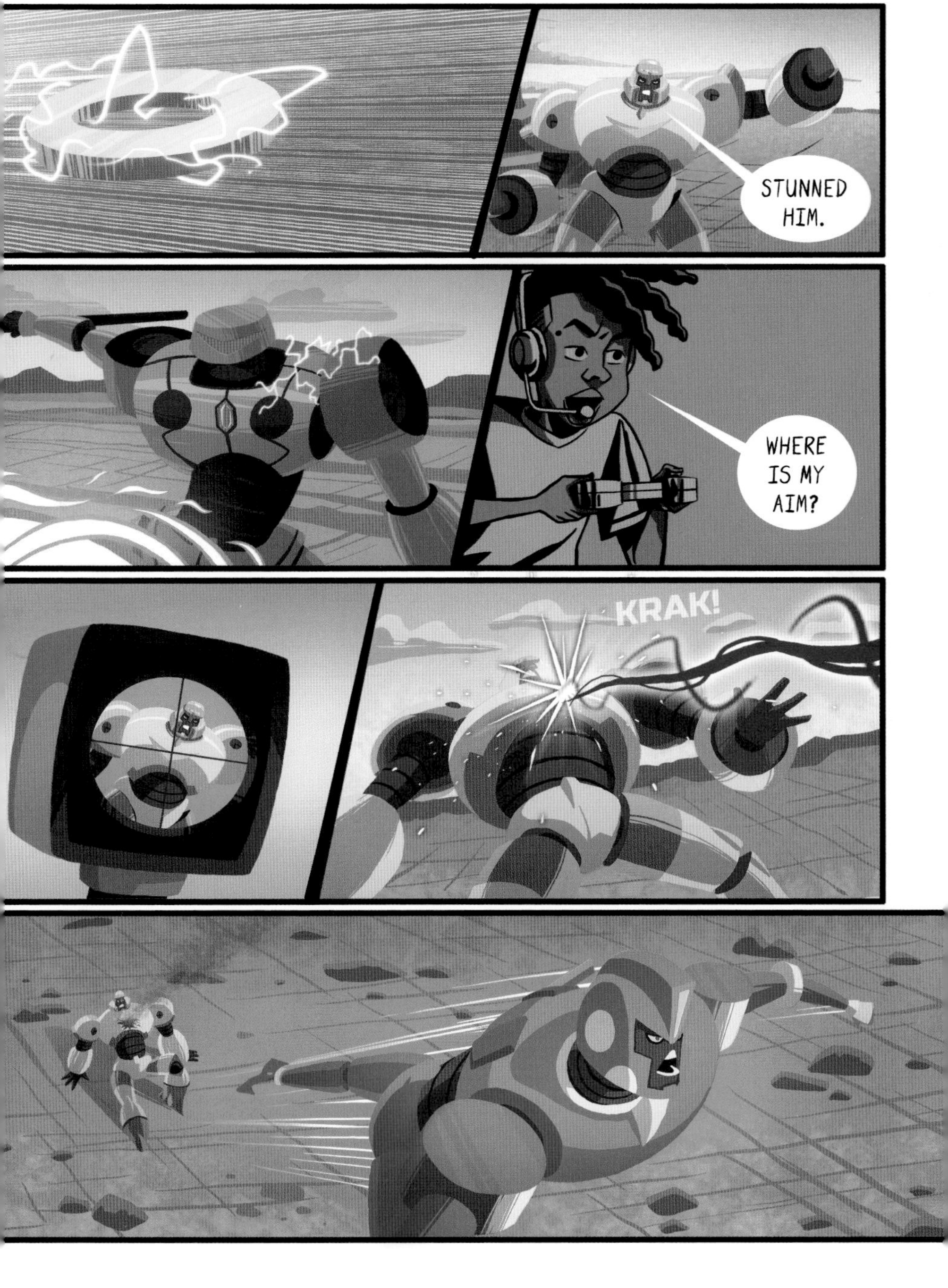
STUNNED HIM.
WHERE IS MY AIM?
KRAK!

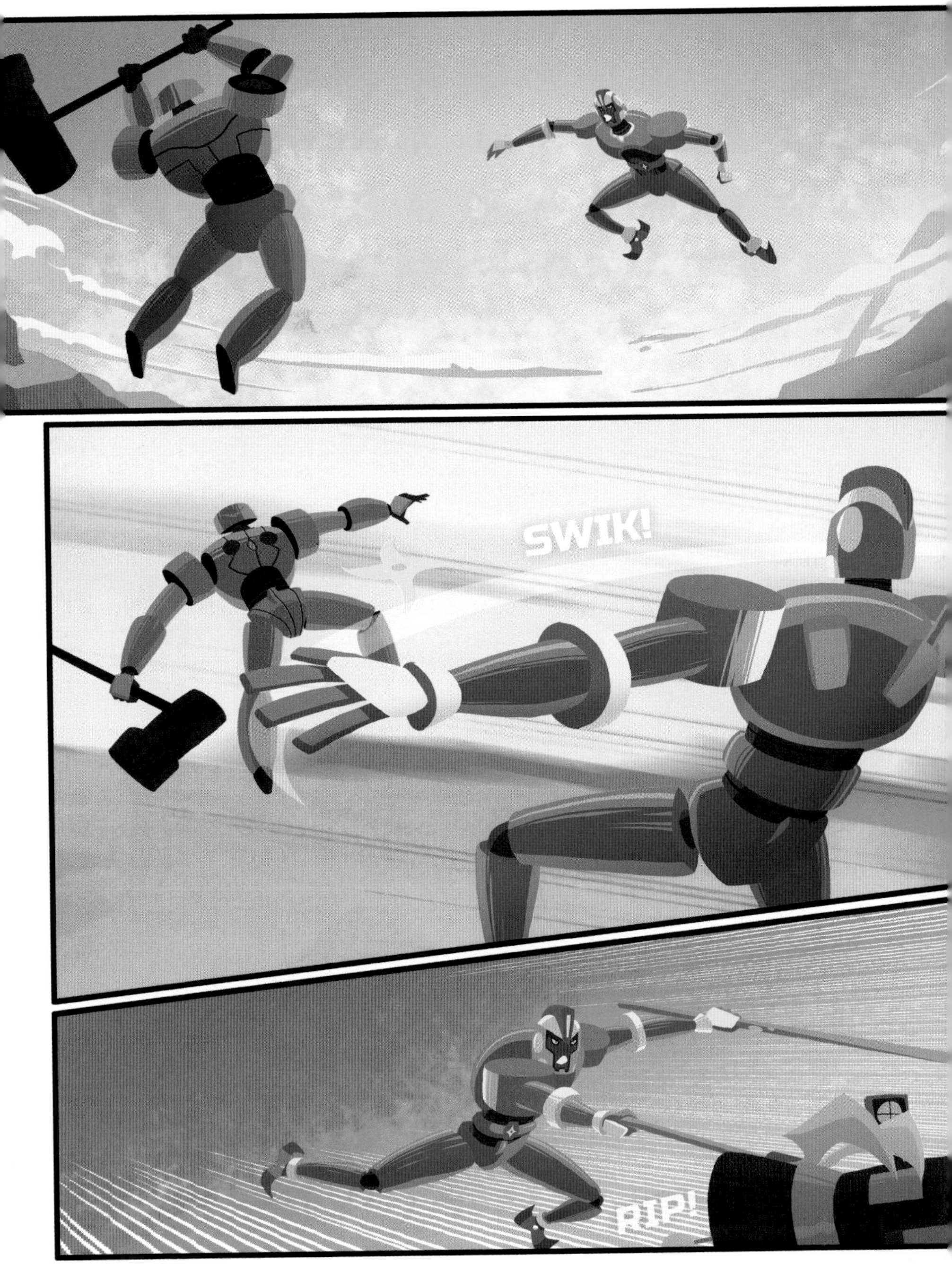
SWIK!
RIP!

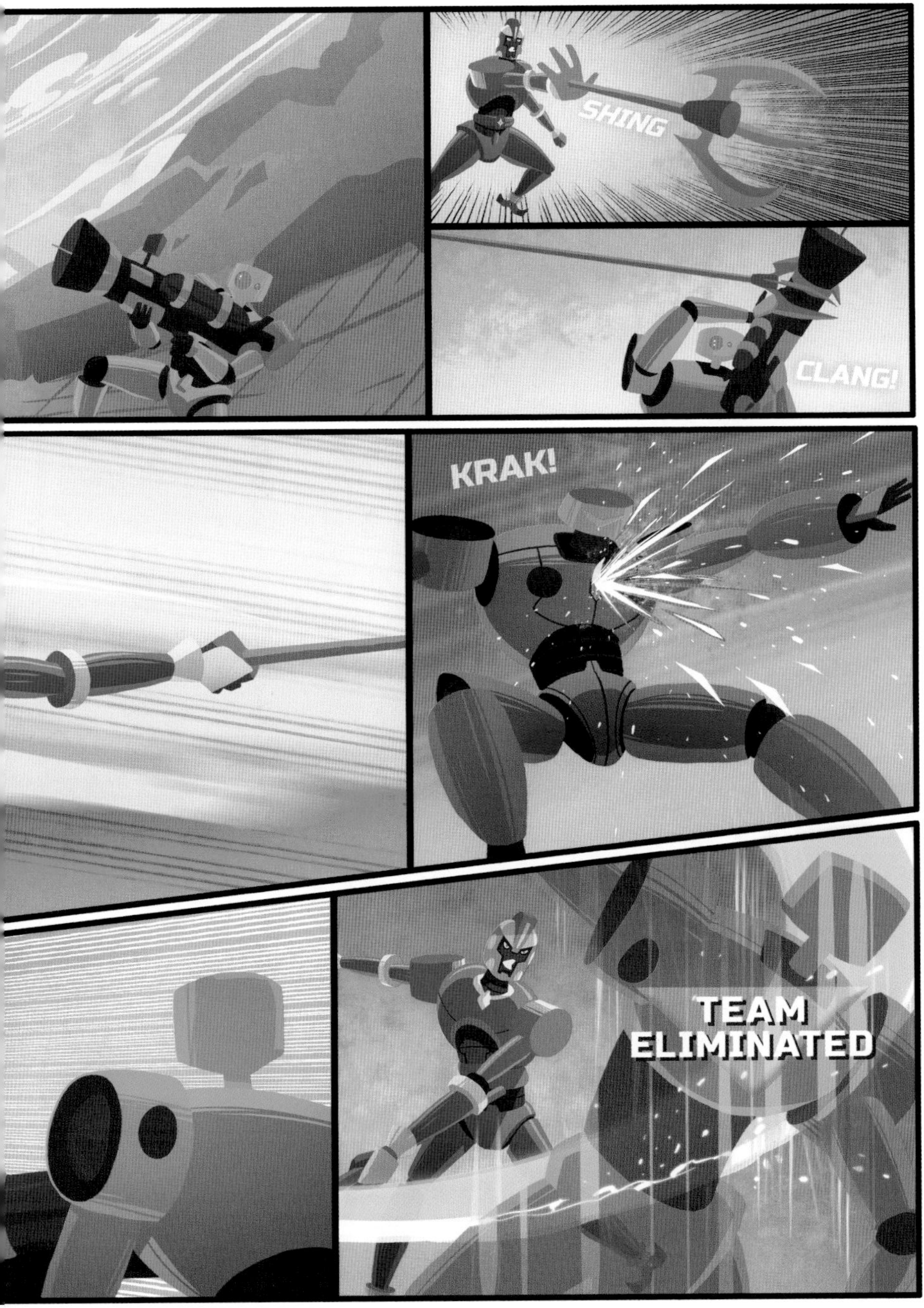
SHING
CLANG!
KRAK!
TEAM ELIMINATED

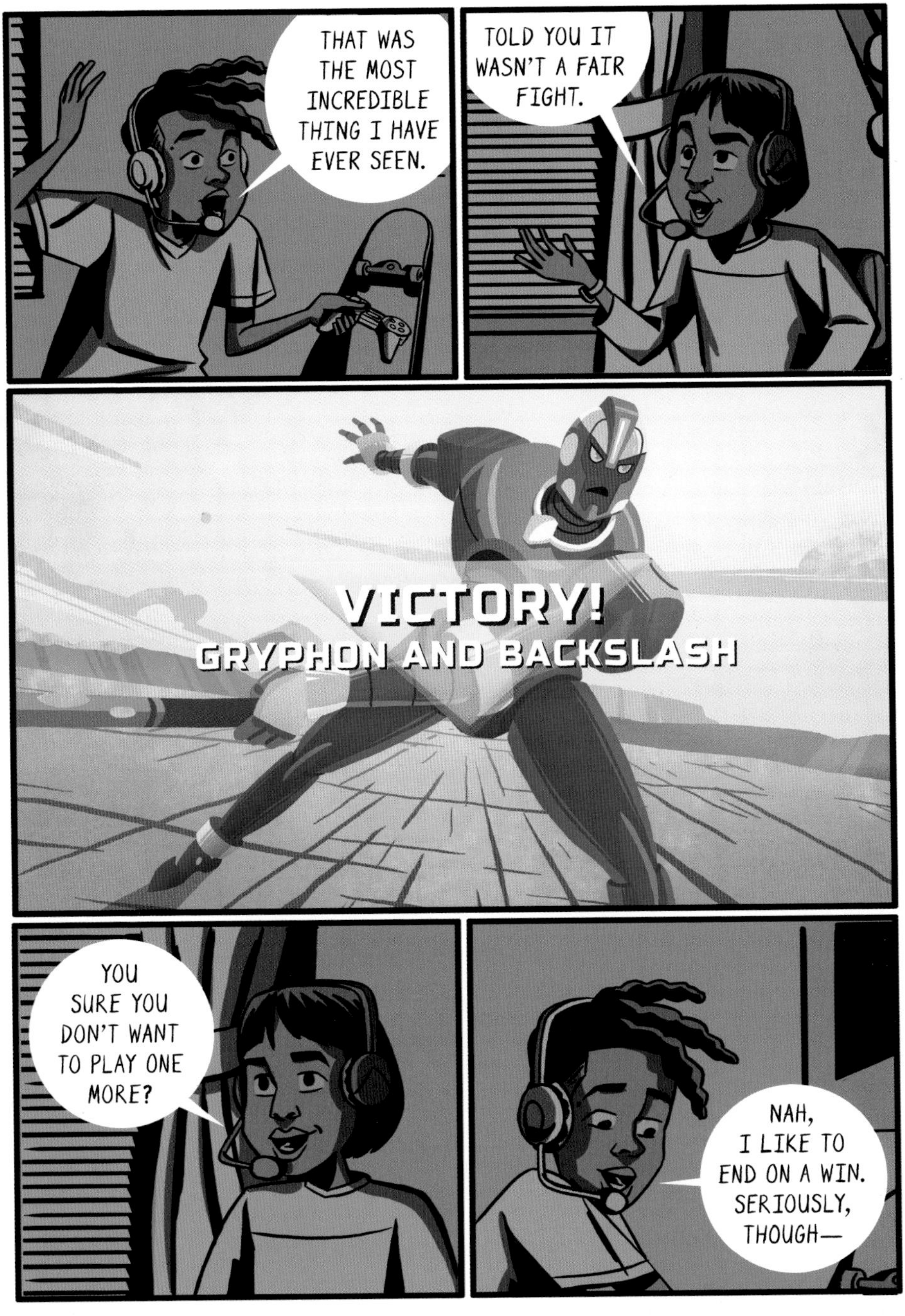
THAT WAS THE MOST INCREDIBLE THING I HAVE EVER SEEN.
TOLD YOU IT WASN'T A FAIR FIGHT.
VICTORY!
GRYPHON AND BACKSLASH
YOU SURE YOU DON'T WANT TO PLAY ONE MORE?
NAH, I LIKE TO END ON A WIN. SERIOUSLY, THOUGH—

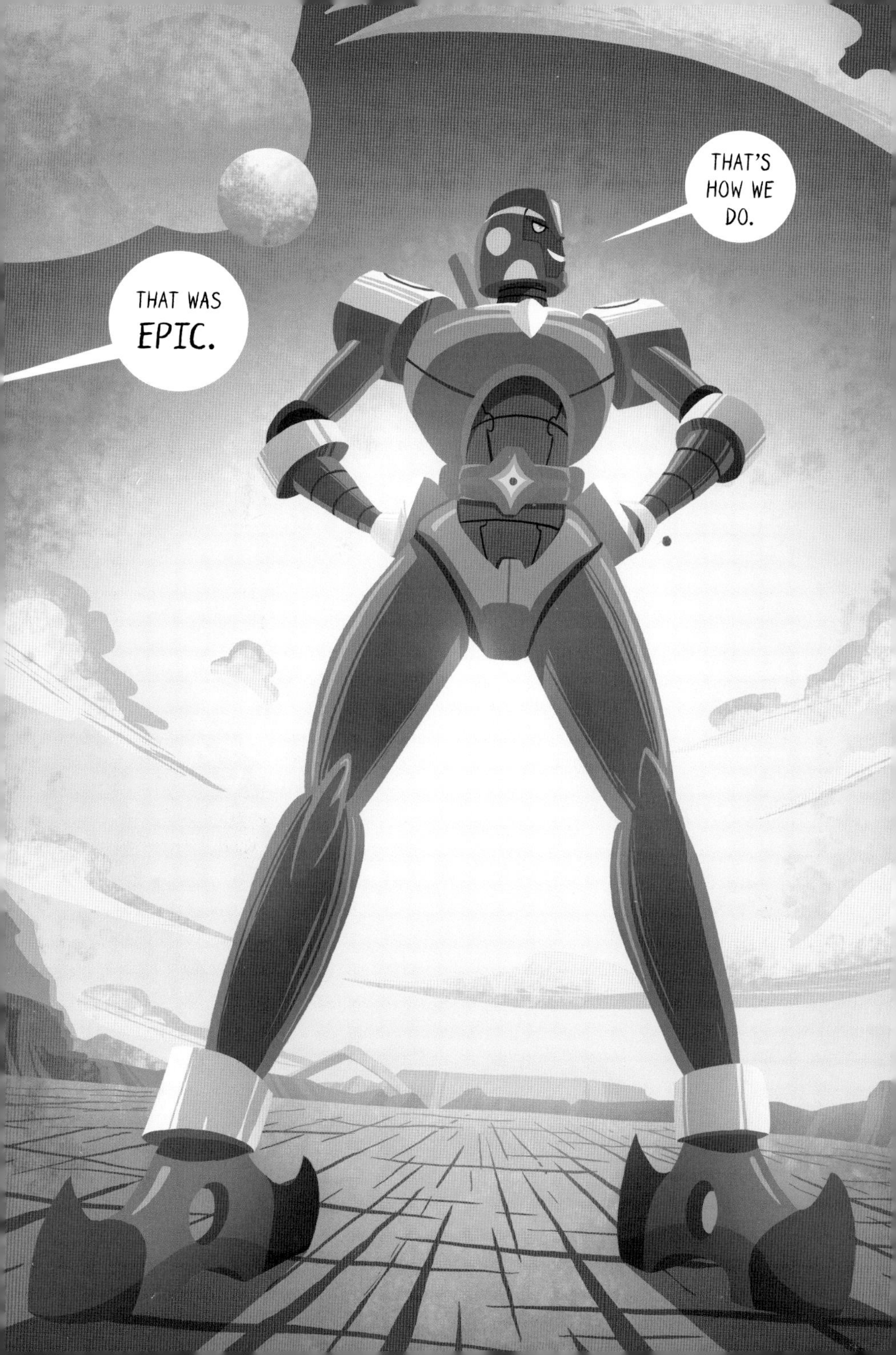
THAT WAS EPIC.
THAT'S HOW WE DO.

CHAPTER 2
IRL

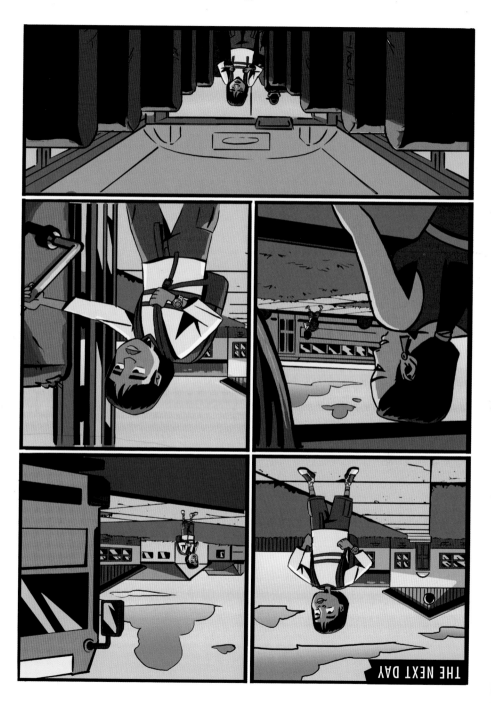

THE NEXT DAY

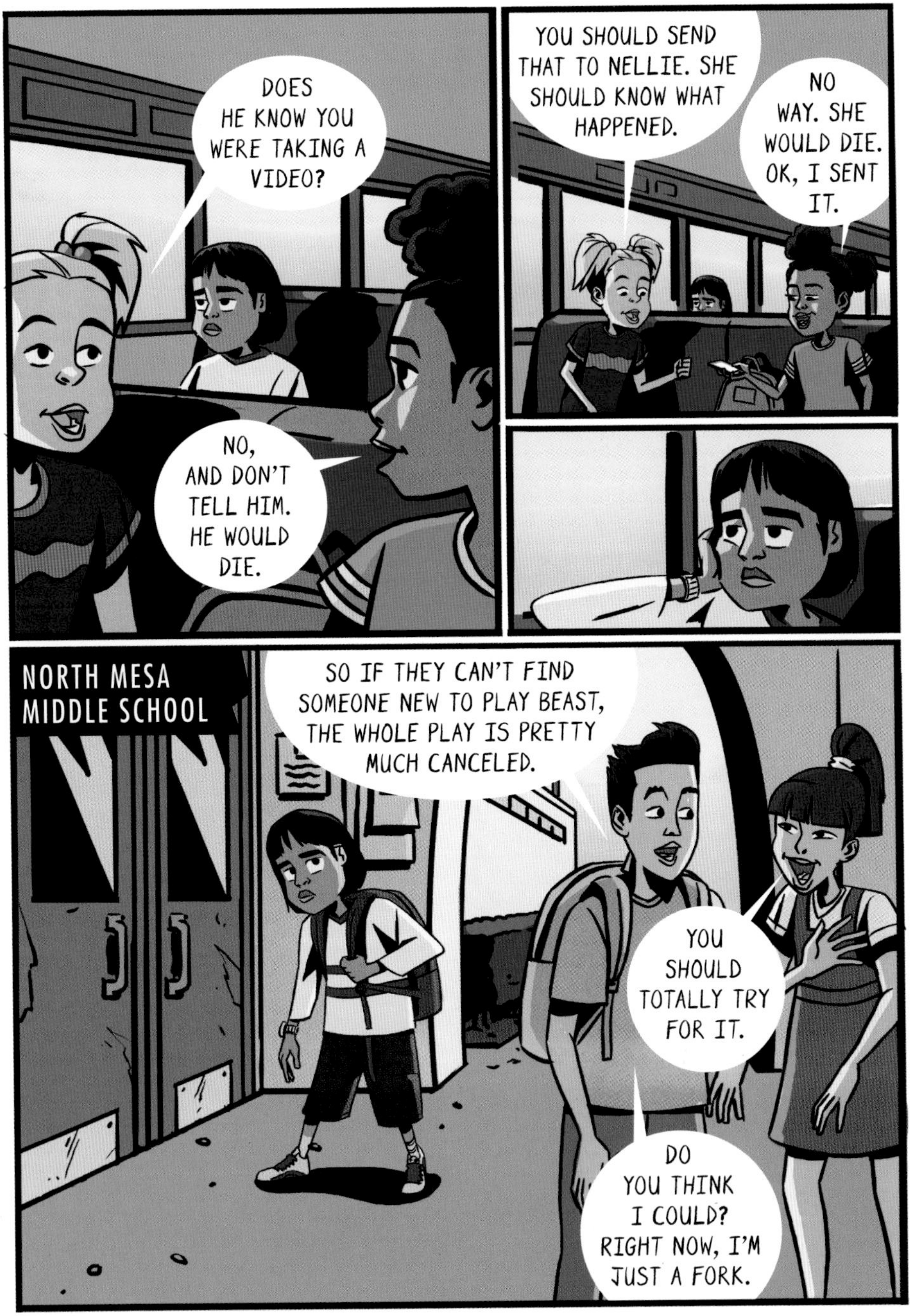
DOES HE KNOW YOU WERE TAKING A VIDEO?
NO, AND DON'T TELL HIM. HE WOULD DIE.
YOU SHOULD SEND THAT TO NELLIE. SHE SHOULD KNOW WHAT HAPPENED.
NO WAY. SHE WOULD DIE. OK, I SENT IT.
NORTH MESA MIDDLE SCHOOL
SO IF THEY CAN'T FIND SOMEONE NEW TO PLAY BEAST, THE WHOLE PLAY IS PRETTY MUCH CANCELED.
YOU SHOULD TOTALLY TRY FOR IT.
DO YOU THINK I COULD? RIGHT NOW, I'M JUST A FORK.

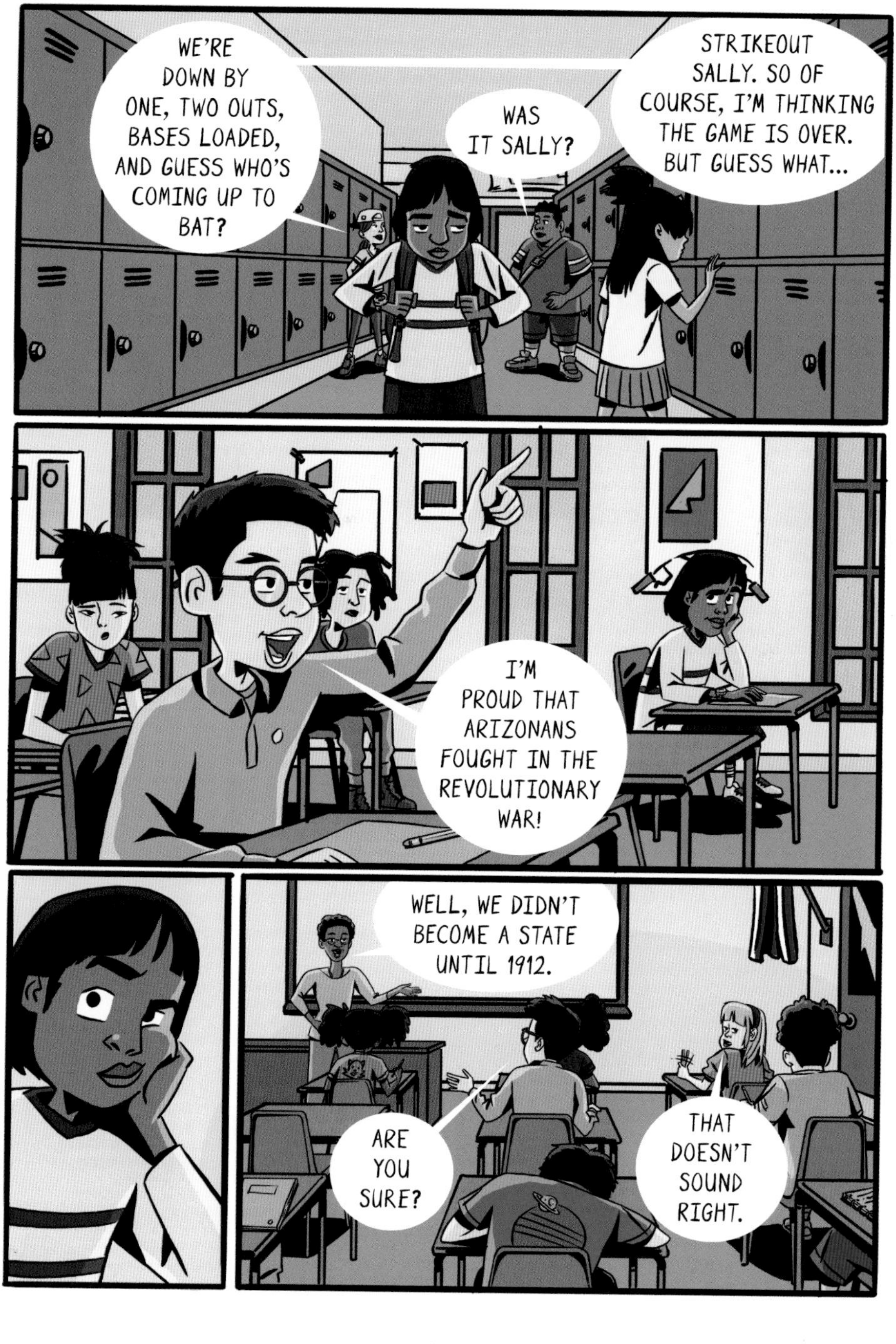
WE'RE DOWN BY ONE, TWO OUTS, BASES LOADED, AND GUESS WHO'S COMING UP TO BAT?
WAS IT SALLY?
STRIKEOUT SALLY. SO OF COURSE, I'M THINKING THE GAME IS OVER. BUT GUESS WHAT...
I'M PROUD THAT ARIZONANS FOUGHT IN THE REVOLUTIONARY WAR!
WELL, WE DIDN'T BECOME A STATE UNTIL 1912.
ARE YOU SURE?
THAT DOESN'T SOUND RIGHT.

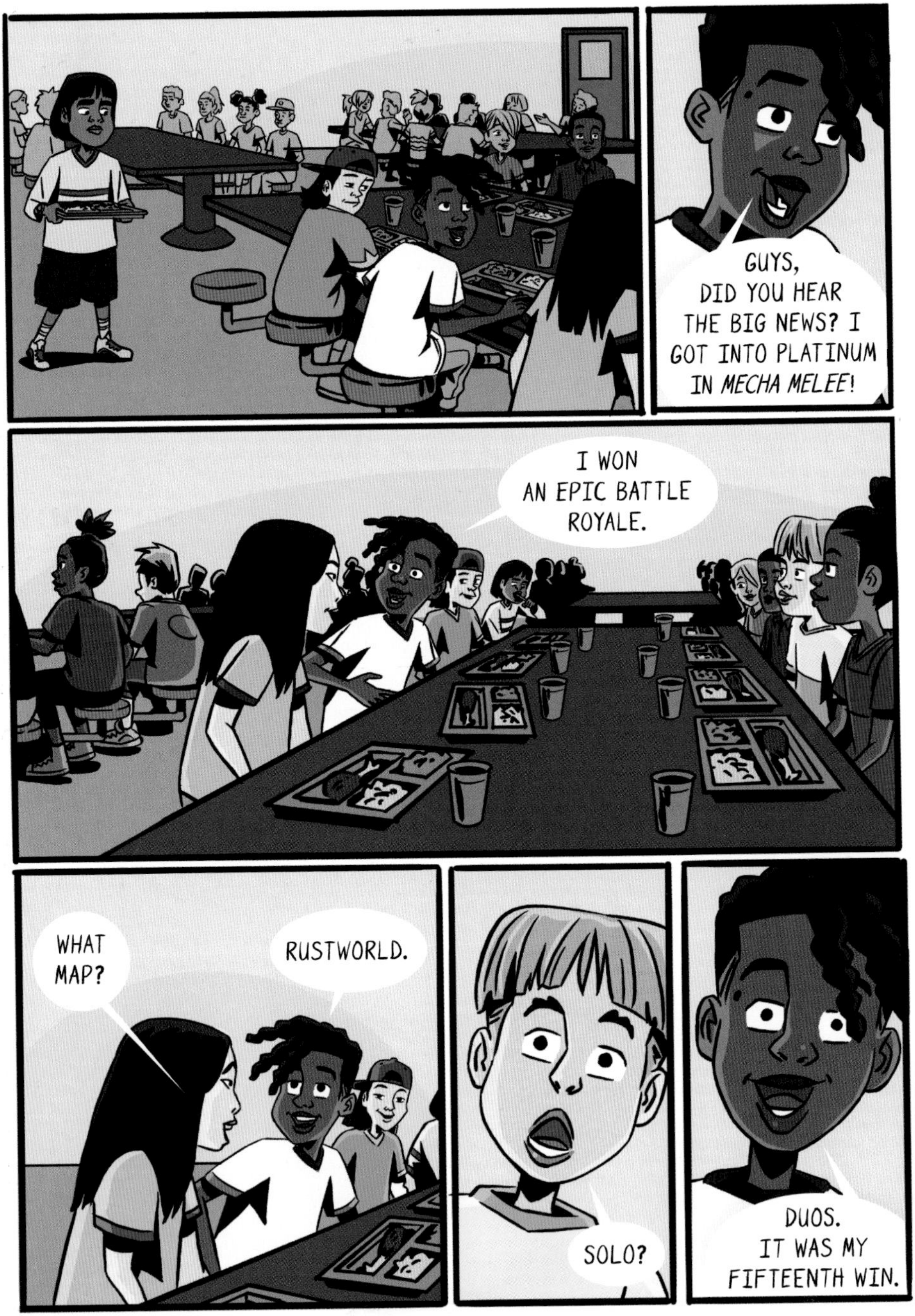
GUYS, DID YOU HEAR THE BIG NEWS? I GOT INTO PLATINUM IN *MECHA MELEE*!
I WON AN EPIC BATTLE ROYALE.
WHAT MAP?
RUSTWORLD.
SOLO?
DUOS. IT WAS MY FIFTEENTH WIN.

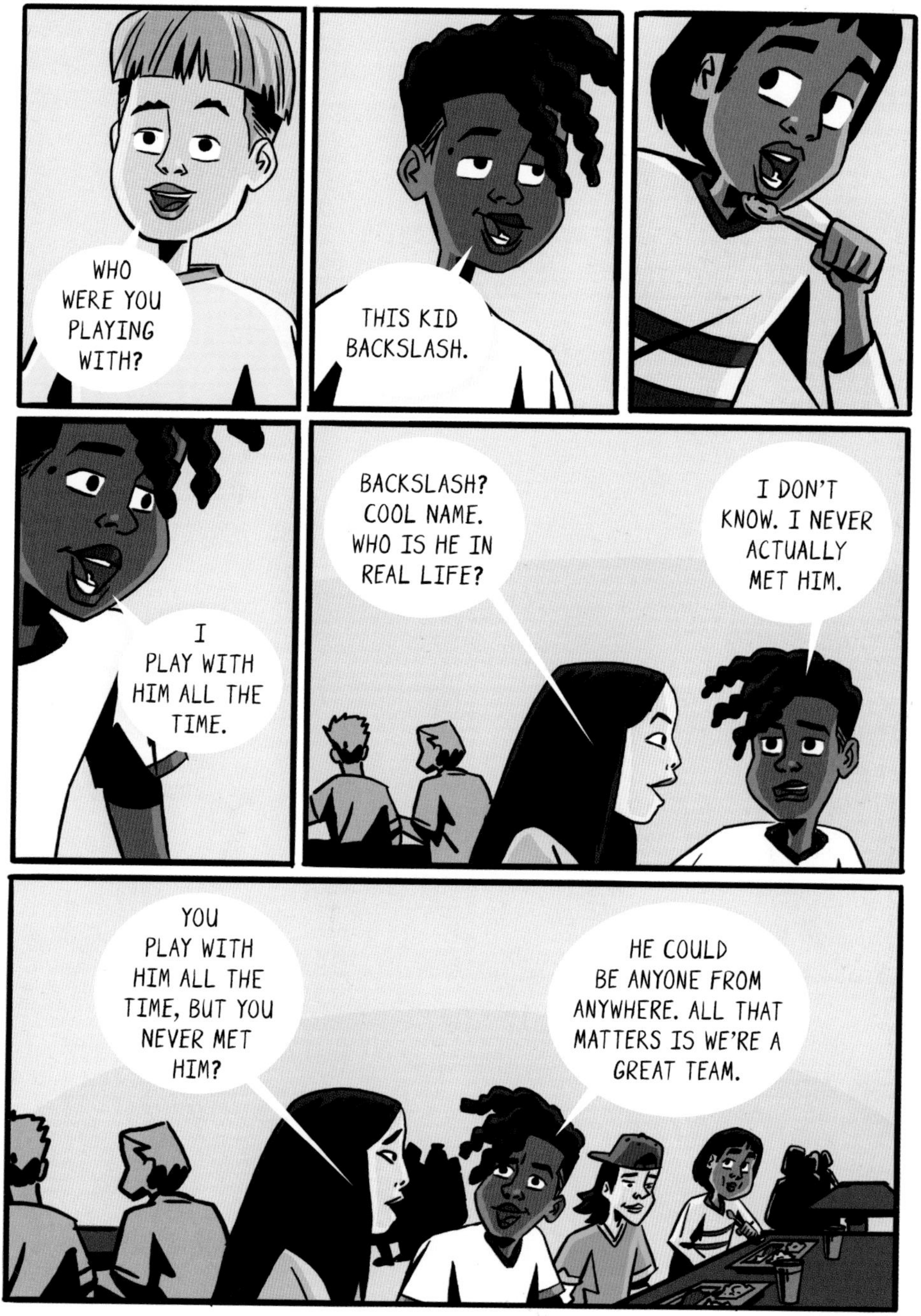
WHO WERE YOU PLAYING WITH?
THIS KID BACKSLASH.
I PLAY WITH HIM ALL THE TIME.
BACKSLASH? COOL NAME. WHO IS HE IN REAL LIFE?
I DON'T KNOW. I NEVER ACTUALLY MET HIM.
YOU PLAY WITH HIM ALL THE TIME, BUT YOU NEVER MET HIM?
HE COULD BE ANYONE FROM ANYWHERE. ALL THAT MATTERS IS WE'RE A GREAT TEAM.

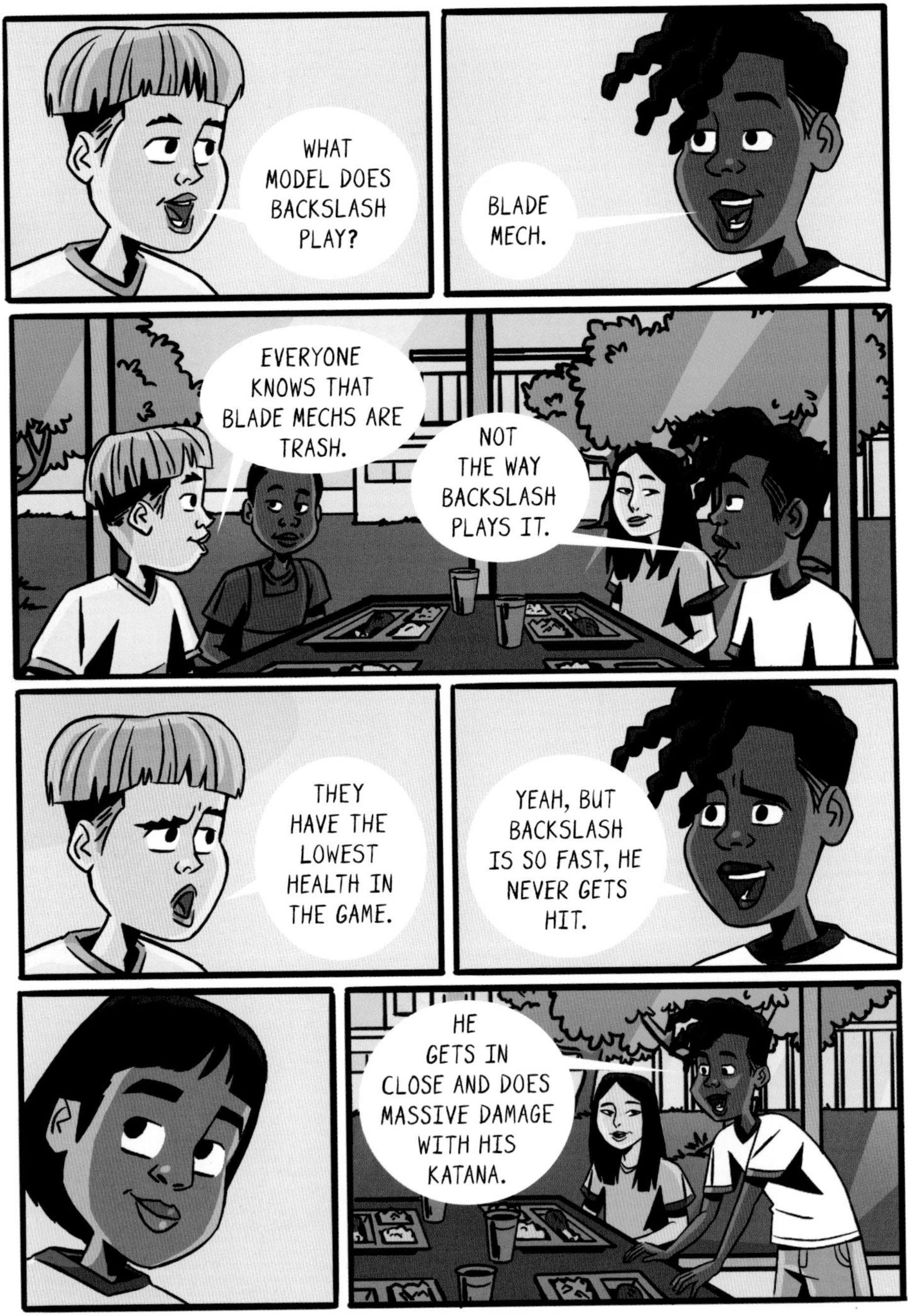
WHAT MODEL DOES BACKSLASH PLAY?
BLADE MECH.
EVERYONE KNOWS THAT BLADE MECHS ARE TRASH.
NOT THE WAY BACKSLASH PLAYS IT.
THEY HAVE THE LOWEST HEALTH IN THE GAME.
YEAH, BUT BACKSLASH IS SO FAST, HE NEVER GETS HIT.
HE GETS IN CLOSE AND DOES MASSIVE DAMAGE WITH HIS KATANA.

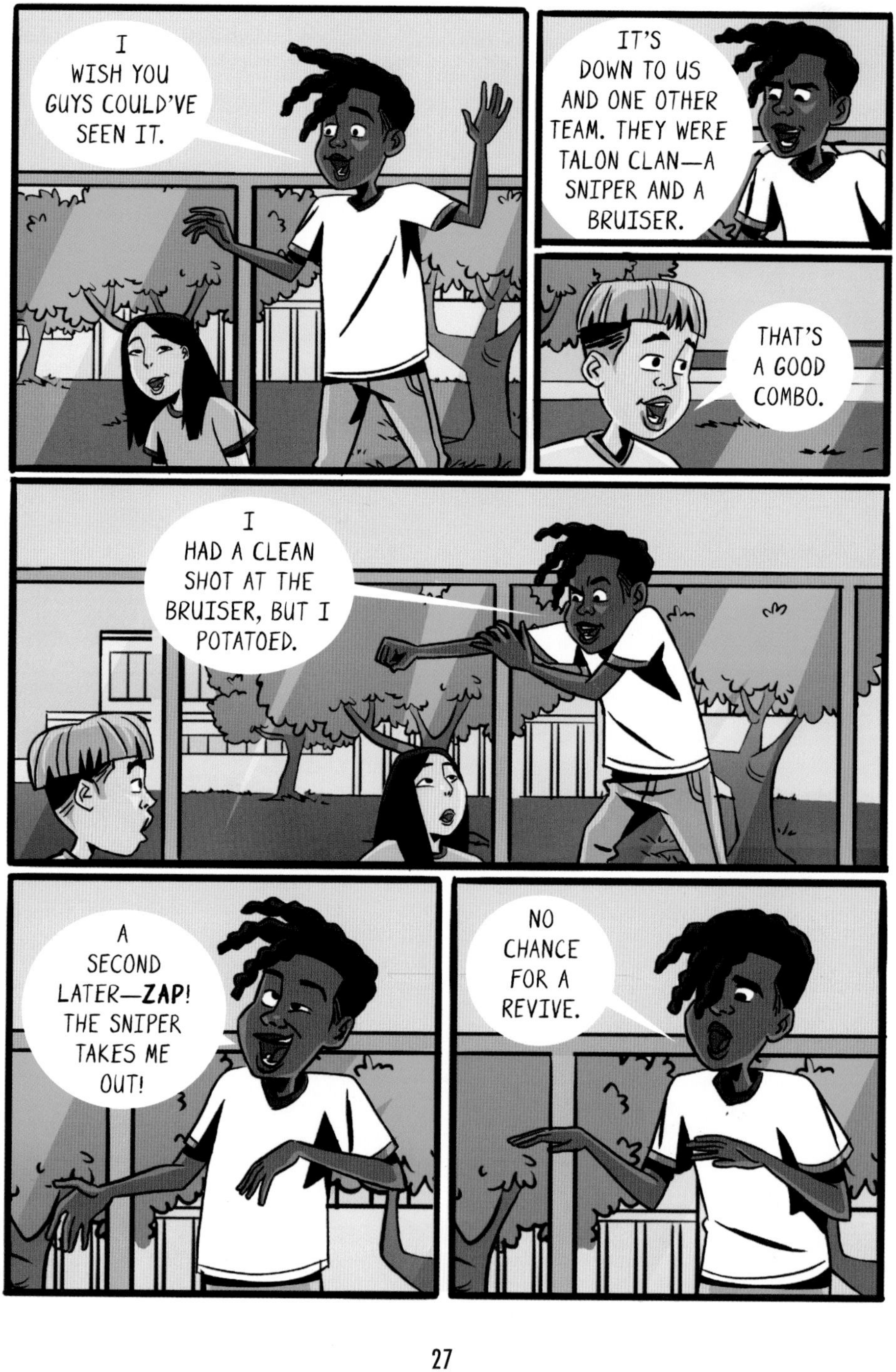
I WISH YOU GUYS COULD'VE SEEN IT.
IT'S DOWN TO US AND ONE OTHER TEAM. THEY WERE TALON CLAN—A SNIPER AND A BRUISER.
THAT'S A GOOD COMBO.
I HAD A CLEAN SHOT AT THE BRUISER, BUT I POTATOED.
A SECOND LATER—**ZAP**! THE SNIPER TAKES ME OUT!
NO CHANCE FOR A REVIVE.

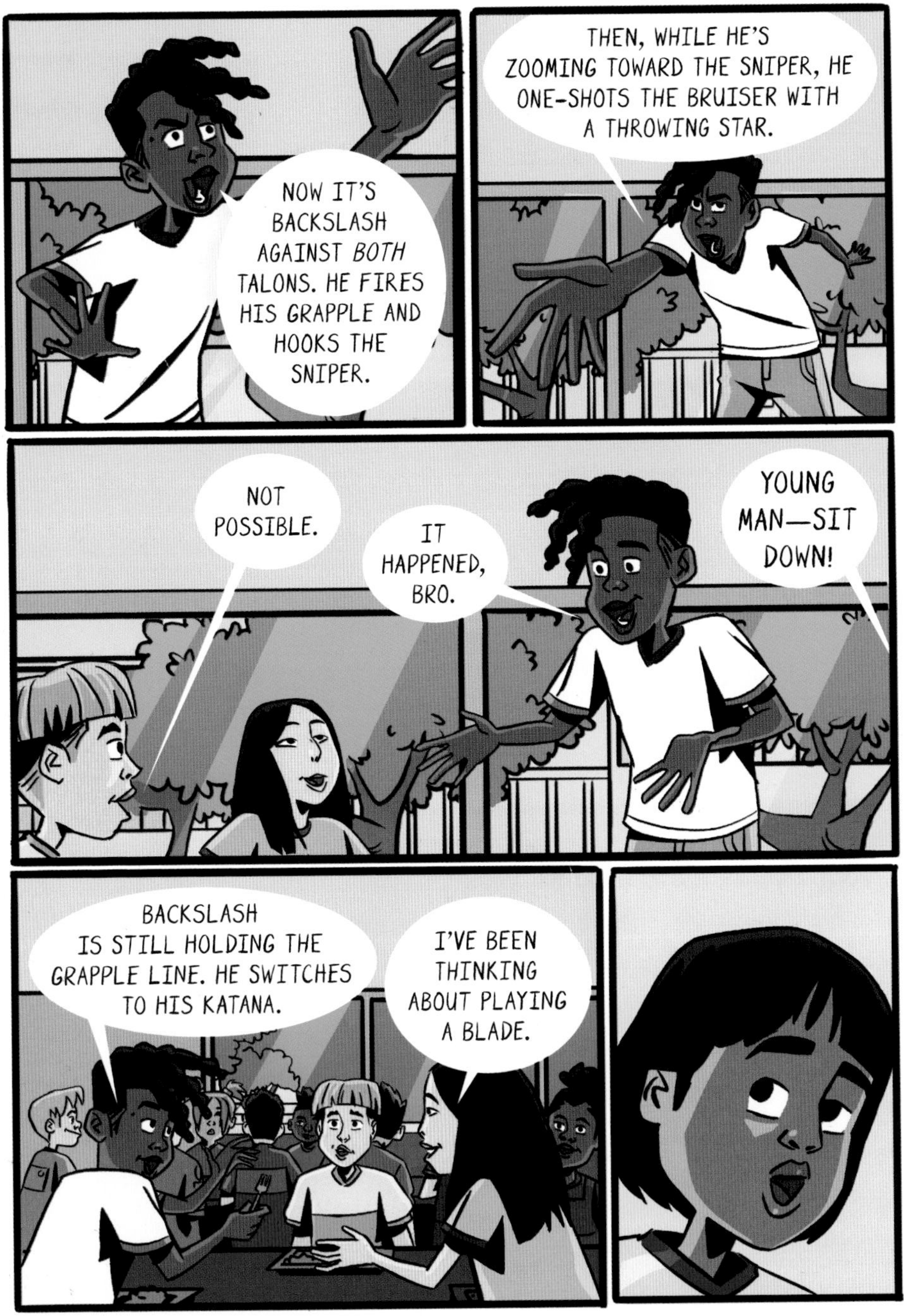
NOW IT'S BACKSLASH AGAINST *BOTH* TALONS. HE FIRES HIS GRAPPLE AND HOOKS THE SNIPER.
THEN, WHILE HE'S ZOOMING TOWARD THE SNIPER, HE ONE-SHOTS THE BRUISER WITH A THROWING STAR.
NOT POSSIBLE.
IT HAPPENED, BRO.
YOUNG MAN—SIT DOWN!
BACKSLASH IS STILL HOLDING THE GRAPPLE LINE. HE SWITCHES TO HIS KATANA.
I'VE BEEN THINKING ABOUT PLAYING A BLADE.

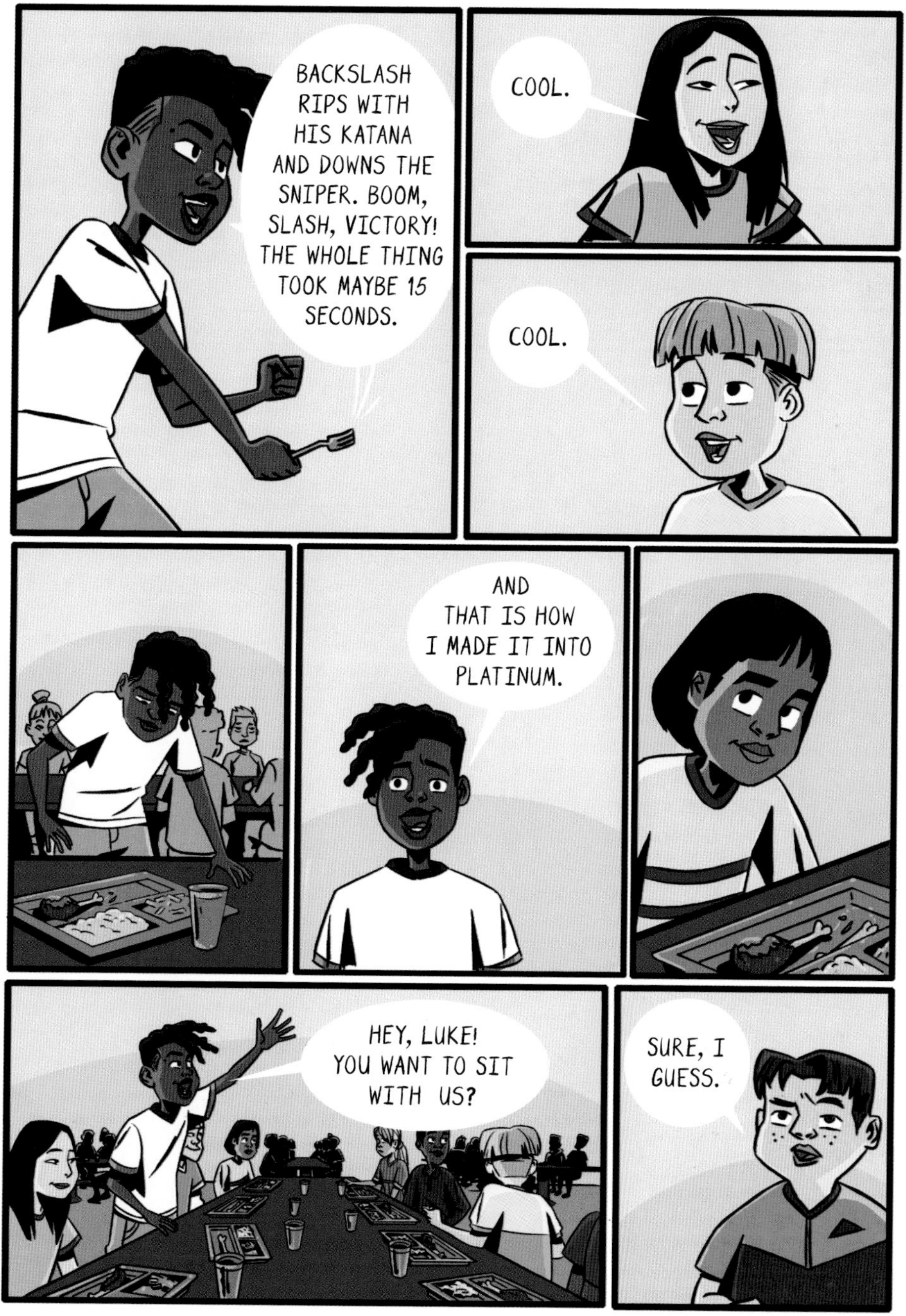
BACKSLASH RIPS WITH HIS KATANA AND DOWNS THE SNIPER. BOOM, SLASH, VICTORY! THE WHOLE THING TOOK MAYBE 15 SECONDS.
COOL.
COOL.
AND THAT IS HOW I MADE IT INTO PLATINUM.
HEY, LUKE! YOU WANT TO SIT WITH US?
SURE, I GUESS.

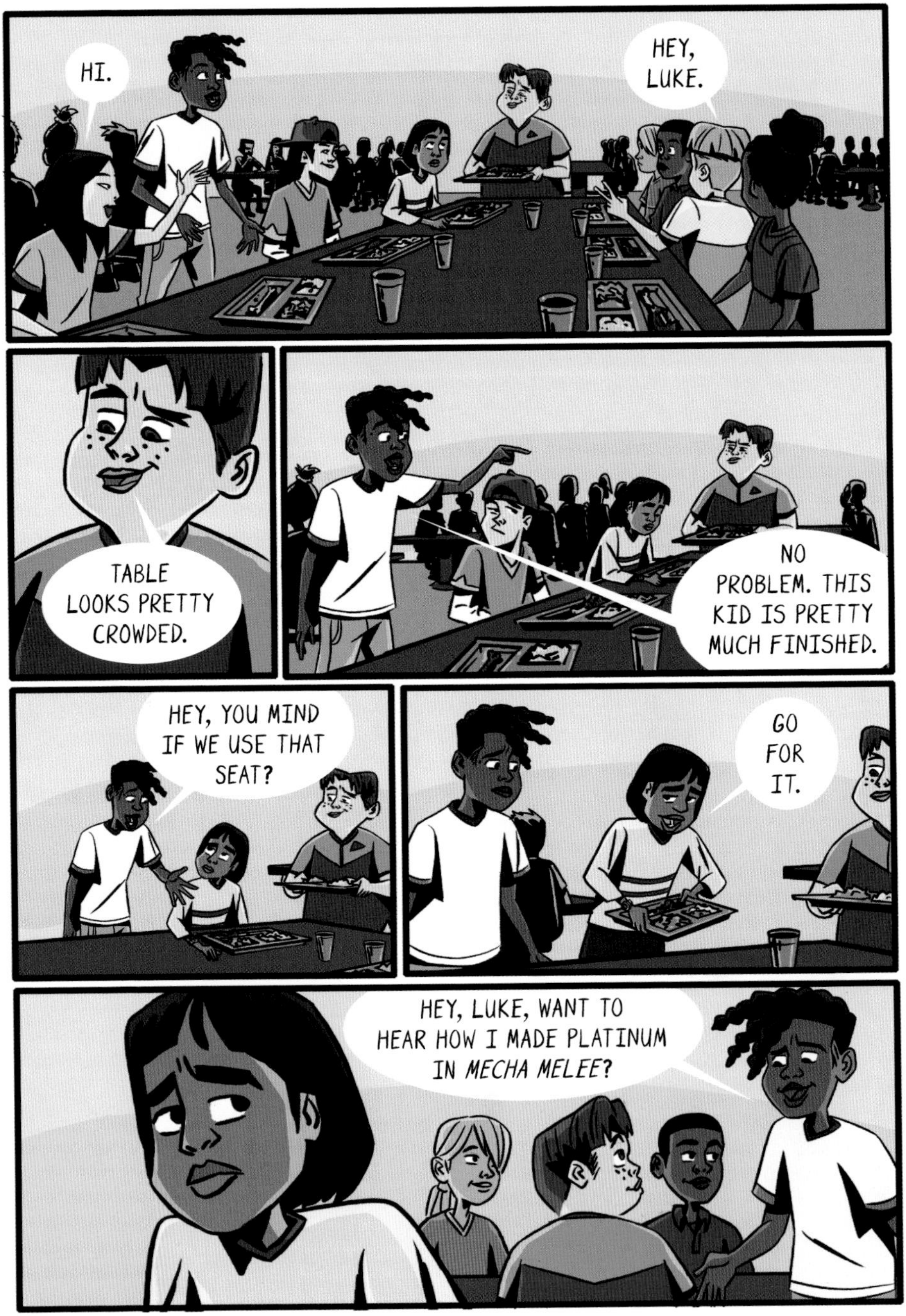
HI.
HEY, LUKE.
TABLE LOOKS PRETTY CROWDED.
NO PROBLEM. THIS KID IS PRETTY MUCH FINISHED.
HEY, YOU MIND IF WE USE THAT SEAT?
GO FOR IT.
HEY, LUKE, WANT TO HEAR HOW I MADE PLATINUM IN *MECHA MELEE*?

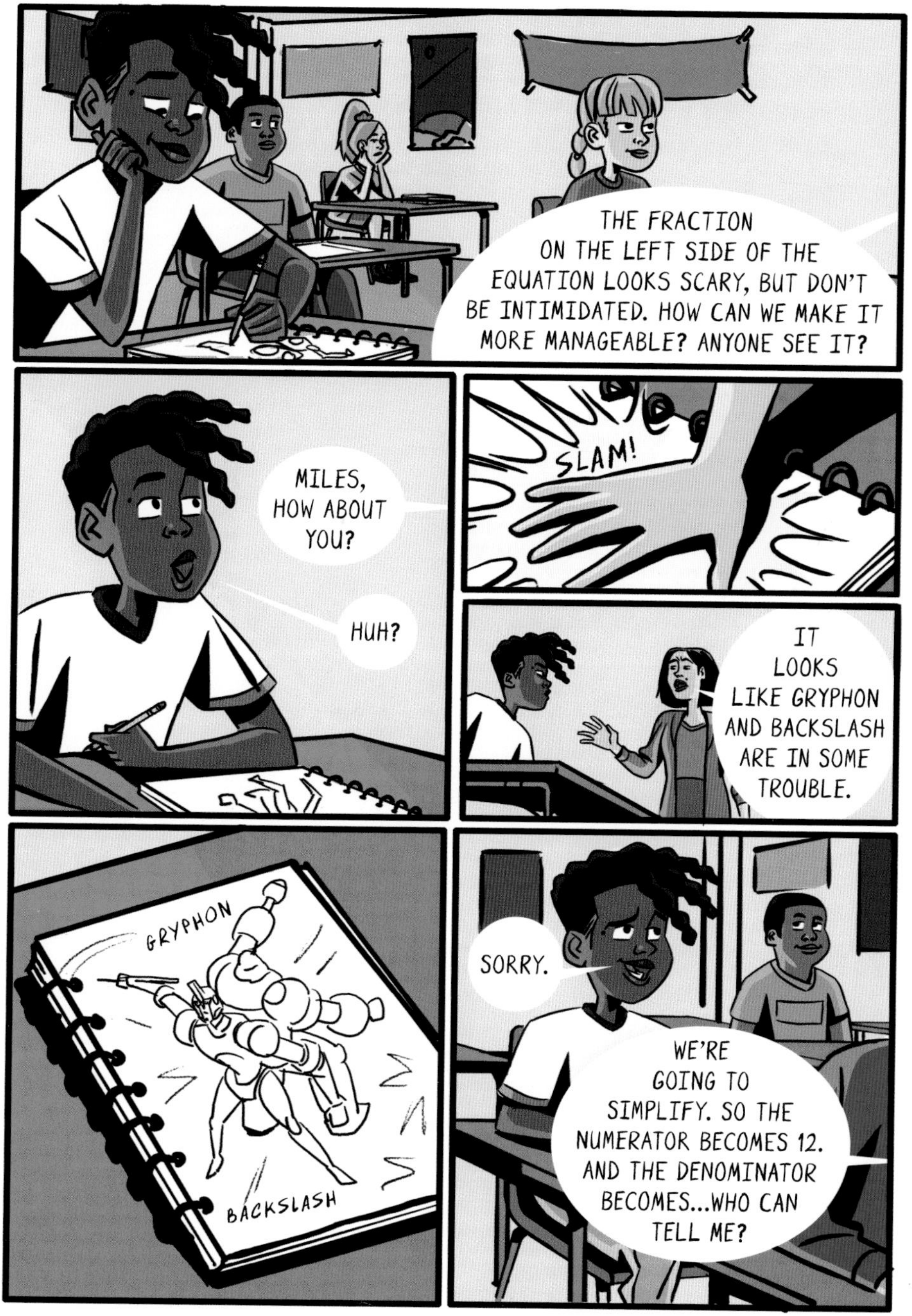
THE FRACTION ON THE LEFT SIDE OF THE EQUATION LOOKS SCARY, BUT DON'T BE INTIMIDATED. HOW CAN WE MAKE IT MORE MANAGEABLE? ANYONE SEE IT?
MILES, HOW ABOUT YOU?
HUH?
SLAM!
IT LOOKS LIKE GRYPHON AND BACKSLASH ARE IN SOME TROUBLE.
GRYPHON
BACKSLASH
SORRY.
WE'RE GOING TO SIMPLIFY. SO THE NUMERATOR BECOMES 12. AND THE DENOMINATOR BECOMES...WHO CAN TELL ME?

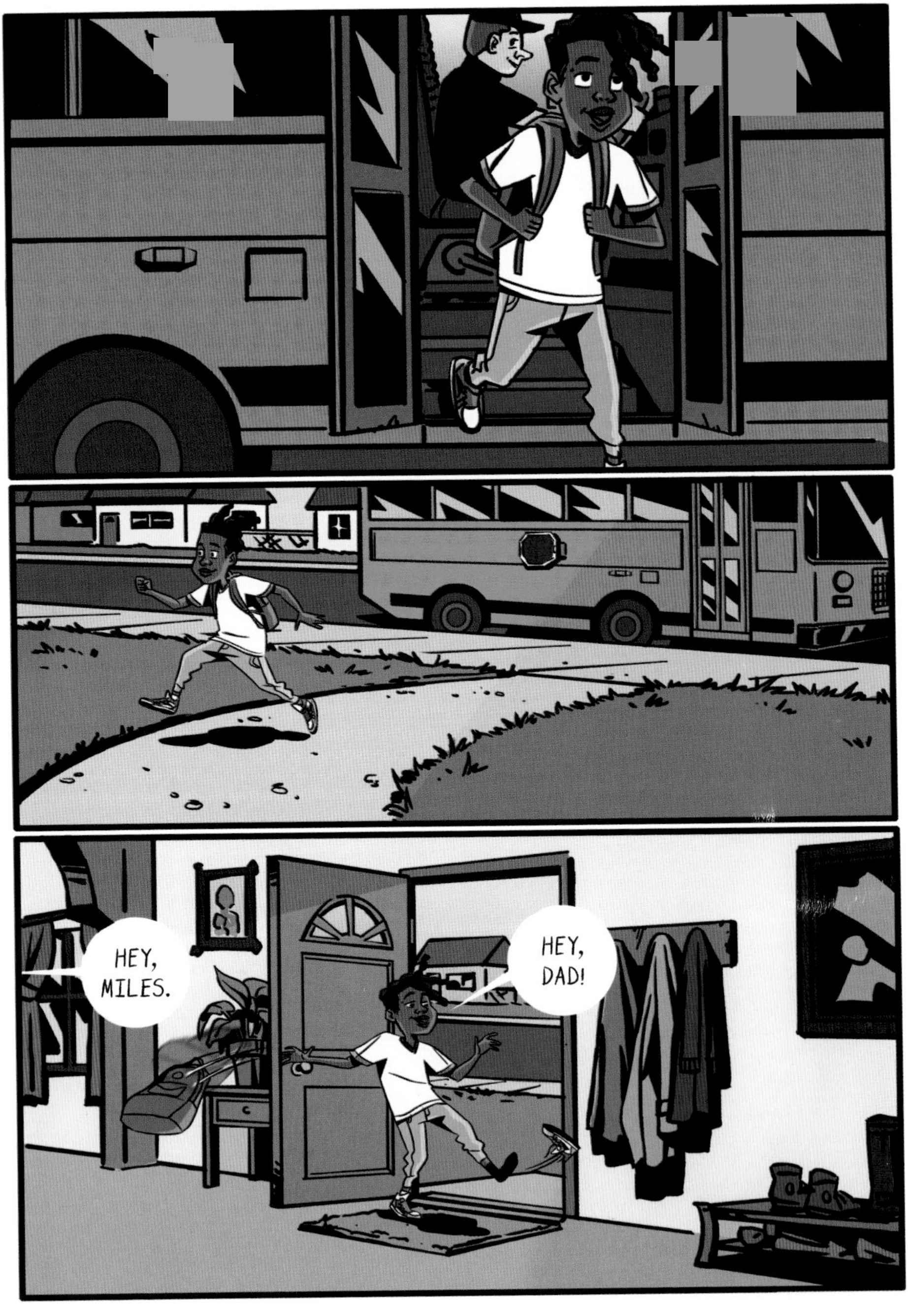
HEY, MILES.
HEY, DAD!

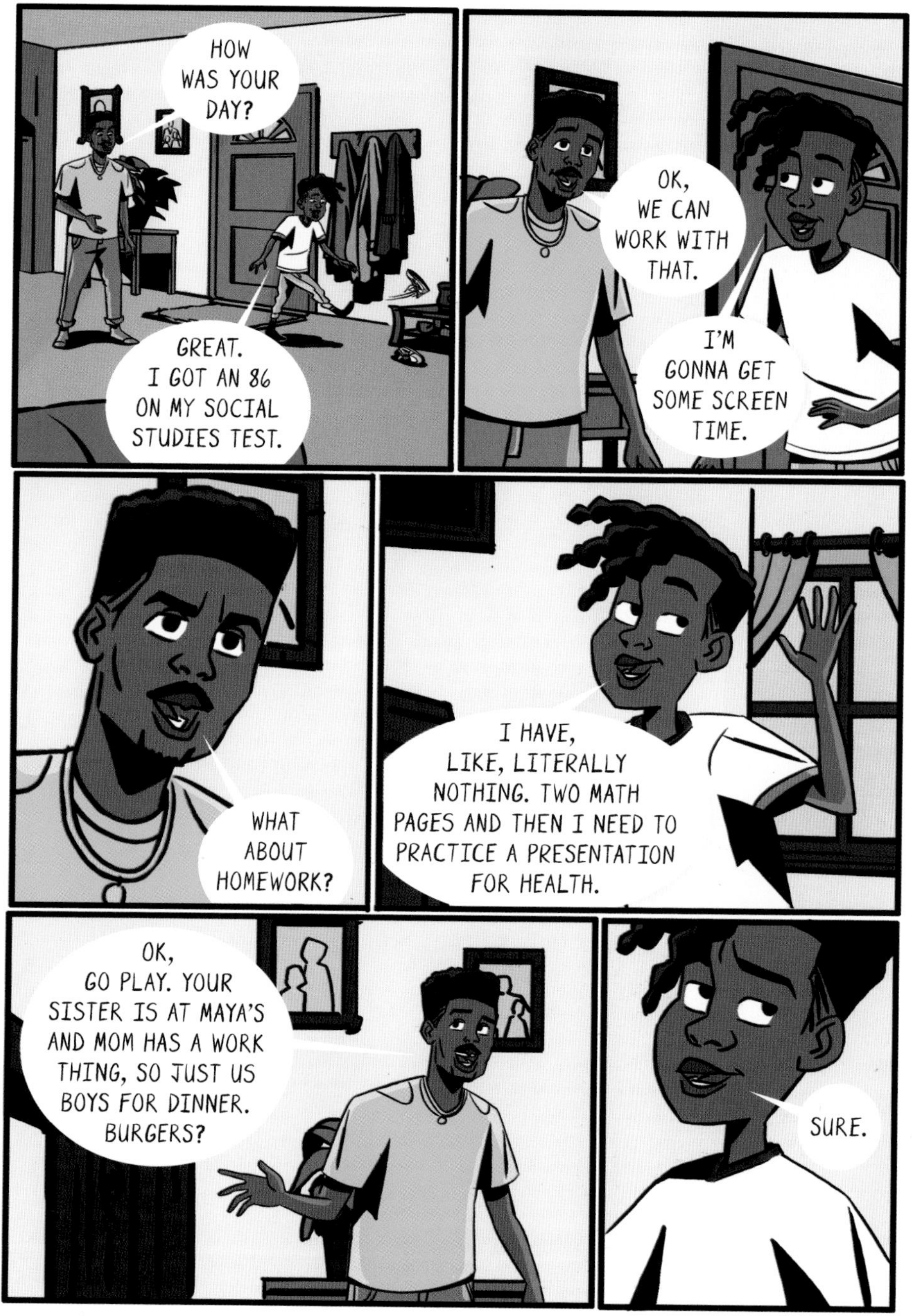
HOW WAS YOUR DAY?
GREAT. I GOT AN 86 ON MY SOCIAL STUDIES TEST.
OK, WE CAN WORK WITH THAT.
I'M GONNA GET SOME SCREEN TIME.
WHAT ABOUT HOMEWORK?
I HAVE, LIKE, LITERALLY NOTHING. TWO MATH PAGES AND THEN I NEED TO PRACTICE A PRESENTATION FOR HEALTH.
OK, GO PLAY. YOUR SISTER IS AT MAYA'S AND MOM HAS A WORK THING, SO JUST US BOYS FOR DINNER. BURGERS?
SURE.

CHAPTER 3
RAID

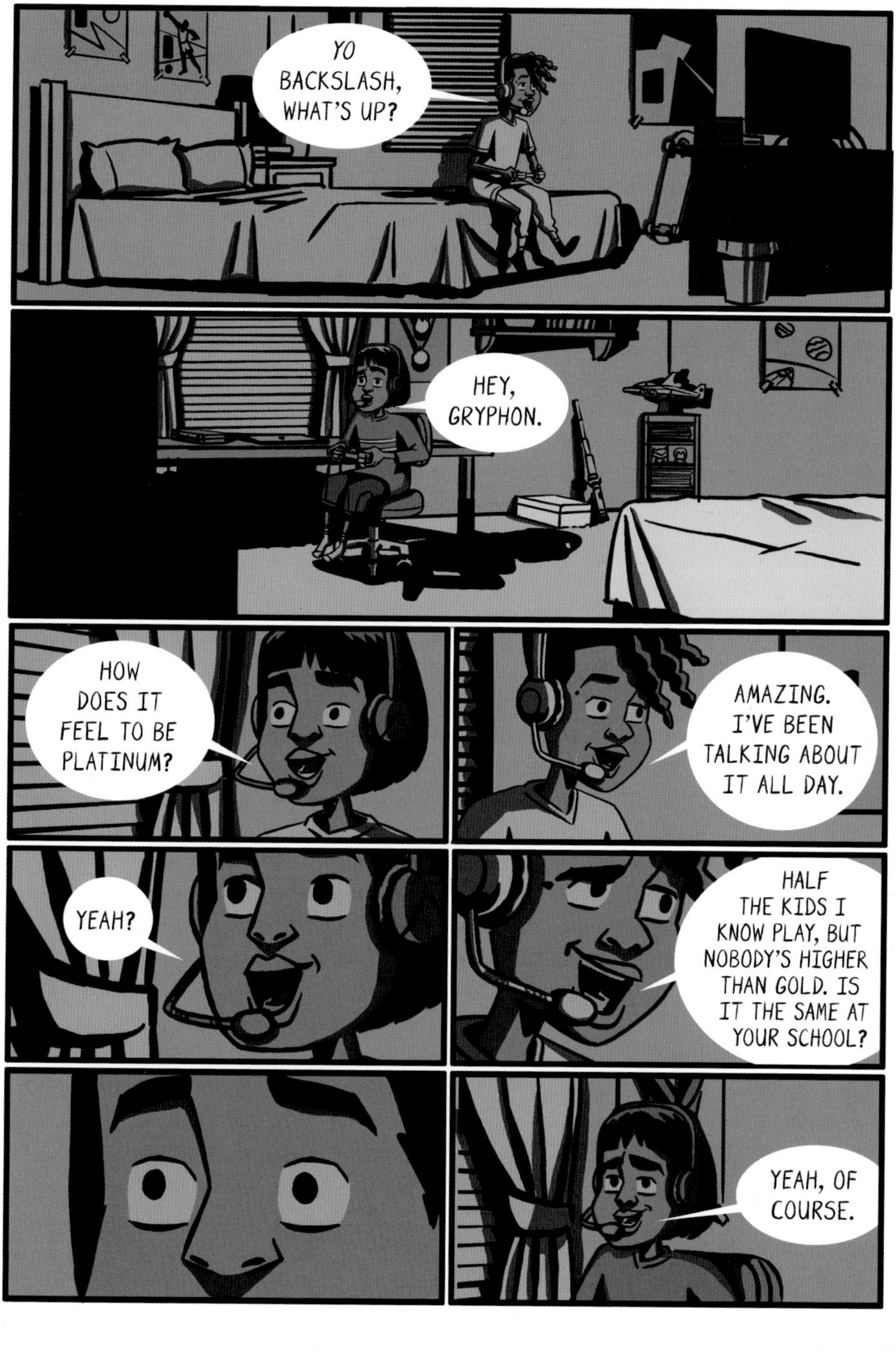
YO BACKSLASH, WHAT'S UP?
HEY, GRYPHON.
HOW DOES IT FEEL TO BE PLATINUM?
AMAZING. I'VE BEEN TALKING ABOUT IT ALL DAY.
YEAH?
HALF THE KIDS I KNOW PLAY, BUT NOBODY'S HIGHER THAN GOLD. IS IT THE SAME AT YOUR SCHOOL?
YEAH, OF COURSE.

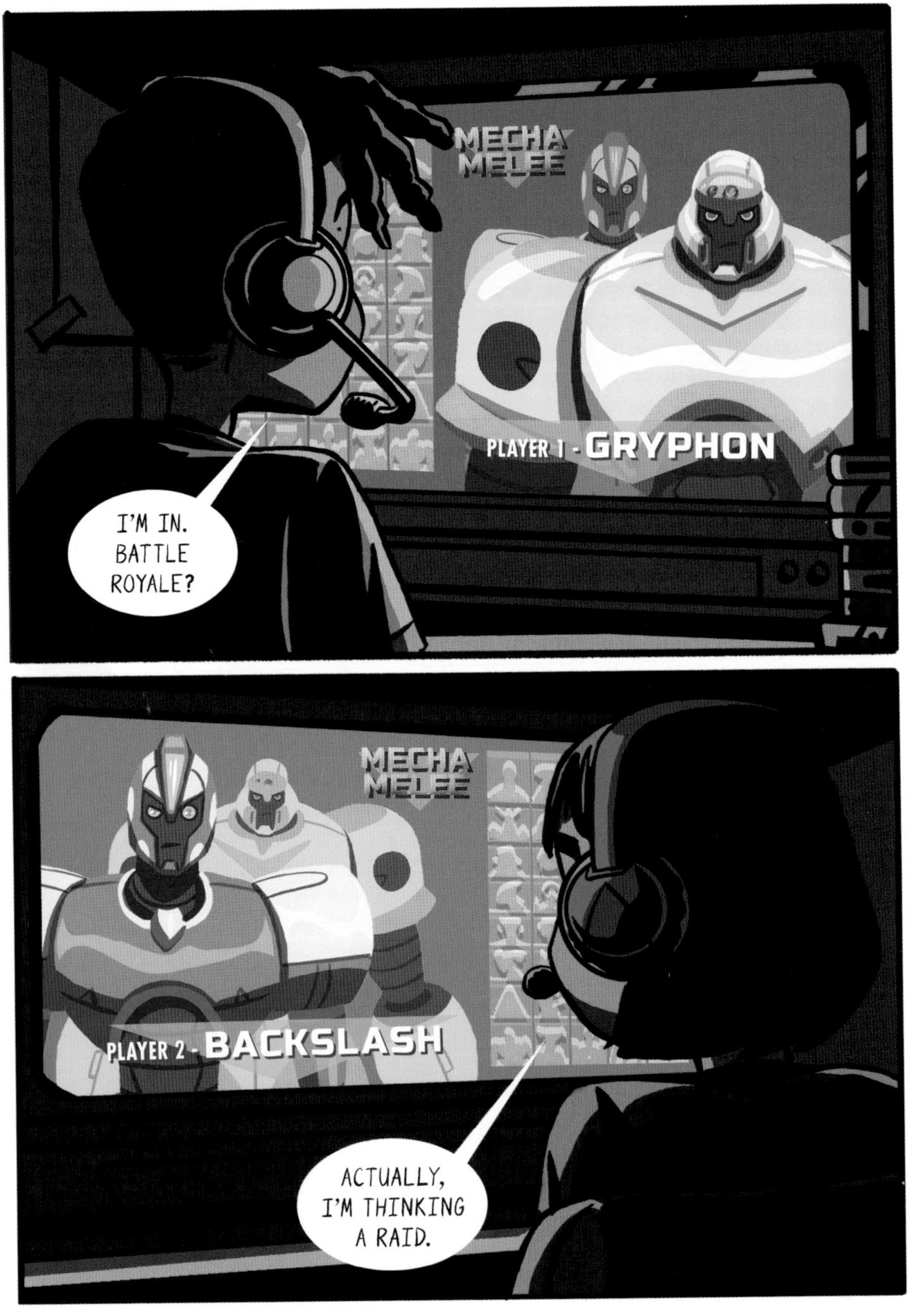
MECHA MELEE
PLAYER 1 - GRYPHON
I'M IN. BATTLE ROYALE?
MECHA MELEE
PLAYER 2 - BACKSLASH
ACTUALLY, I'M THINKING A RAID.

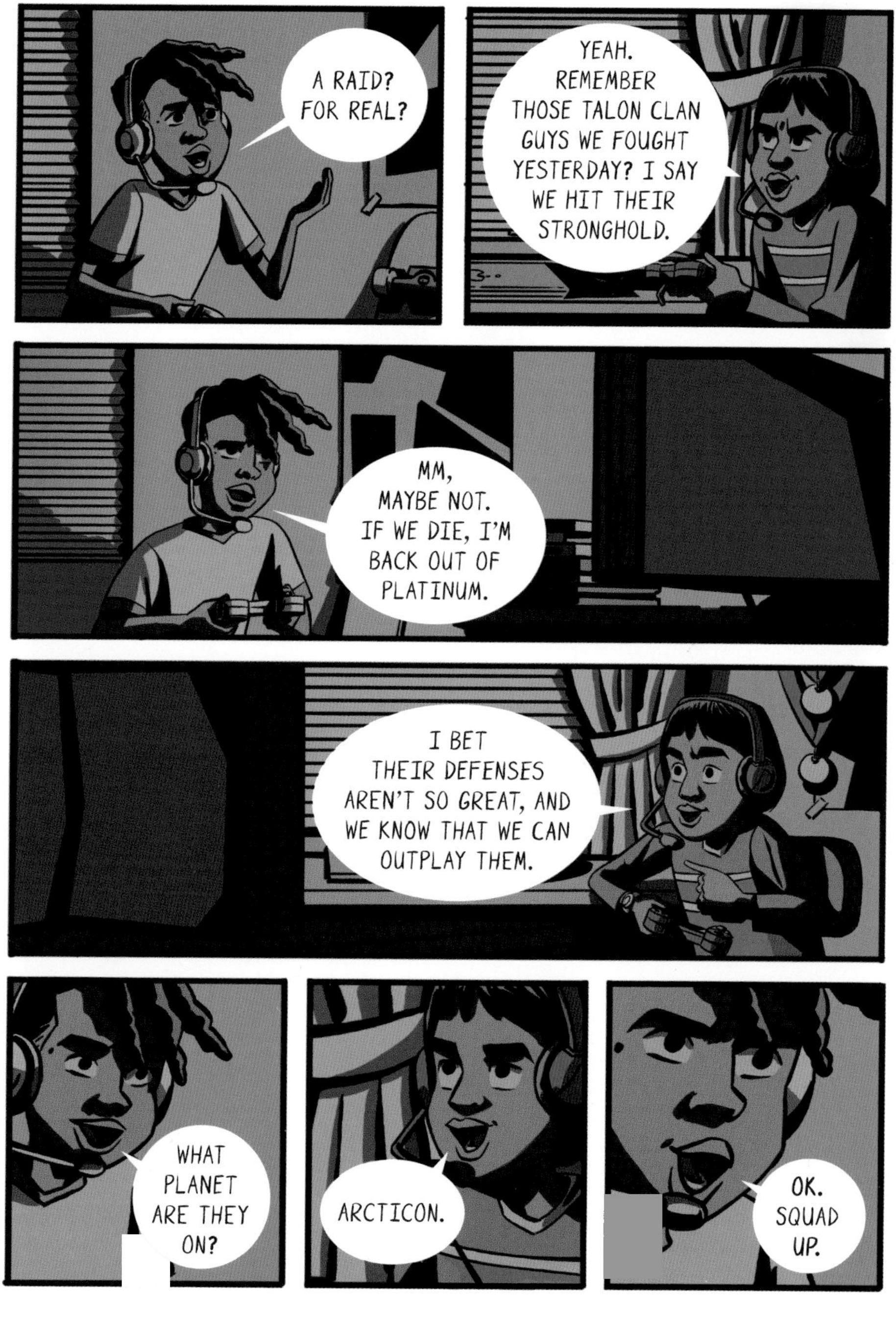
A RAID? FOR REAL?
YEAH. REMEMBER THOSE TALON CLAN GUYS WE FOUGHT YESTERDAY? I SAY WE HIT THEIR STRONGHOLD.
MM, MAYBE NOT. IF WE DIE, I'M BACK OUT OF PLATINUM.
I BET THEIR DEFENSES AREN'T SO GREAT, AND WE KNOW THAT WE CAN OUTPLAY THEM.
WHAT PLANET ARE THEY ON?
ARCTICON.
OK. SQUAD UP.

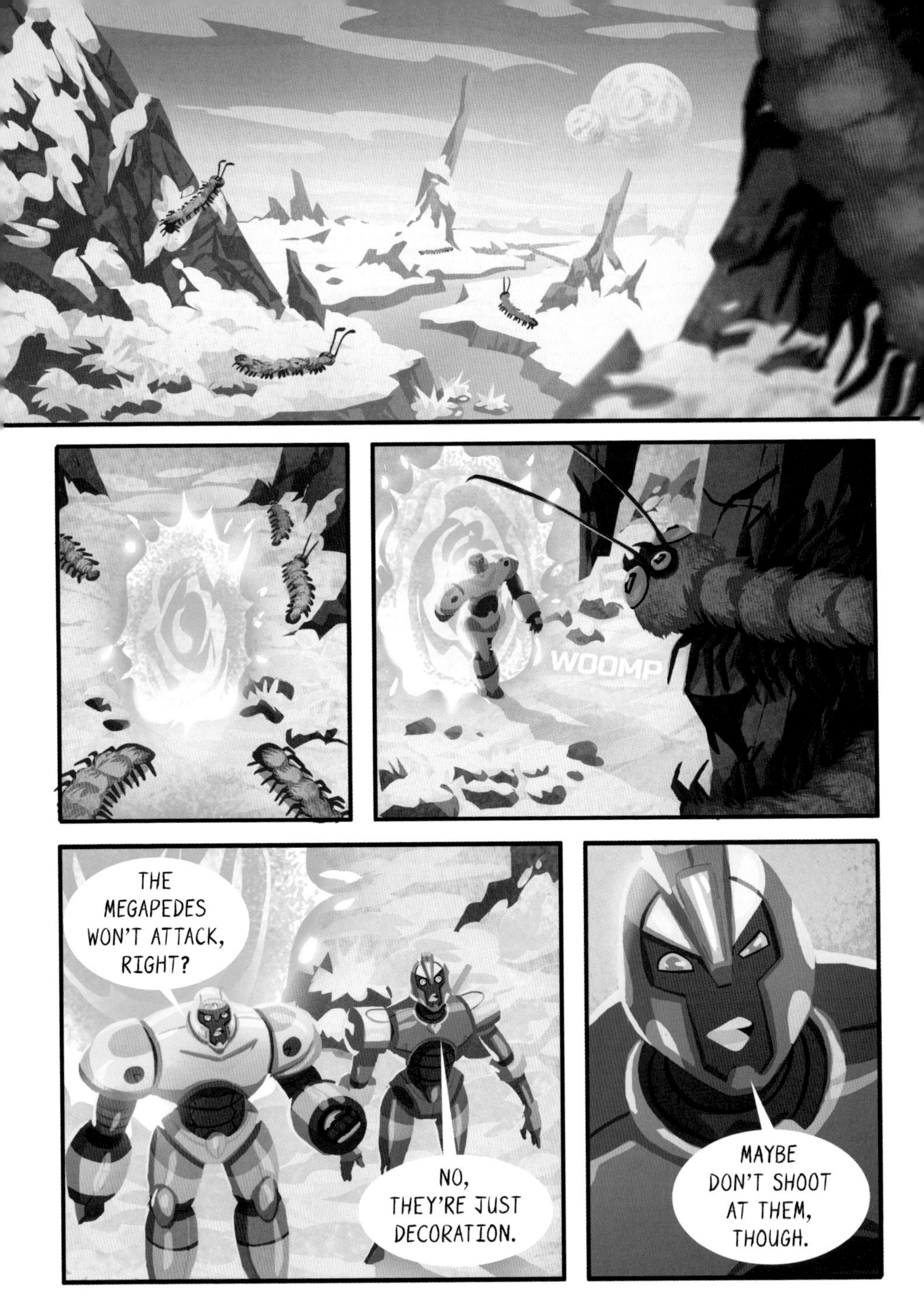
WOOMP
THE MEGAPEDES WON'T ATTACK, RIGHT?
NO, THEY'RE JUST DECORATION.
MAYBE DON'T SHOOT AT THEM, THOUGH.

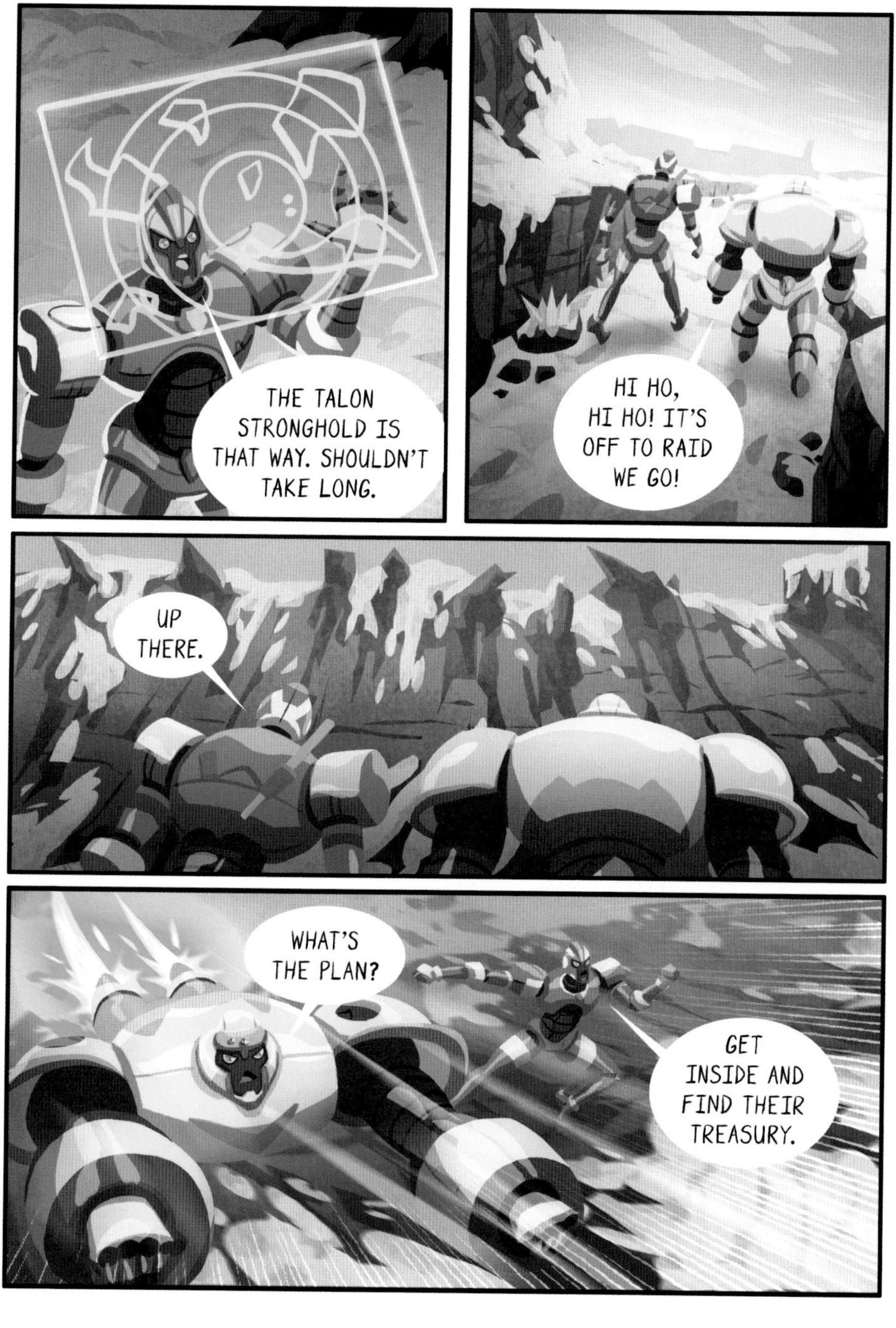
THE TALON STRONGHOLD IS THAT WAY. SHOULDN'T TAKE LONG.
HI HO, HI HO! IT'S OFF TO RAID WE GO!
UP THERE.
WHAT'S THE PLAN?
GET INSIDE AND FIND THEIR TREASURY.

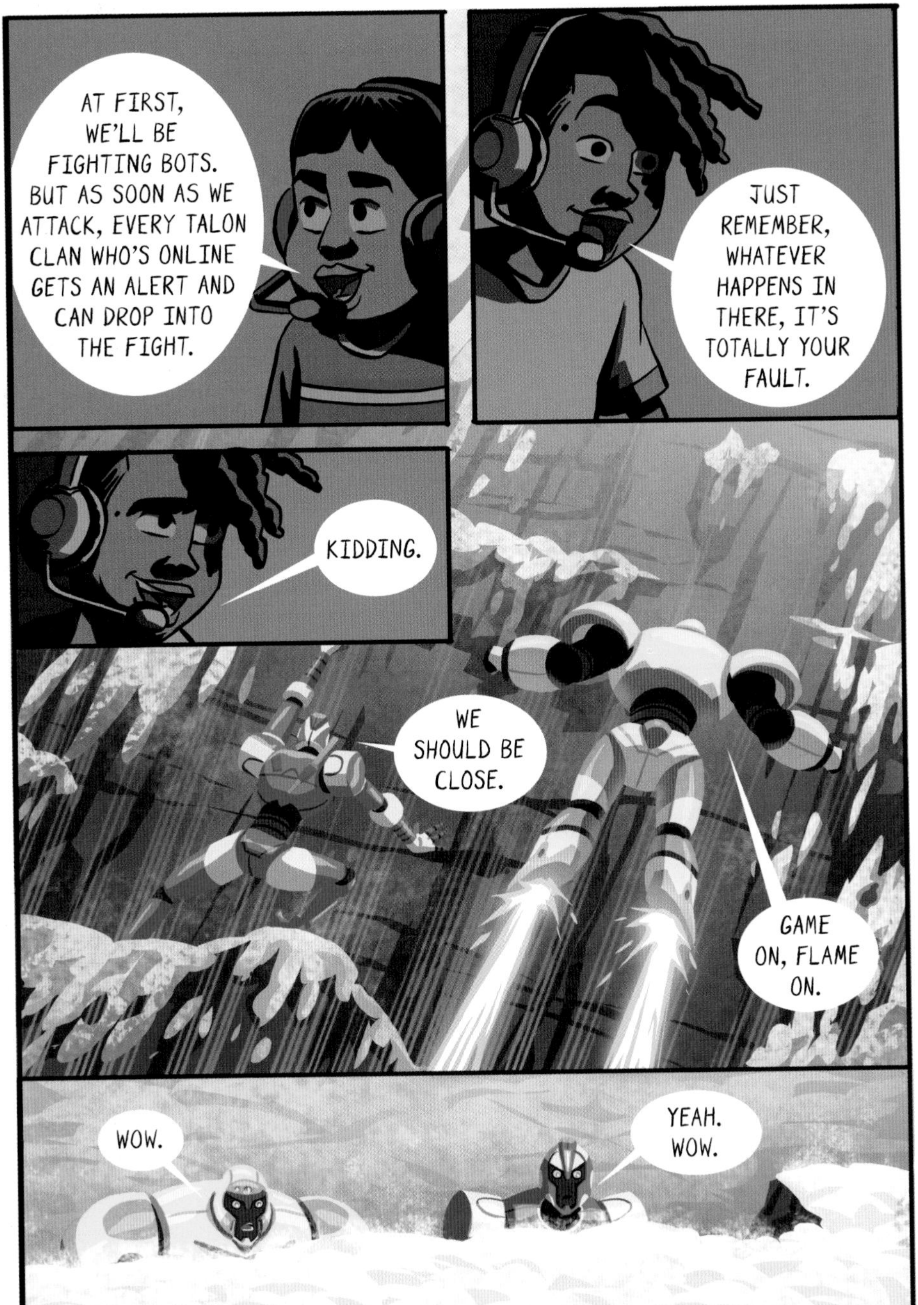
AT FIRST, WE'LL BE FIGHTING BOTS. BUT AS SOON AS WE ATTACK, EVERY TALON CLAN WHO'S ONLINE GETS AN ALERT AND CAN DROP INTO THE FIGHT.
JUST REMEMBER, WHATEVER HAPPENS IN THERE, IT'S TOTALLY YOUR FAULT.
KIDDING.
WE SHOULD BE CLOSE.
GAME ON, FLAME ON.
WOW.
YEAH. WOW.

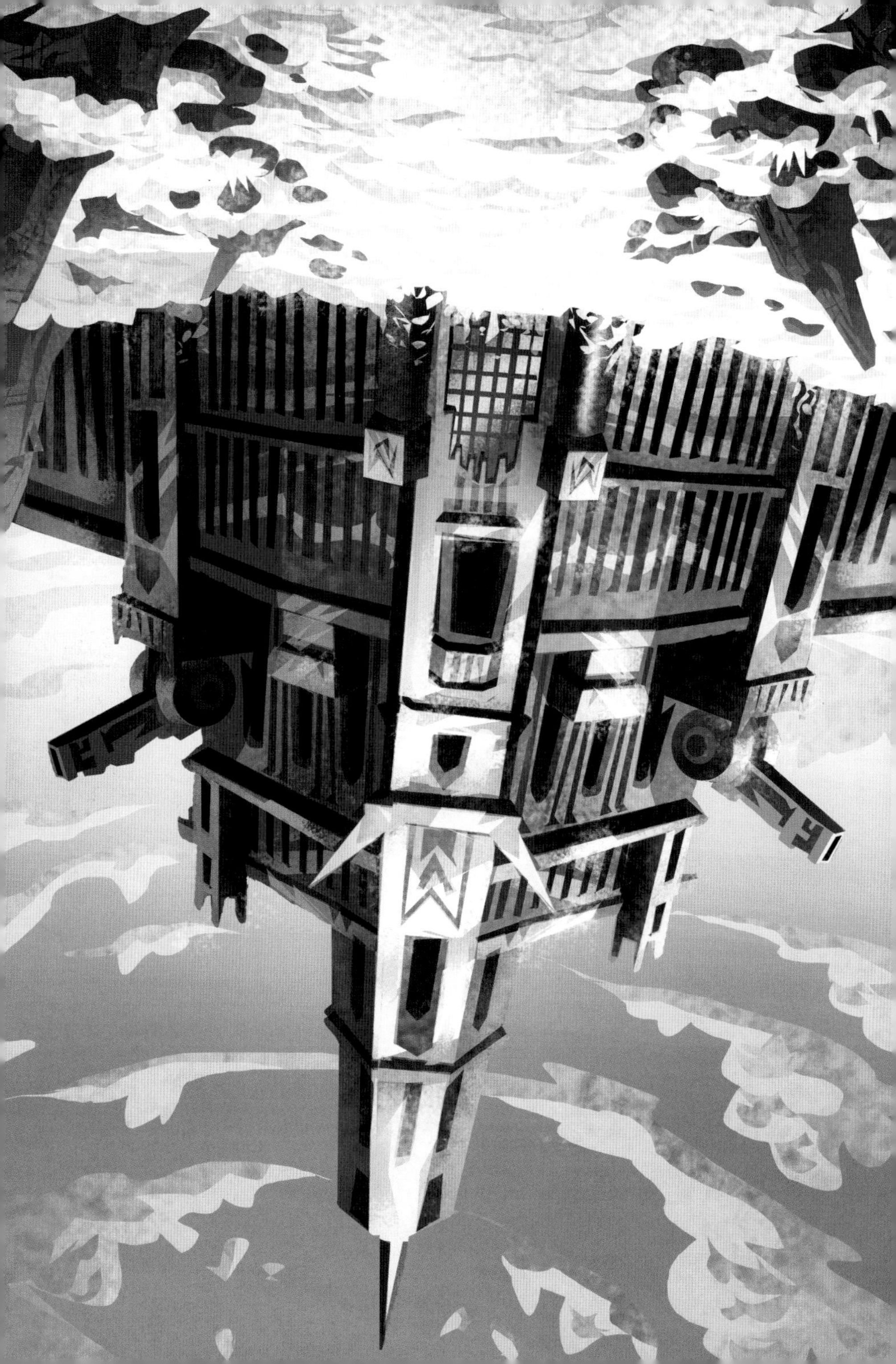

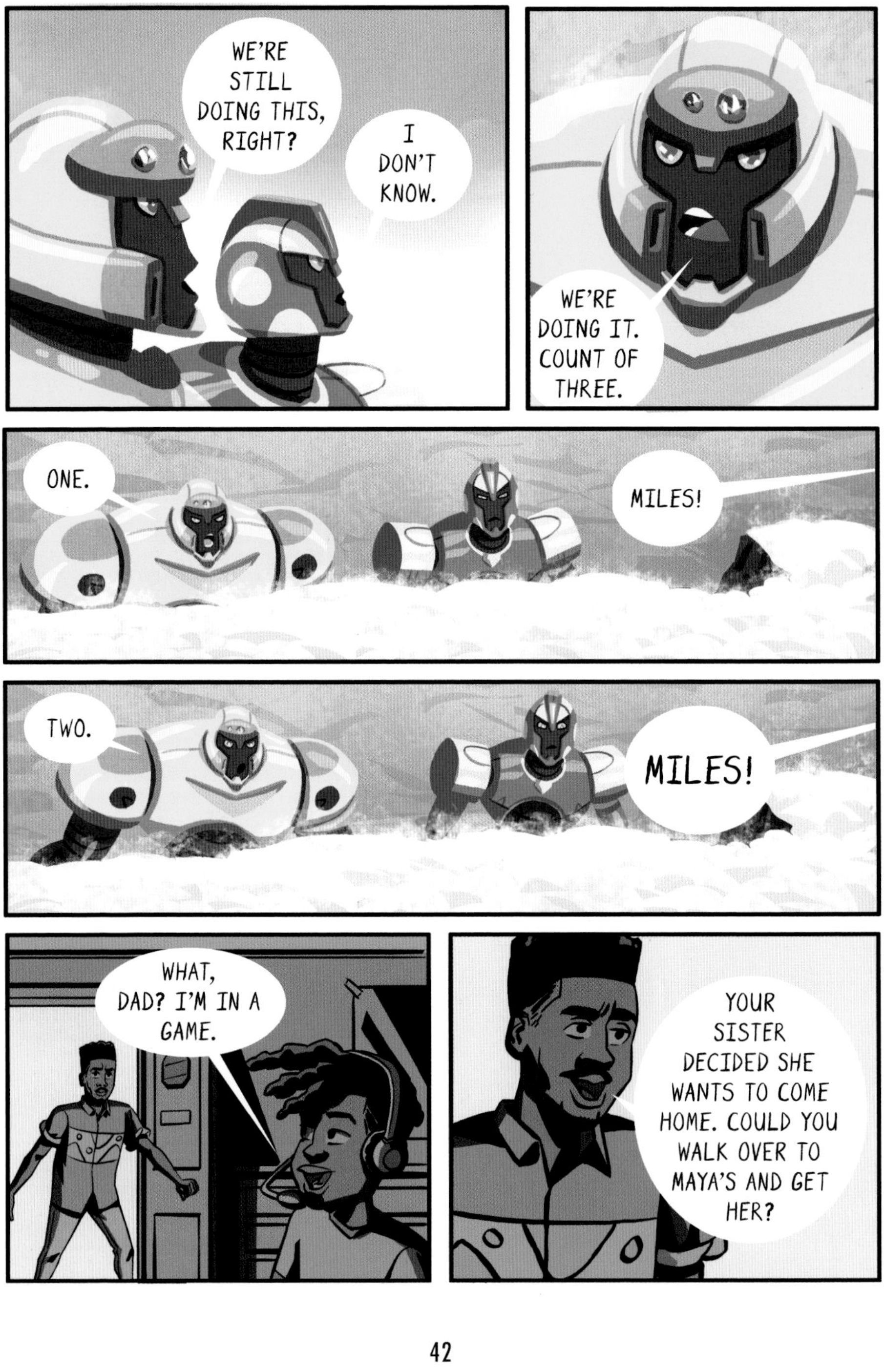
WE'RE STILL DOING THIS, RIGHT?
I DON'T KNOW.
WE'RE DOING IT. COUNT OF THREE.
ONE.
MILES!
TWO.
MILES!
WHAT, DAD? I'M IN A GAME.
YOUR SISTER DECIDED SHE WANTS TO COME HOME. COULD YOU WALK OVER TO MAYA'S AND GET HER?

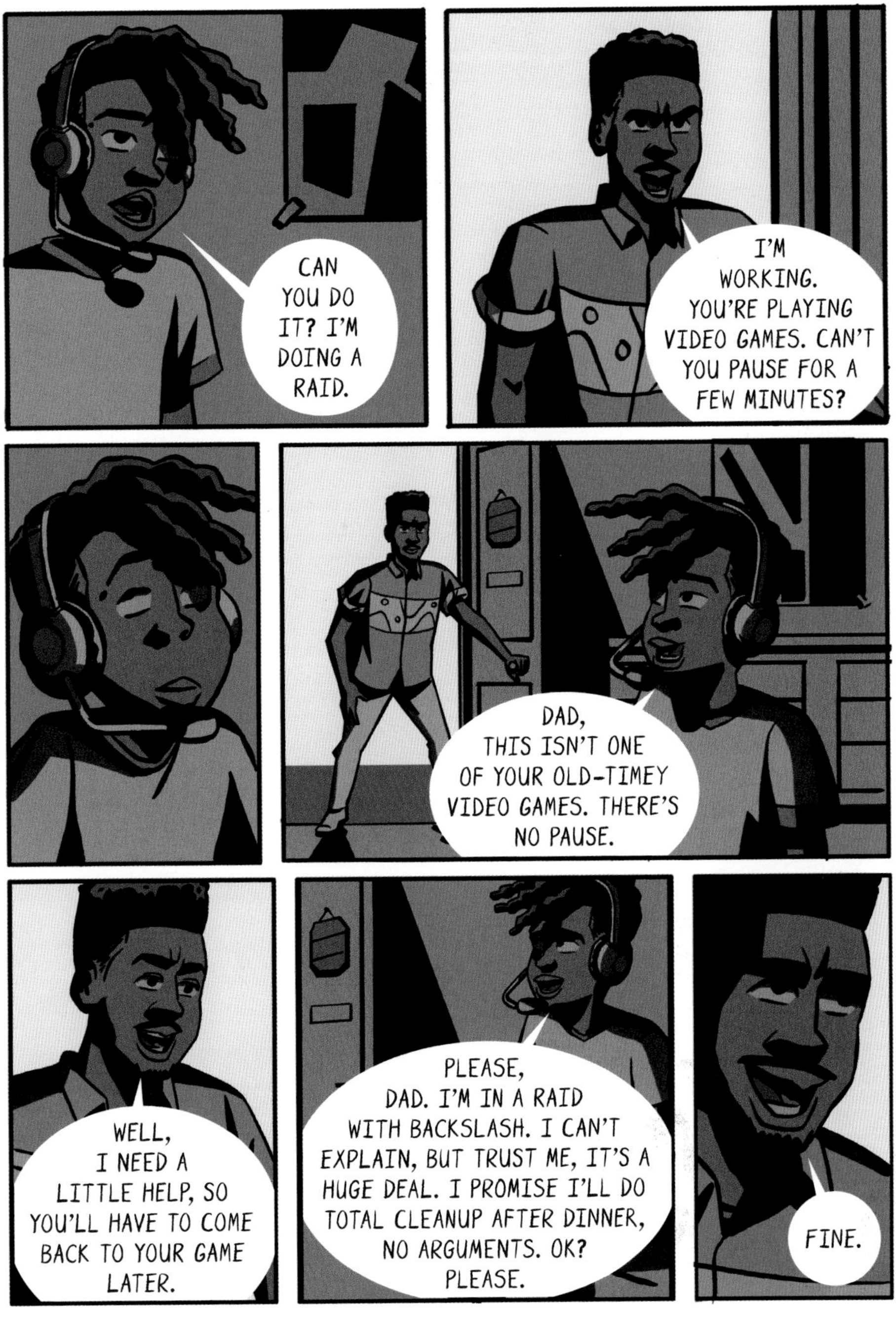
CAN YOU DO IT? I'M DOING A RAID.
I'M WORKING. YOU'RE PLAYING VIDEO GAMES. CAN'T YOU PAUSE FOR A FEW MINUTES?
DAD, THIS ISN'T ONE OF YOUR OLD-TIMEY VIDEO GAMES. THERE'S NO PAUSE.
WELL, I NEED A LITTLE HELP, SO YOU'LL HAVE TO COME BACK TO YOUR GAME LATER.
PLEASE, DAD. I'M IN A RAID WITH BACKSLASH. I CAN'T EXPLAIN, BUT TRUST ME, IT'S A HUGE DEAL. I PROMISE I'LL DO TOTAL CLEANUP AFTER DINNER, NO ARGUMENTS. OK? PLEASE.
FINE.

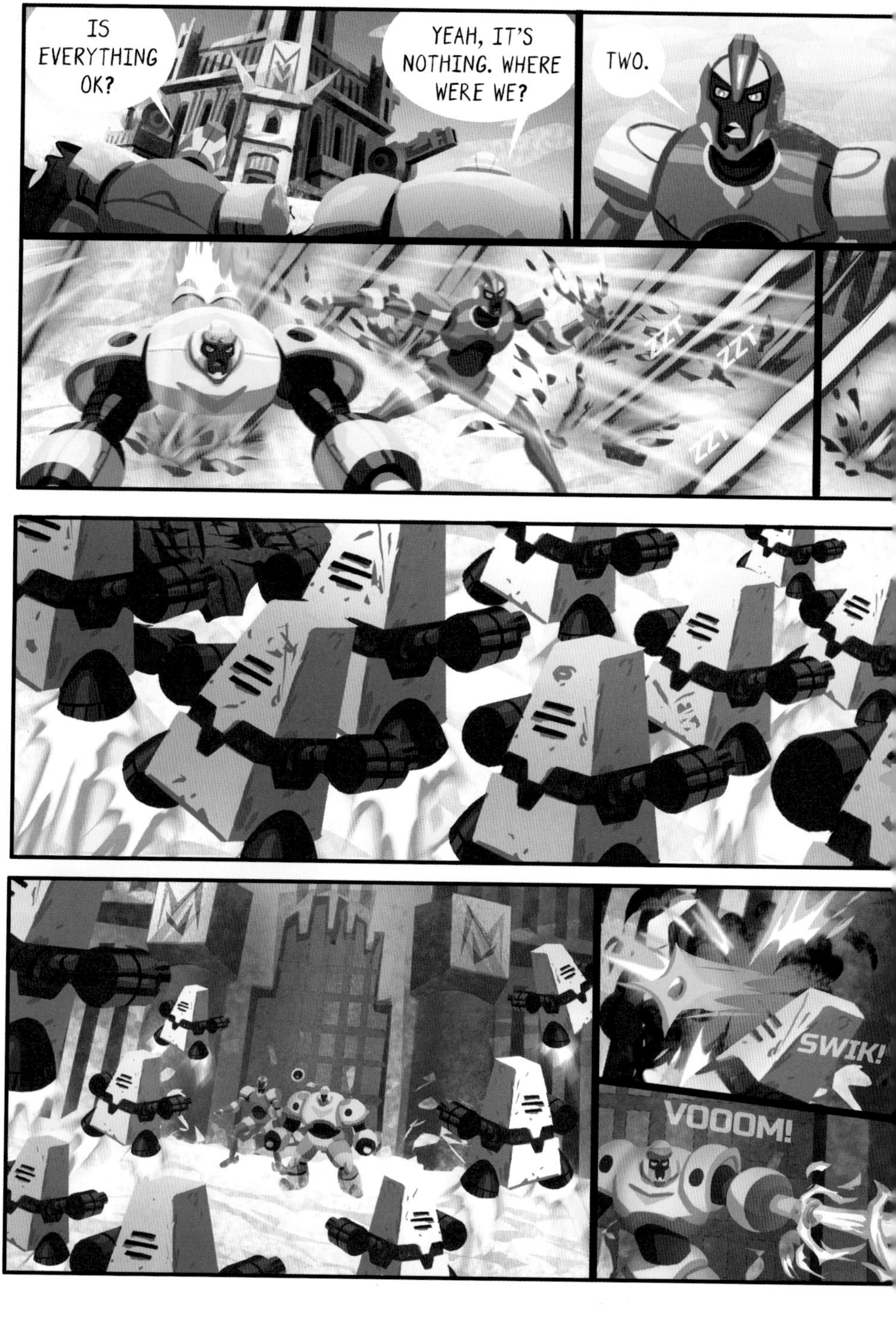
IS EVERYTHING OK?
YEAH, IT'S NOTHING. WHERE WERE WE?
TWO.
ZZT
ZZT
ZZT
SWIK!
VOOOM!

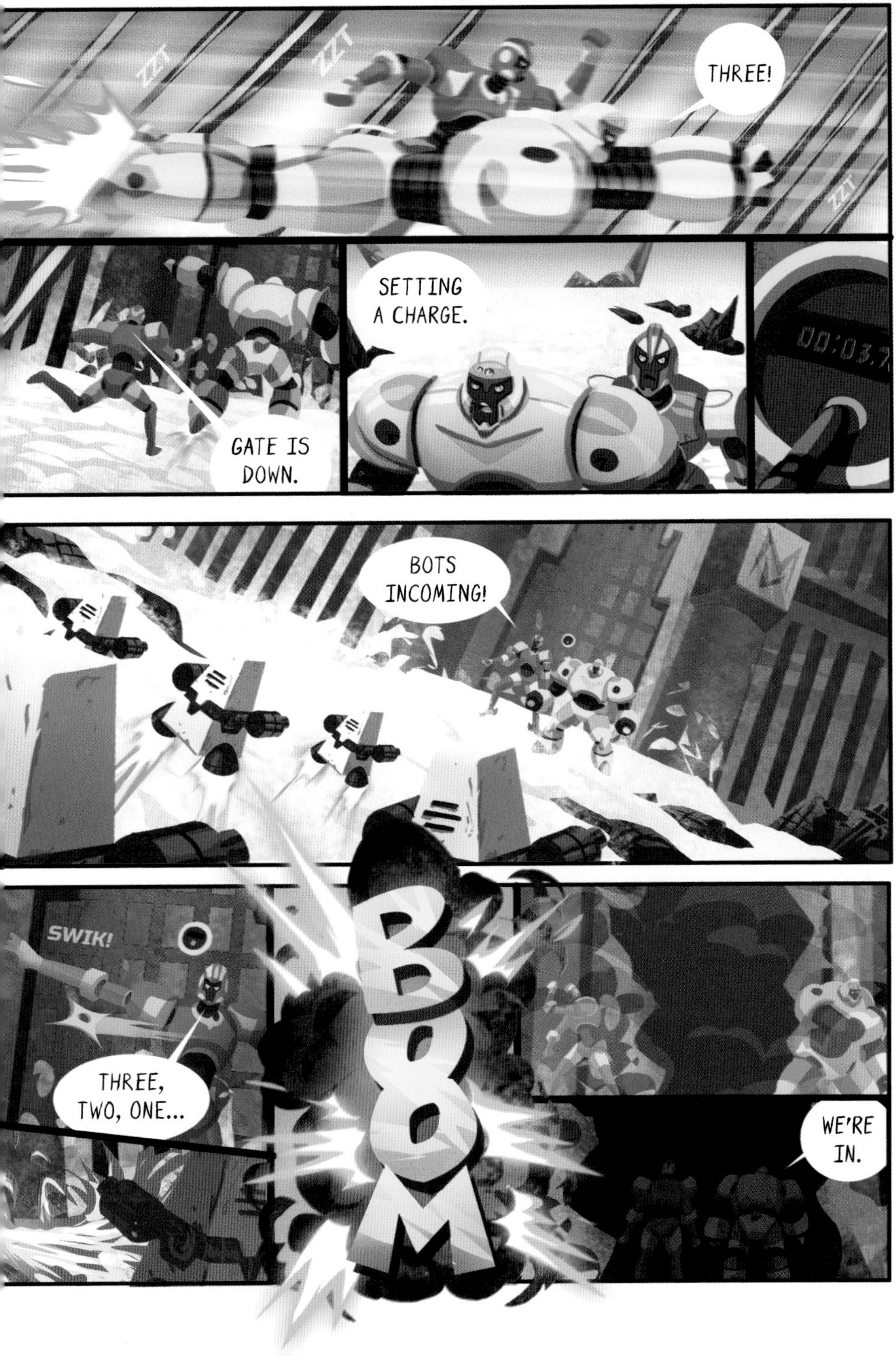
ZZT
ZZT
THREE!
ZZT
GATE IS DOWN.
SETTING A CHARGE.
00:03.7
BOTS INCOMING!
SWIK!
THREE, TWO, ONE...
BOOM
WE'RE IN.

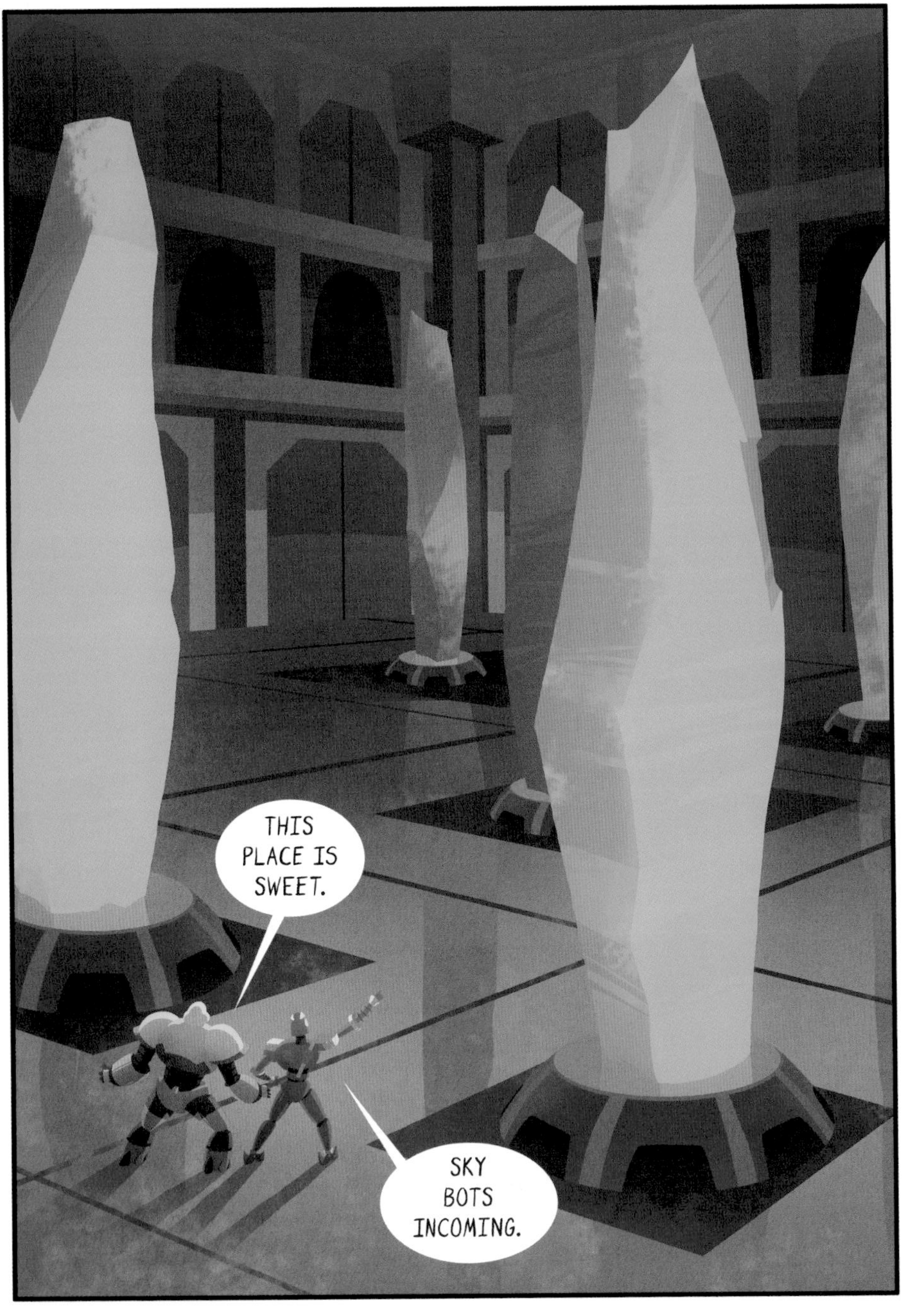
THIS PLACE IS SWEET.
SKY BOTS INCOMING.

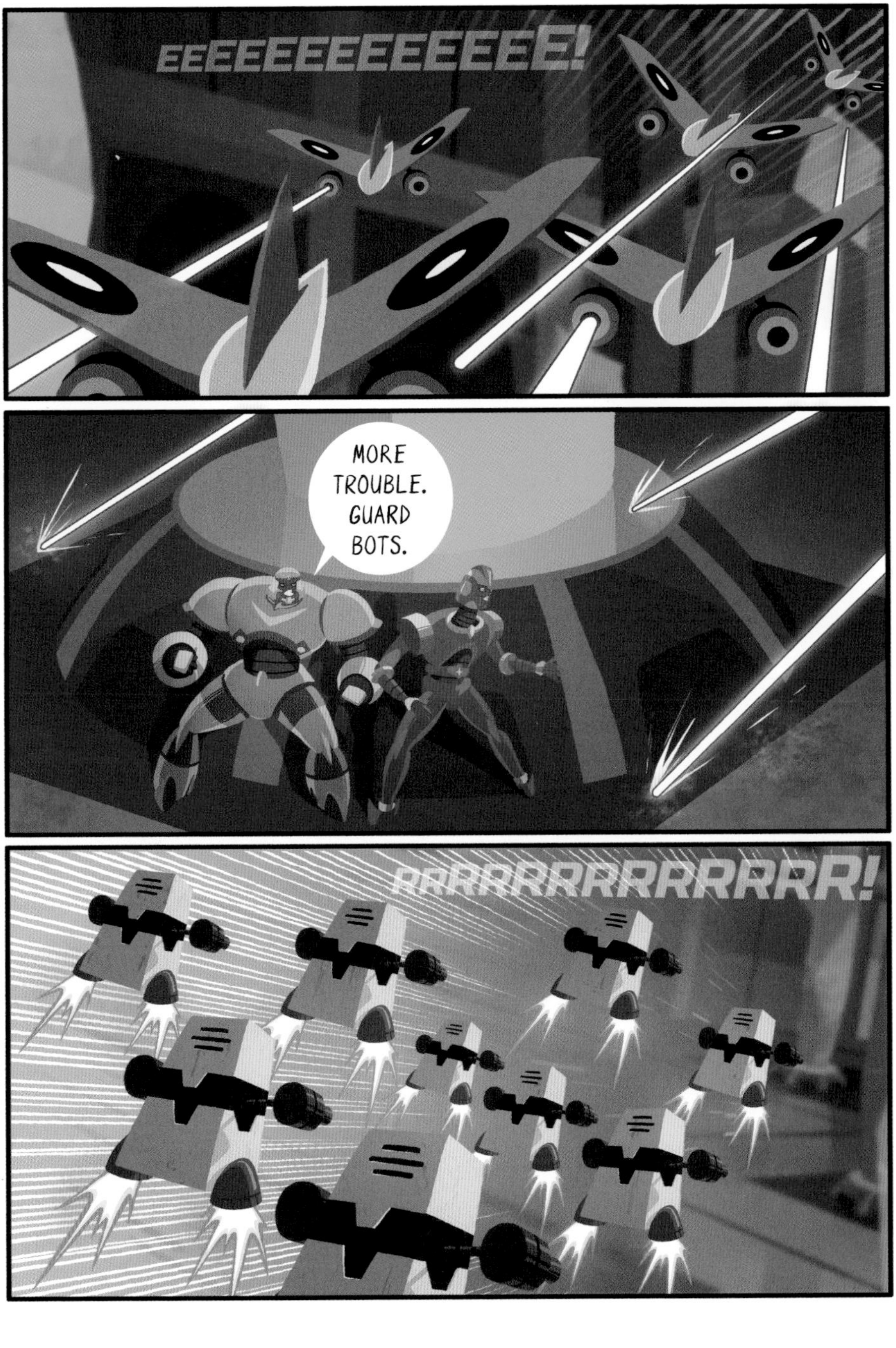
EEEEEEEEEEEEEE!
MORE TROUBLE. GUARD BOTS.
RRRRRRRRRRRRRRR!

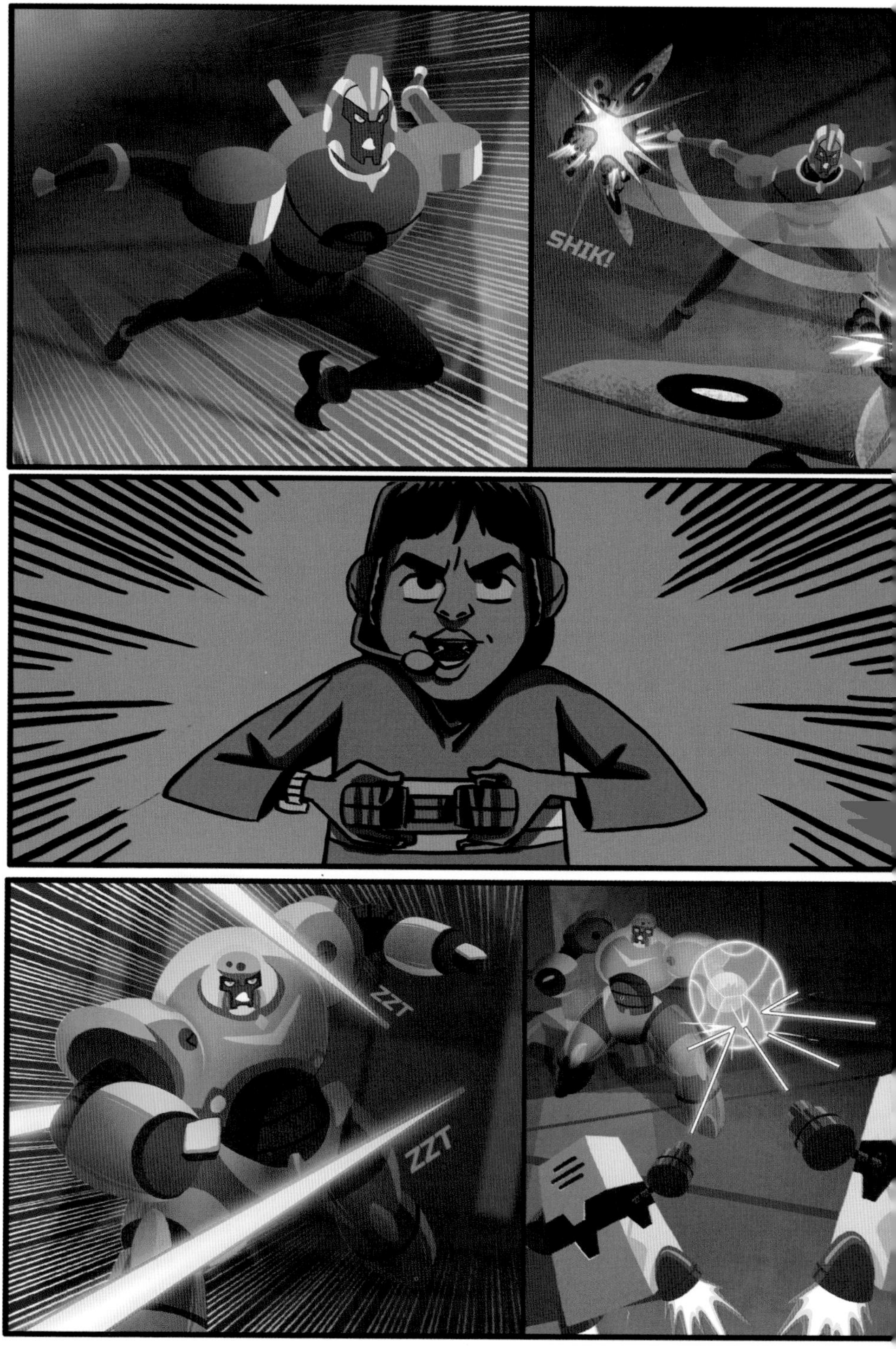
SHIK!
ZZT
ZZT

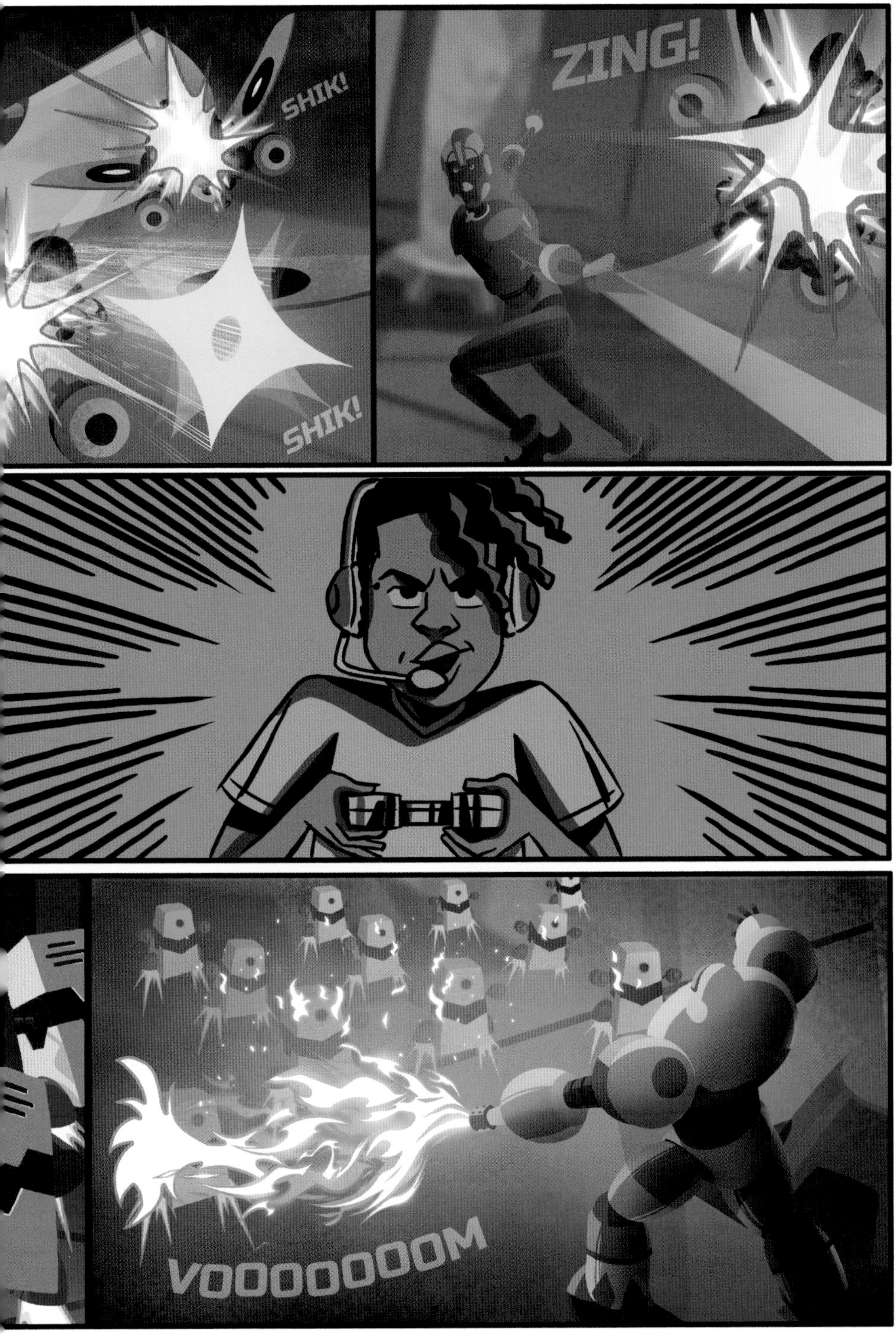
SHIK!
SHIK!
ZING!
VOOOOOOOM

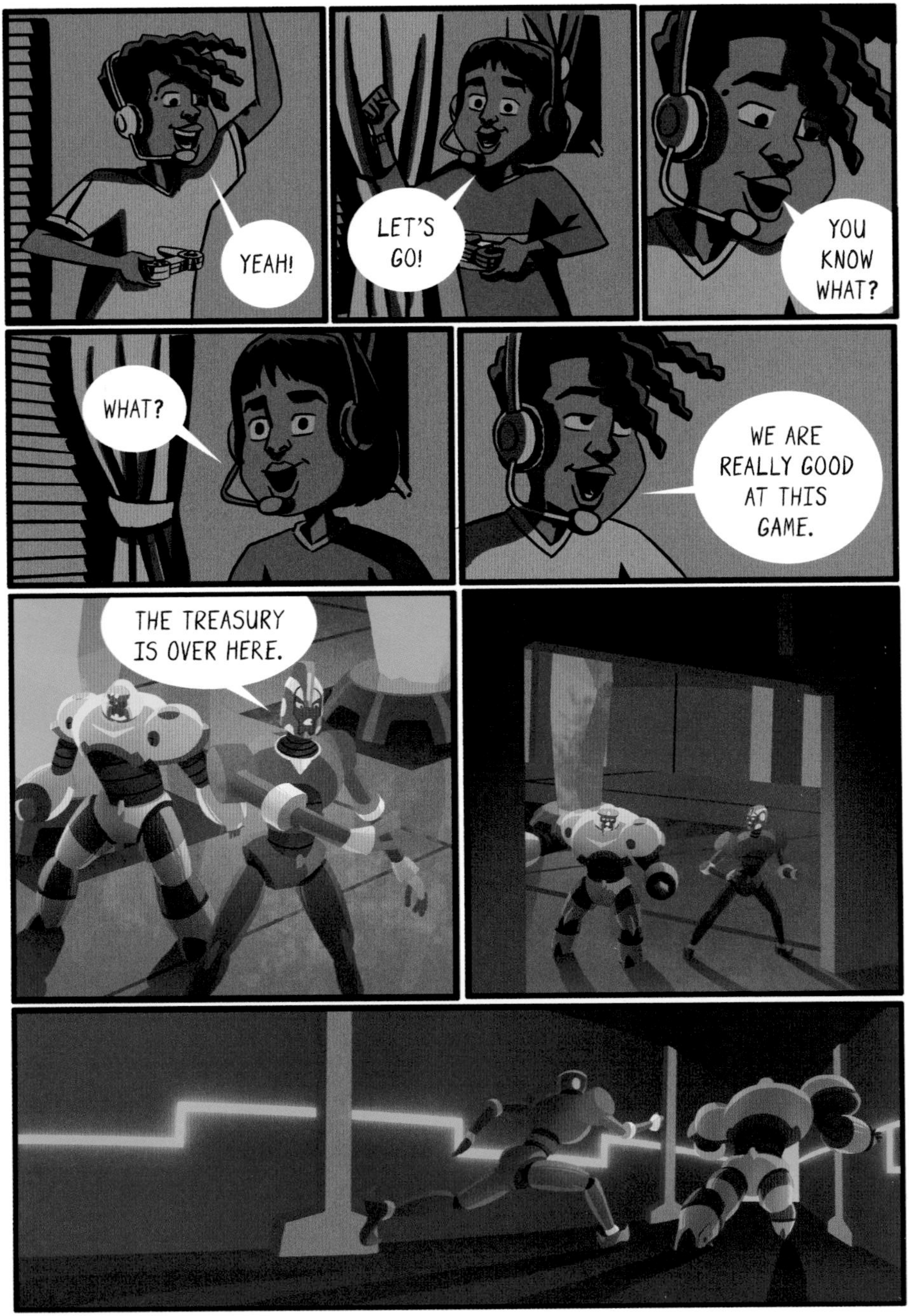
YEAH!
LET'S GO!
YOU KNOW WHAT?
WHAT?
WE ARE REALLY GOOD AT THIS GAME.
THE TREASURY IS OVER HERE.

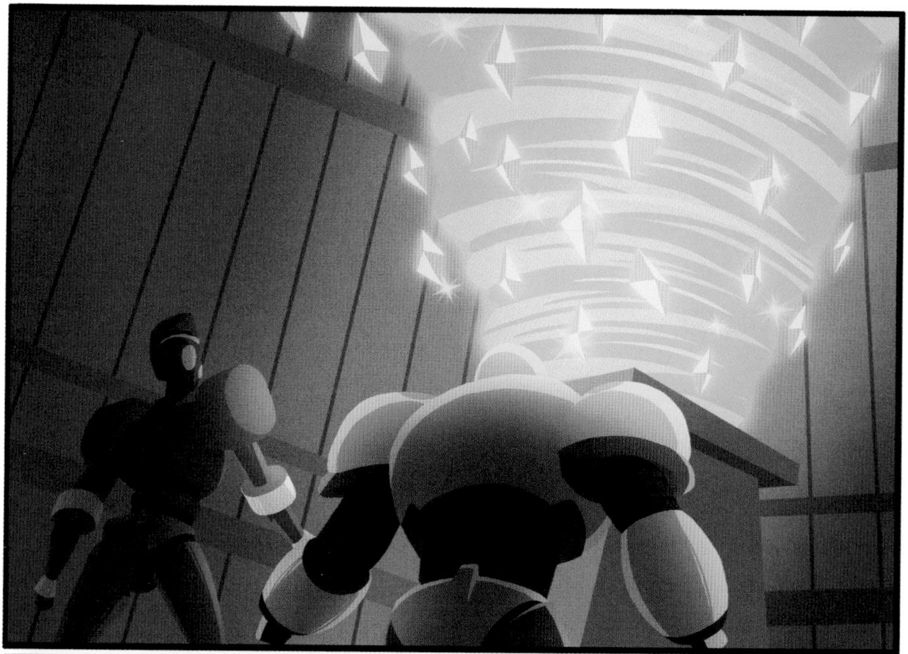

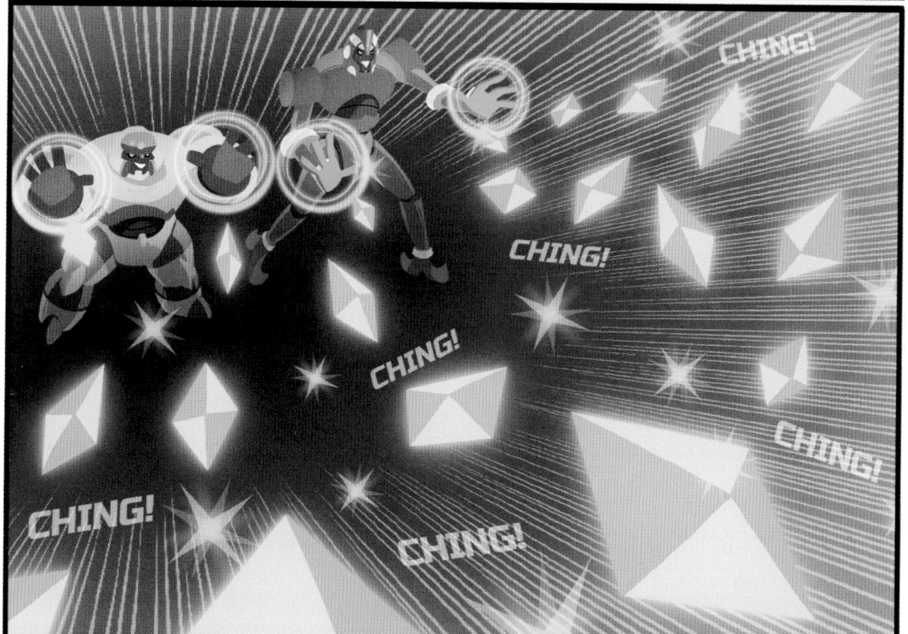
CHING!
CHING!
CHING!
CHING!
CHING!
CHING!

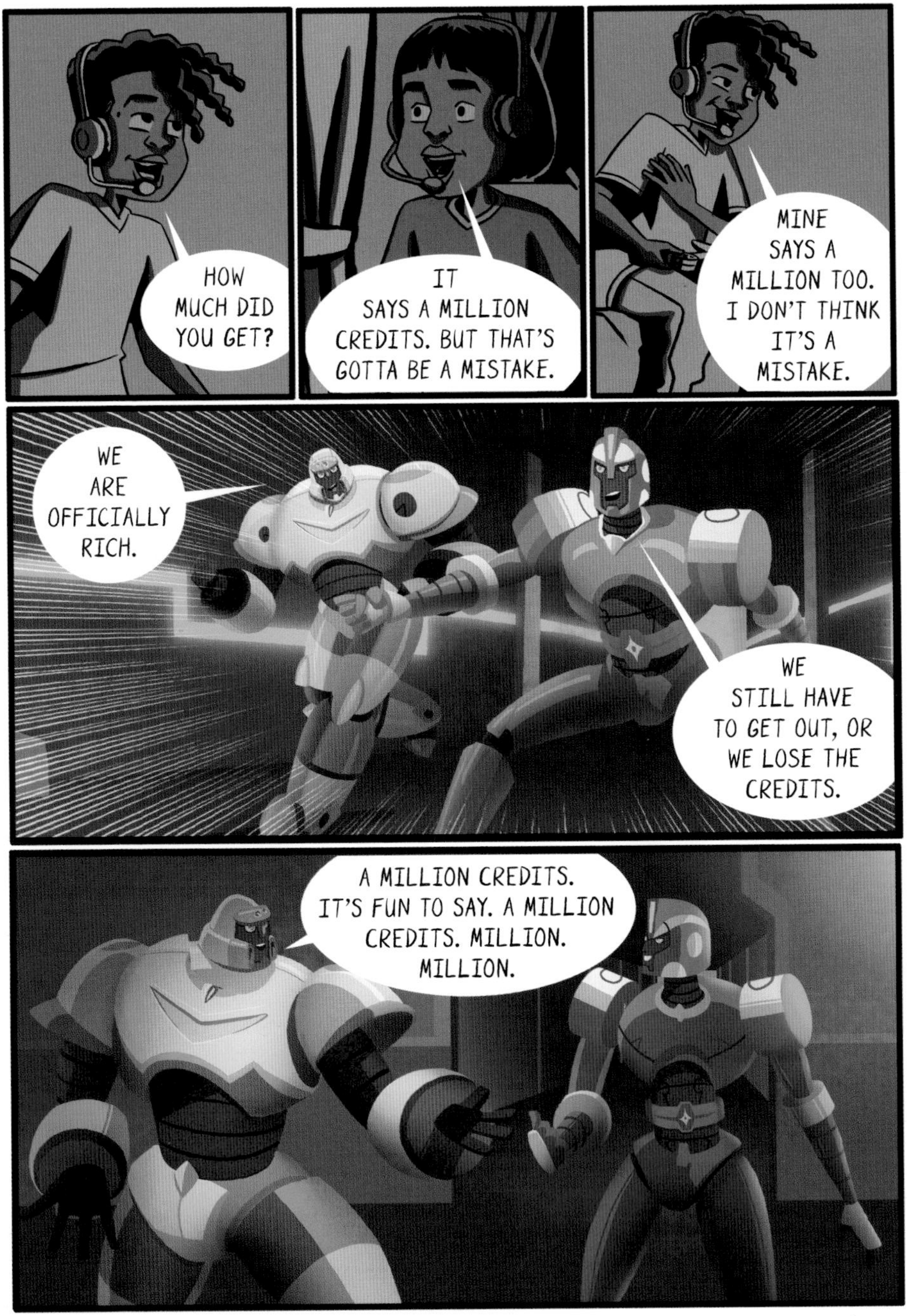
HOW MUCH DID YOU GET?
IT SAYS A MILLION CREDITS. BUT THAT'S GOTTA BE A MISTAKE.
MINE SAYS A MILLION TOO. I DON'T THINK IT'S A MISTAKE.
WE ARE OFFICIALLY RICH.
WE STILL HAVE TO GET OUT, OR WE LOSE THE CREDITS.
A MILLION CREDITS. IT'S FUN TO SAY. A MILLION CREDITS. MILLION. MILLION.

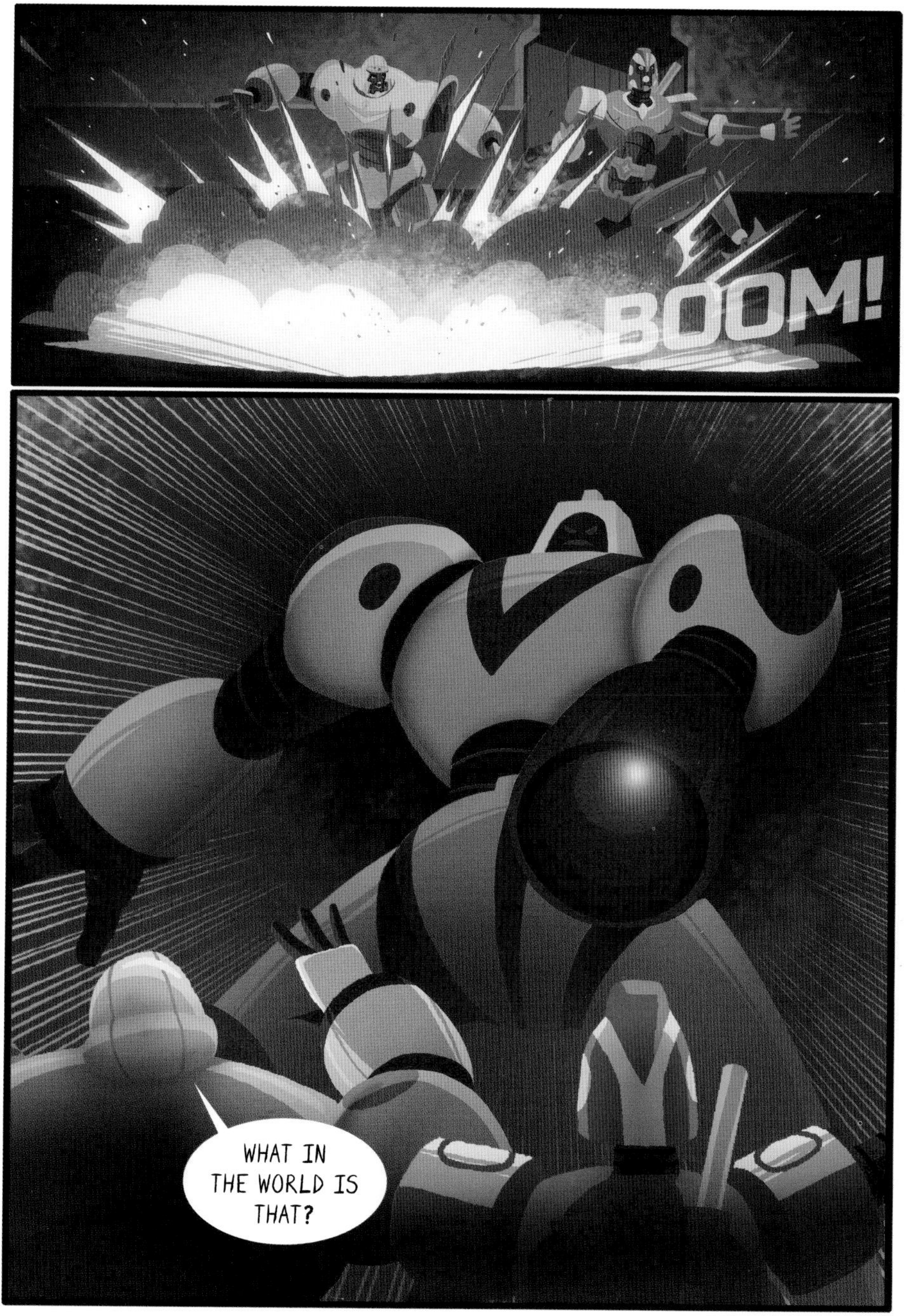
BOOM!
WHAT IN THE WORLD IS THAT?

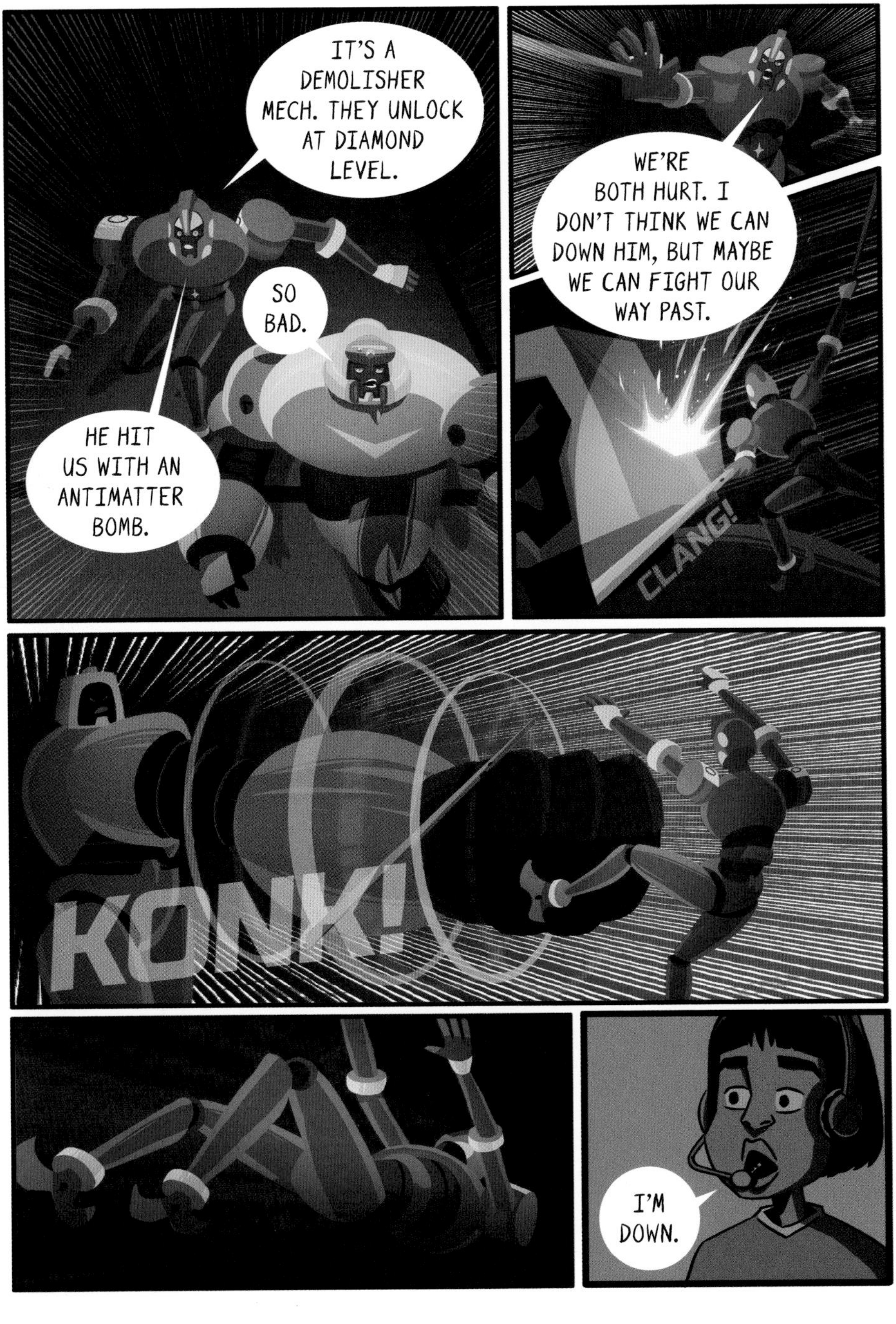
IT'S A DEMOLISHER MECH. THEY UNLOCK AT DIAMOND LEVEL.
HE HIT US WITH AN ANTIMATTER BOMB.
SO BAD.
WE'RE BOTH HURT. I DON'T THINK WE CAN DOWN HIM, BUT MAYBE WE CAN FIGHT OUR WAY PAST.
CLANG!
KONK!
I'M DOWN.

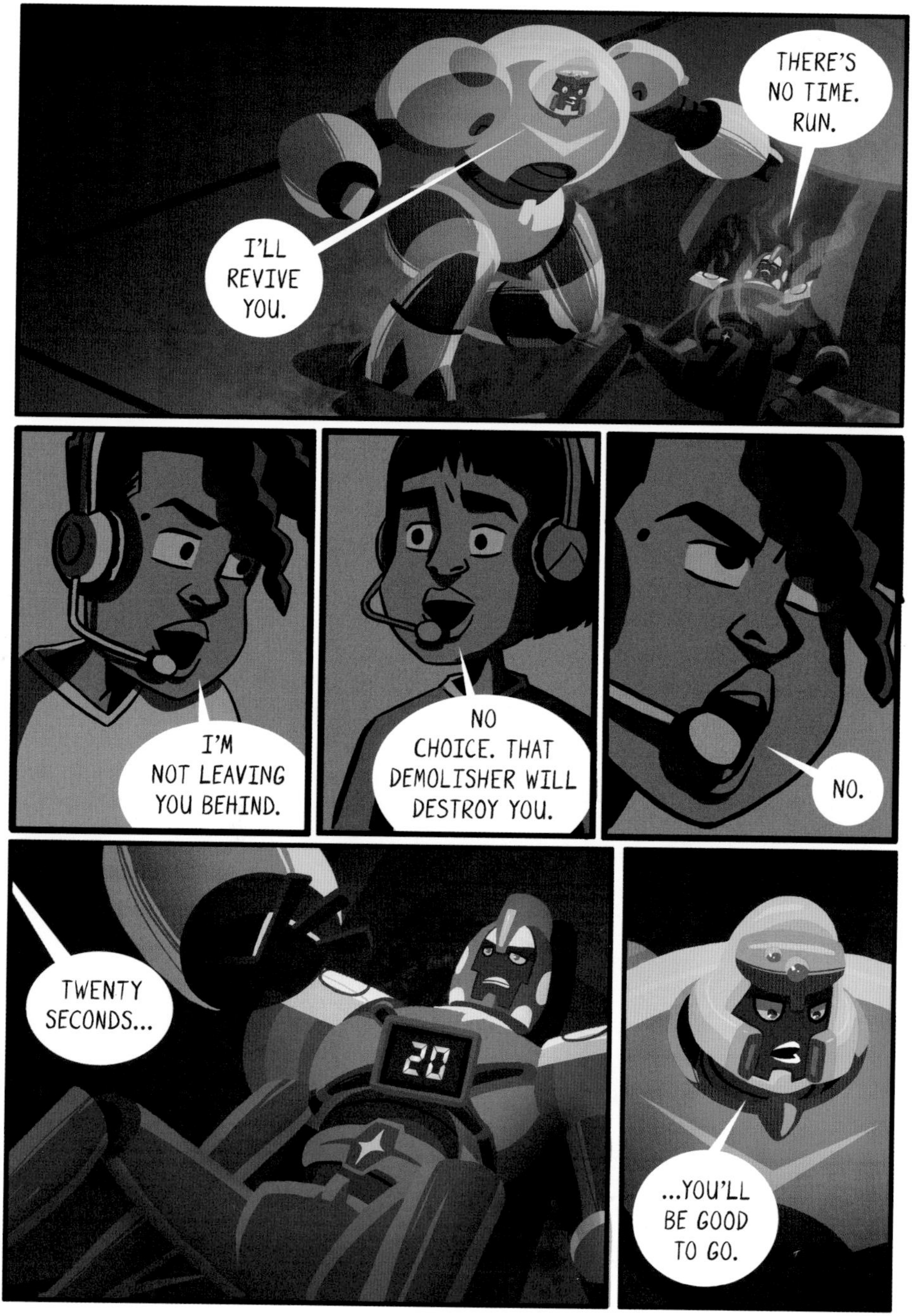
I'LL REVIVE YOU.
THERE'S NO TIME. RUN.
I'M NOT LEAVING YOU BEHIND.
NO CHOICE. THAT DEMOLISHER WILL DESTROY YOU.
NO.
TWENTY SECONDS...
20
...YOU'LL BE GOOD TO GO.

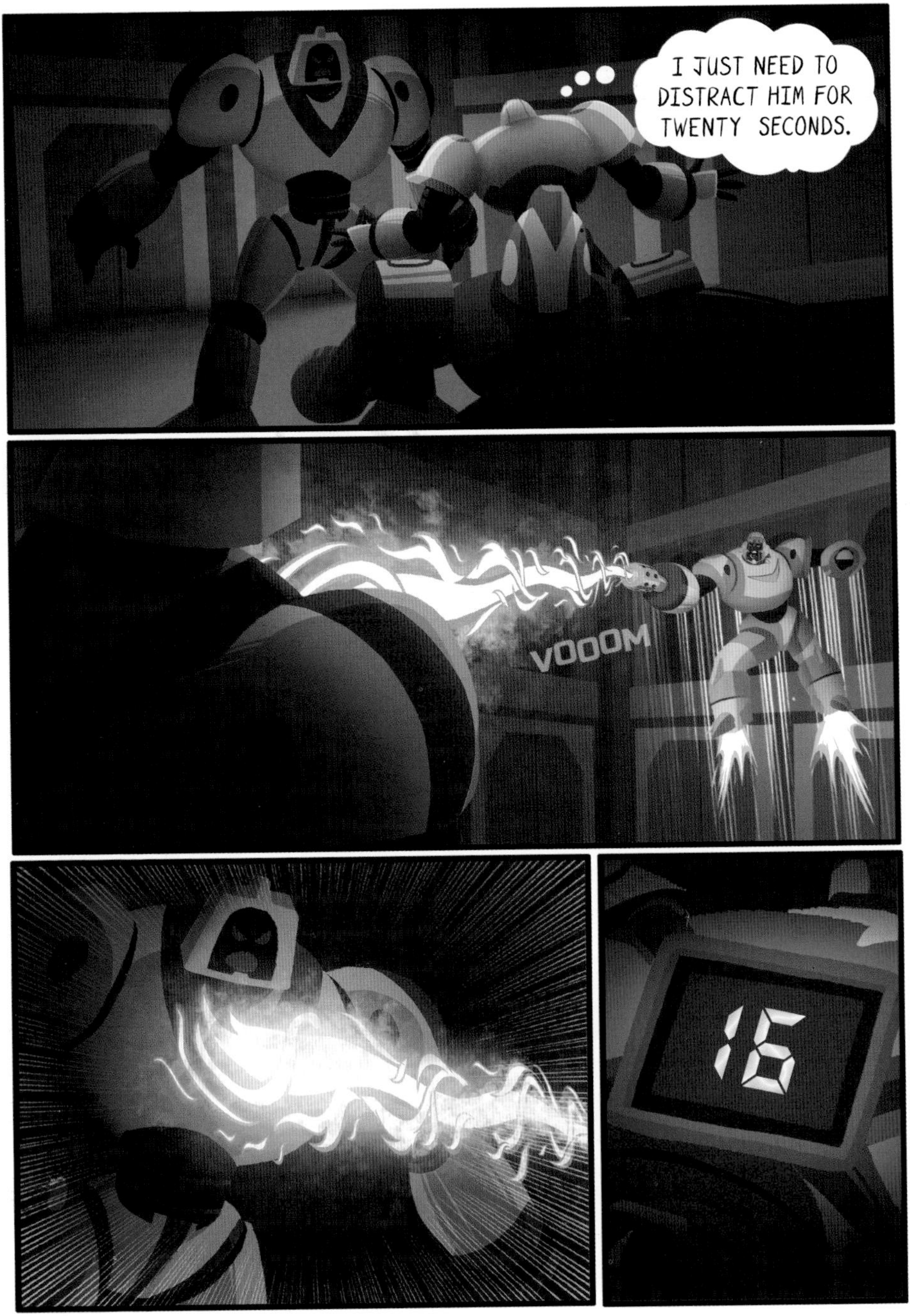
I JUST NEED TO DISTRACT HIM FOR TWENTY SECONDS.
VOOOM
16

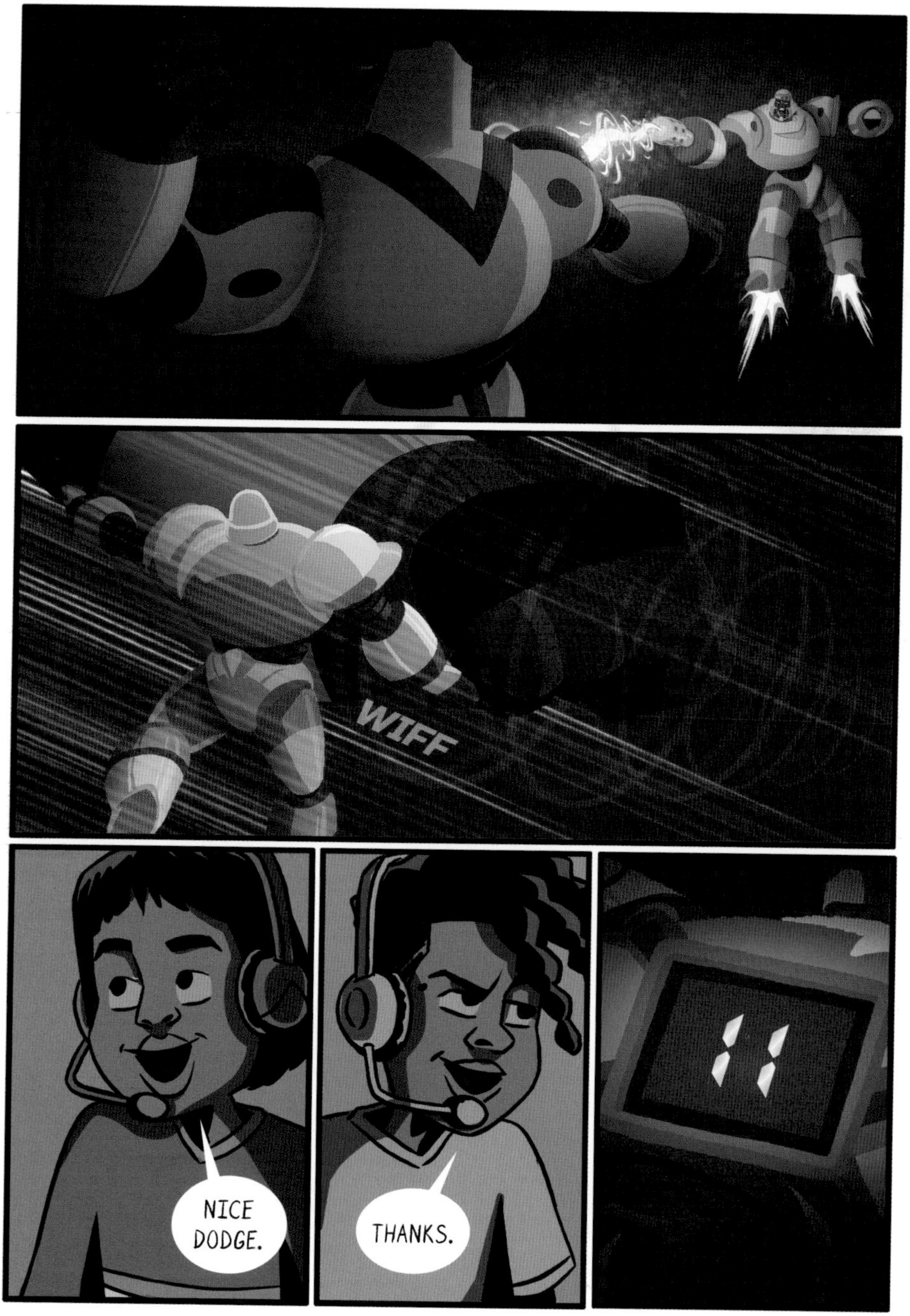
WIFF
NICE DODGE.
THANKS.
11

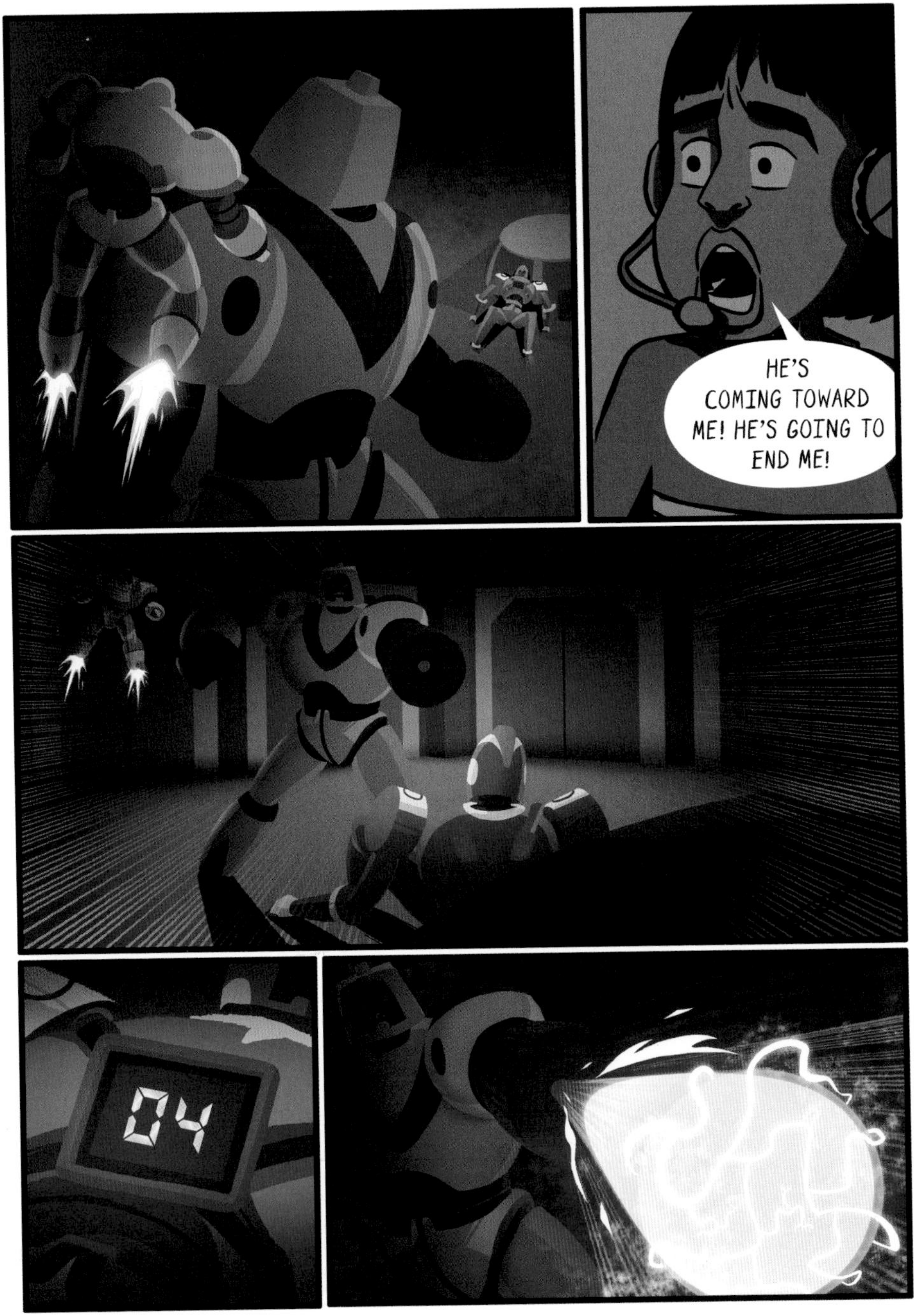
HE'S COMING TOWARD ME! HE'S GOING TO END ME!
04

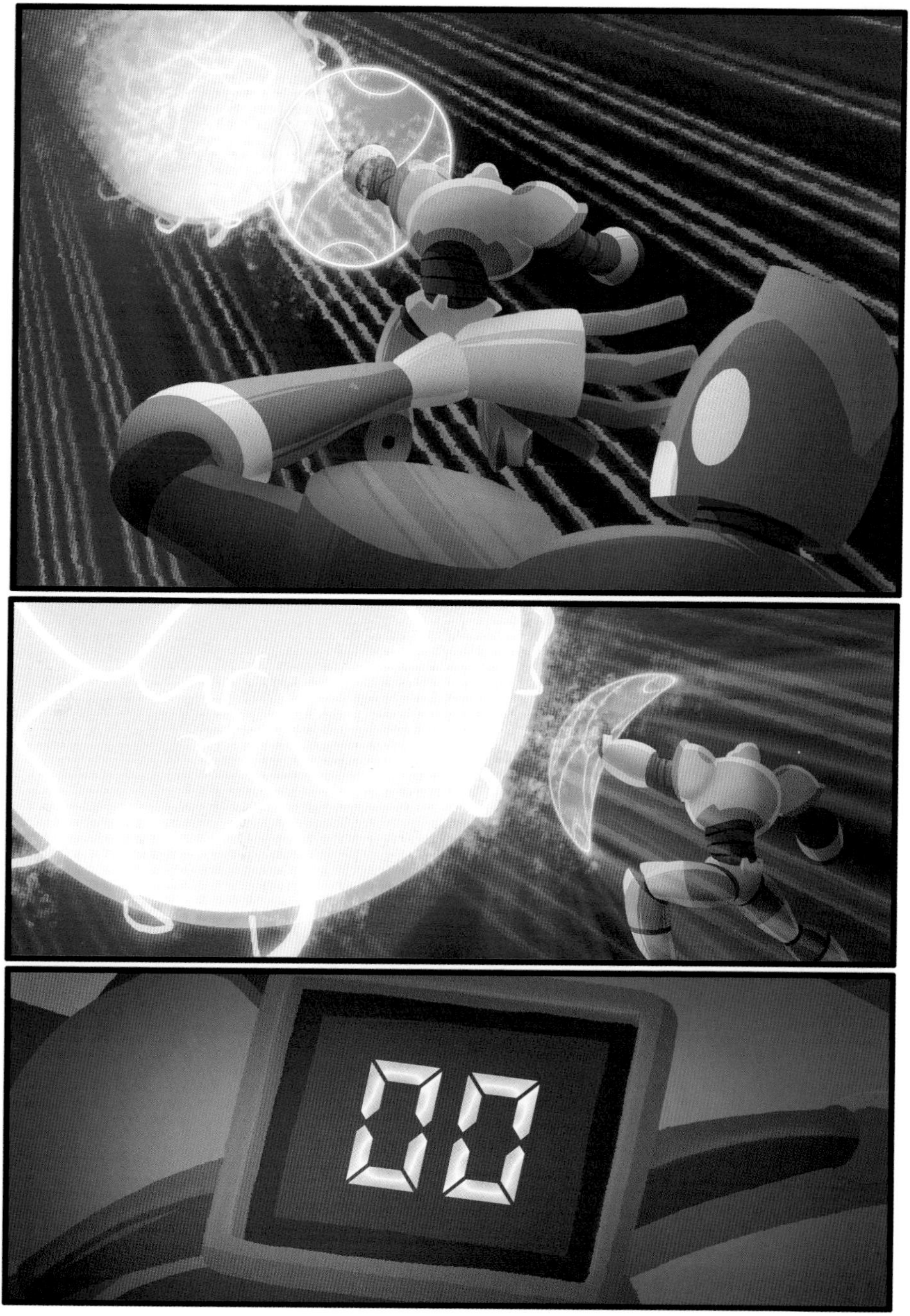
00

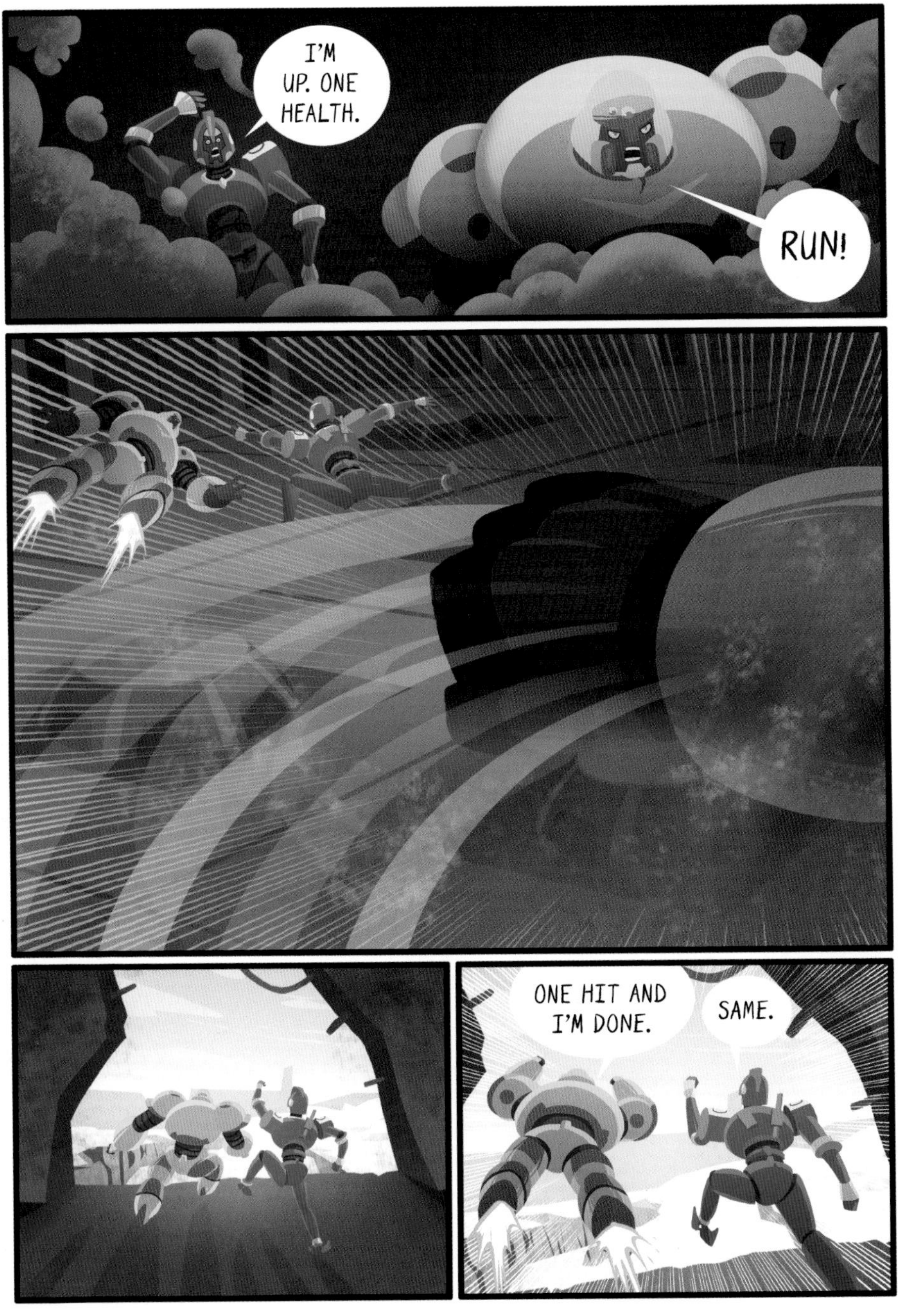
I'M UP. ONE HEALTH.
RUN!
ONE HIT AND I'M DONE.
SAME.

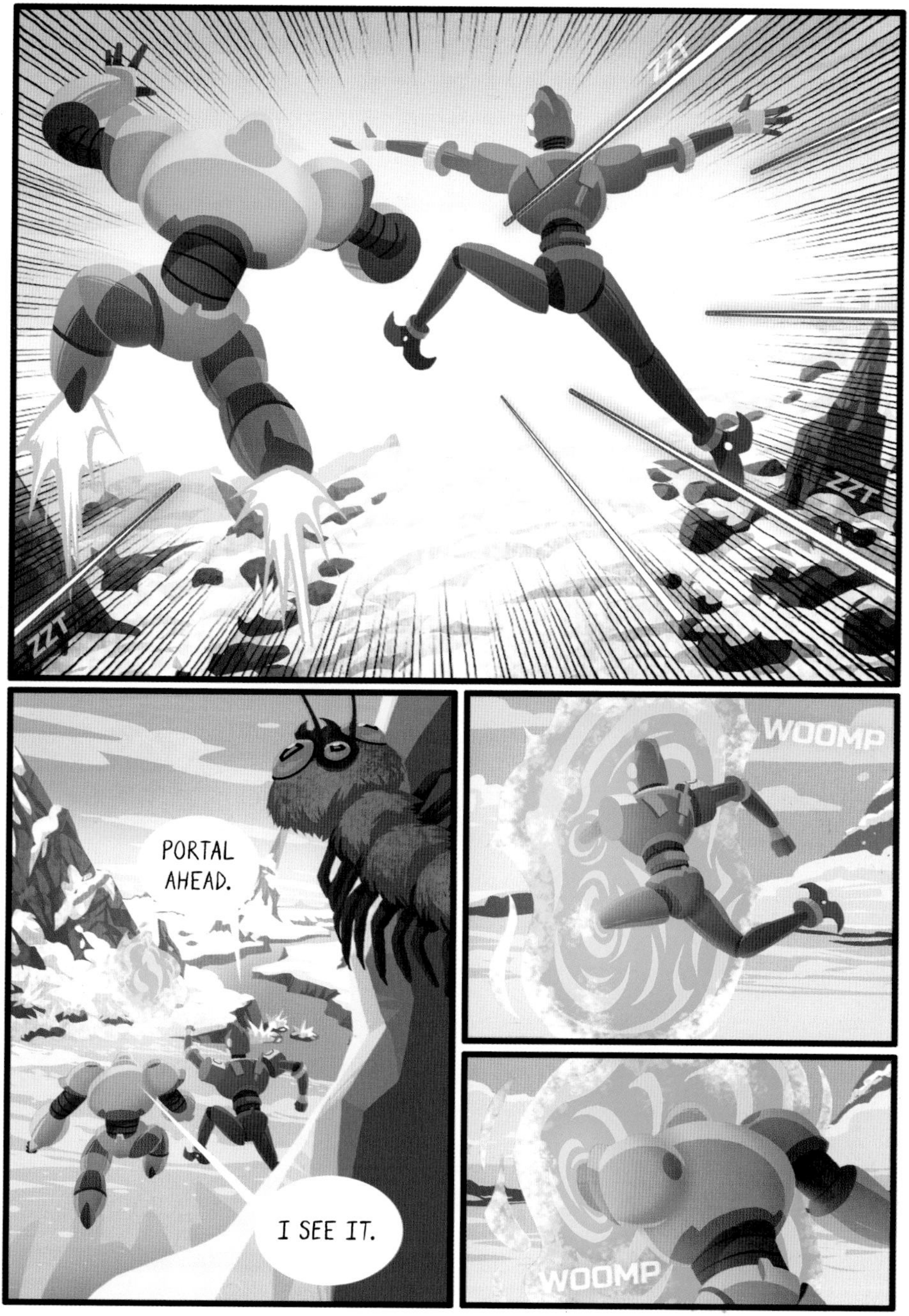
ZZT
ZZT
ZZT
PORTAL AHEAD.
I SEE IT.
WOOMP
WOOMP

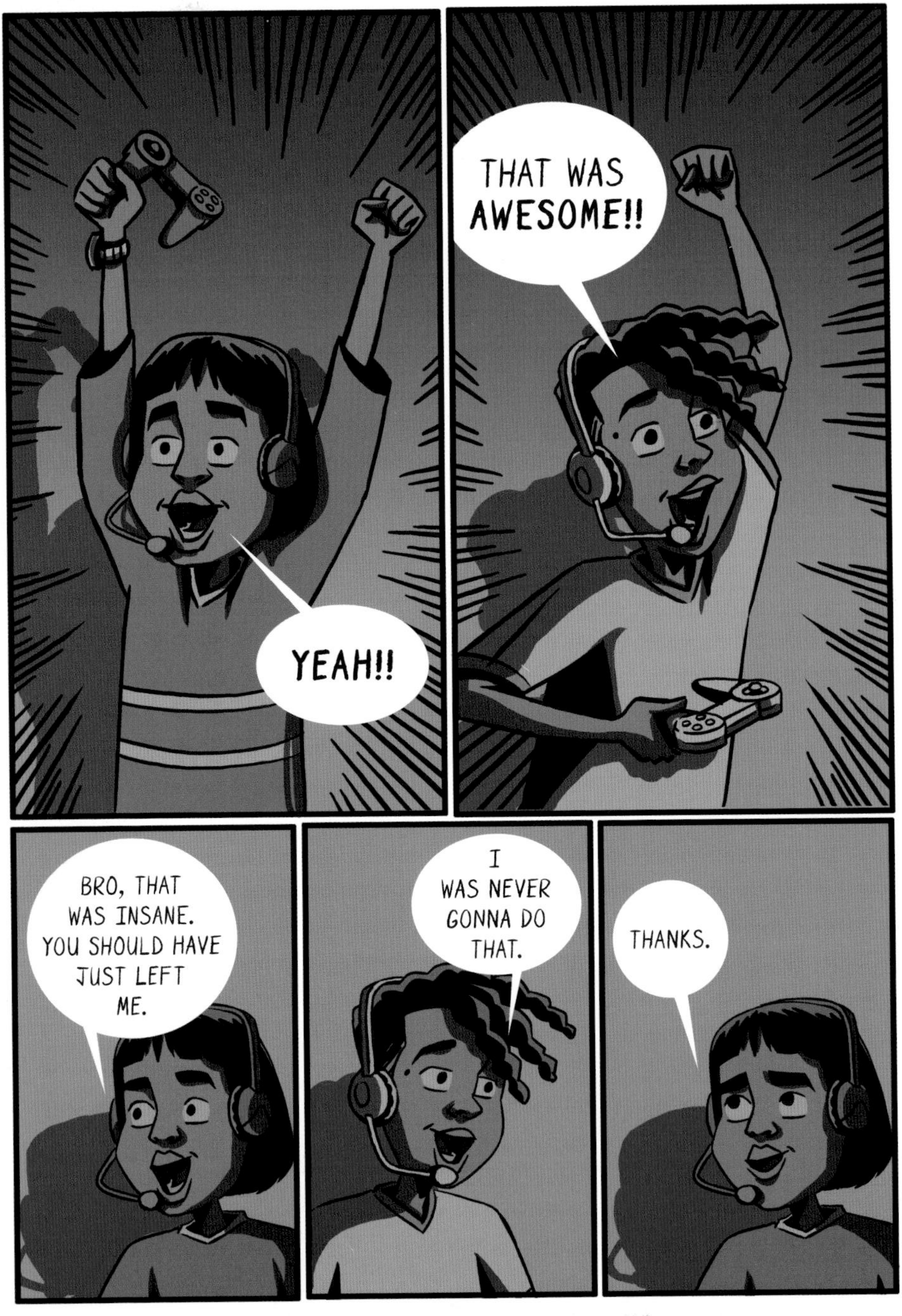
YEAH!!
THAT WAS AWESOME!!
BRO, THAT WAS INSANE. YOU SHOULD HAVE JUST LEFT ME.
I WAS NEVER GONNA DO THAT.
THANKS.

CHAPTER 4

BALANCE

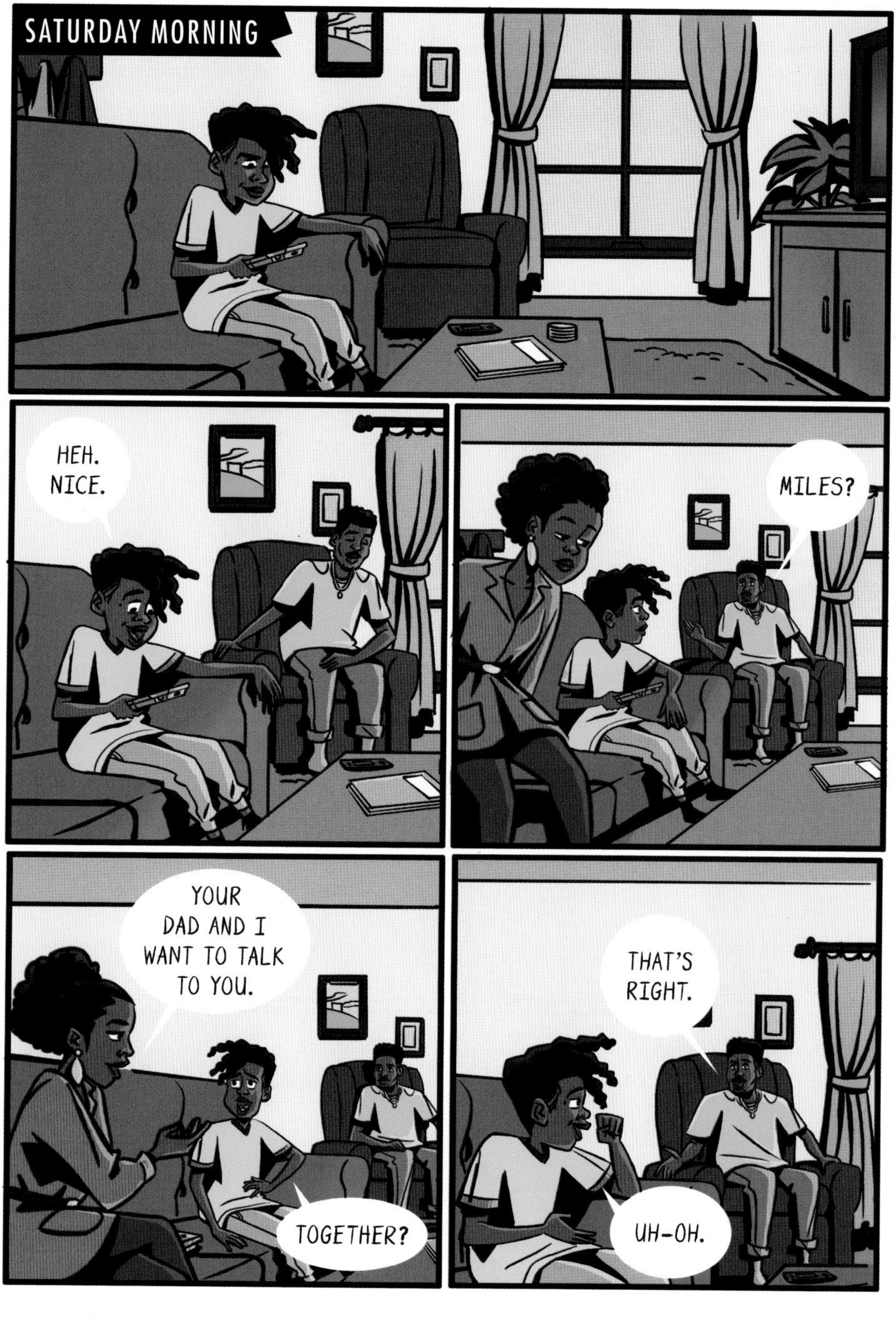
SATURDAY MORNING
HEH. NICE.
MILES?
YOUR DAD AND I WANT TO TALK TO YOU.
TOGETHER?
THAT'S RIGHT.
UH-OH.

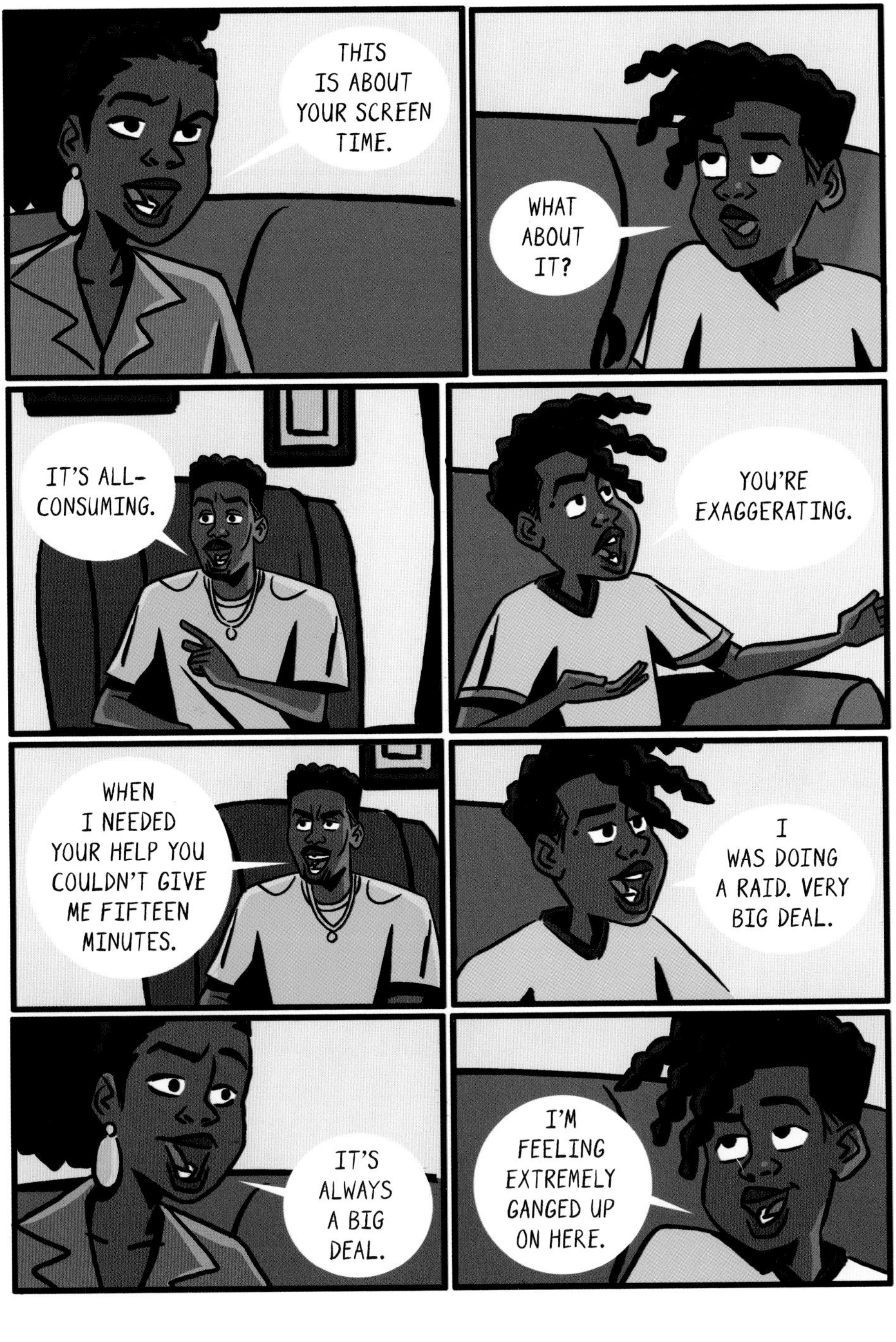
THIS IS ABOUT YOUR SCREEN TIME.
WHAT ABOUT IT?
IT'S ALL-CONSUMING.
YOU'RE EXAGGERATING.
WHEN I NEEDED YOUR HELP YOU COULDN'T GIVE ME FIFTEEN MINUTES.
I WAS DOING A RAID. VERY BIG DEAL.
IT'S ALWAYS A BIG DEAL.
I'M FEELING EXTREMELY GANGED UP ON HERE.

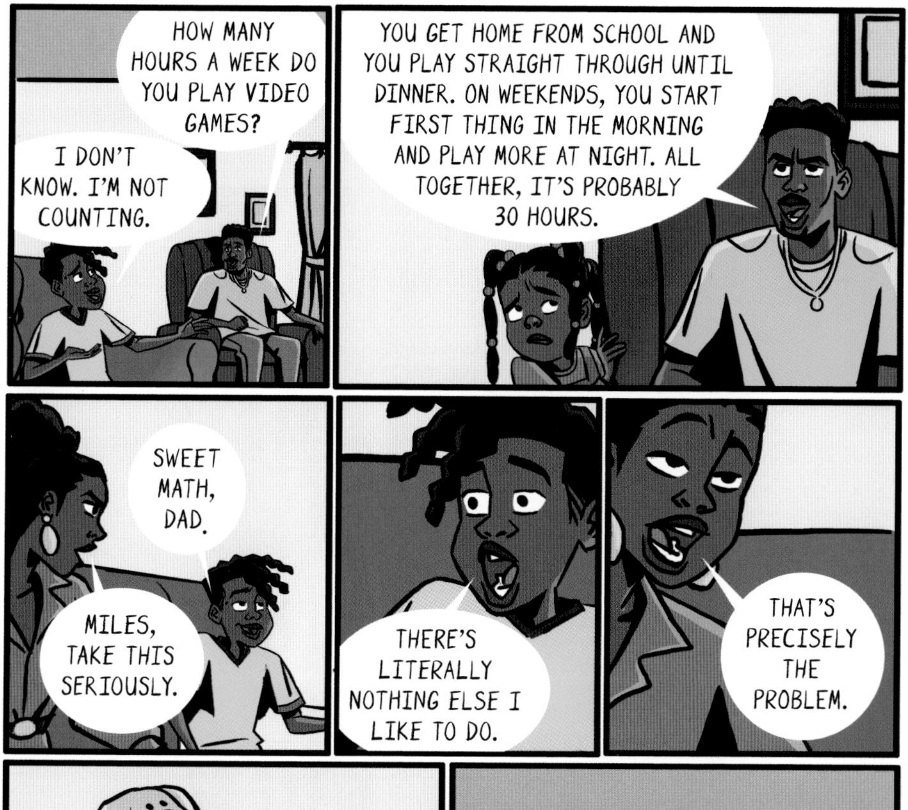
HOW MANY HOURS A WEEK DO YOU PLAY VIDEO GAMES?
I DON'T KNOW. I'M NOT COUNTING.
YOU GET HOME FROM SCHOOL AND YOU PLAY STRAIGHT THROUGH UNTIL DINNER. ON WEEKENDS, YOU START FIRST THING IN THE MORNING AND PLAY MORE AT NIGHT. ALL TOGETHER, IT'S PROBABLY 30 HOURS.
SWEET MATH, DAD.
MILES, TAKE THIS SERIOUSLY.
THERE'S LITERALLY NOTHING ELSE I LIKE TO DO.
THAT'S PRECISELY THE PROBLEM.
NOT NOW, GLORIA.

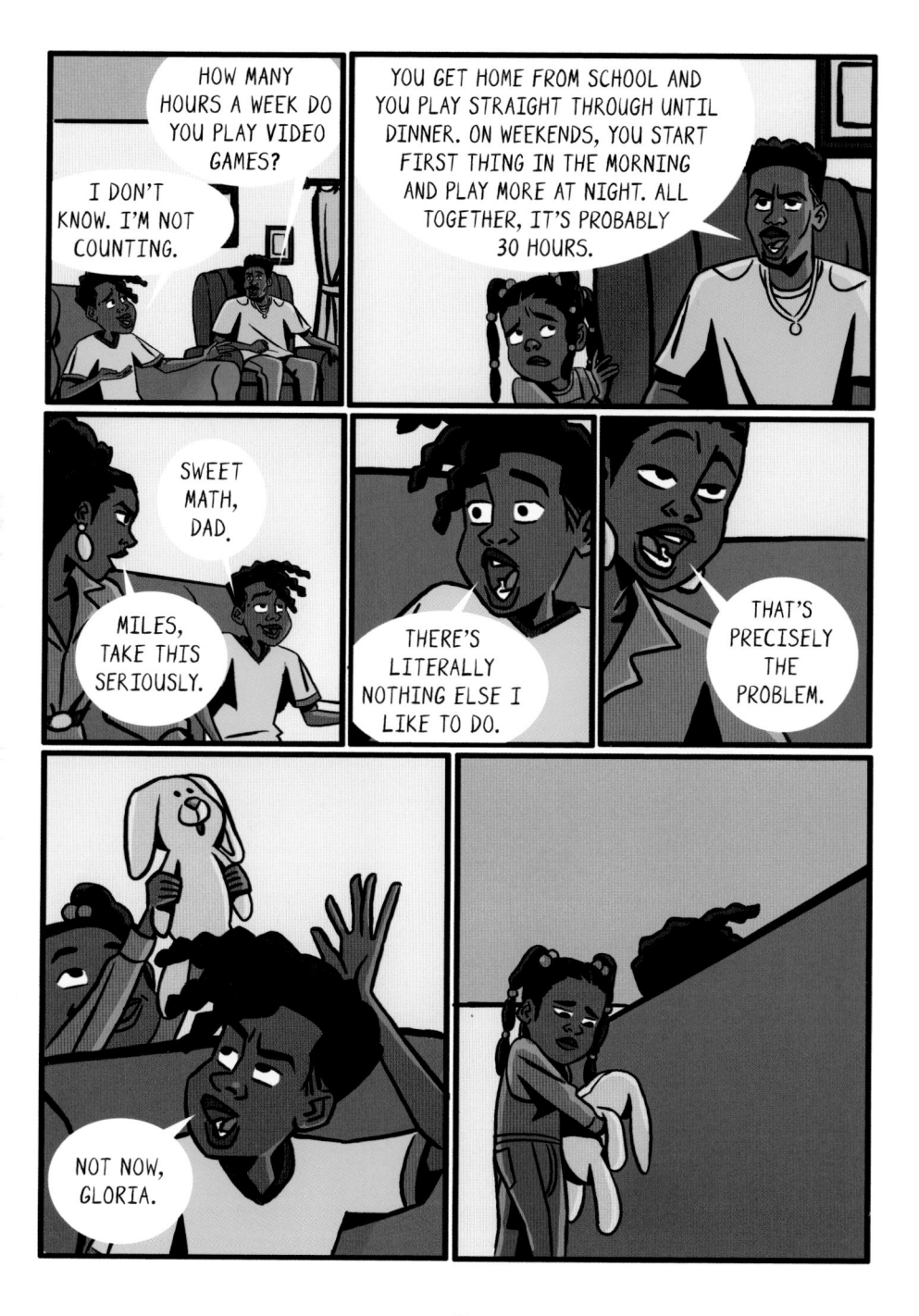

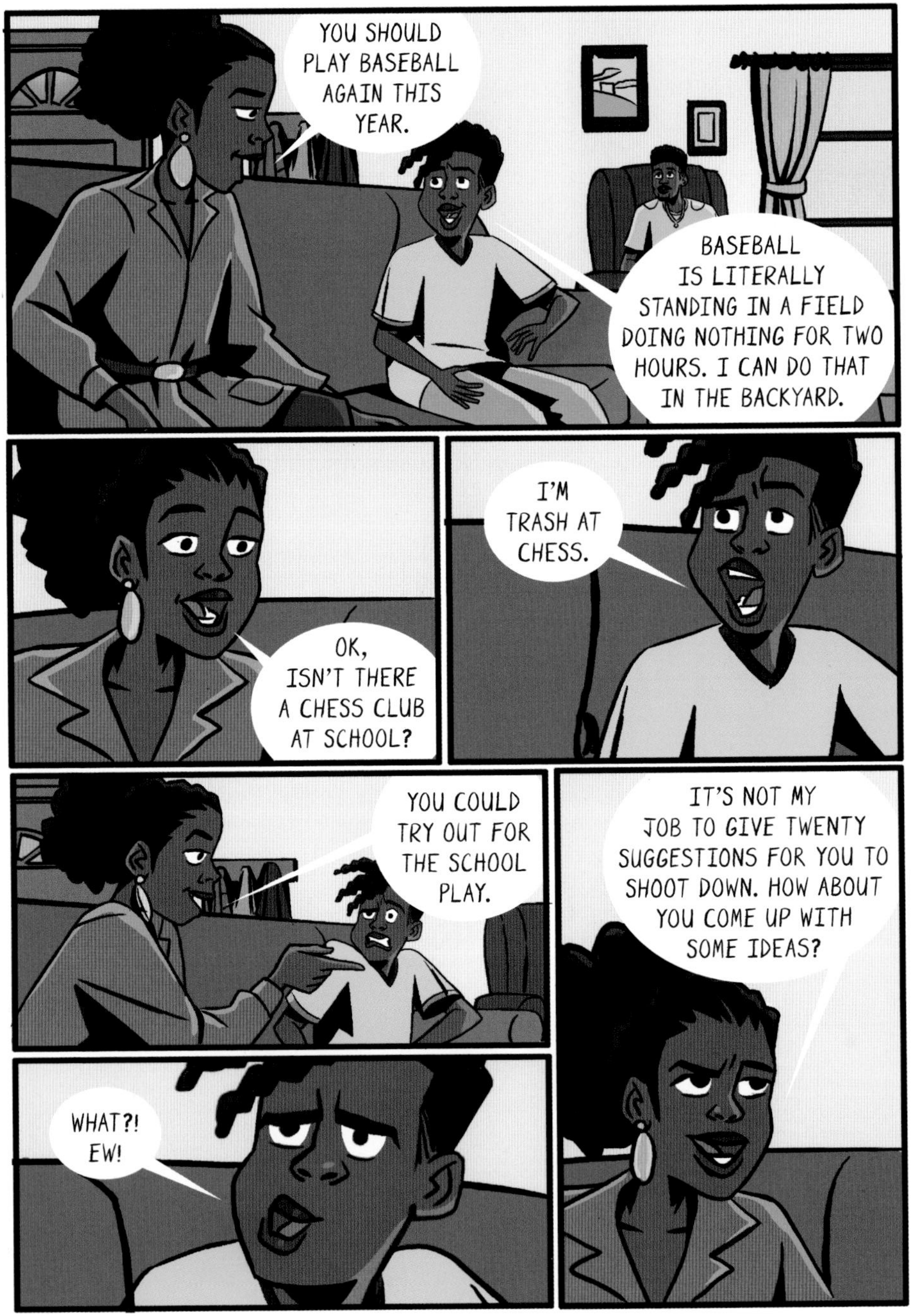
YOU SHOULD PLAY BASEBALL AGAIN THIS YEAR.
BASEBALL IS LITERALLY STANDING IN A FIELD DOING NOTHING FOR TWO HOURS. I CAN DO THAT IN THE BACKYARD.
OK, ISN'T THERE A CHESS CLUB AT SCHOOL?
I'M TRASH AT CHESS.
YOU COULD TRY OUT FOR THE SCHOOL PLAY.
WHAT?! EW!
IT'S NOT MY JOB TO GIVE TWENTY SUGGESTIONS FOR YOU TO SHOOT DOWN. HOW ABOUT YOU COME UP WITH SOME IDEAS?

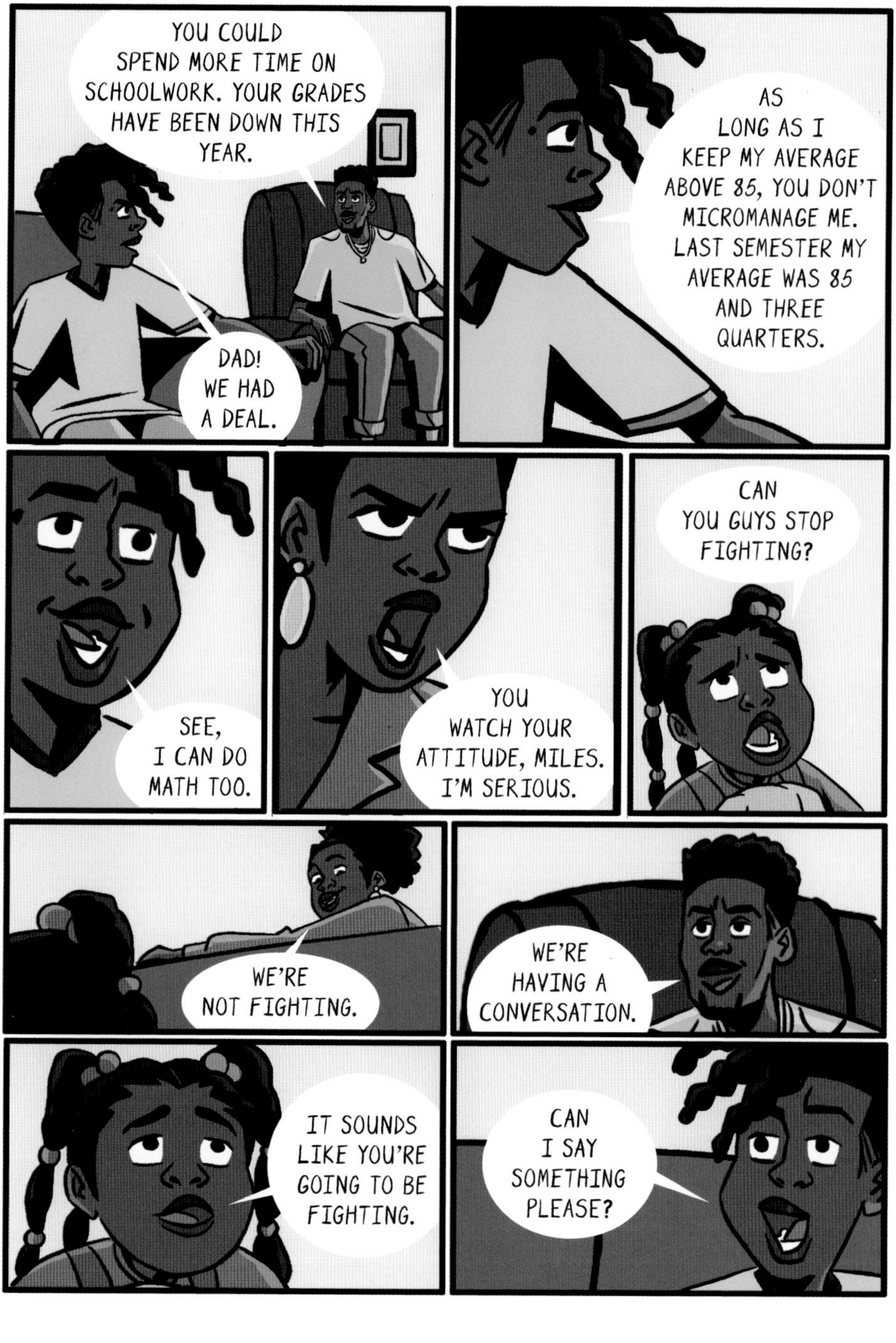
YOU COULD SPEND MORE TIME ON SCHOOLWORK. YOUR GRADES HAVE BEEN DOWN THIS YEAR.
DAD! WE HAD A DEAL.
AS LONG AS I KEEP MY AVERAGE ABOVE 85, YOU DON'T MICROMANAGE ME. LAST SEMESTER MY AVERAGE WAS 85 AND THREE QUARTERS.
SEE, I CAN DO MATH TOO.
YOU WATCH YOUR ATTITUDE, MILES. I'M SERIOUS.
CAN YOU GUYS STOP FIGHTING?
WE'RE NOT FIGHTING.
WE'RE HAVING A CONVERSATION.
IT SOUNDS LIKE YOU'RE GOING TO BE FIGHTING.
CAN I SAY SOMETHING PLEASE?

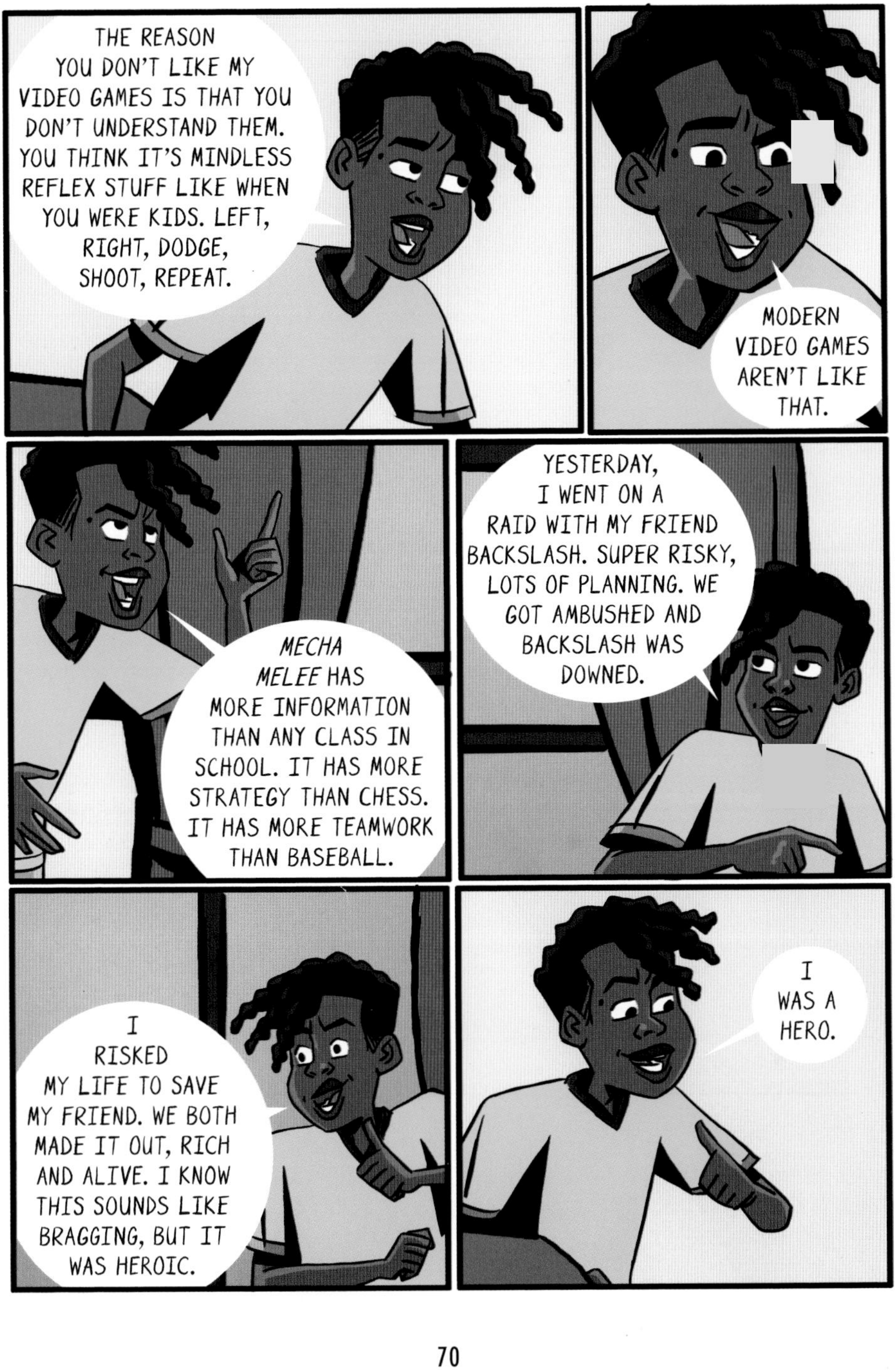
THE REASON YOU DON'T LIKE MY VIDEO GAMES IS THAT YOU DON'T UNDERSTAND THEM. YOU THINK IT'S MINDLESS REFLEX STUFF LIKE WHEN YOU WERE KIDS. LEFT, RIGHT, DODGE, SHOOT, REPEAT.
MODERN VIDEO GAMES AREN'T LIKE THAT.
MECHA MELEE HAS MORE INFORMATION THAN ANY CLASS IN SCHOOL. IT HAS MORE STRATEGY THAN CHESS. IT HAS MORE TEAMWORK THAN BASEBALL.
YESTERDAY, I WENT ON A RAID WITH MY FRIEND BACKSLASH. SUPER RISKY, LOTS OF PLANNING. WE GOT AMBUSHED AND BACKSLASH WAS DOWNED.
I RISKED MY LIFE TO SAVE MY FRIEND. WE BOTH MADE IT OUT, RICH AND ALIVE. I KNOW THIS SOUNDS LIKE BRAGGING, BUT IT WAS HEROIC.
I WAS A HERO.

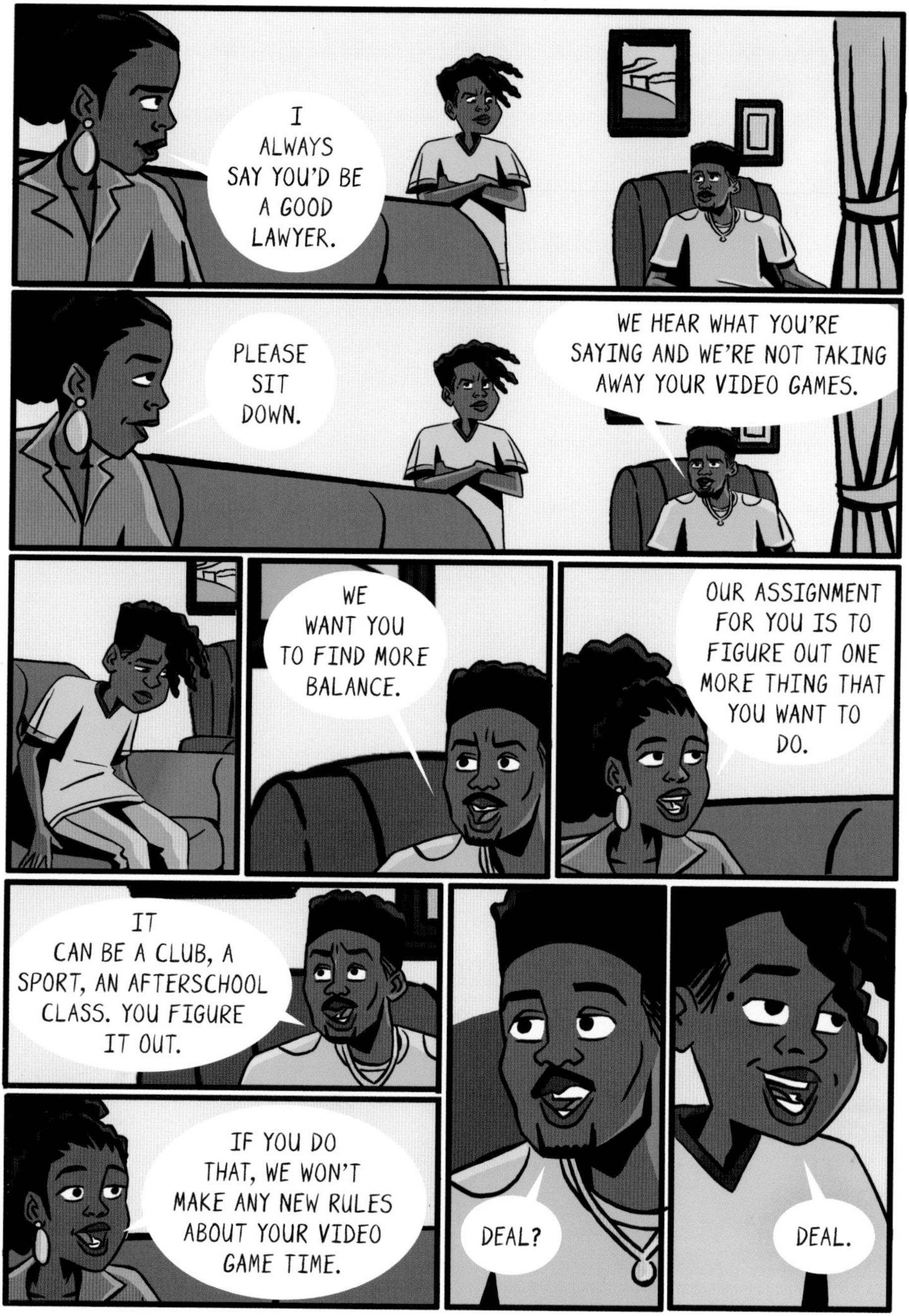
I ALWAYS SAY YOU'D BE A GOOD LAWYER.
PLEASE SIT DOWN.
WE HEAR WHAT YOU'RE SAYING AND WE'RE NOT TAKING AWAY YOUR VIDEO GAMES.
WE WANT YOU TO FIND MORE BALANCE.
OUR ASSIGNMENT FOR YOU IS TO FIGURE OUT ONE MORE THING THAT YOU WANT TO DO.
IT CAN BE A CLUB, A SPORT, AN AFTERSCHOOL CLASS. YOU FIGURE IT OUT.
IF YOU DO THAT, WE WON'T MAKE ANY NEW RULES ABOUT YOUR VIDEO GAME TIME.
DEAL?
DEAL.

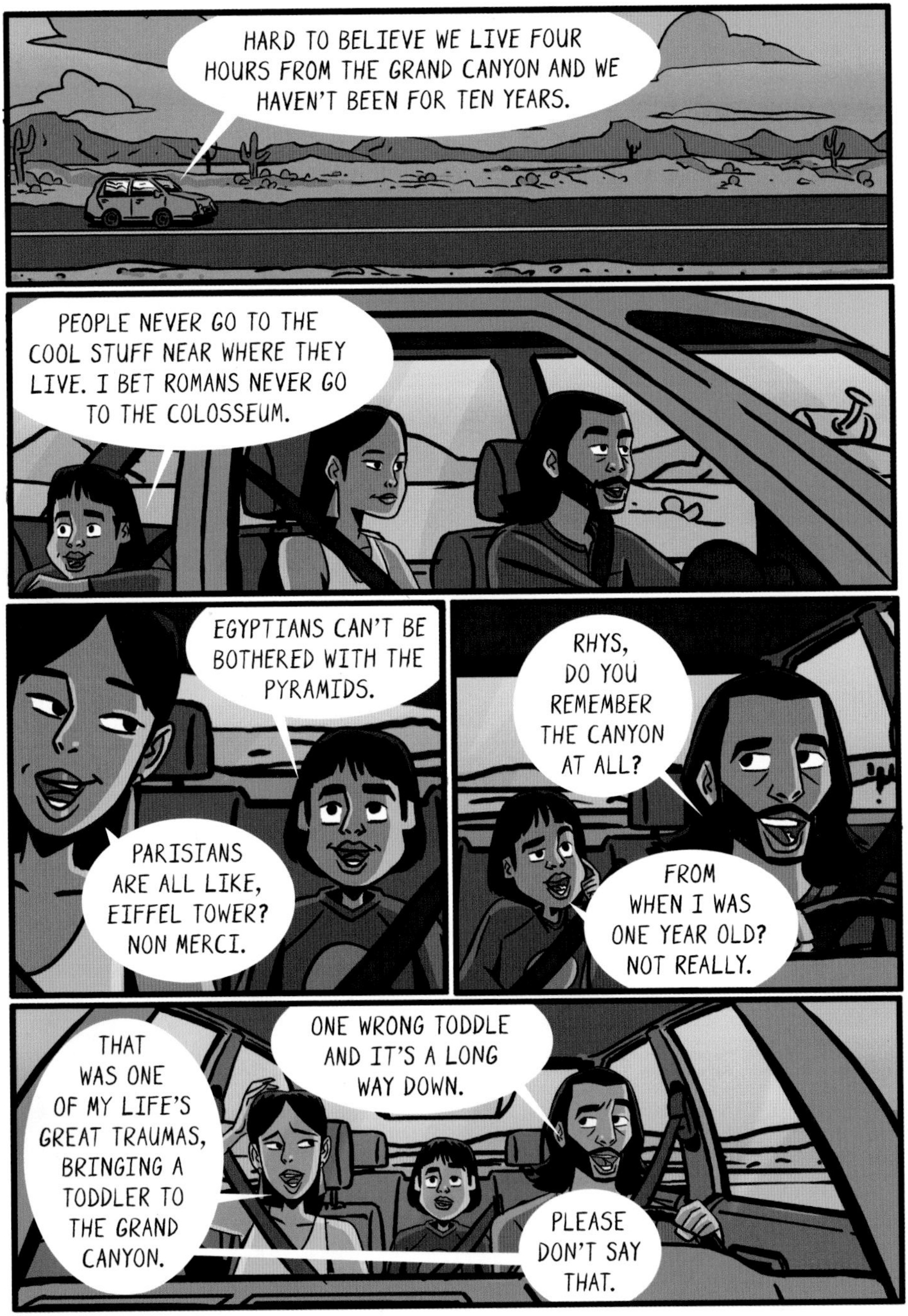
HARD TO BELIEVE WE LIVE FOUR HOURS FROM THE GRAND CANYON AND WE HAVEN'T BEEN FOR TEN YEARS.
PEOPLE NEVER GO TO THE COOL STUFF NEAR WHERE THEY LIVE. I BET ROMANS NEVER GO TO THE COLOSSEUM.
EGYPTIANS CAN'T BE BOTHERED WITH THE PYRAMIDS.
PARISIANS ARE ALL LIKE, EIFFEL TOWER? NON MERCI.
RHYS, DO YOU REMEMBER THE CANYON AT ALL?
FROM WHEN I WAS ONE YEAR OLD? NOT REALLY.
THAT WAS ONE OF MY LIFE'S GREAT TRAUMAS, BRINGING A TODDLER TO THE GRAND CANYON.
ONE WRONG TODDLE AND IT'S A LONG WAY DOWN.
PLEASE DON'T SAY THAT.

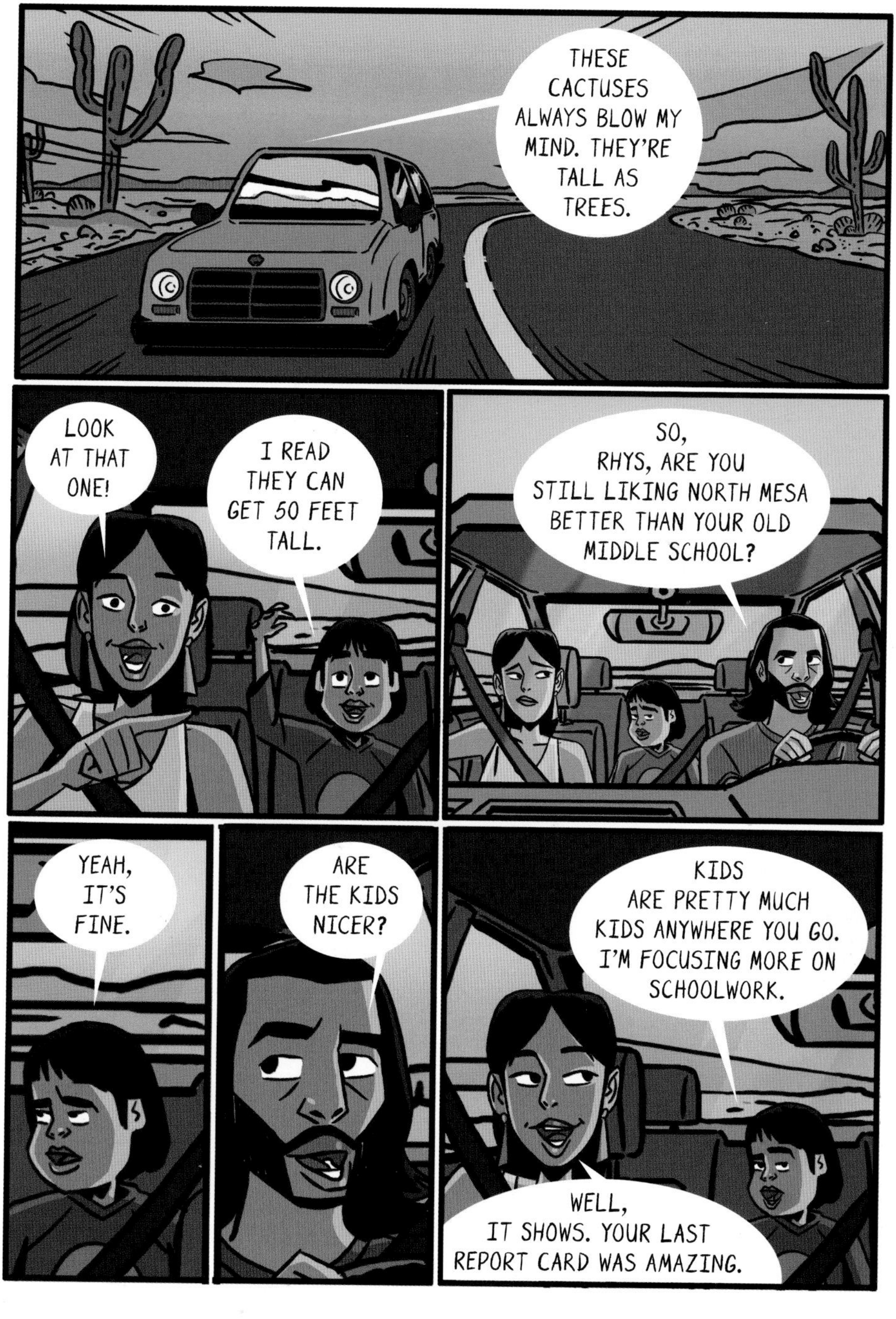
THESE CACTUSES ALWAYS BLOW MY MIND. THEY'RE TALL AS TREES.
LOOK AT THAT ONE!
I READ THEY CAN GET 50 FEET TALL.
SO, RHYS, ARE YOU STILL LIKING NORTH MESA BETTER THAN YOUR OLD MIDDLE SCHOOL?
YEAH, IT'S FINE.
ARE THE KIDS NICER?
KIDS ARE PRETTY MUCH KIDS ANYWHERE YOU GO. I'M FOCUSING MORE ON SCHOOLWORK.
WELL, IT SHOWS. YOUR LAST REPORT CARD WAS AMAZING.

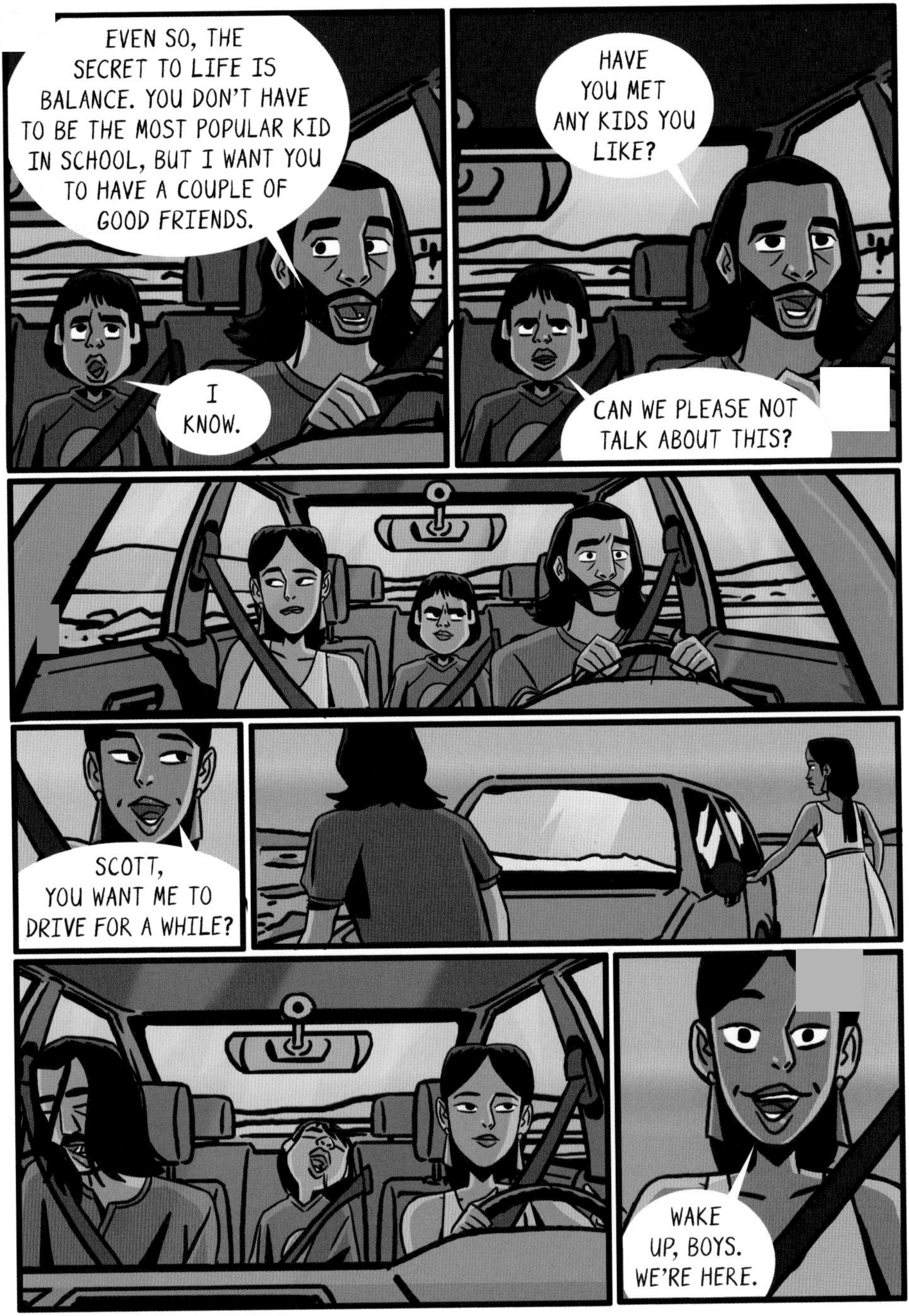
EVEN SO, THE SECRET TO LIFE IS BALANCE. YOU DON'T HAVE TO BE THE MOST POPULAR KID IN SCHOOL, BUT I WANT YOU TO HAVE A COUPLE OF GOOD FRIENDS.
I KNOW.
HAVE YOU MET ANY KIDS YOU LIKE?
CAN WE PLEASE NOT TALK ABOUT THIS?
SCOTT, YOU WANT ME TO DRIVE FOR A WHILE?
WAKE UP, BOYS. WE'RE HERE.

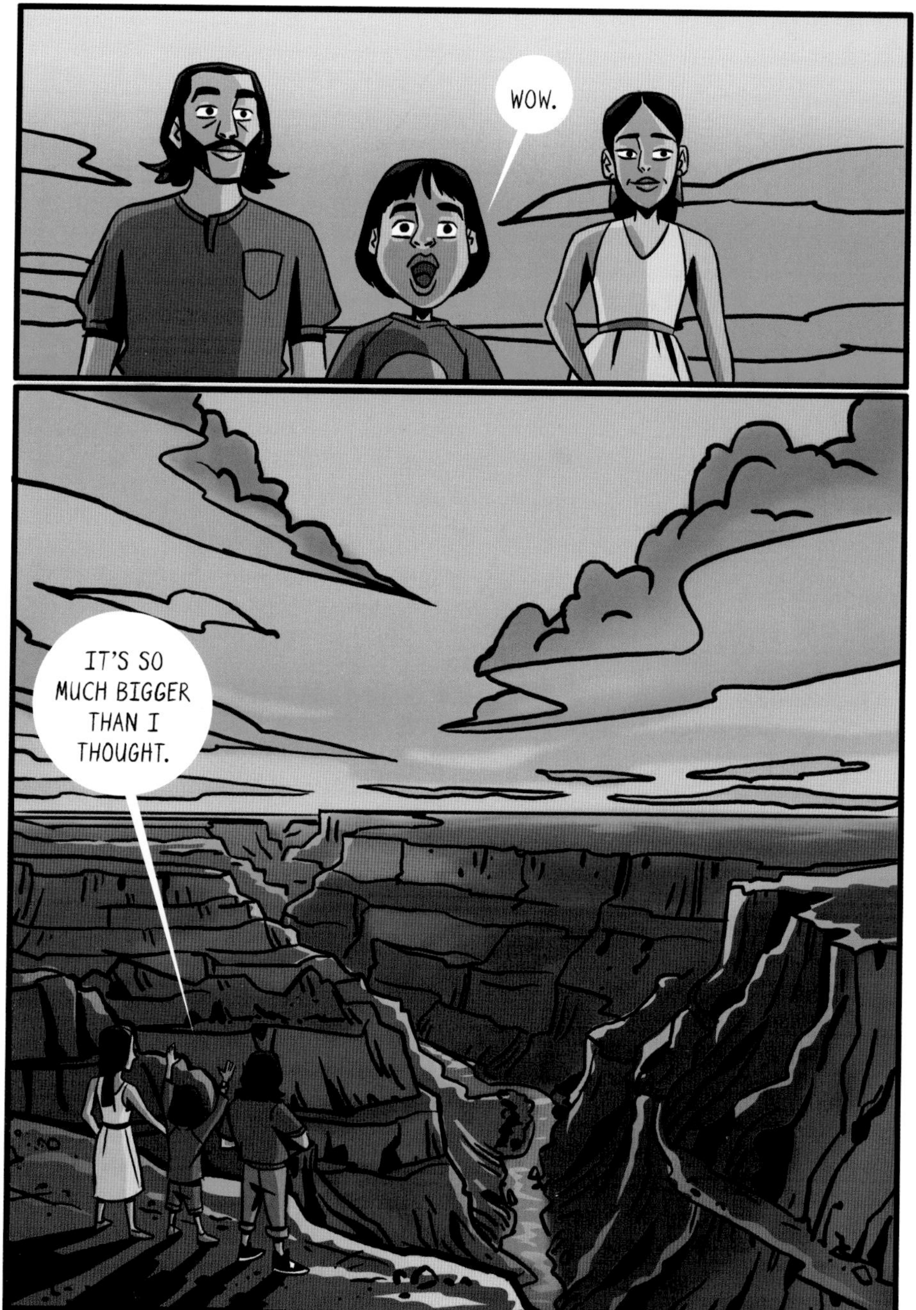
WOW.
IT'S SO MUCH BIGGER THAN I THOUGHT.

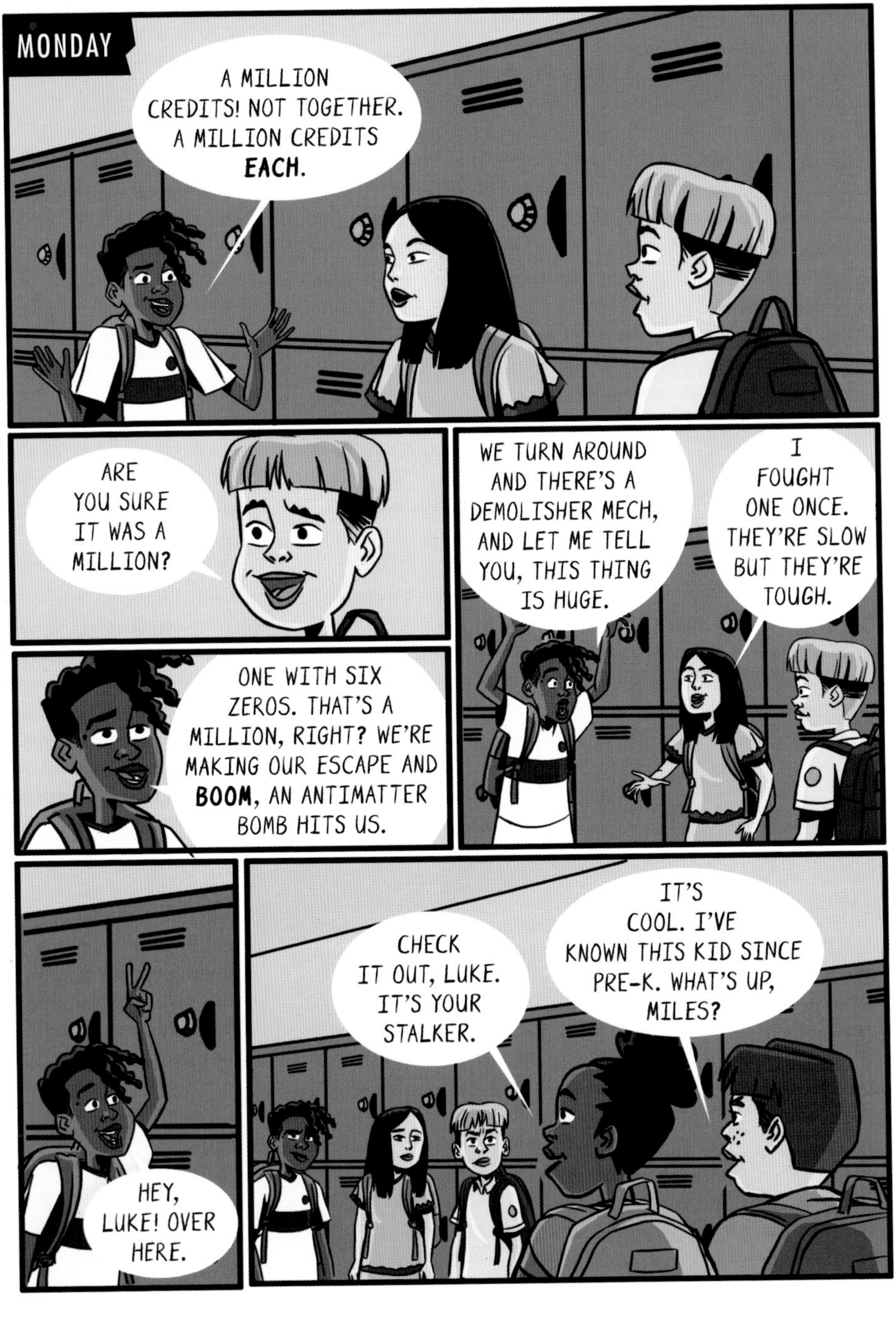
MONDAY
A MILLION CREDITS! NOT TOGETHER. A MILLION CREDITS **EACH**.
ARE YOU SURE IT WAS A MILLION?
ONE WITH SIX ZEROS. THAT'S A MILLION, RIGHT? WE'RE MAKING OUR ESCAPE AND **BOOM**, AN ANTIMATTER BOMB HITS US.
WE TURN AROUND AND THERE'S A DEMOLISHER MECH, AND LET ME TELL YOU, THIS THING IS HUGE.
I FOUGHT ONE ONCE. THEY'RE SLOW BUT THEY'RE TOUGH.
HEY, LUKE! OVER HERE.
CHECK IT OUT, LUKE. IT'S YOUR STALKER.
IT'S COOL. I'VE KNOWN THIS KID SINCE PRE-K. WHAT'S UP, MILES?

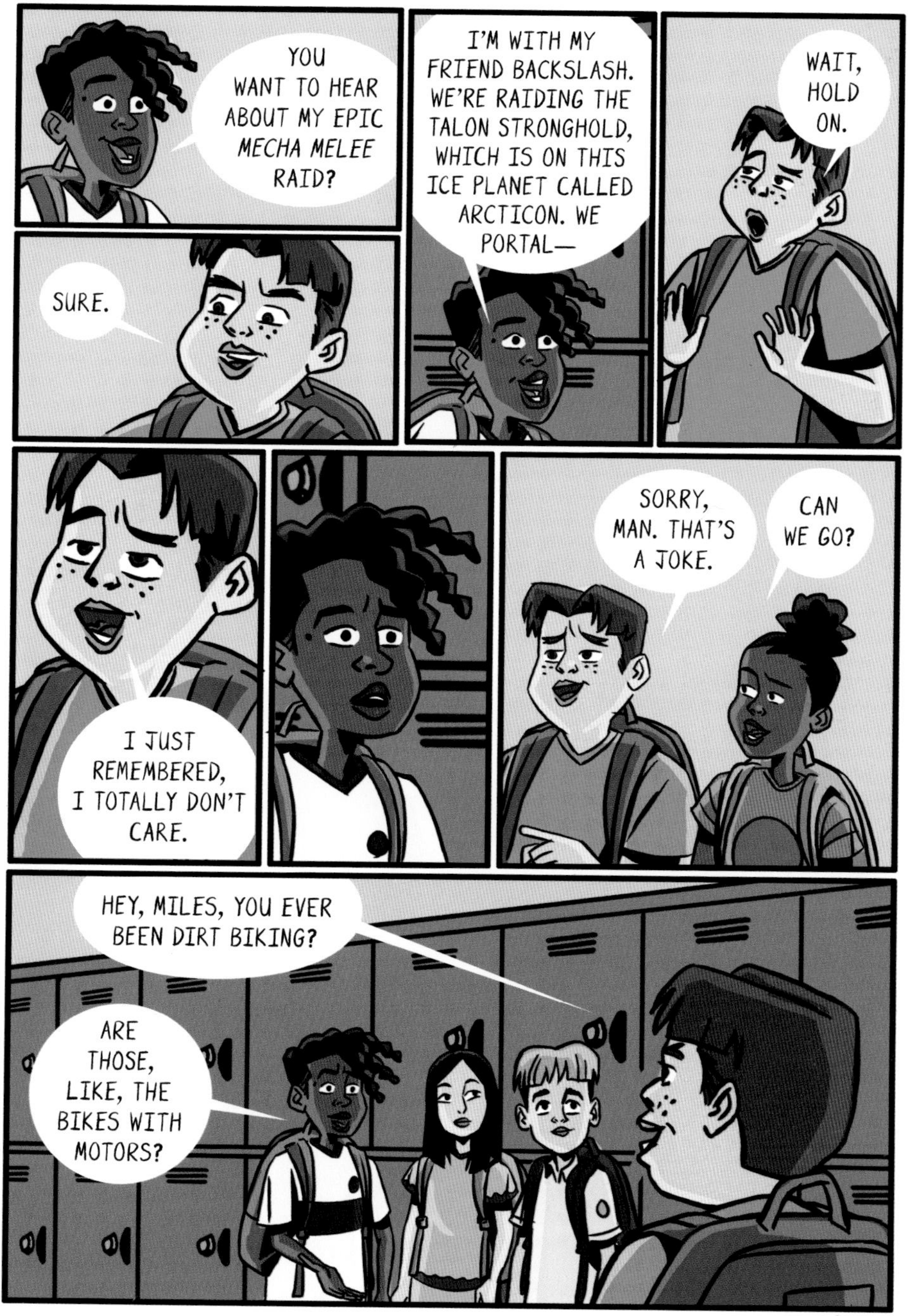
YOU WANT TO HEAR ABOUT MY EPIC *MECHA MELEE* RAID?
SURE.
I'M WITH MY FRIEND BACKSLASH. WE'RE RAIDING THE TALON STRONGHOLD, WHICH IS ON THIS ICE PLANET CALLED ARCTICON. WE PORTAL—
WAIT, HOLD ON.
I JUST REMEMBERED, I TOTALLY DON'T CARE.
SORRY, MAN. THAT'S A JOKE.
CAN WE GO?
HEY, MILES, YOU EVER BEEN DIRT BIKING?
ARE THOSE, LIKE, THE BIKES WITH MOTORS?

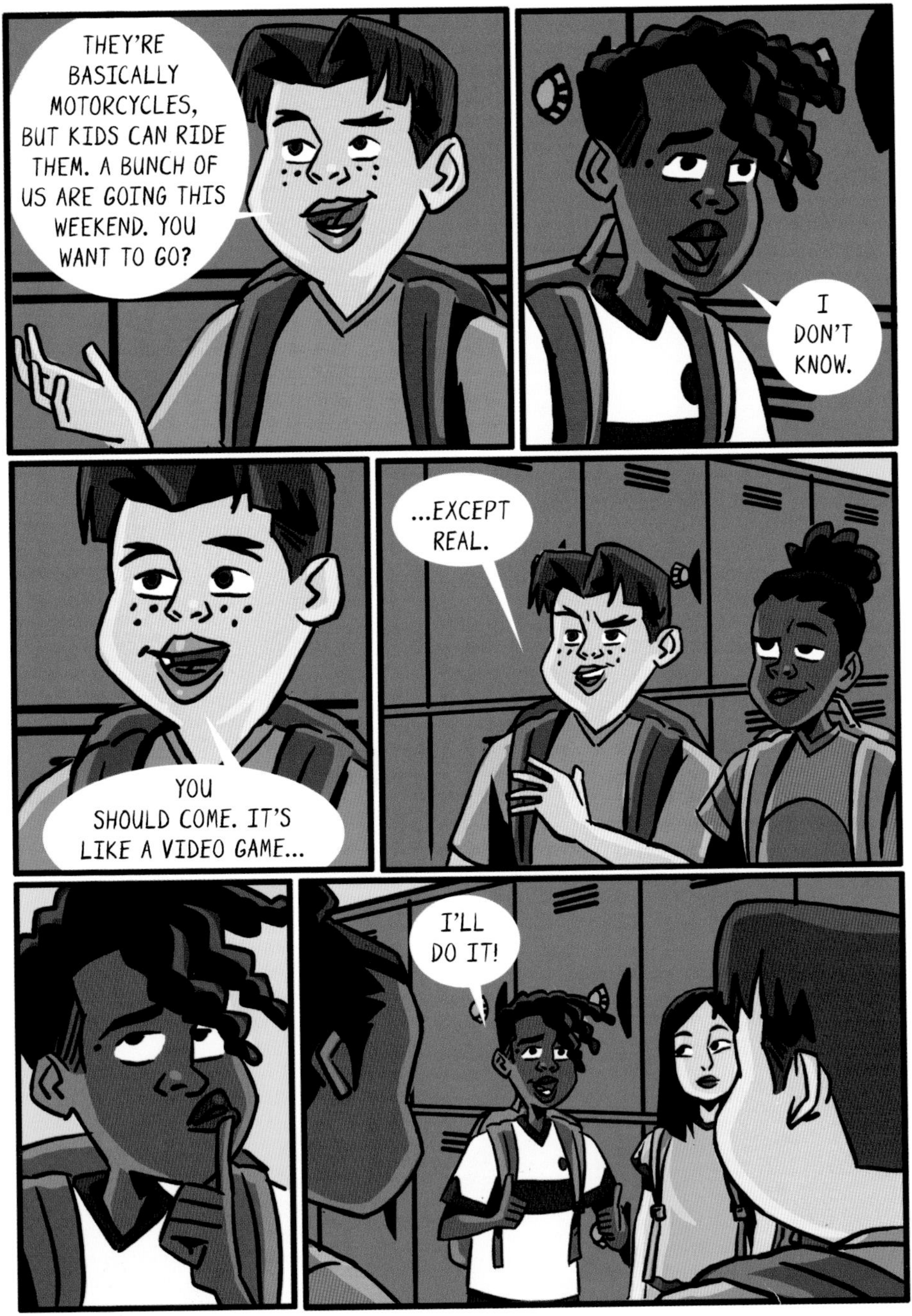
THEY'RE BASICALLY MOTORCYCLES, BUT KIDS CAN RIDE THEM. A BUNCH OF US ARE GOING THIS WEEKEND. YOU WANT TO GO?
I DON'T KNOW.
YOU SHOULD COME. IT'S LIKE A VIDEO GAME...
...EXCEPT REAL.
I'LL DO IT!

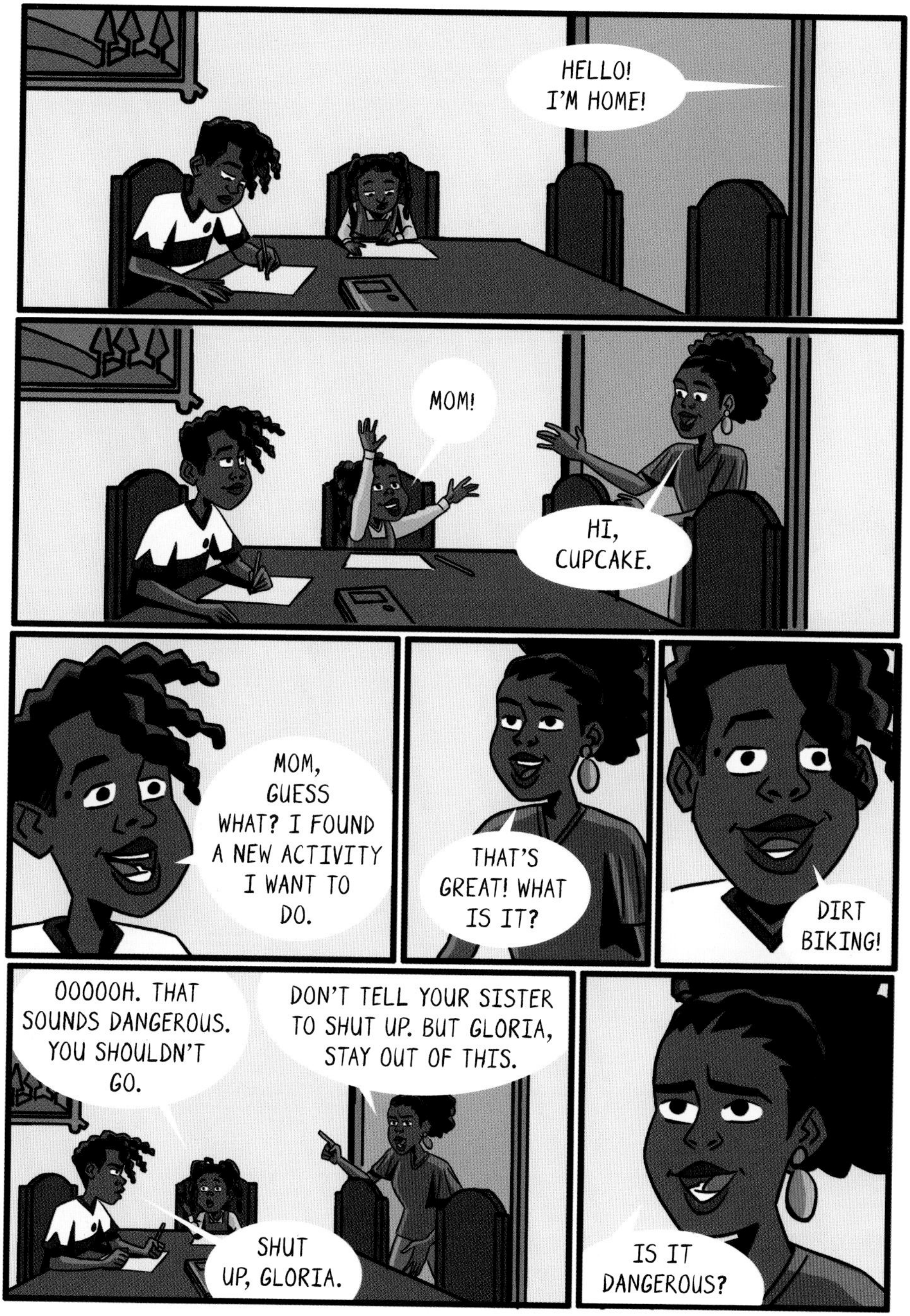
HELLO! I'M HOME!
MOM!
HI, CUPCAKE.
MOM, GUESS WHAT? I FOUND A NEW ACTIVITY I WANT TO DO.
THAT'S GREAT! WHAT IS IT?
DIRT BIKING!
OOOOOH. THAT SOUNDS DANGEROUS. YOU SHOULDN'T GO.
SHUT UP, GLORIA.
DON'T TELL YOUR SISTER TO SHUT UP. BUT GLORIA, STAY OUT OF THIS.
IS IT DANGEROUS?

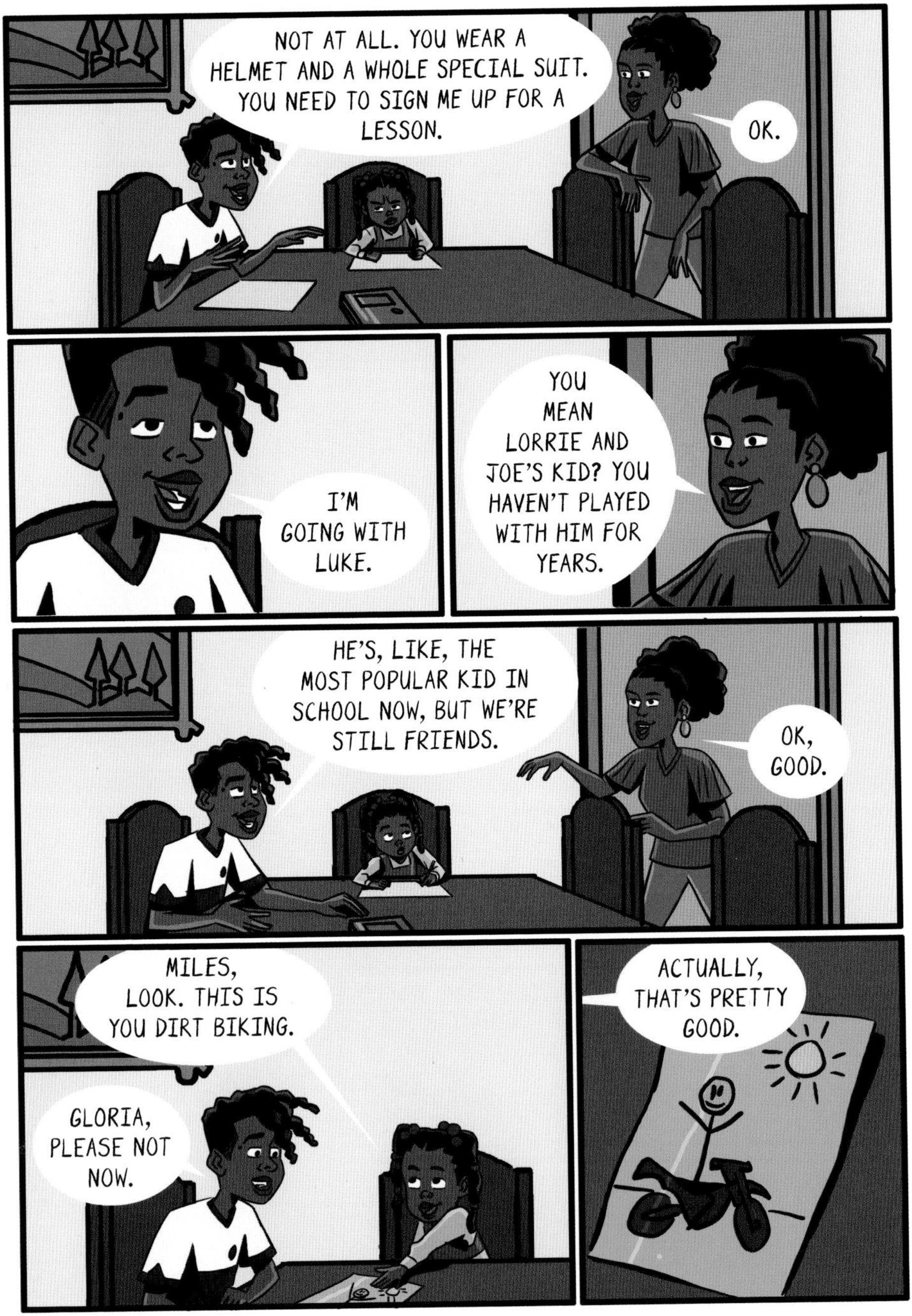
NOT AT ALL. YOU WEAR A HELMET AND A WHOLE SPECIAL SUIT. YOU NEED TO SIGN ME UP FOR A LESSON.
OK.
I'M GOING WITH LUKE.
YOU MEAN LORRIE AND JOE'S KID? YOU HAVEN'T PLAYED WITH HIM FOR YEARS.
HE'S, LIKE, THE MOST POPULAR KID IN SCHOOL NOW, BUT WE'RE STILL FRIENDS.
OK, GOOD.
MILES, LOOK. THIS IS YOU DIRT BIKING.
GLORIA, PLEASE NOT NOW.
ACTUALLY, THAT'S PRETTY GOOD.

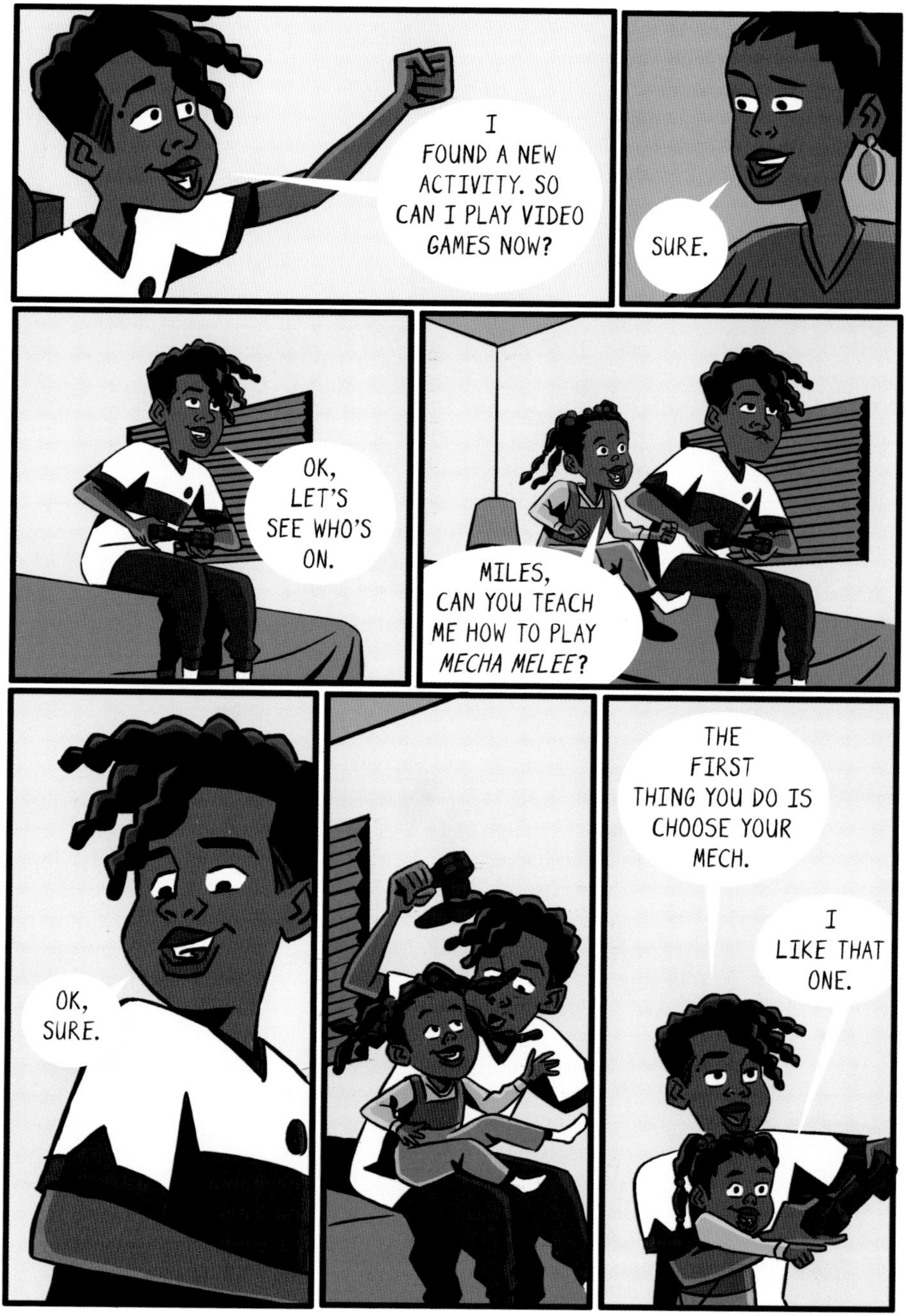
I FOUND A NEW ACTIVITY. SO CAN I PLAY VIDEO GAMES NOW?
SURE.
OK, LET'S SEE WHO'S ON.
MILES, CAN YOU TEACH ME HOW TO PLAY *MECHA MELEE*?
OK, SURE.
THE FIRST THING YOU DO IS CHOOSE YOUR MECH.
I LIKE THAT ONE.

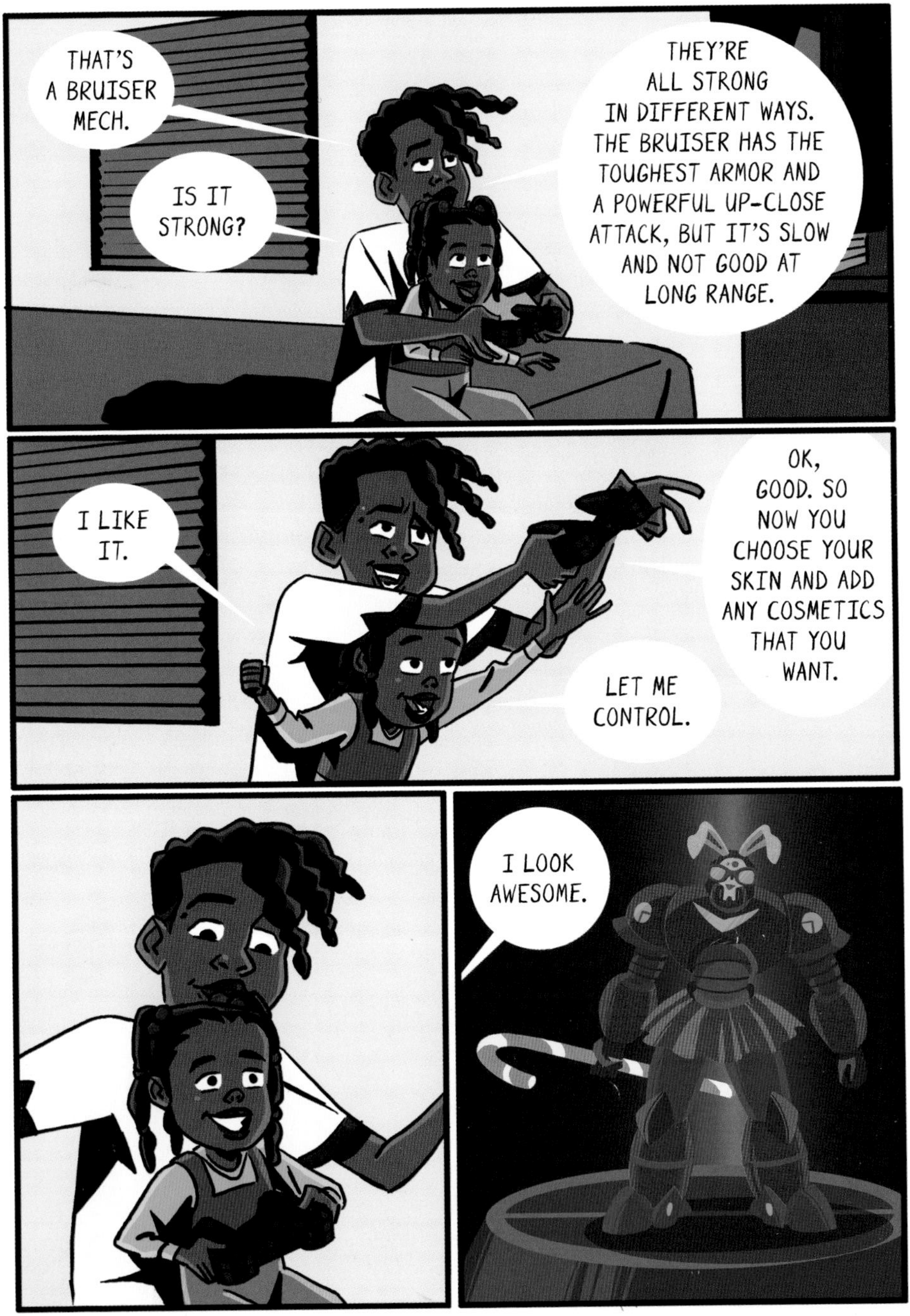
THAT'S A BRUISER MECH.
IS IT STRONG?
THEY'RE ALL STRONG IN DIFFERENT WAYS. THE BRUISER HAS THE TOUGHEST ARMOR AND A POWERFUL UP-CLOSE ATTACK, BUT IT'S SLOW AND NOT GOOD AT LONG RANGE.
I LIKE IT.
OK, GOOD. SO NOW YOU CHOOSE YOUR SKIN AND ADD ANY COSMETICS THAT YOU WANT.
LET ME CONTROL.
I LOOK AWESOME.

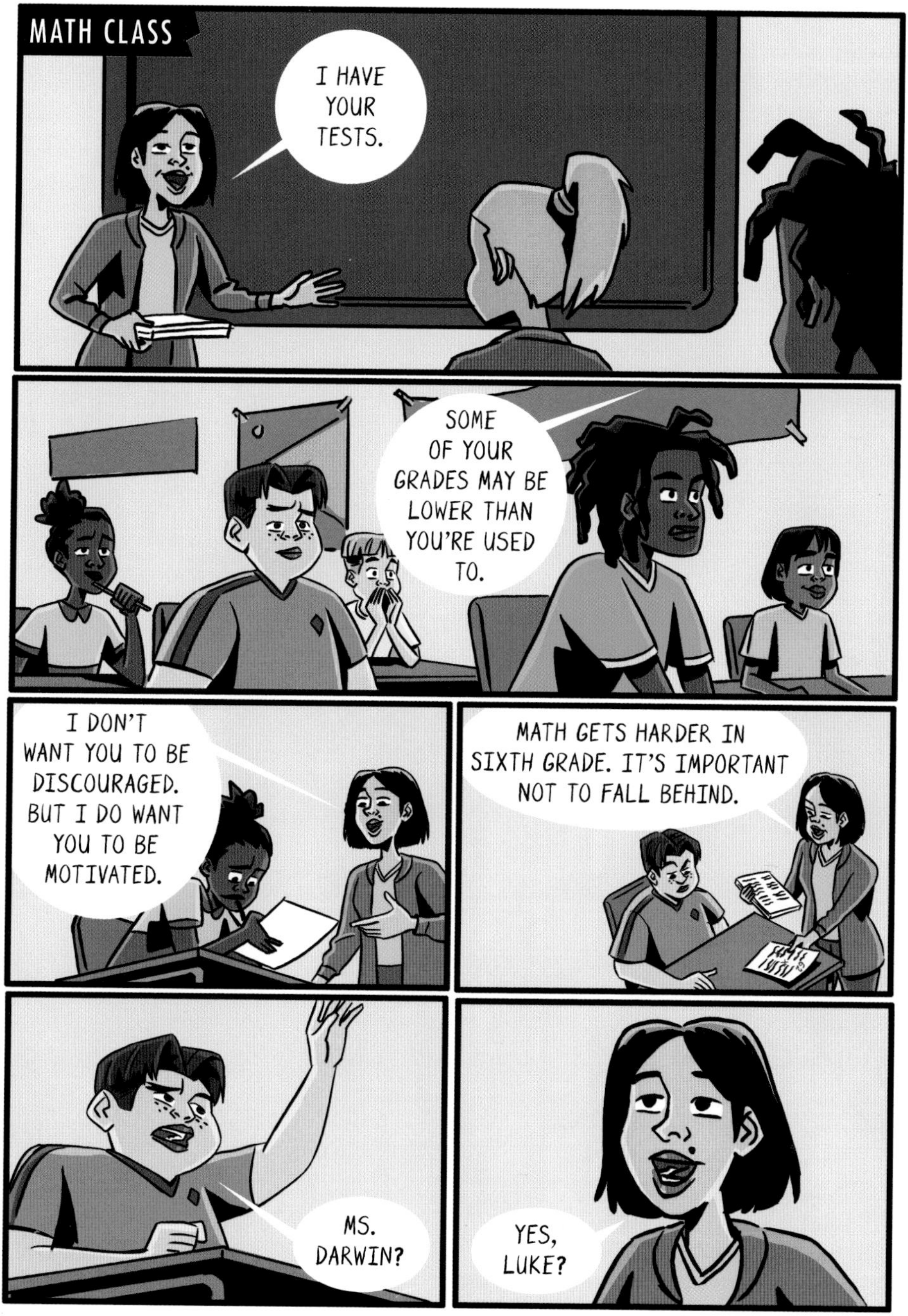
MATH CLASS
I HAVE YOUR TESTS.
SOME OF YOUR GRADES MAY BE LOWER THAN YOU'RE USED TO.
I DON'T WANT YOU TO BE DISCOURAGED. BUT I DO WANT YOU TO BE MOTIVATED.
MATH GETS HARDER IN SIXTH GRADE. IT'S IMPORTANT NOT TO FALL BEHIND.
MS. DARWIN?
YES, LUKE?

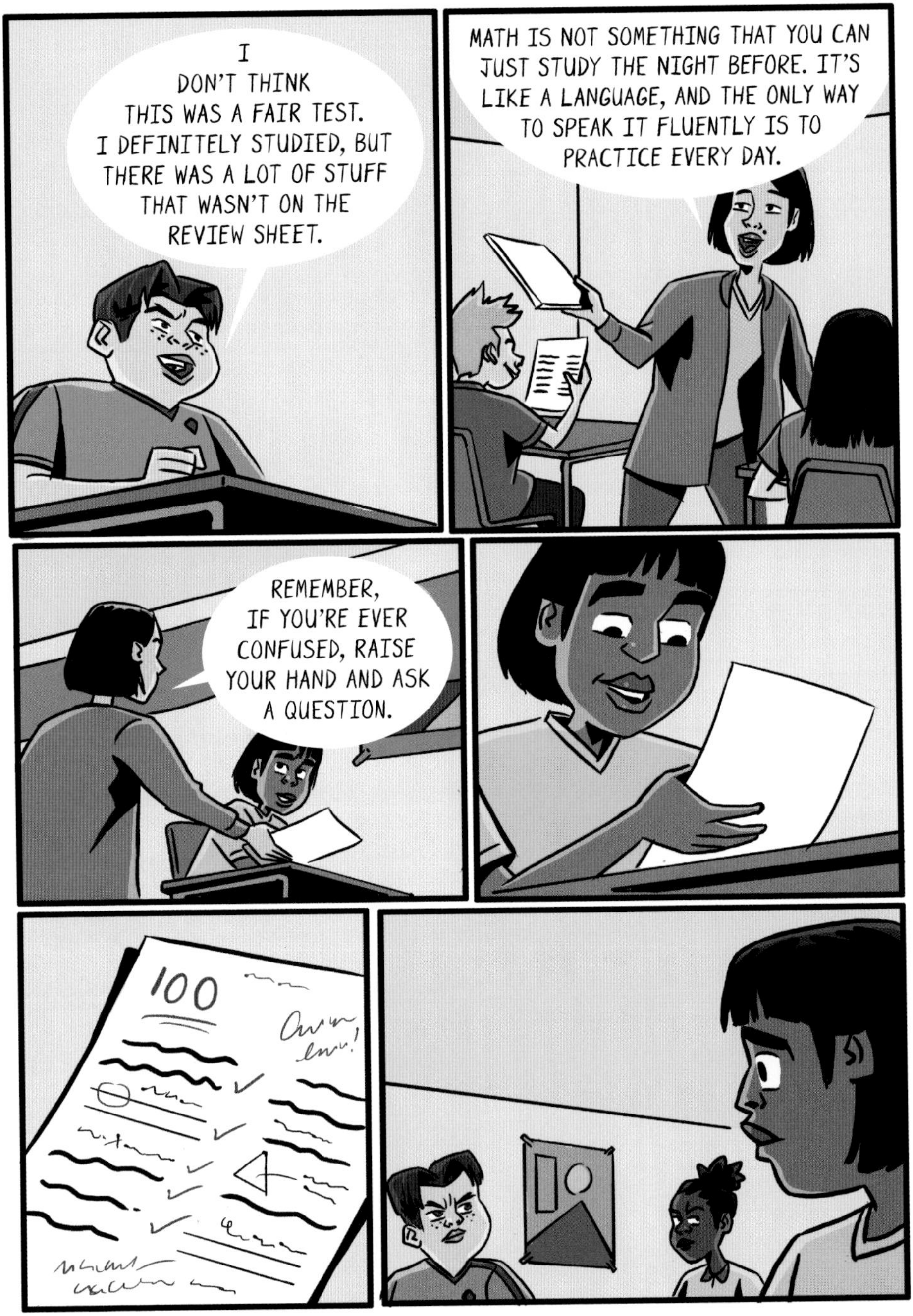
I DON'T THINK THIS WAS A FAIR TEST. I DEFINITELY STUDIED, BUT THERE WAS A LOT OF STUFF THAT WASN'T ON THE REVIEW SHEET.
MATH IS NOT SOMETHING THAT YOU CAN JUST STUDY THE NIGHT BEFORE. IT'S LIKE A LANGUAGE, AND THE ONLY WAY TO SPEAK IT FLUENTLY IS TO PRACTICE EVERY DAY.
REMEMBER, IF YOU'RE EVER CONFUSED, RAISE YOUR HAND AND ASK A QUESTION.
100

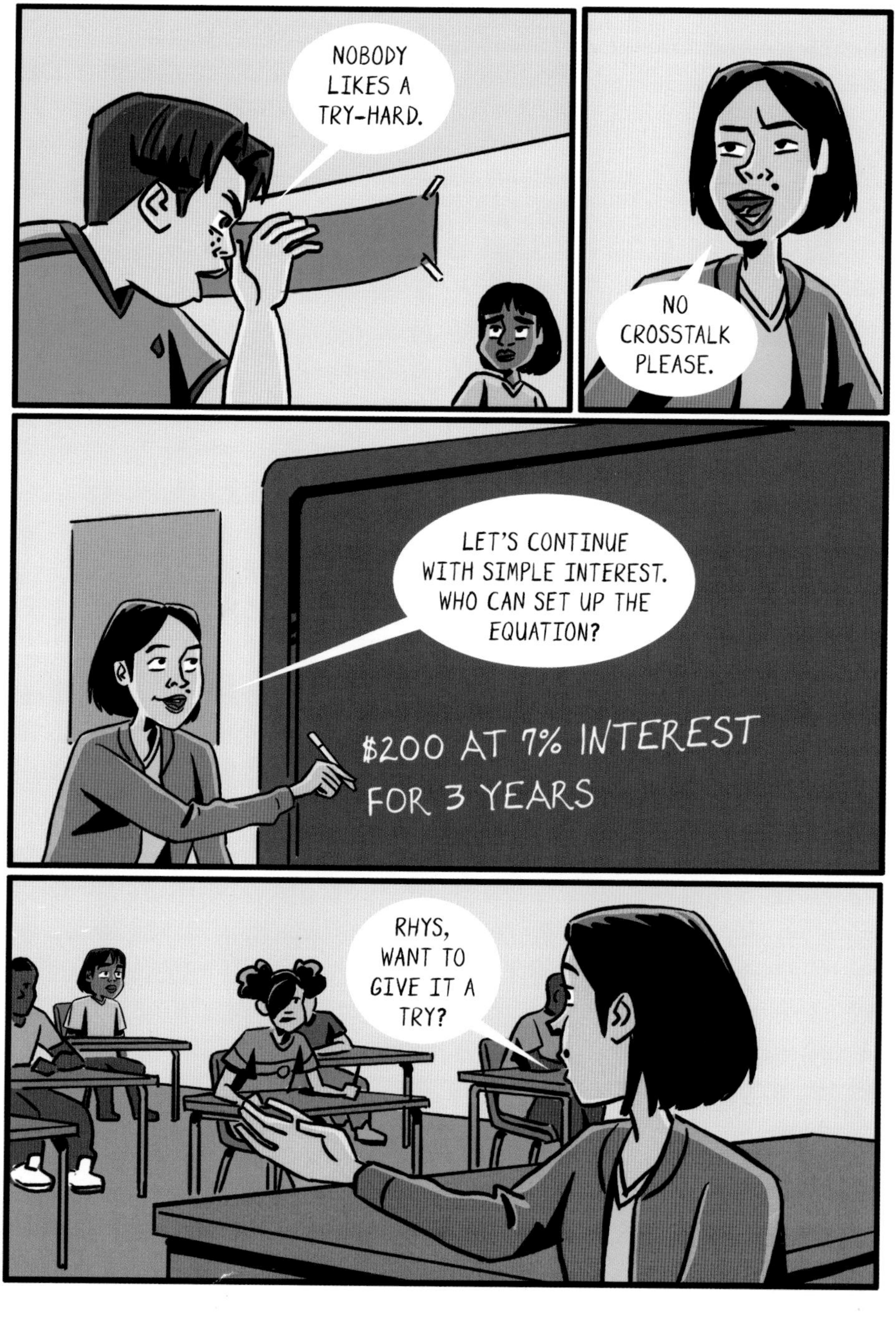
NOBODY LIKES A TRY-HARD.
NO CROSSTALK PLEASE.
LET'S CONTINUE WITH SIMPLE INTEREST. WHO CAN SET UP THE EQUATION?
$200 AT 7% INTEREST FOR 3 YEARS
RHYS, WANT TO GIVE IT A TRY?

STRONGHOLD

CHAPTER 5

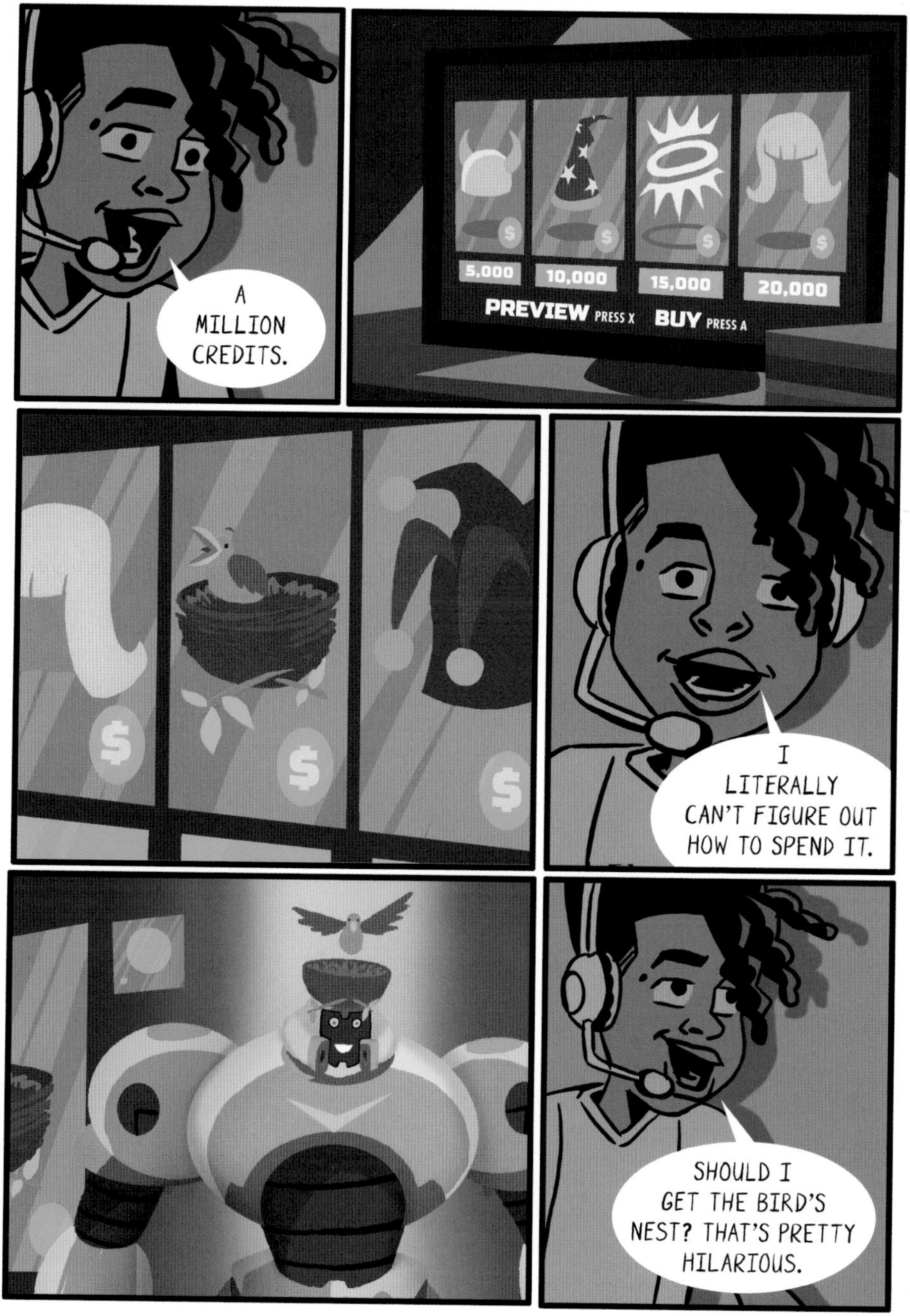
A MILLION CREDITS.
5,000
10,000
15,000
20,000
PREVIEW PRESS X BUY PRESS A
I LITERALLY CAN'T FIGURE OUT HOW TO SPEND IT.
SHOULD I GET THE BIRD'S NEST? THAT'S PRETTY HILARIOUS.

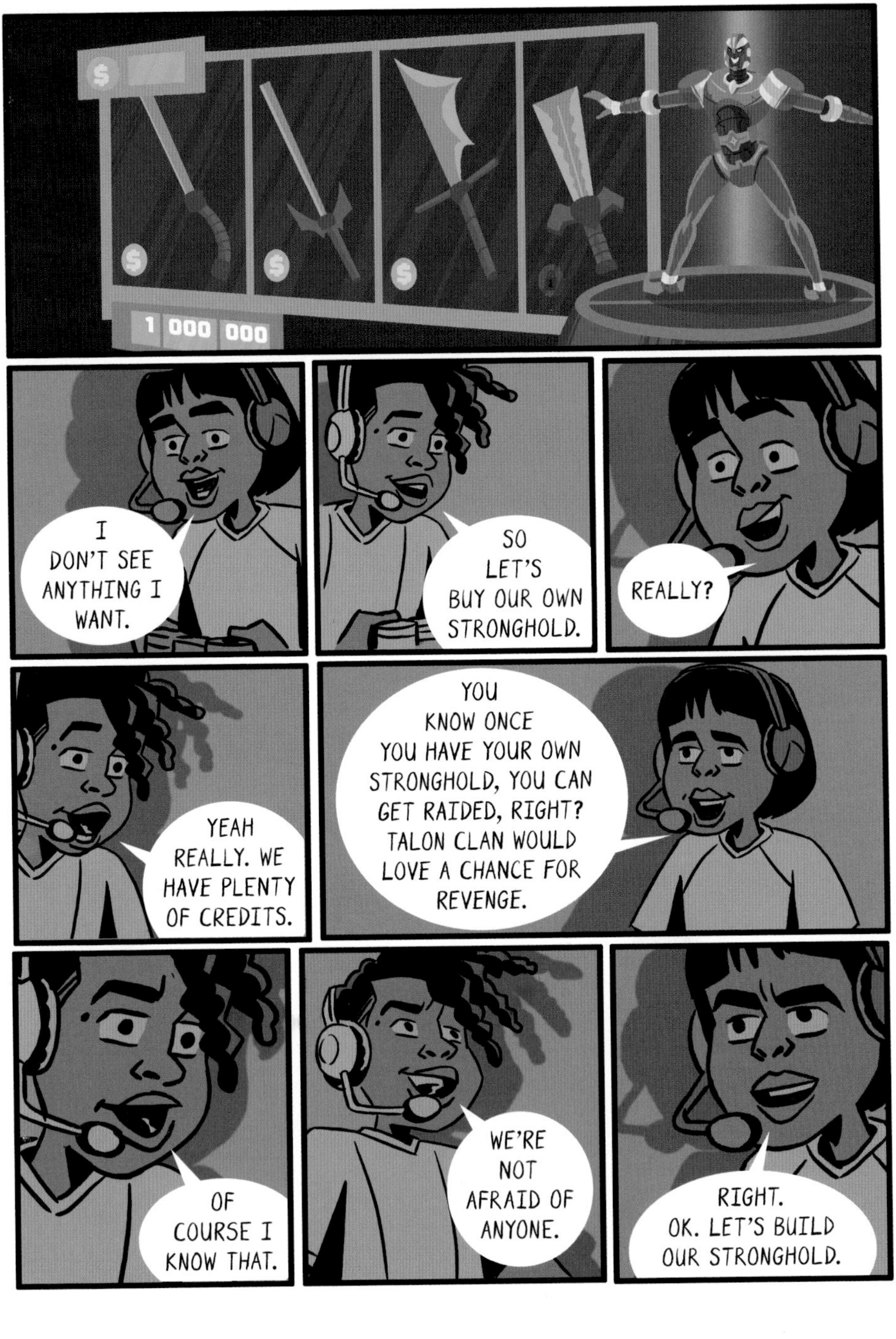
1 000 000
I DON'T SEE ANYTHING I WANT.
SO LET'S BUY OUR OWN STRONGHOLD.
REALLY?
YEAH REALLY. WE HAVE PLENTY OF CREDITS.
YOU KNOW ONCE YOU HAVE YOUR OWN STRONGHOLD, YOU CAN GET RAIDED, RIGHT? TALON CLAN WOULD LOVE A CHANCE FOR REVENGE.
OF COURSE I KNOW THAT.
WE'RE NOT AFRAID OF ANYONE.
RIGHT. OK. LET'S BUILD OUR STRONGHOLD.

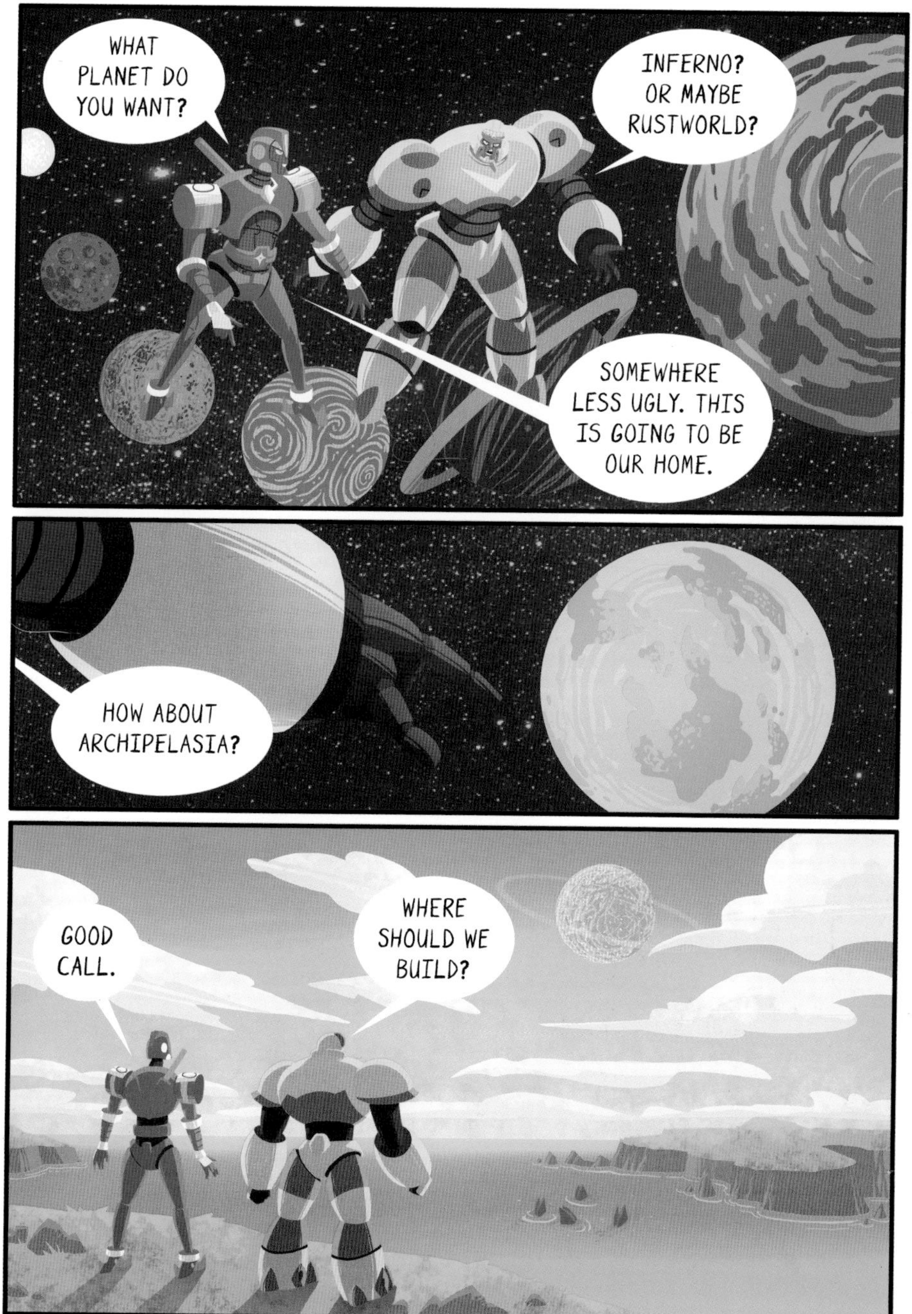
WHAT PLANET DO YOU WANT?
INFERNO? OR MAYBE RUSTWORLD?
SOMEWHERE LESS UGLY. THIS IS GOING TO BE OUR HOME.
HOW ABOUT ARCHIPELASIA?
WHERE SHOULD WE BUILD?
GOOD CALL.

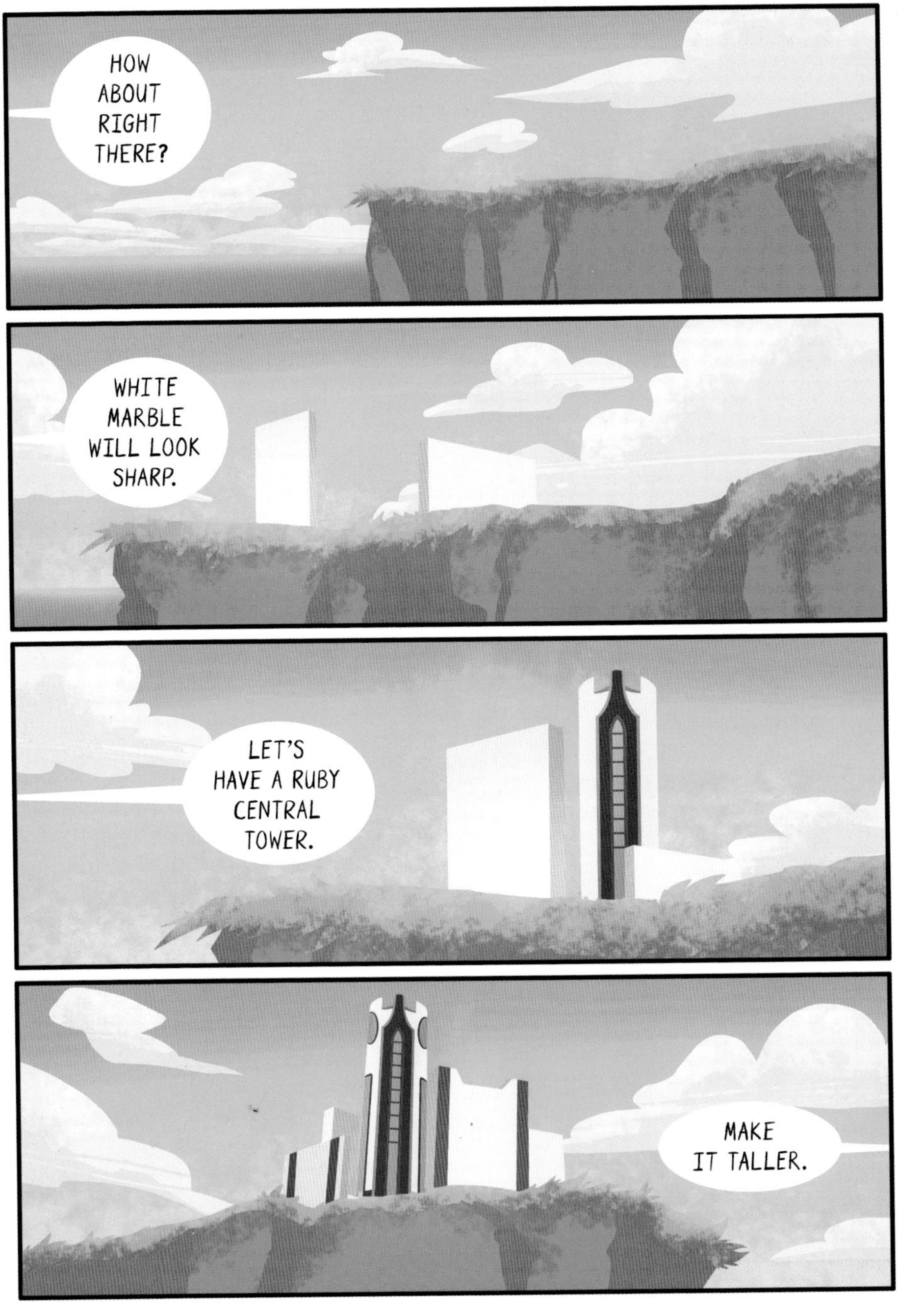
HOW ABOUT RIGHT THERE?
WHITE MARBLE WILL LOOK SHARP.
LET'S HAVE A RUBY CENTRAL TOWER.
MAKE IT TALLER.

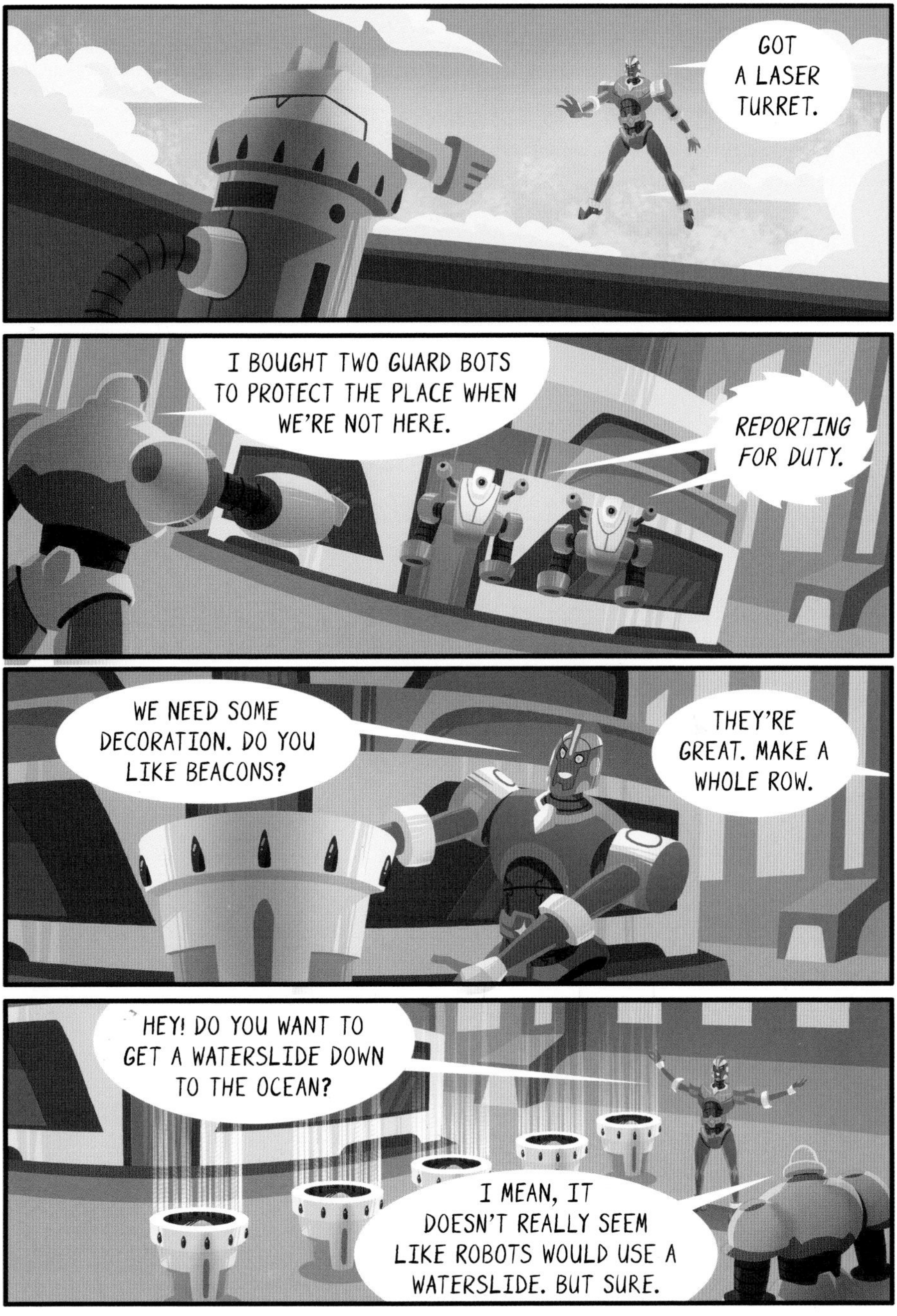
GOT A LASER TURRET.
I BOUGHT TWO GUARD BOTS TO PROTECT THE PLACE WHEN WE'RE NOT HERE.
REPORTING FOR DUTY.
WE NEED SOME DECORATION. DO YOU LIKE BEACONS?
THEY'RE GREAT. MAKE A WHOLE ROW.
HEY! DO YOU WANT TO GET A WATERSLIDE DOWN TO THE OCEAN?
I MEAN, IT DOESN'T REALLY SEEM LIKE ROBOTS WOULD USE A WATERSLIDE. BUT SURE.

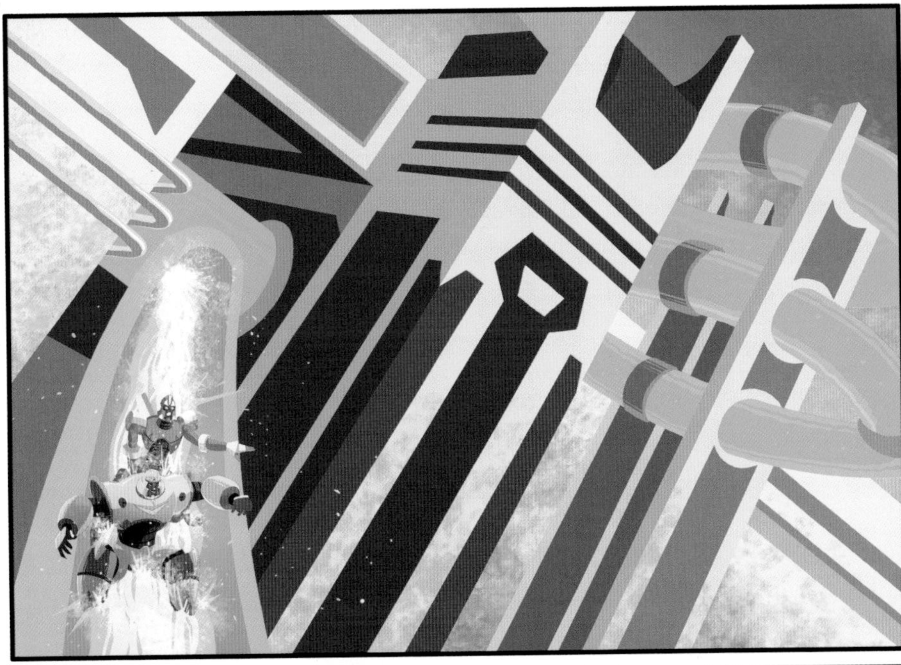

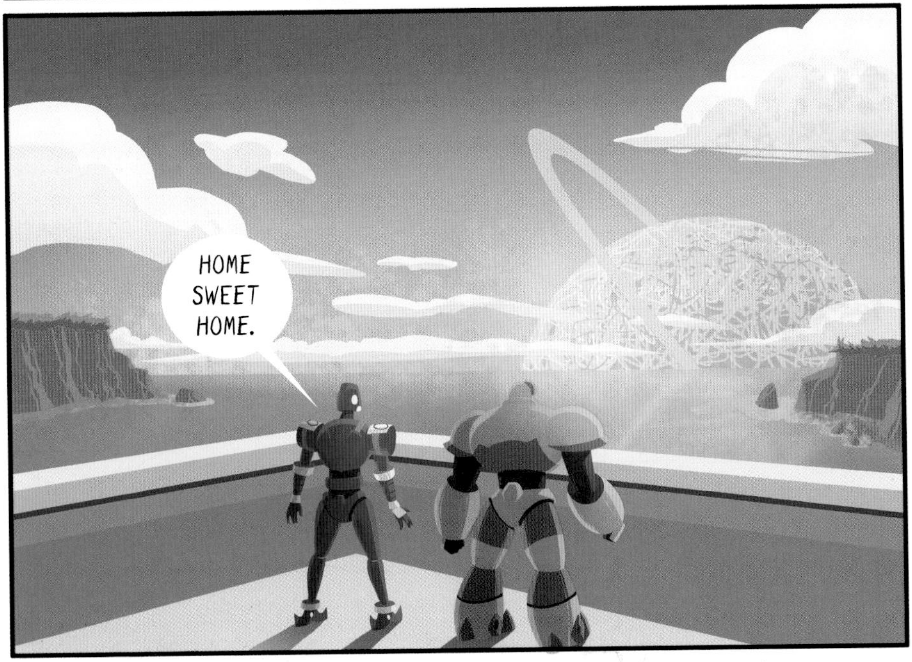
HOME SWEET HOME.

CHAPTER 6
OFF ROAD

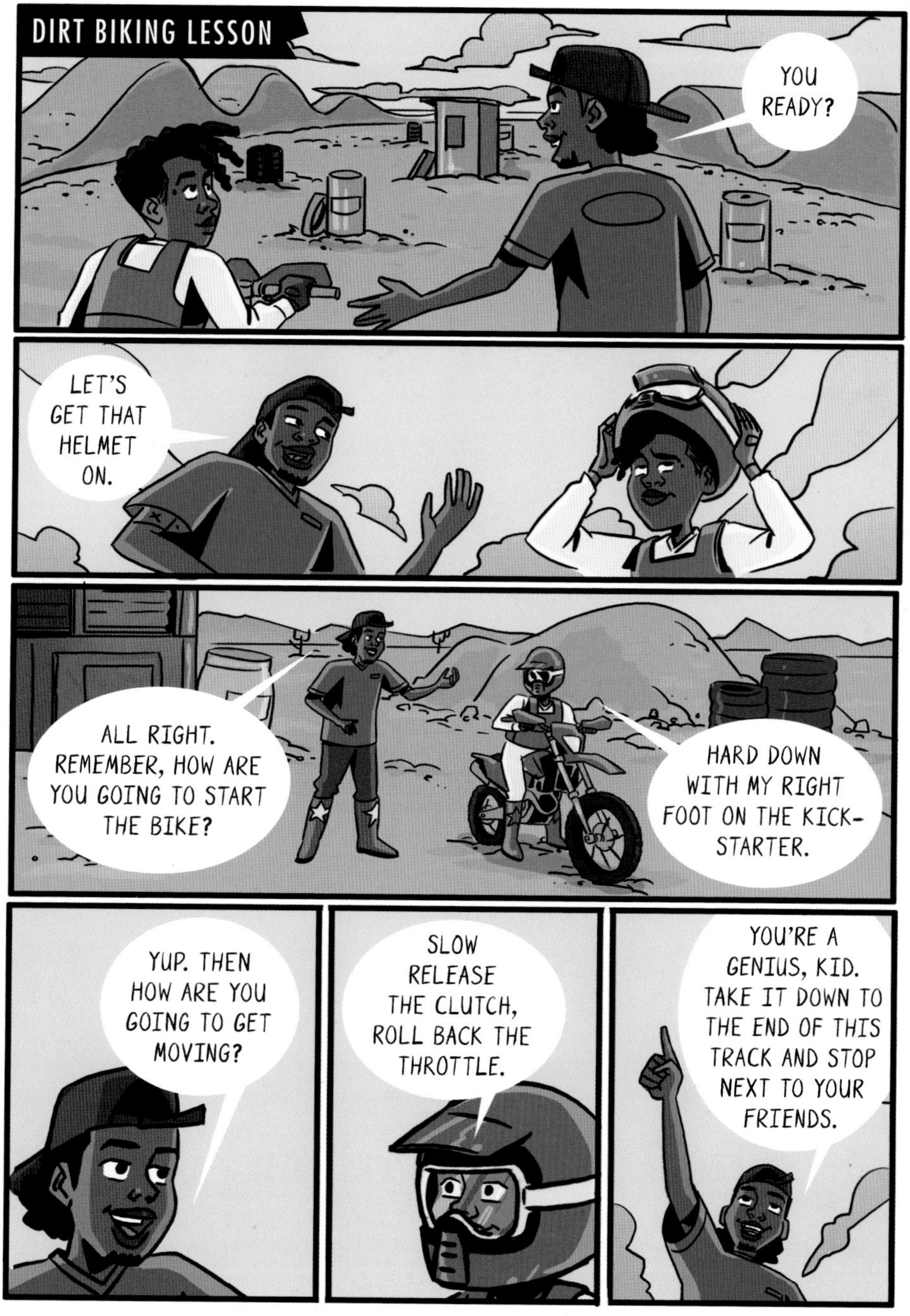
DIRT BIKING LESSON
YOU READY?
LET'S GET THAT HELMET ON.
ALL RIGHT. REMEMBER, HOW ARE YOU GOING TO START THE BIKE?
HARD DOWN WITH MY RIGHT FOOT ON THE KICK-STARTER.
YUP. THEN HOW ARE YOU GOING TO GET MOVING?
SLOW RELEASE THE CLUTCH, ROLL BACK THE THROTTLE.
YOU'RE A GENIUS, KID. TAKE IT DOWN TO THE END OF THIS TRACK AND STOP NEXT TO YOUR FRIENDS.

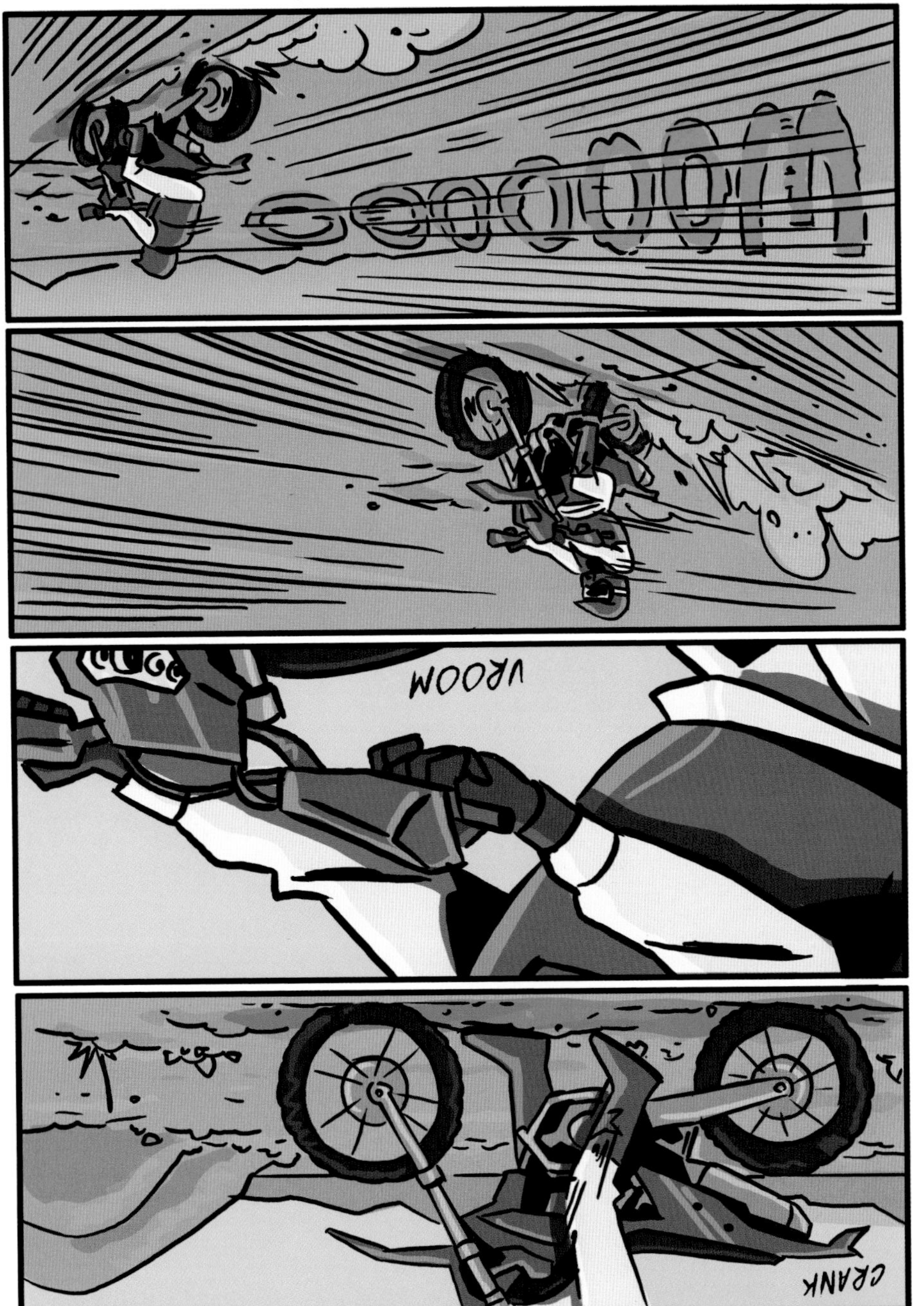
VROOM
CRANK

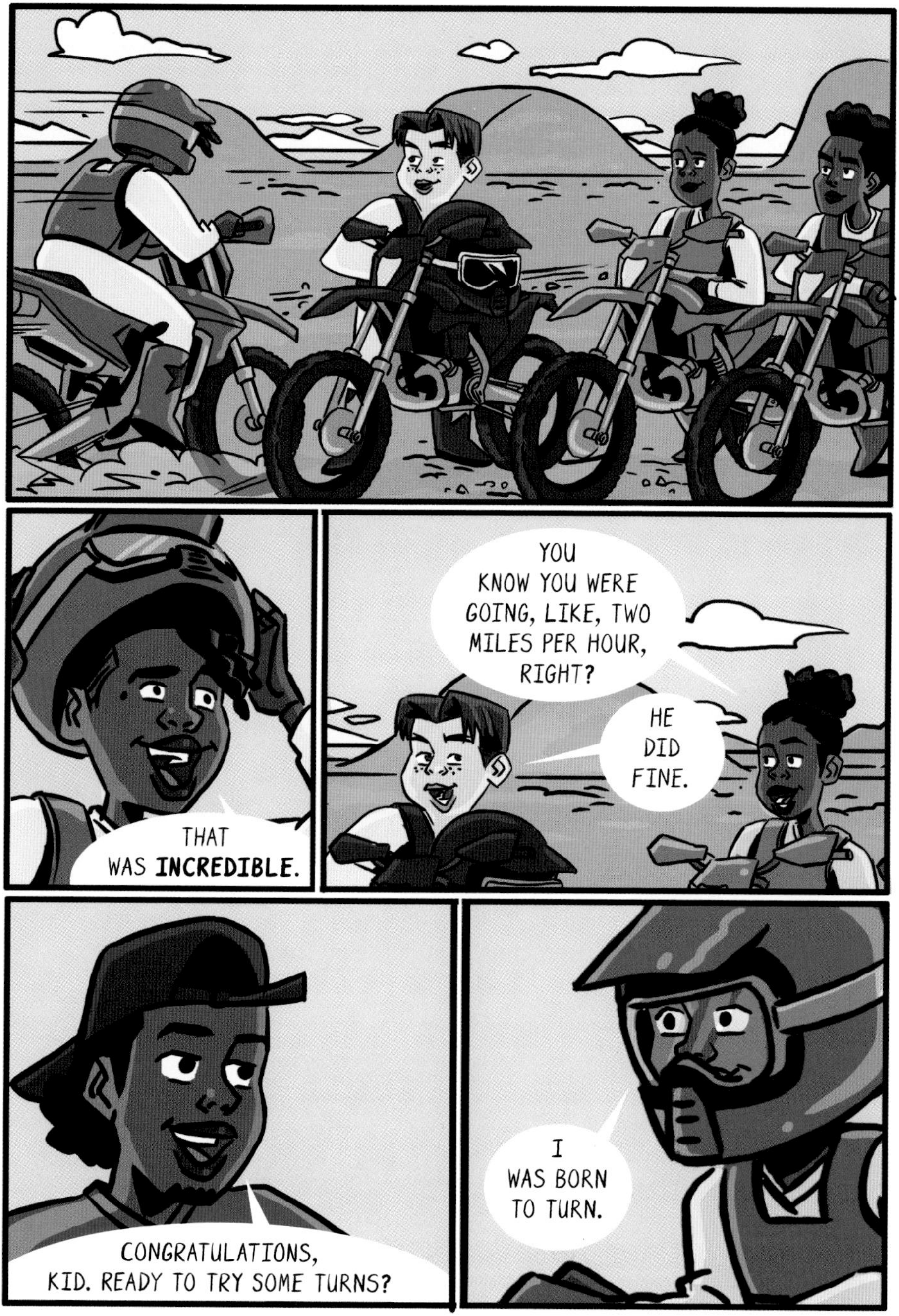
THAT WAS **INCREDIBLE**.
YOU KNOW YOU WERE GOING, LIKE, TWO MILES PER HOUR, RIGHT?
HE DID FINE.
CONGRATULATIONS, KID. READY TO TRY SOME TURNS?
I WAS BORN TO TURN.

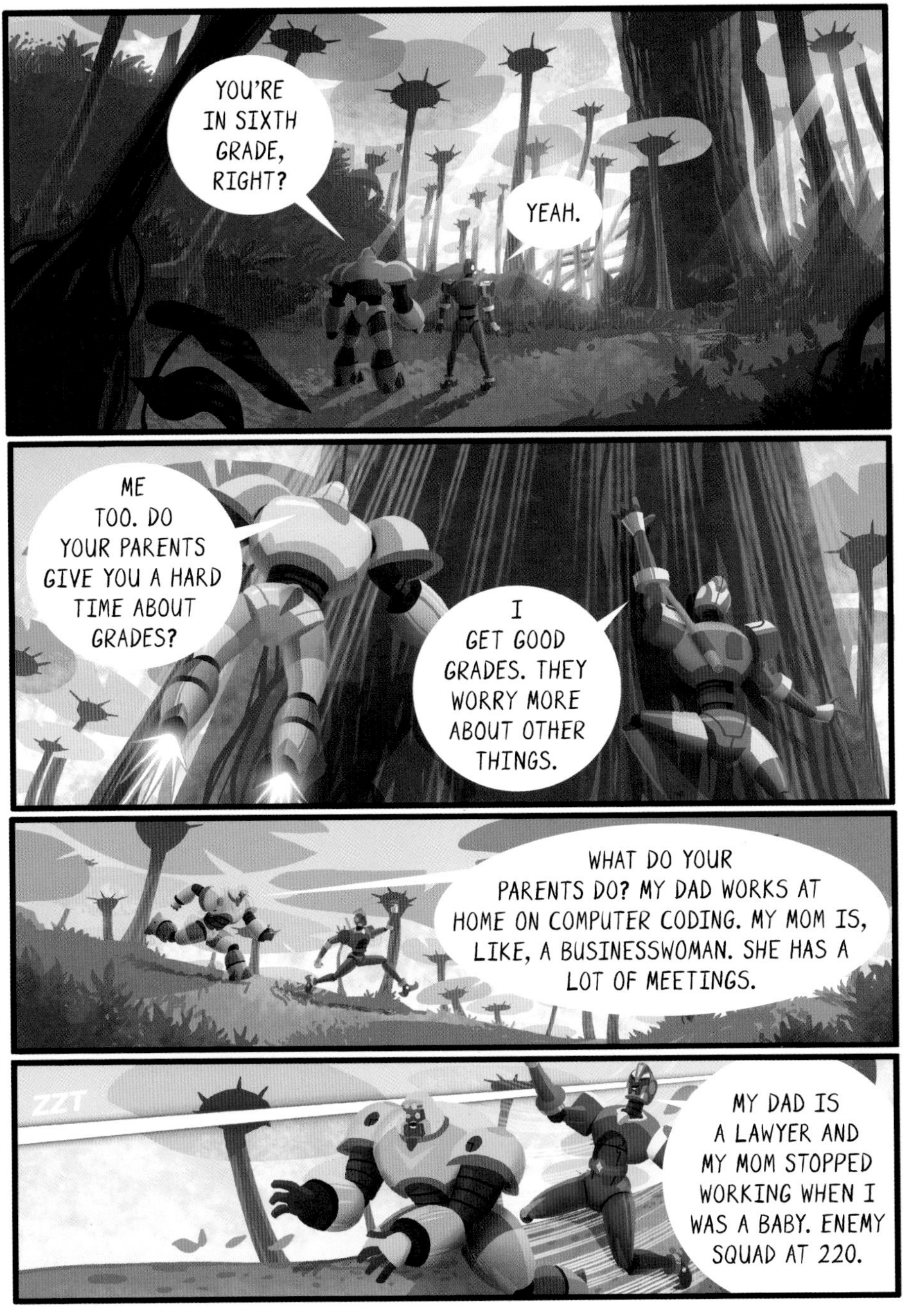
YOU'RE IN SIXTH GRADE, RIGHT?
YEAH.
ME TOO. DO YOUR PARENTS GIVE YOU A HARD TIME ABOUT GRADES?
I GET GOOD GRADES. THEY WORRY MORE ABOUT OTHER THINGS.
WHAT DO YOUR PARENTS DO? MY DAD WORKS AT HOME ON COMPUTER CODING. MY MOM IS, LIKE, A BUSINESSWOMAN. SHE HAS A LOT OF MEETINGS.
ZZT
MY DAD IS A LAWYER AND MY MOM STOPPED WORKING WHEN I WAS A BABY. ENEMY SQUAD AT 220.

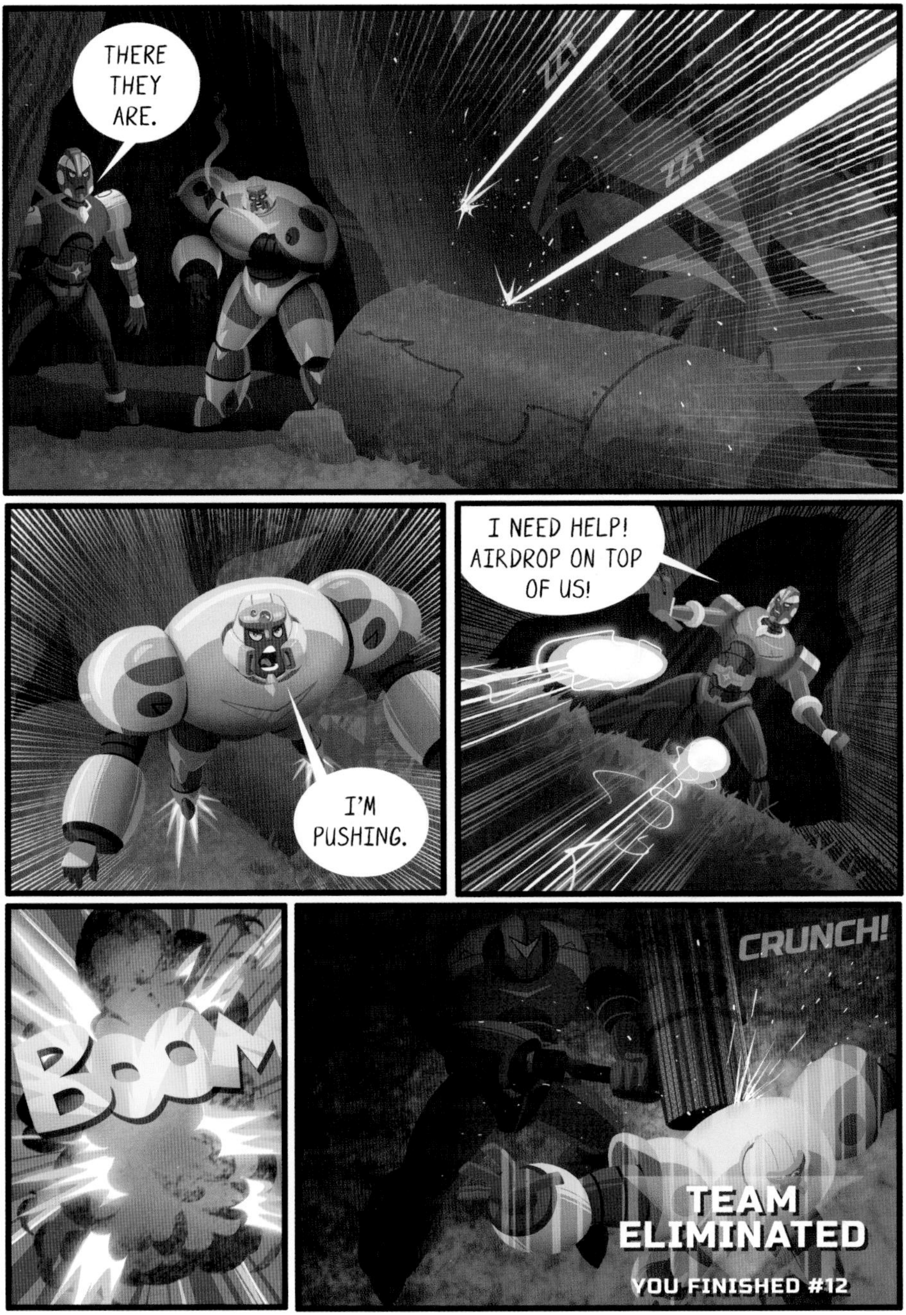
THERE THEY ARE.
ZZT
ZZT
I'M PUSHING.
I NEED HELP! AIRDROP ON TOP OF US!
BOOM
CRUNCH!
TEAM ELIMINATED
YOU FINISHED #12

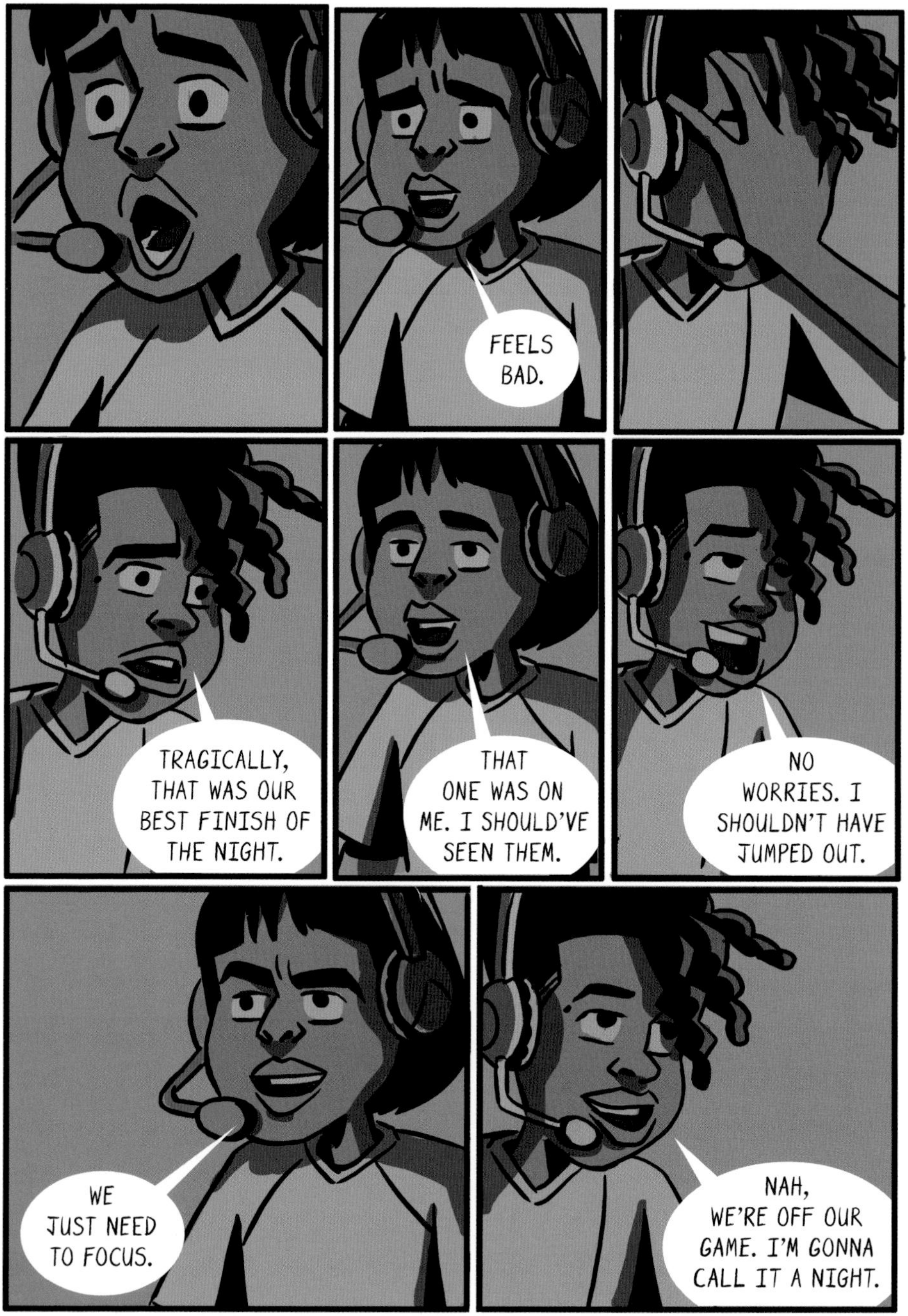
FEELS BAD.
TRAGICALLY, THAT WAS OUR BEST FINISH OF THE NIGHT.
THAT ONE WAS ON ME. I SHOULD'VE SEEN THEM.
NO WORRIES. I SHOULDN'T HAVE JUMPED OUT.
WE JUST NEED TO FOCUS.
NAH, WE'RE OFF OUR GAME. I'M GONNA CALL IT A NIGHT.

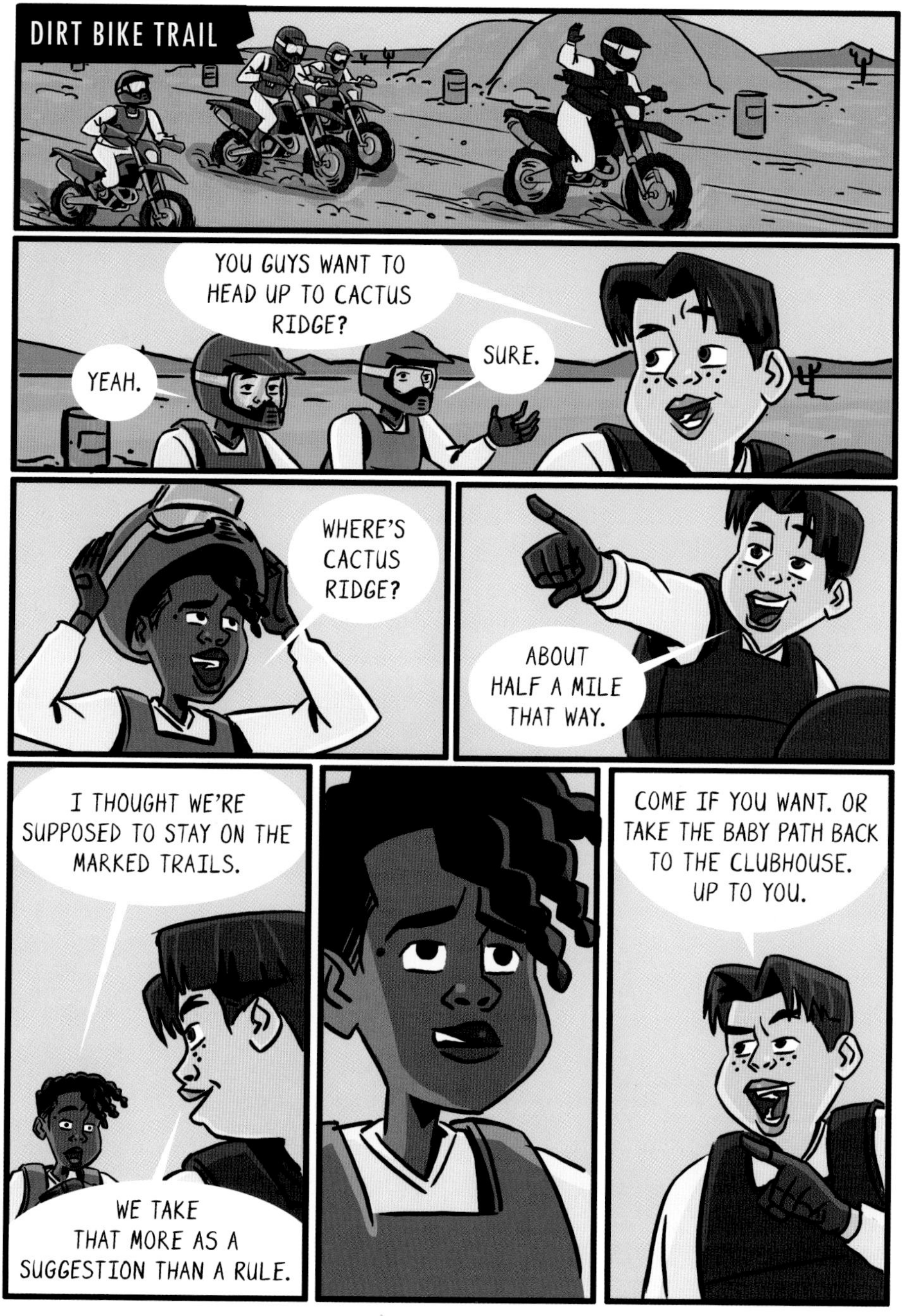
DIRT BIKE TRAIL
YOU GUYS WANT TO HEAD UP TO CACTUS RIDGE?
YEAH.
SURE.
WHERE'S CACTUS RIDGE?
ABOUT HALF A MILE THAT WAY.
I THOUGHT WE'RE SUPPOSED TO STAY ON THE MARKED TRAILS.
WE TAKE THAT MORE AS A SUGGESTION THAN A RULE.
COME IF YOU WANT. OR TAKE THE BABY PATH BACK TO THE CLUBHOUSE. UP TO YOU.

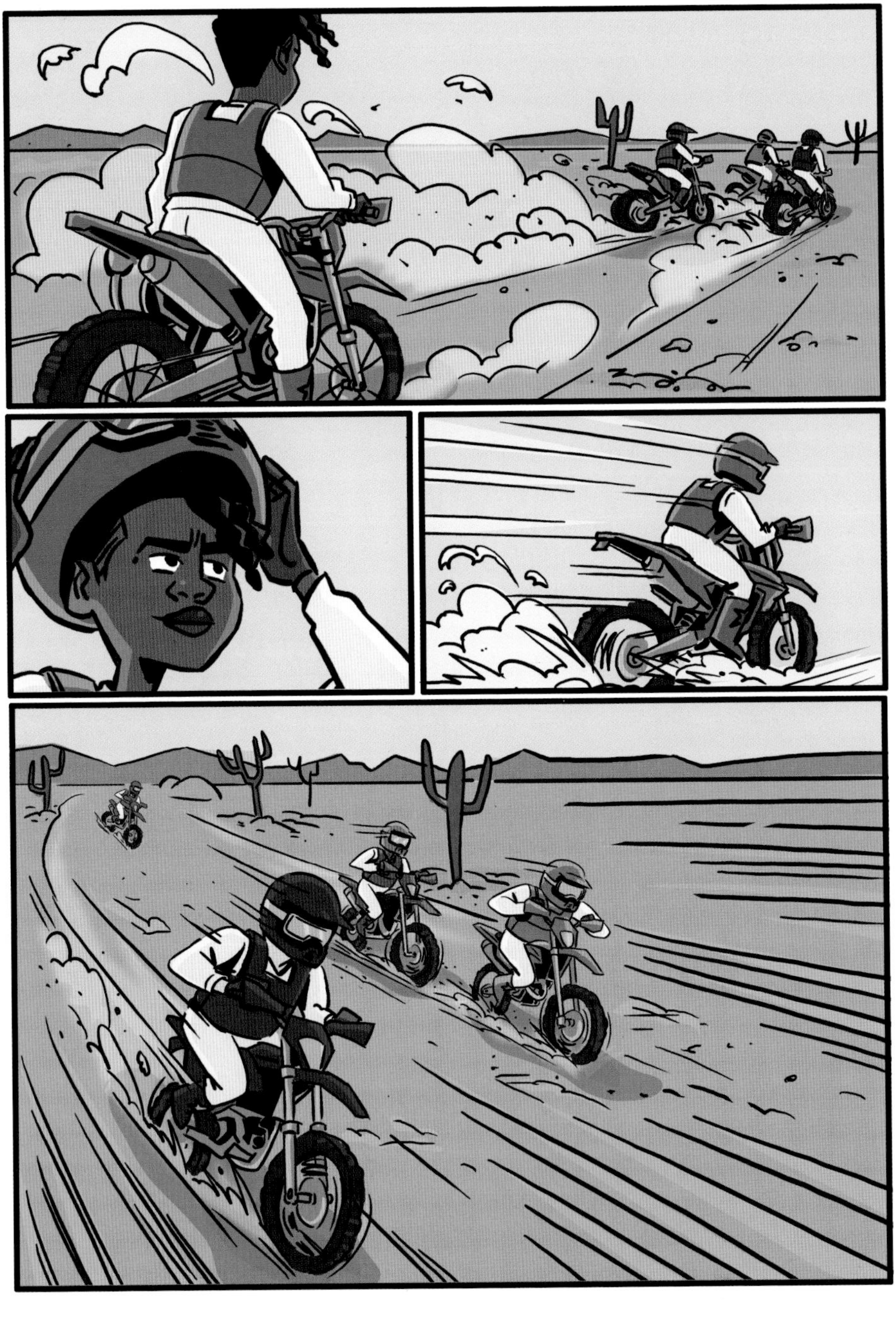

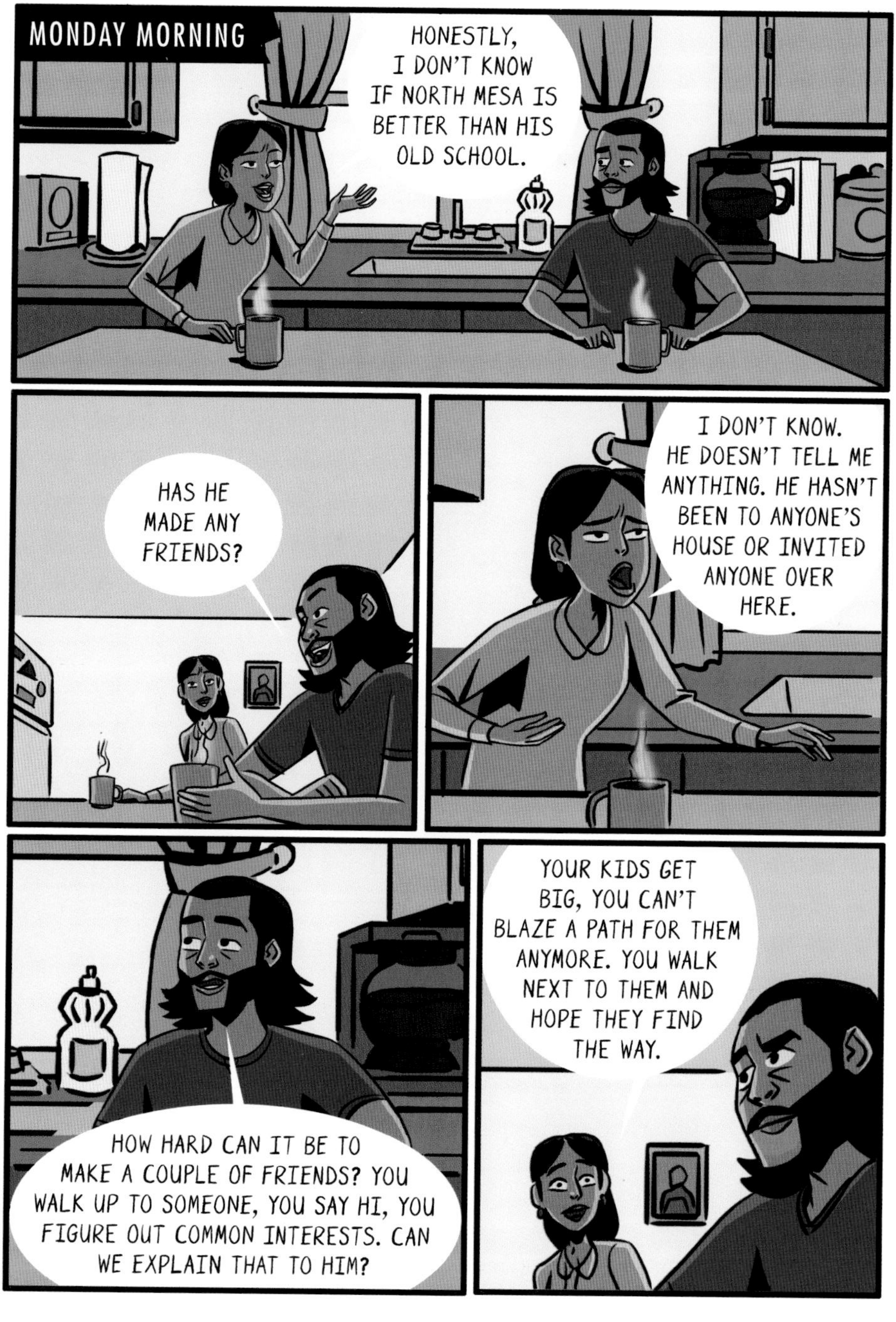
MONDAY MORNING
HONESTLY, I DON'T KNOW IF NORTH MESA IS BETTER THAN HIS OLD SCHOOL.
HAS HE MADE ANY FRIENDS?
I DON'T KNOW. HE DOESN'T TELL ME ANYTHING. HE HASN'T BEEN TO ANYONE'S HOUSE OR INVITED ANYONE OVER HERE.
HOW HARD CAN IT BE TO MAKE A COUPLE OF FRIENDS? YOU WALK UP TO SOMEONE, YOU SAY HI, YOU FIGURE OUT COMMON INTERESTS. CAN WE EXPLAIN THAT TO HIM?
YOUR KIDS GET BIG, YOU CAN'T BLAZE A PATH FOR THEM ANYMORE. YOU WALK NEXT TO THEM AND HOPE THEY FIND THE WAY.

104

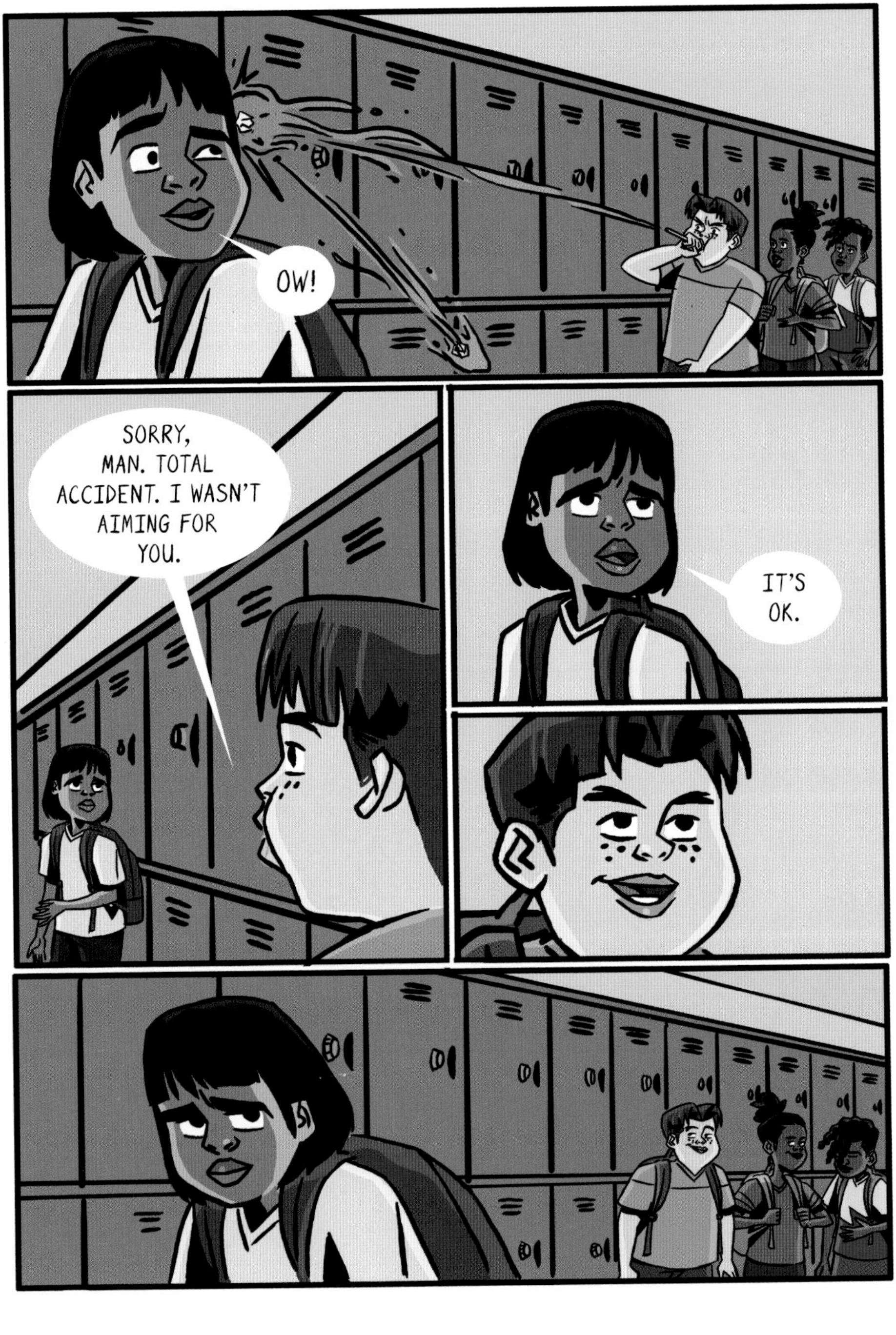
OW!
SORRY, MAN. TOTAL ACCIDENT. I WASN'T AIMING FOR YOU.
IT'S OK.

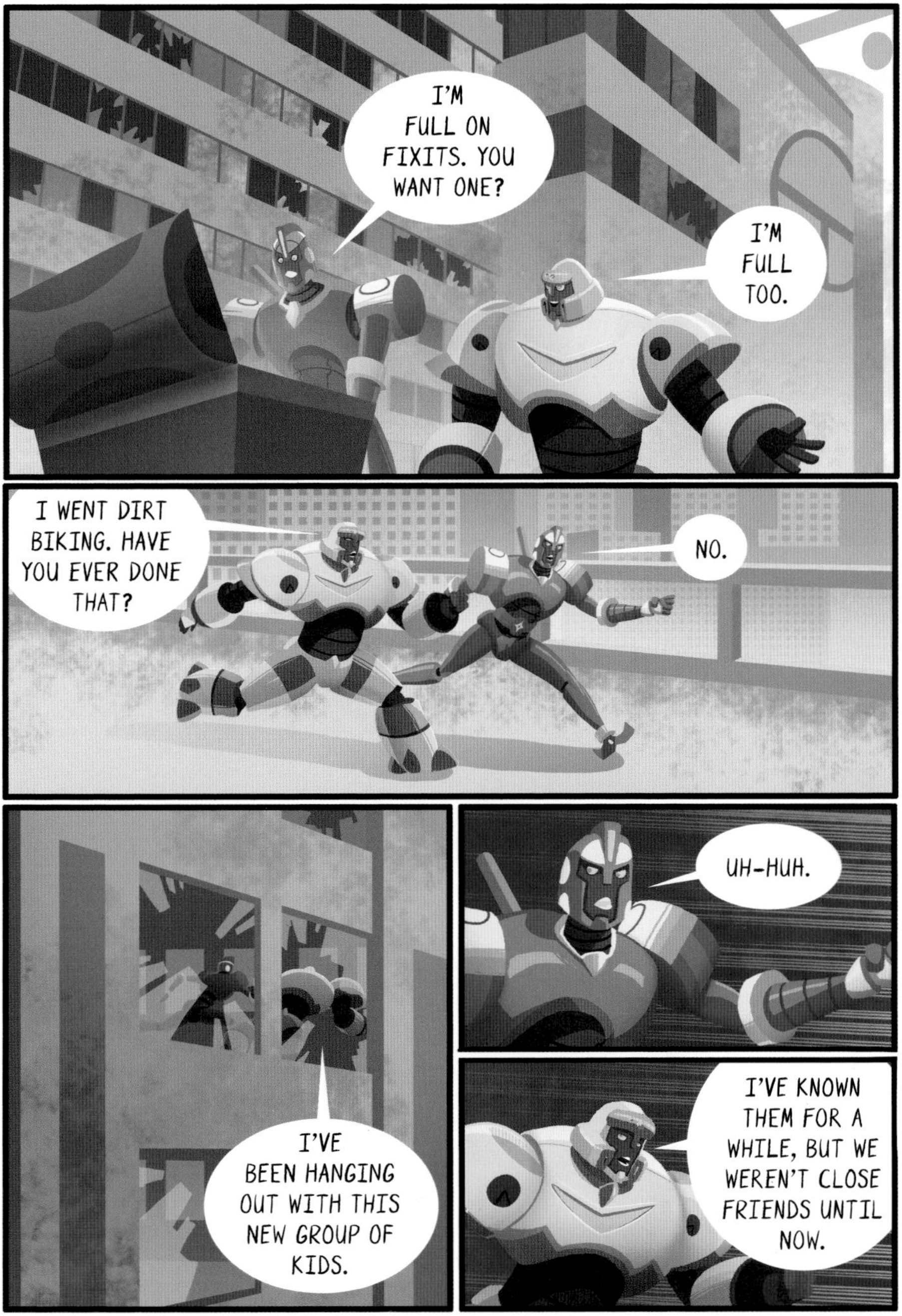
I'M FULL ON FIXITS. YOU WANT ONE?
I'M FULL TOO.
I WENT DIRT BIKING. HAVE YOU EVER DONE THAT?
NO.
I'VE BEEN HANGING OUT WITH THIS NEW GROUP OF KIDS.
UH-HUH.
I'VE KNOWN THEM FOR A WHILE, BUT WE WEREN'T CLOSE FRIENDS UNTIL NOW.

108

CHAPTER 7
KEEP-AWAY

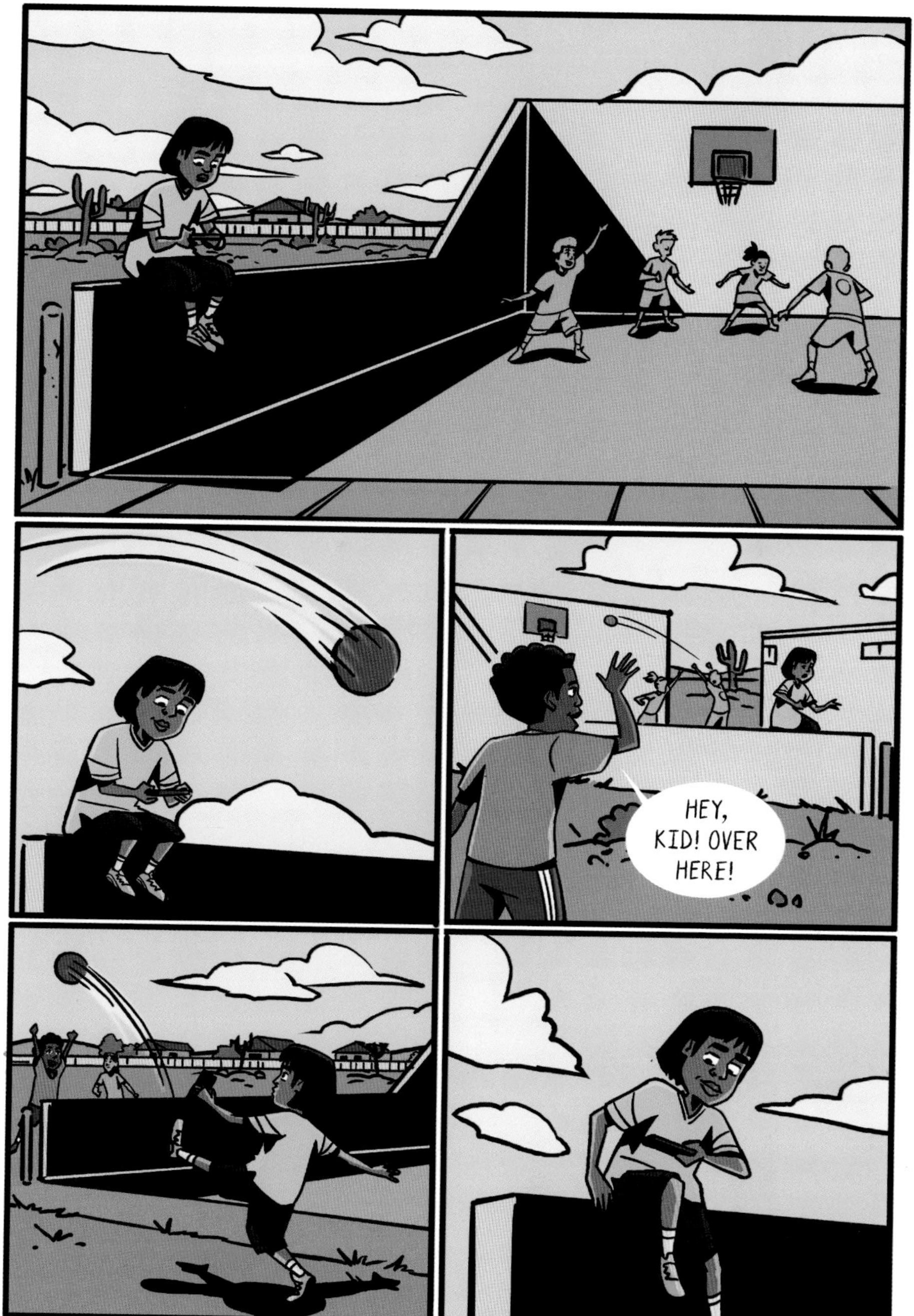
HEY, KID! OVER HERE!

113

114

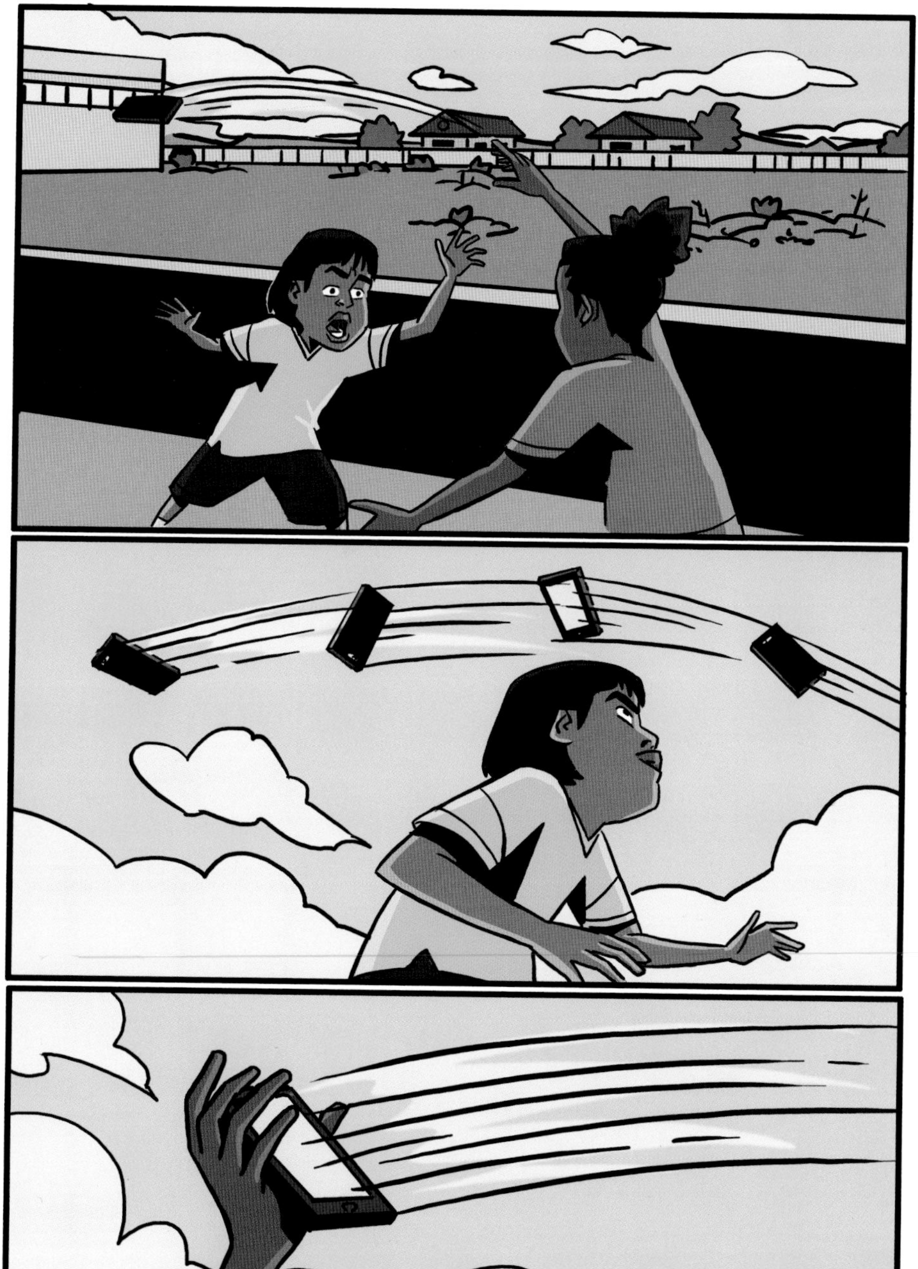

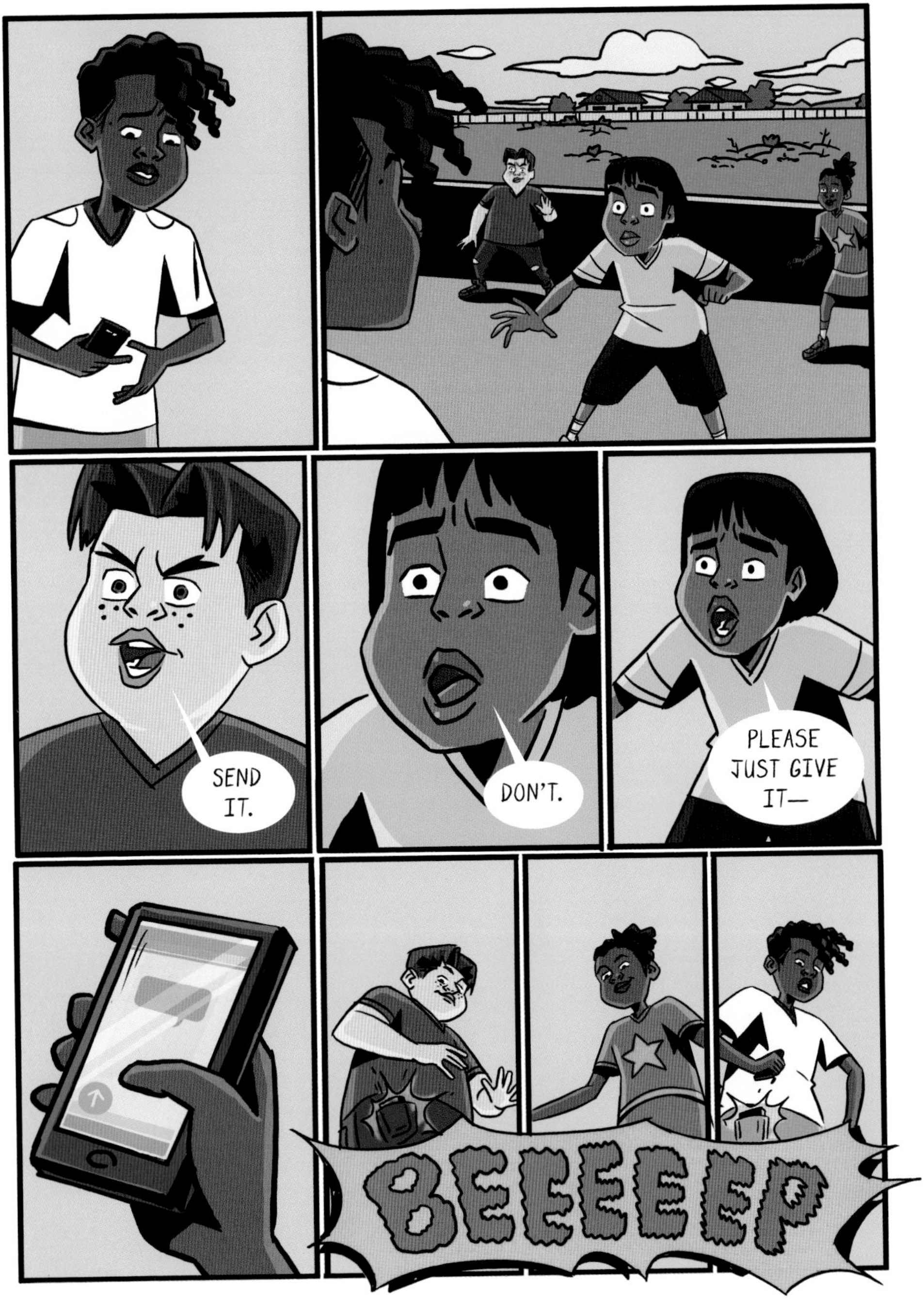
SEND
IT.
DON'T.
PLEASE
JUST GIVE
IT—
BEEEEEP

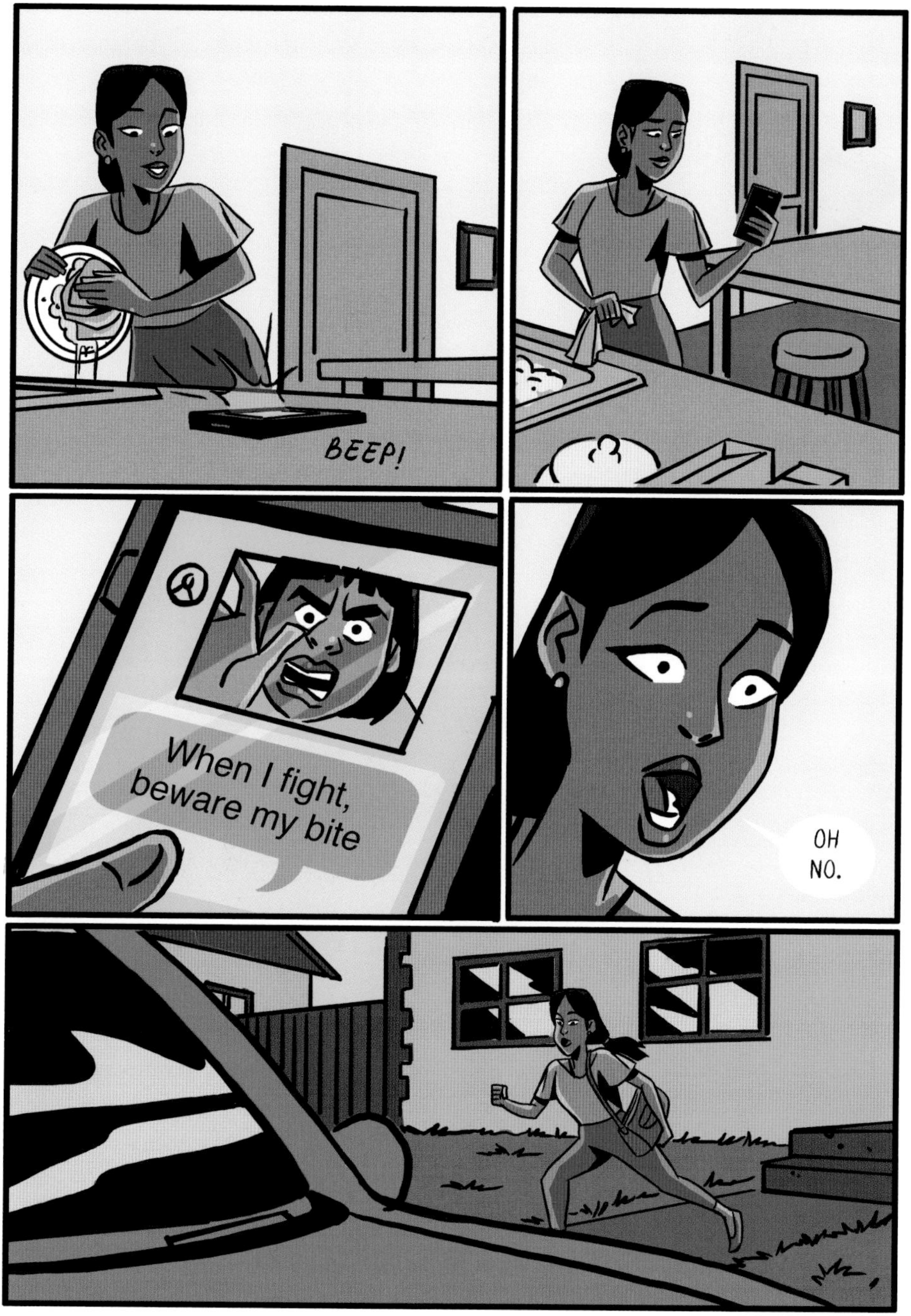
BEEP!
When I fight, beware my bite
OH NO.

118

CHAPTER 8
ANGER ISSUES

122

123

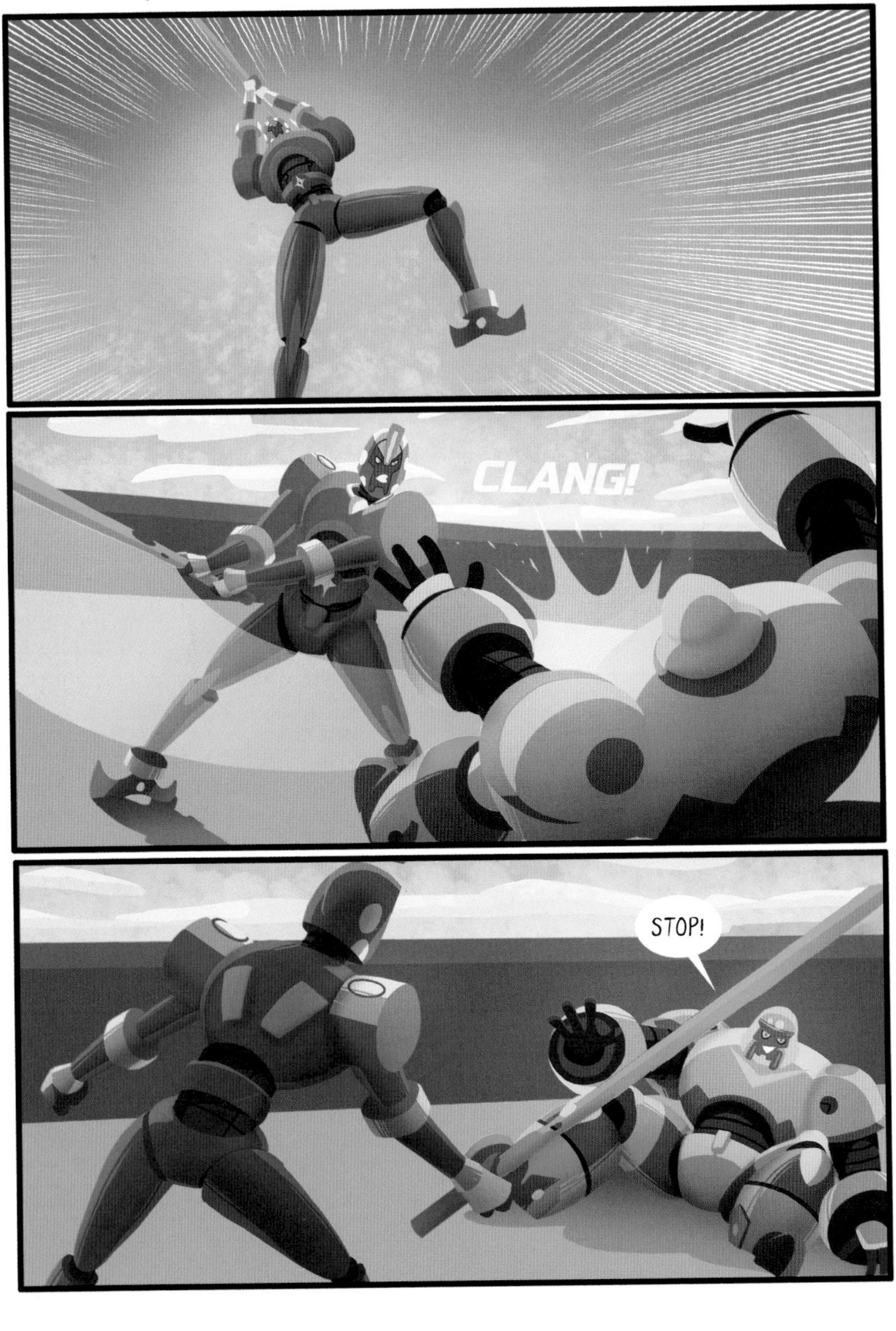
CLANG!
STOP!

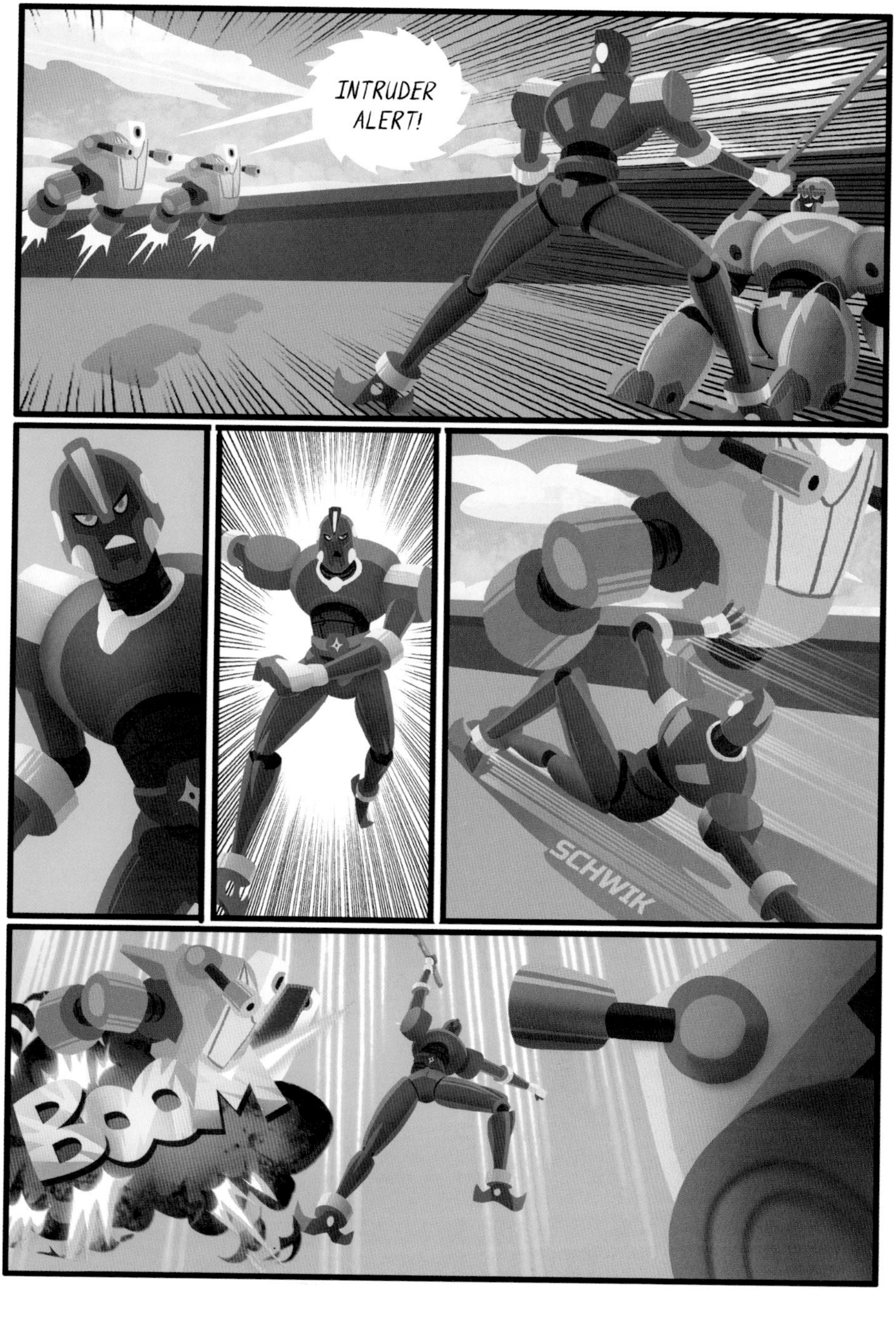
INTRUDER ALERT!
SCHWIK
BOOM

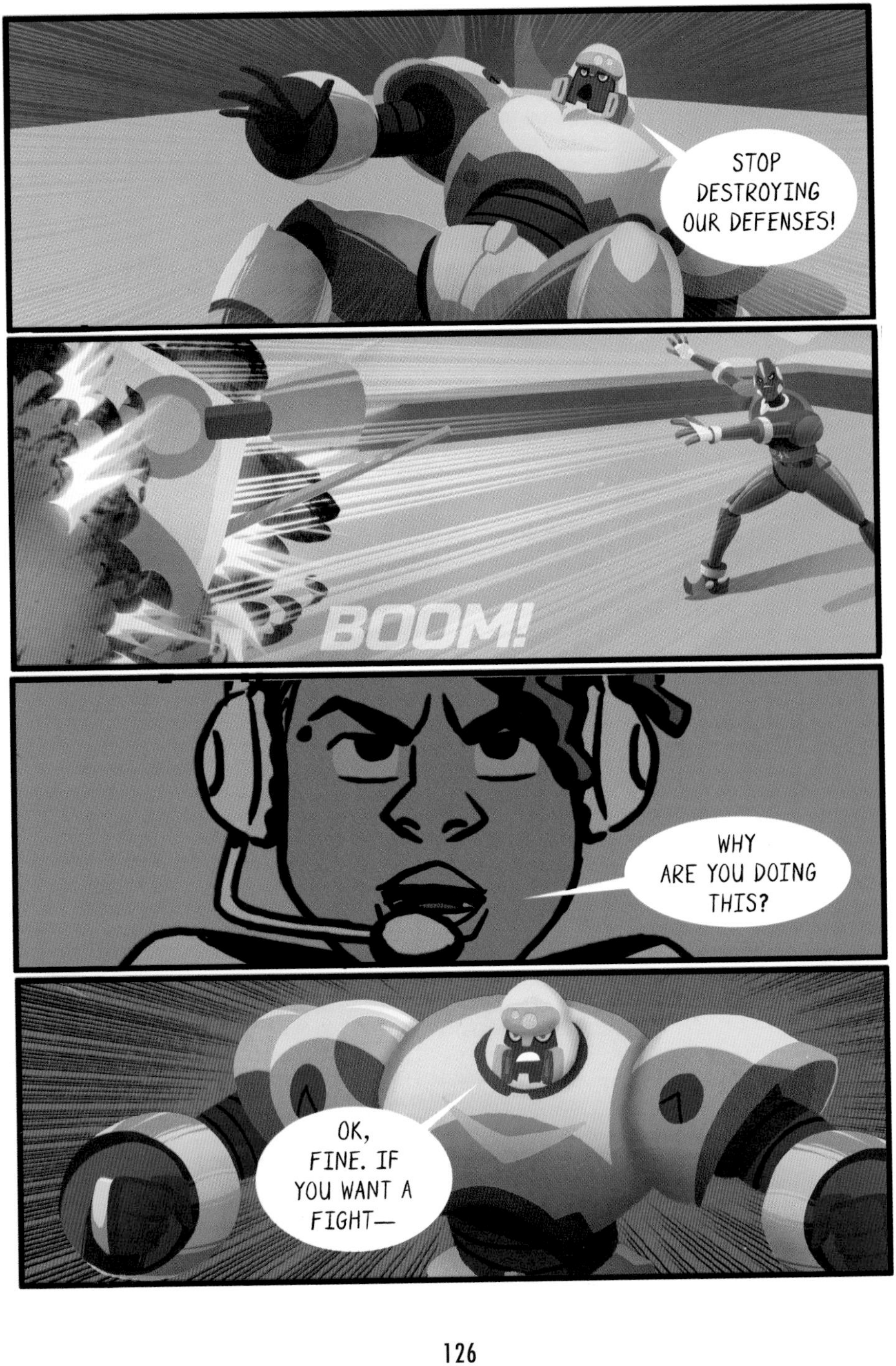
STOP DESTROYING OUR DEFENSES!
BOOM!
WHY ARE YOU DOING THIS?
OK, FINE. IF YOU WANT A FIGHT—

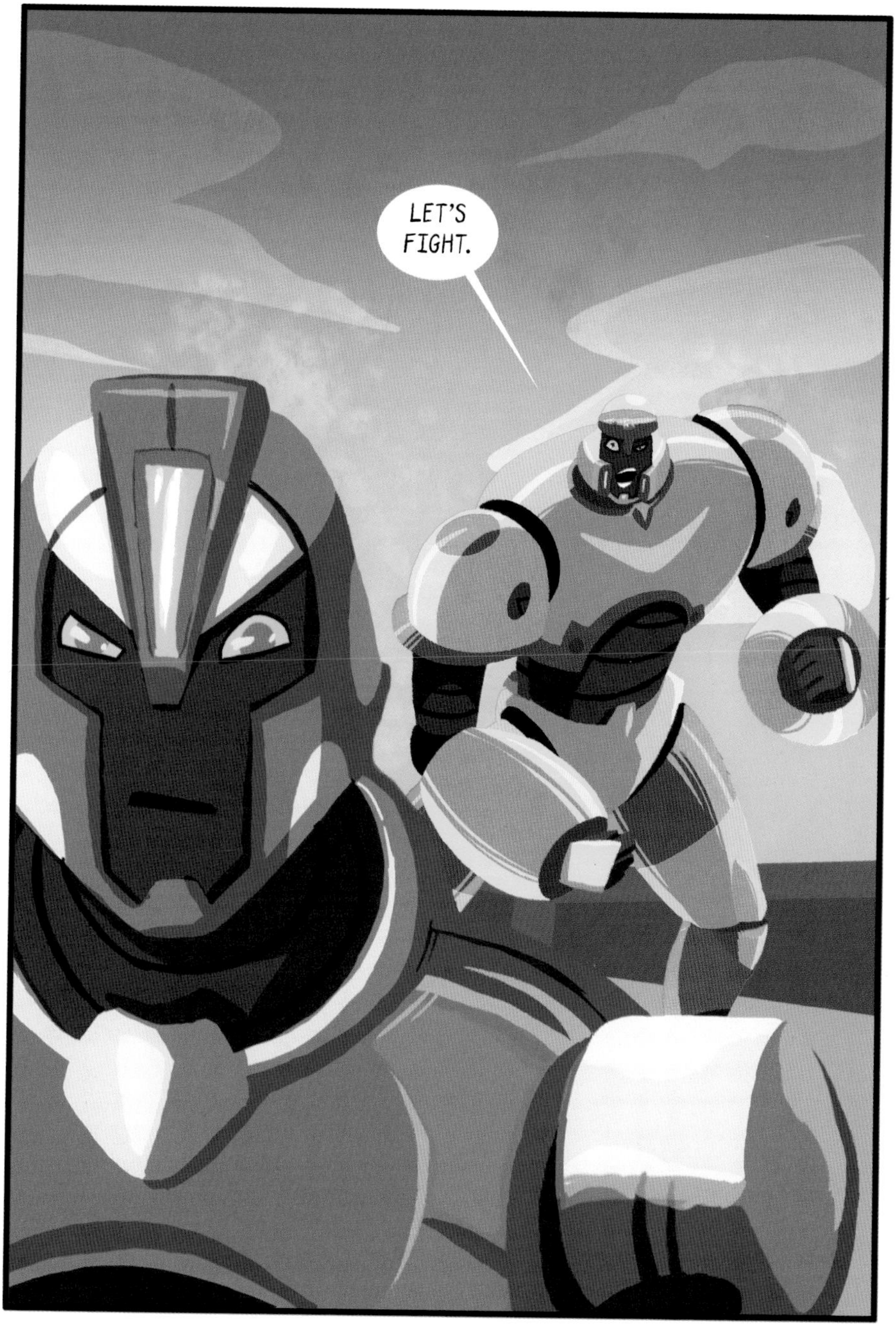
LET'S FIGHT.

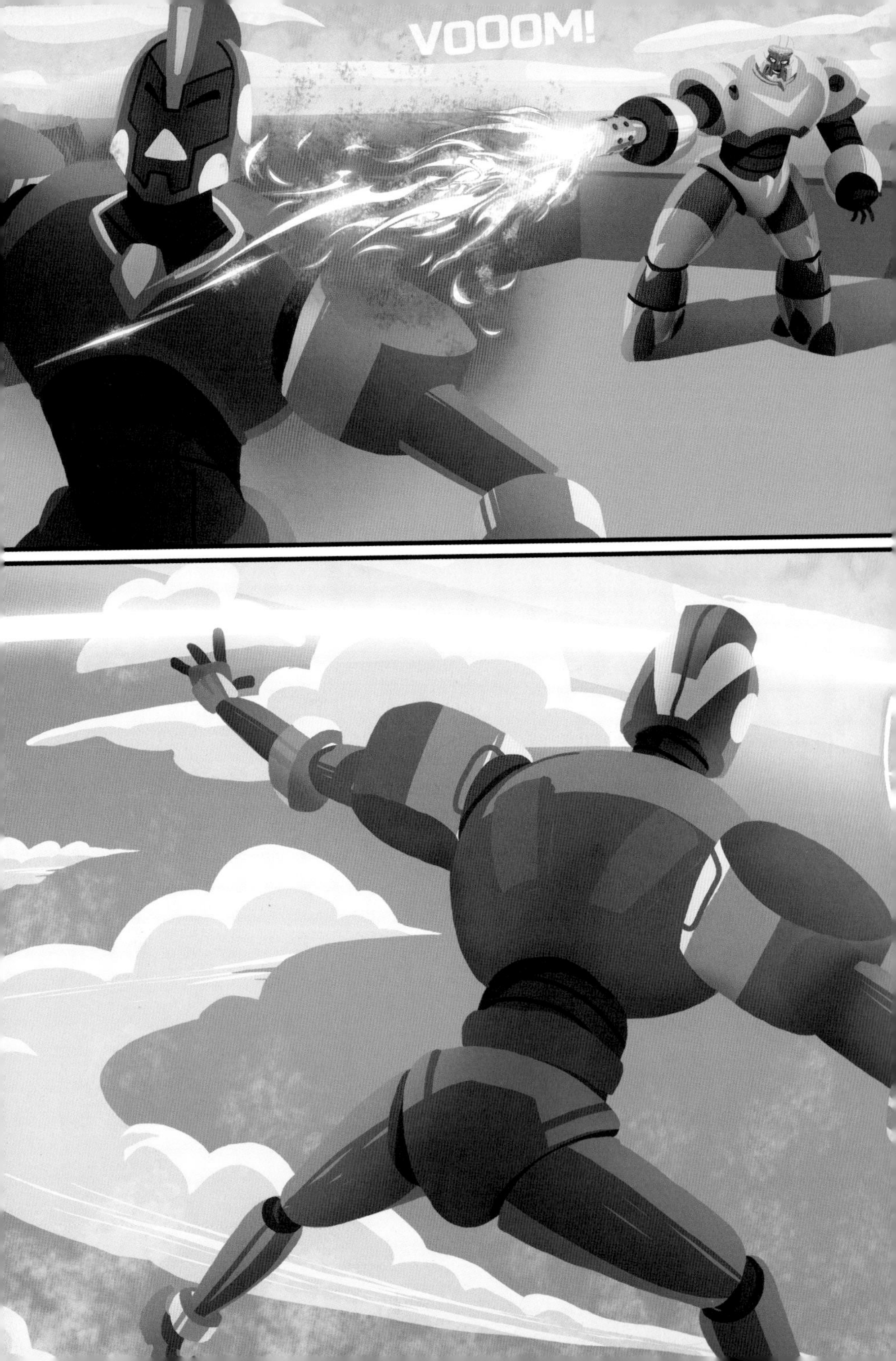
VOOOM!

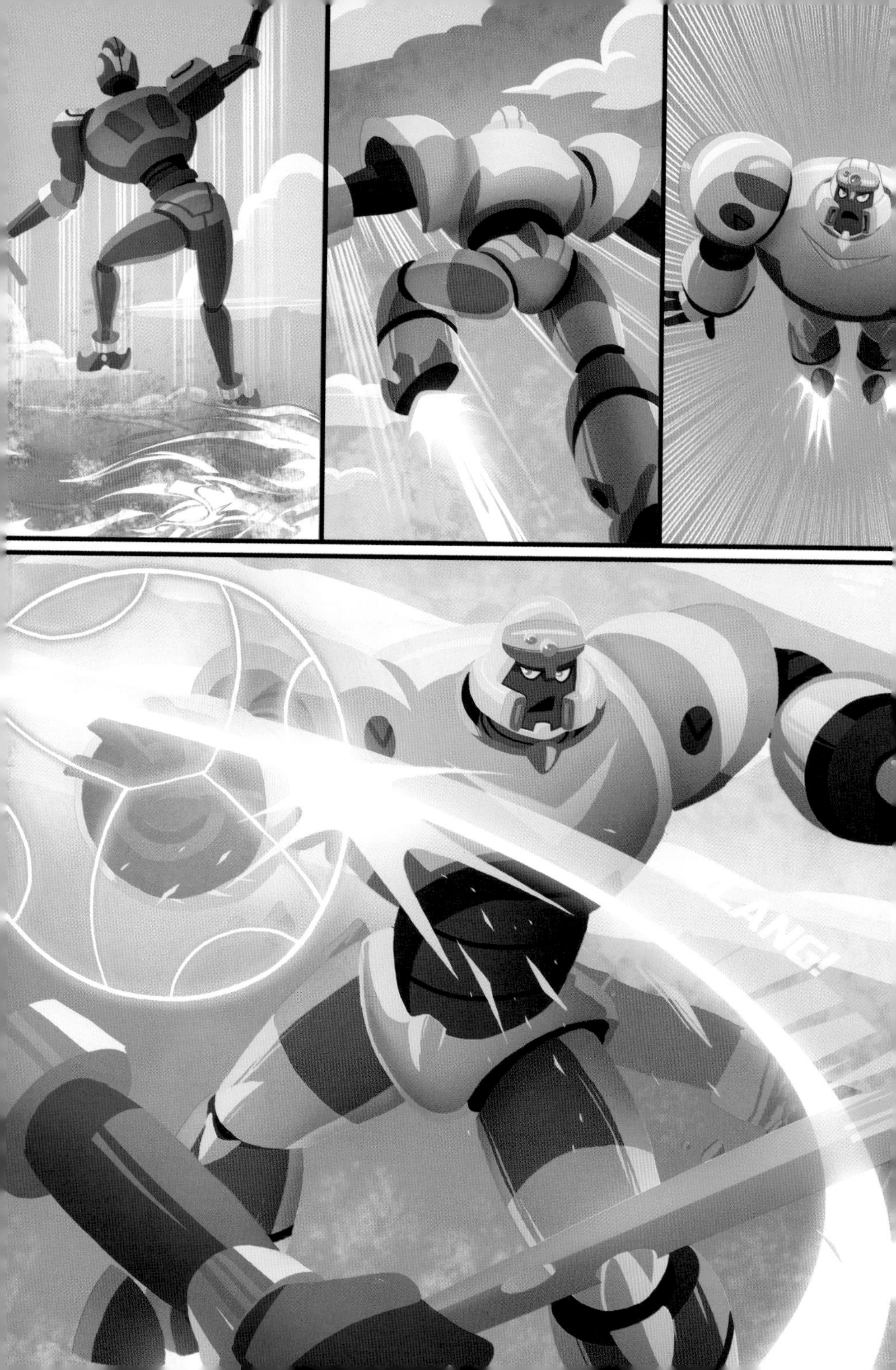
LANG!

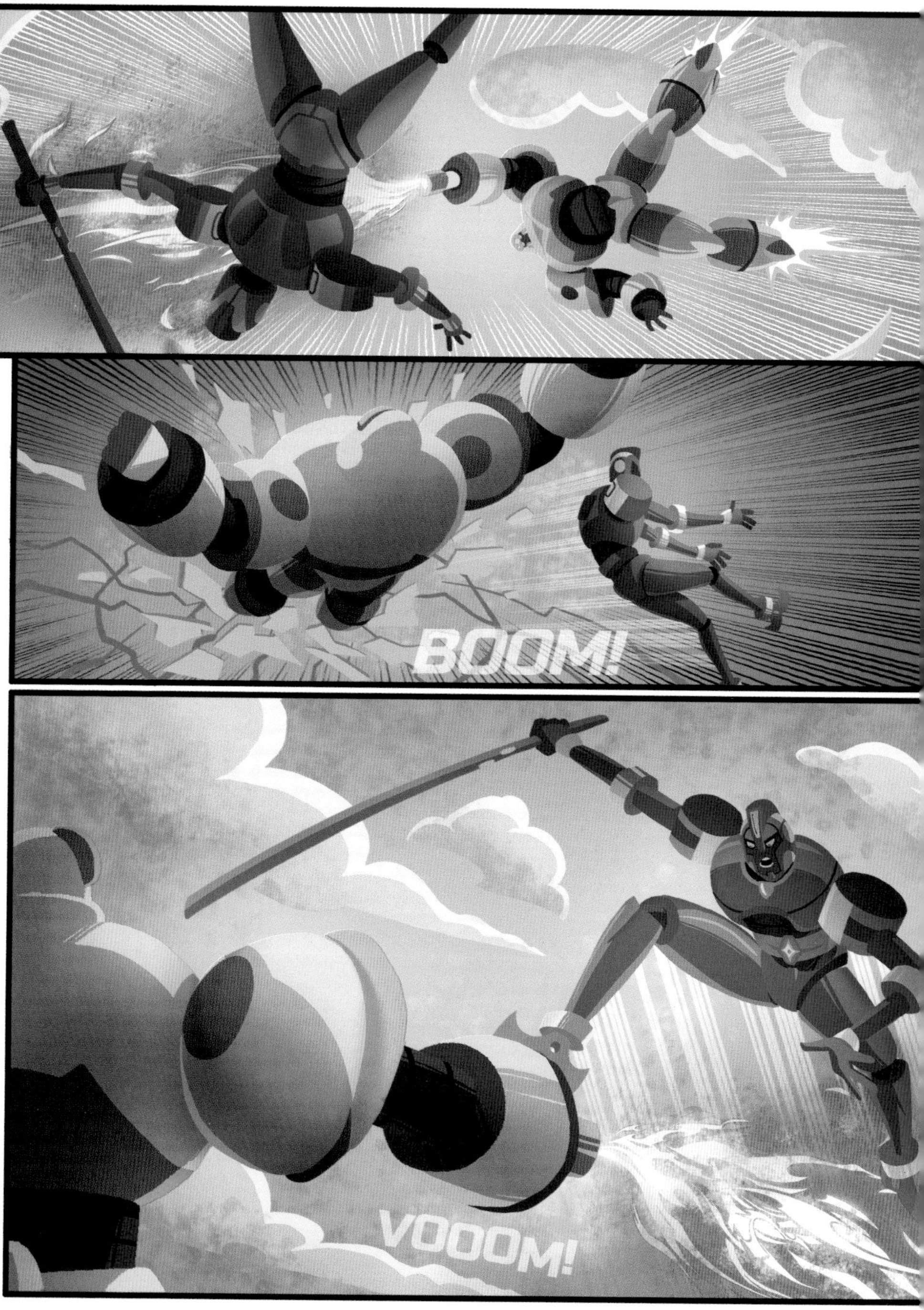
BOOM!
VOOOM!

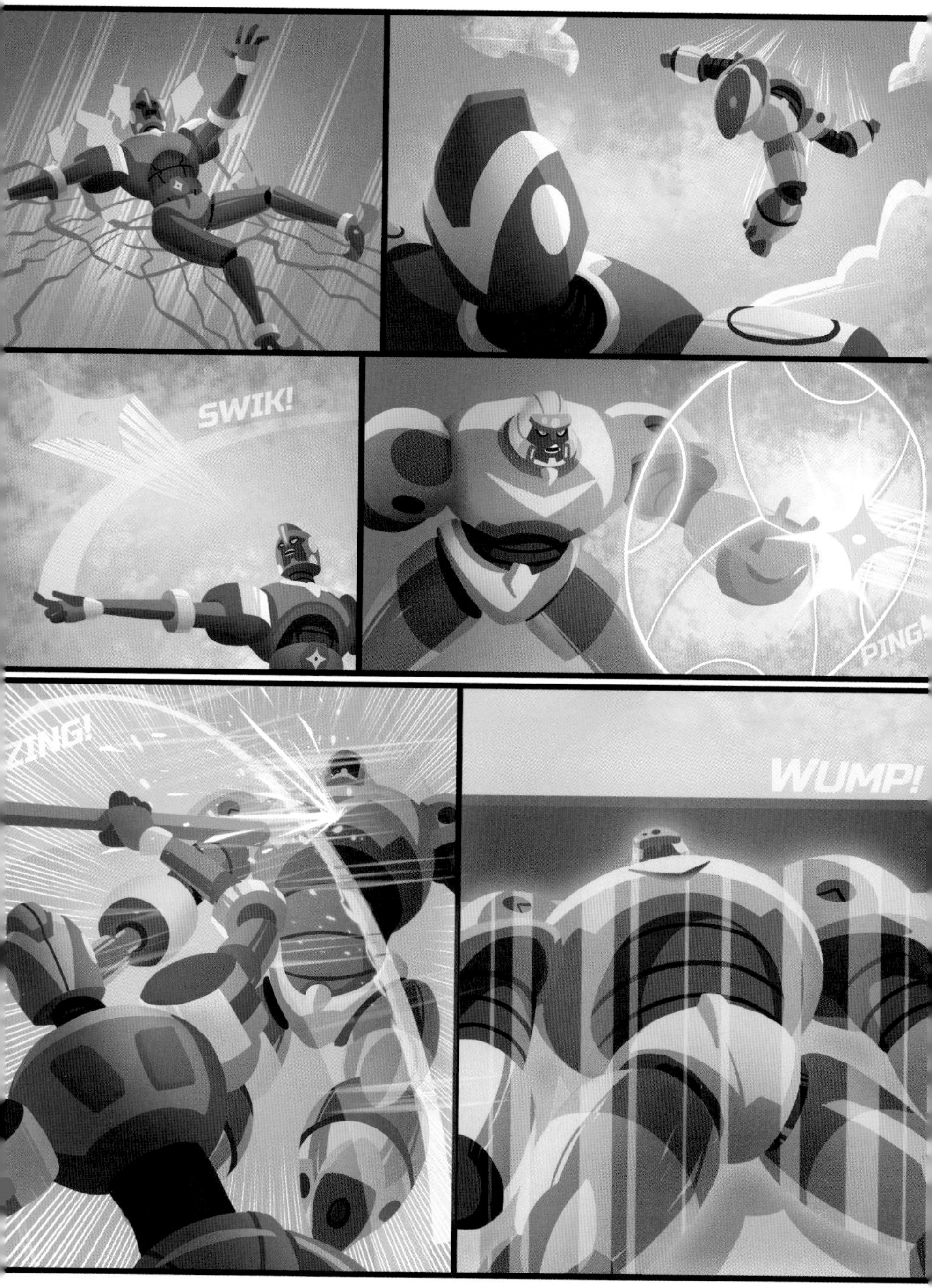
SWIK!
PING!
ZING!
WUMP!

132

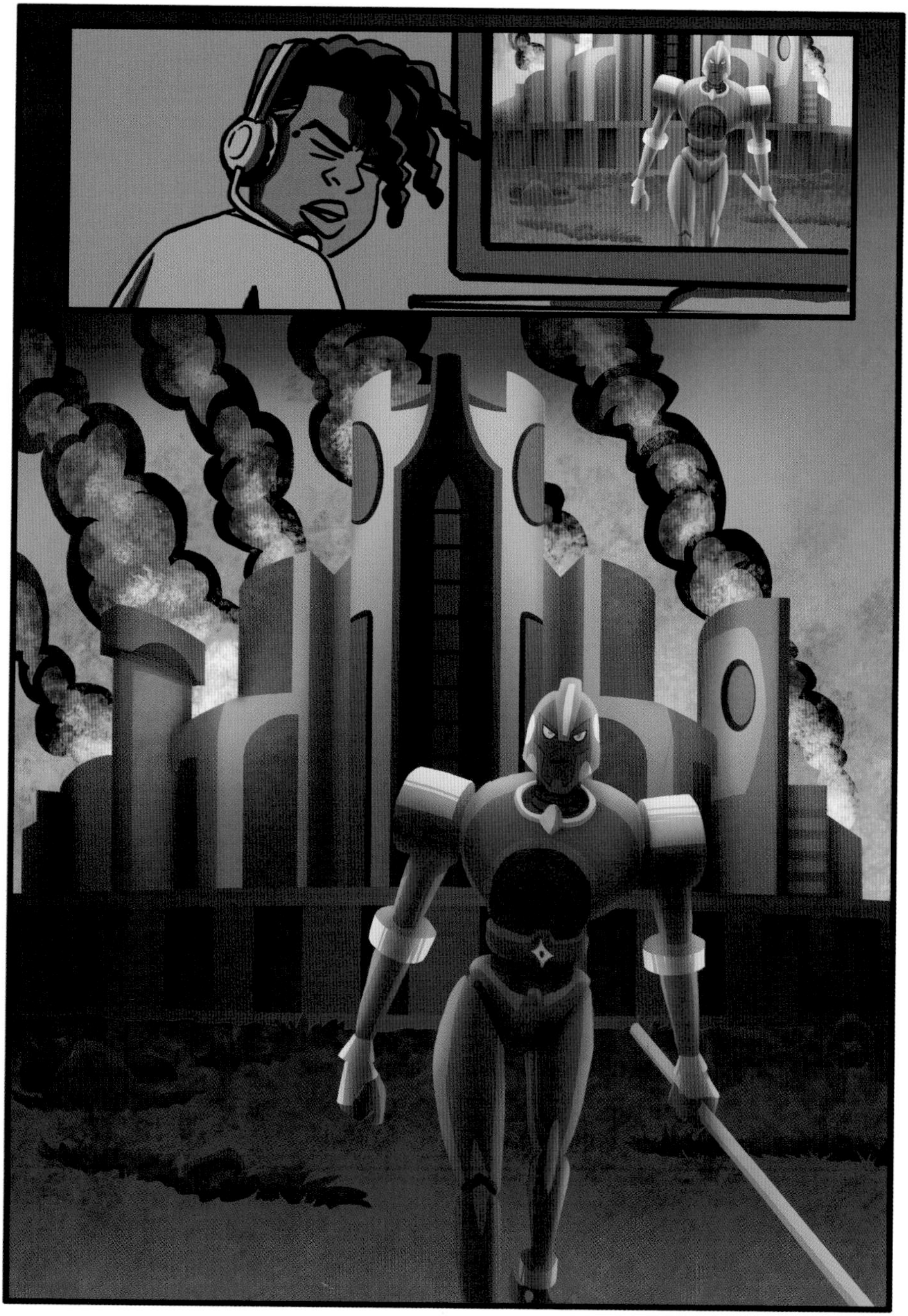

134

135

136

138

139

140

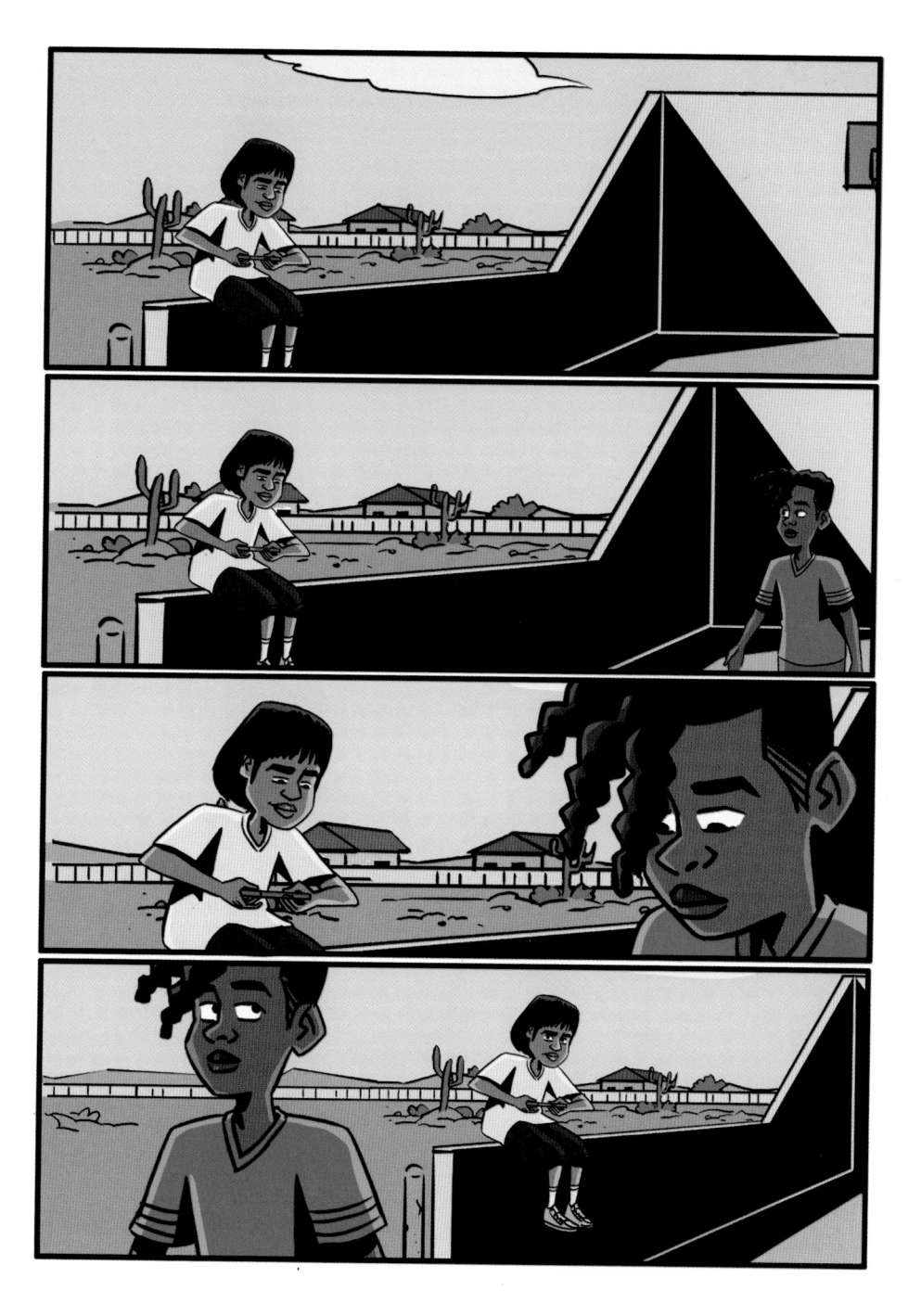

CHAPTER 9
EVERY GAME EVER

143

145

146

147

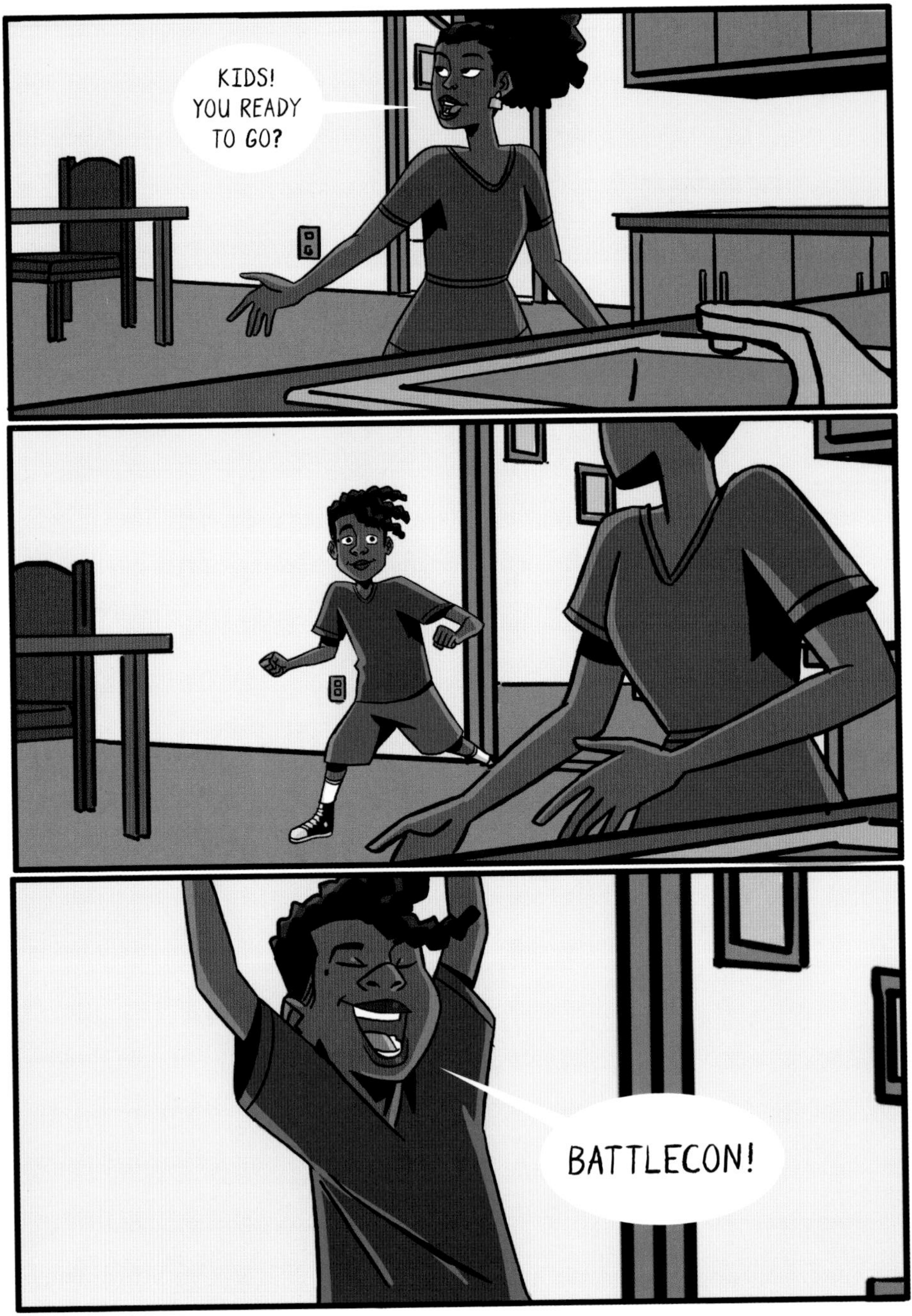
KIDS! YOU READY TO GO?
BATTLECON!

149

151

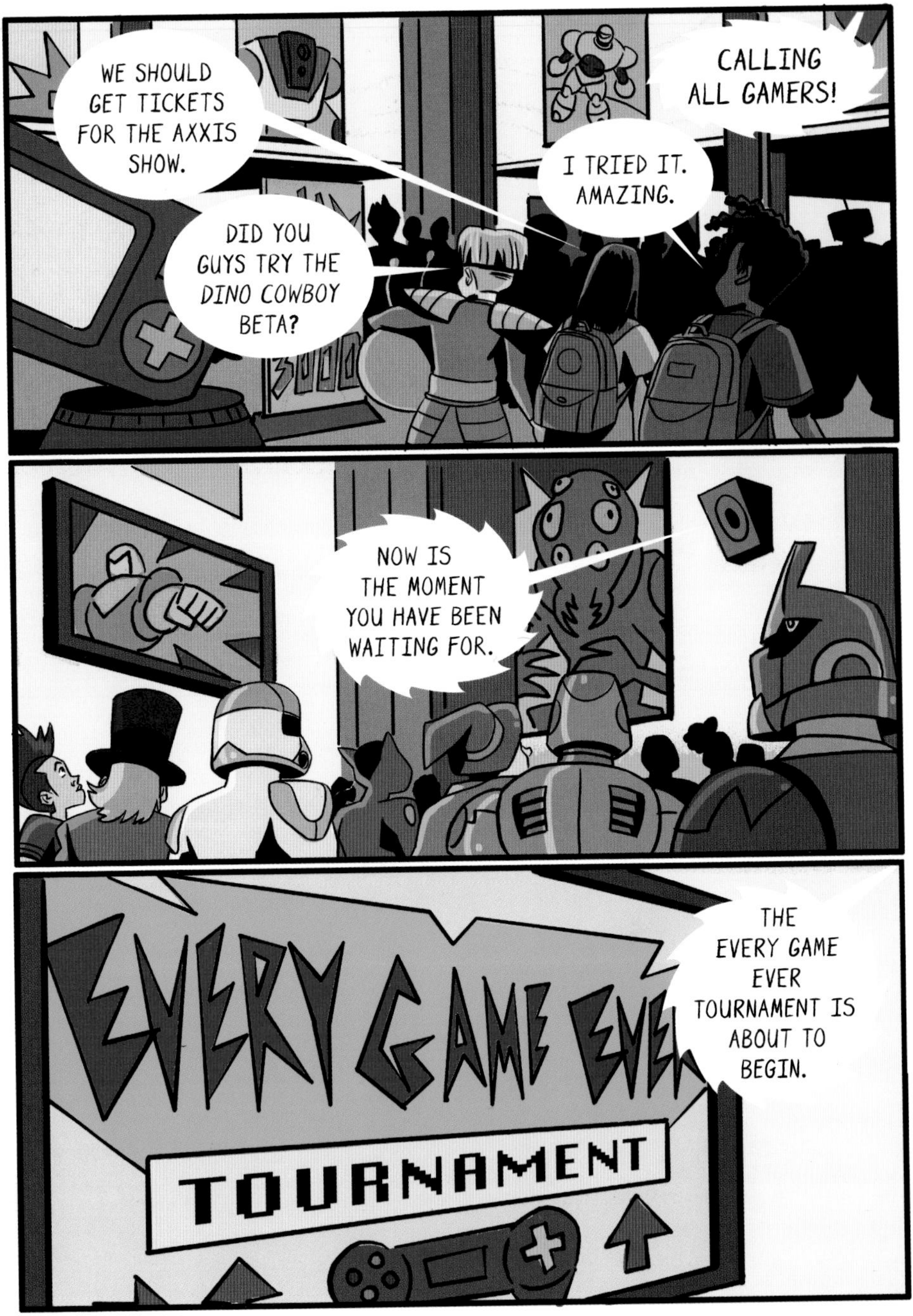
CALLING ALL GAMERS!
WE SHOULD GET TICKETS FOR THE AXXIS SHOW.
I TRIED IT. AMAZING.
DID YOU GUYS TRY THE DINO COWBOY BETA?
NOW IS THE MOMENT YOU HAVE BEEN WAITING FOR.
THE EVERY GAME EVER TOURNAMENT IS ABOUT TO BEGIN.
TOURNAMENT

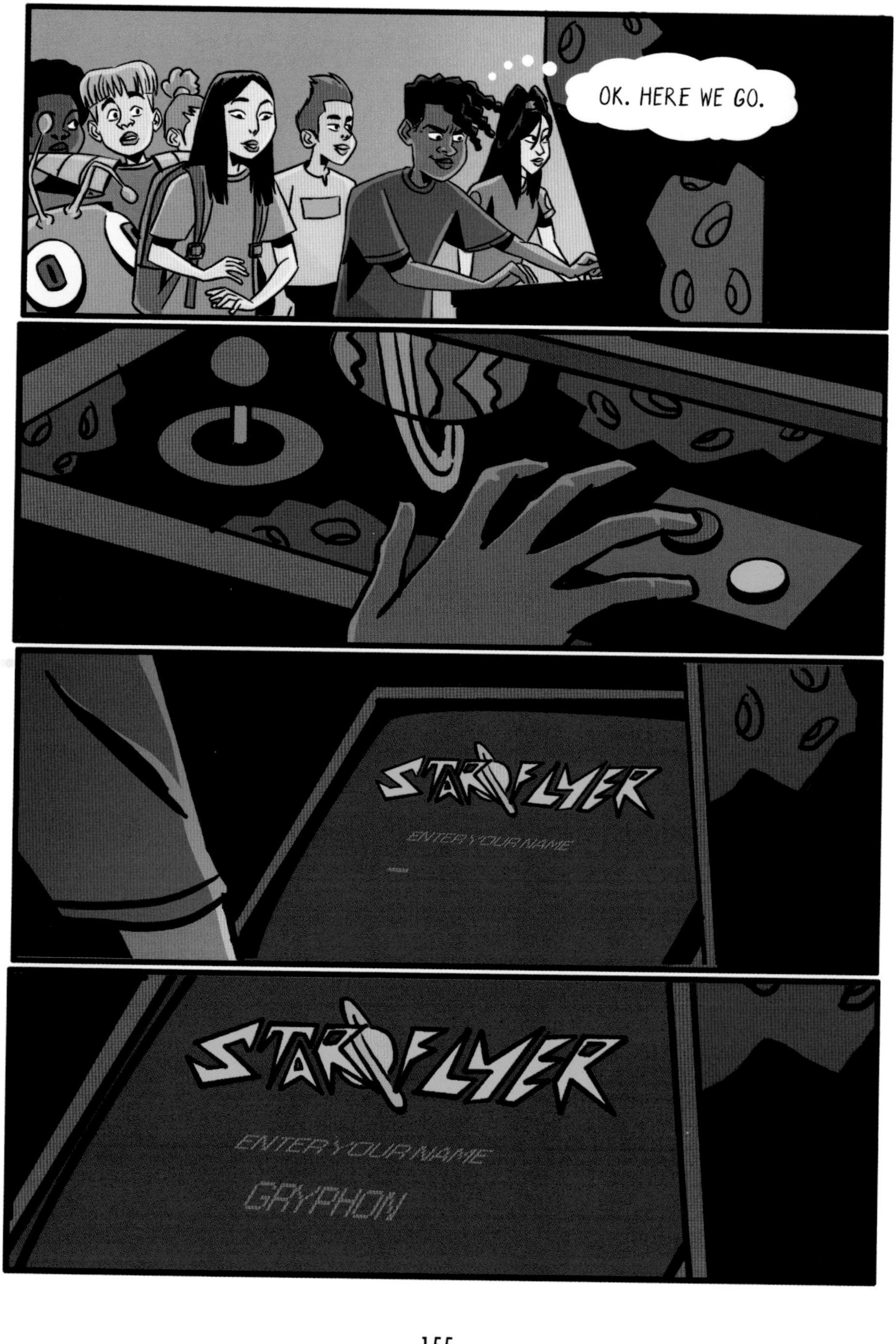
OK. HERE WE GO.
STAR FLYER
ENTER YOUR NAME
STAR FLYER
ENTER YOUR NAME
GRYPHON

156

157

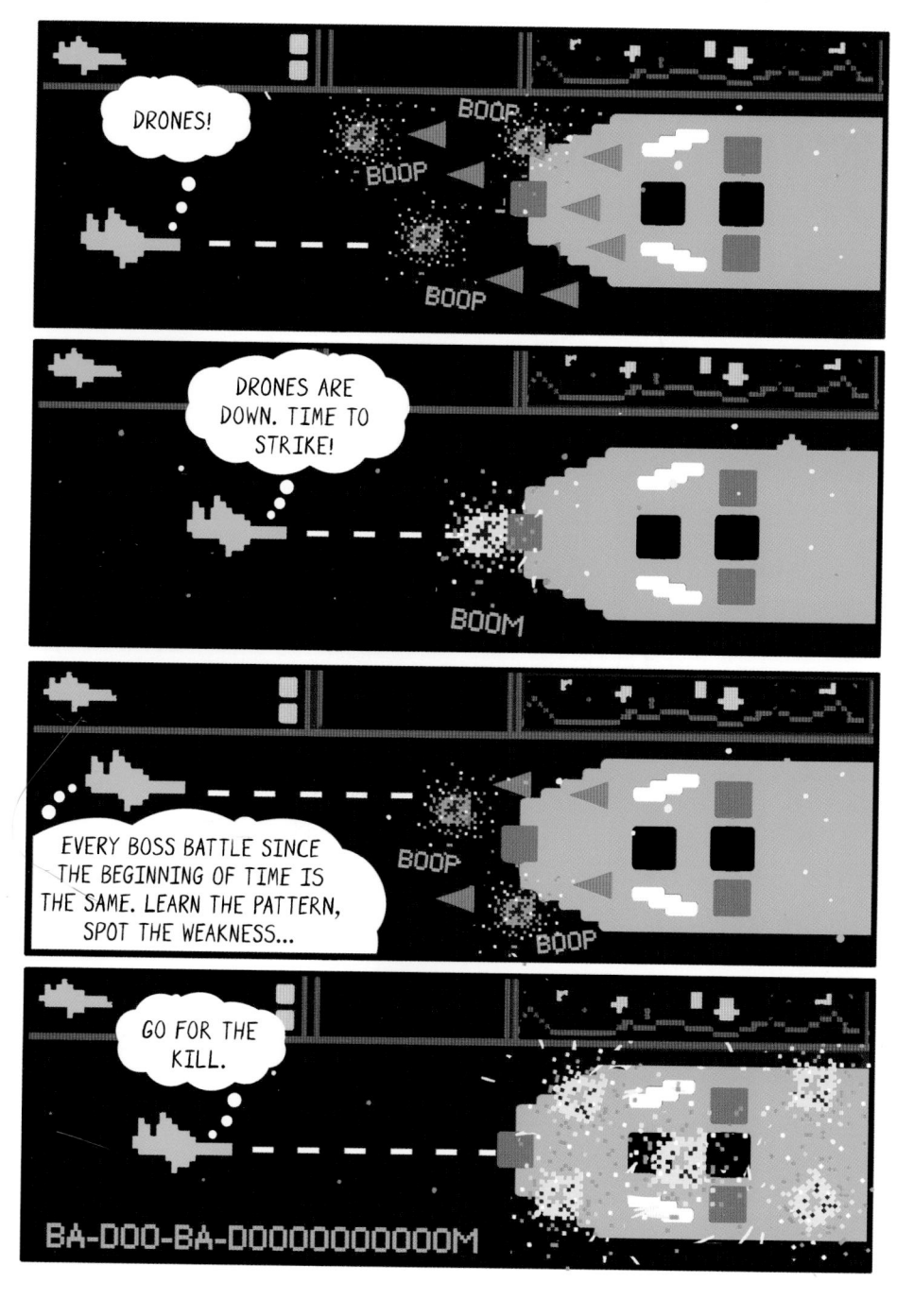

161

162

CHAPTER 10
ELIMINATIONS

165

167

168

170

171

175

176

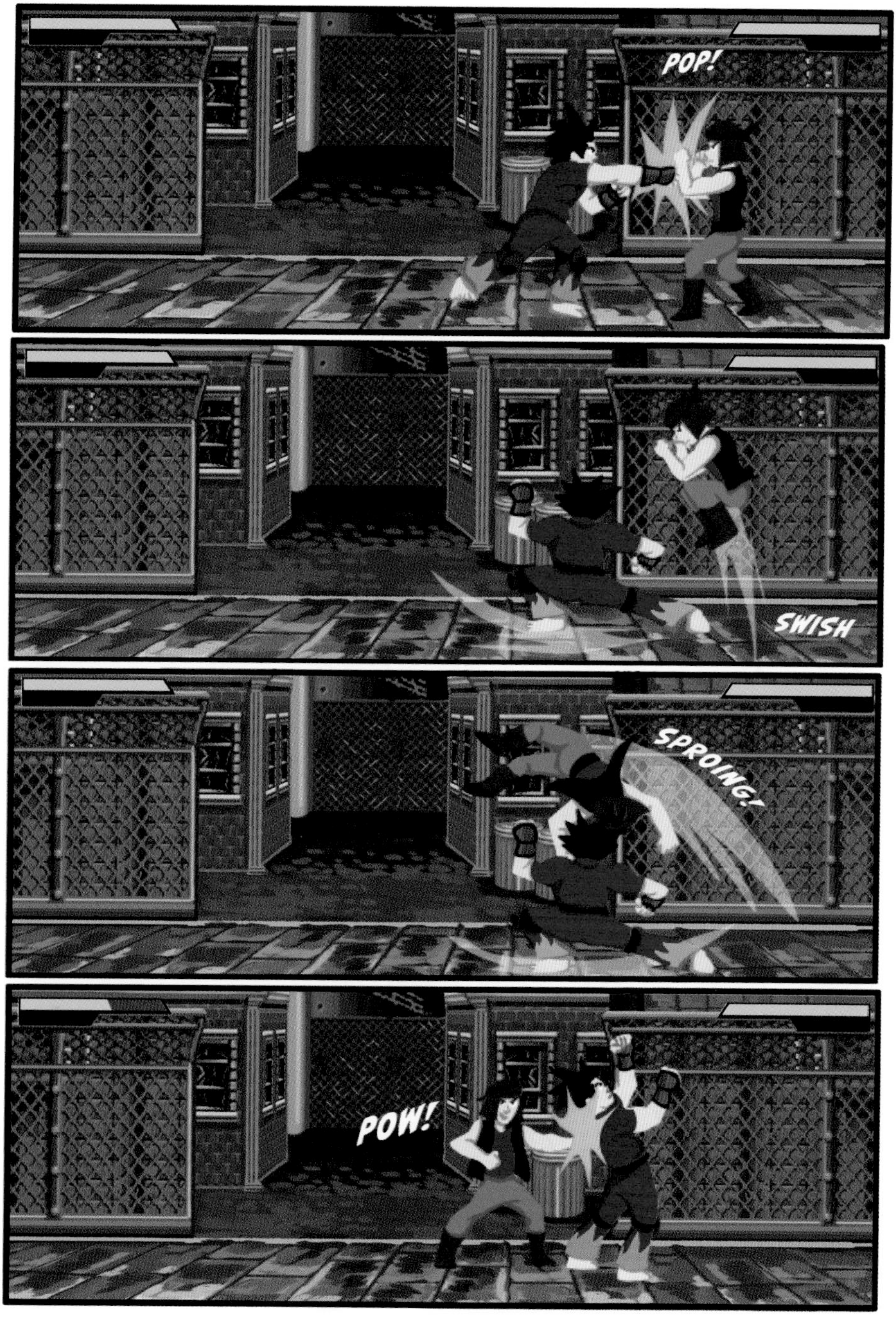
POP!
SWISH
SPROING!
POW!

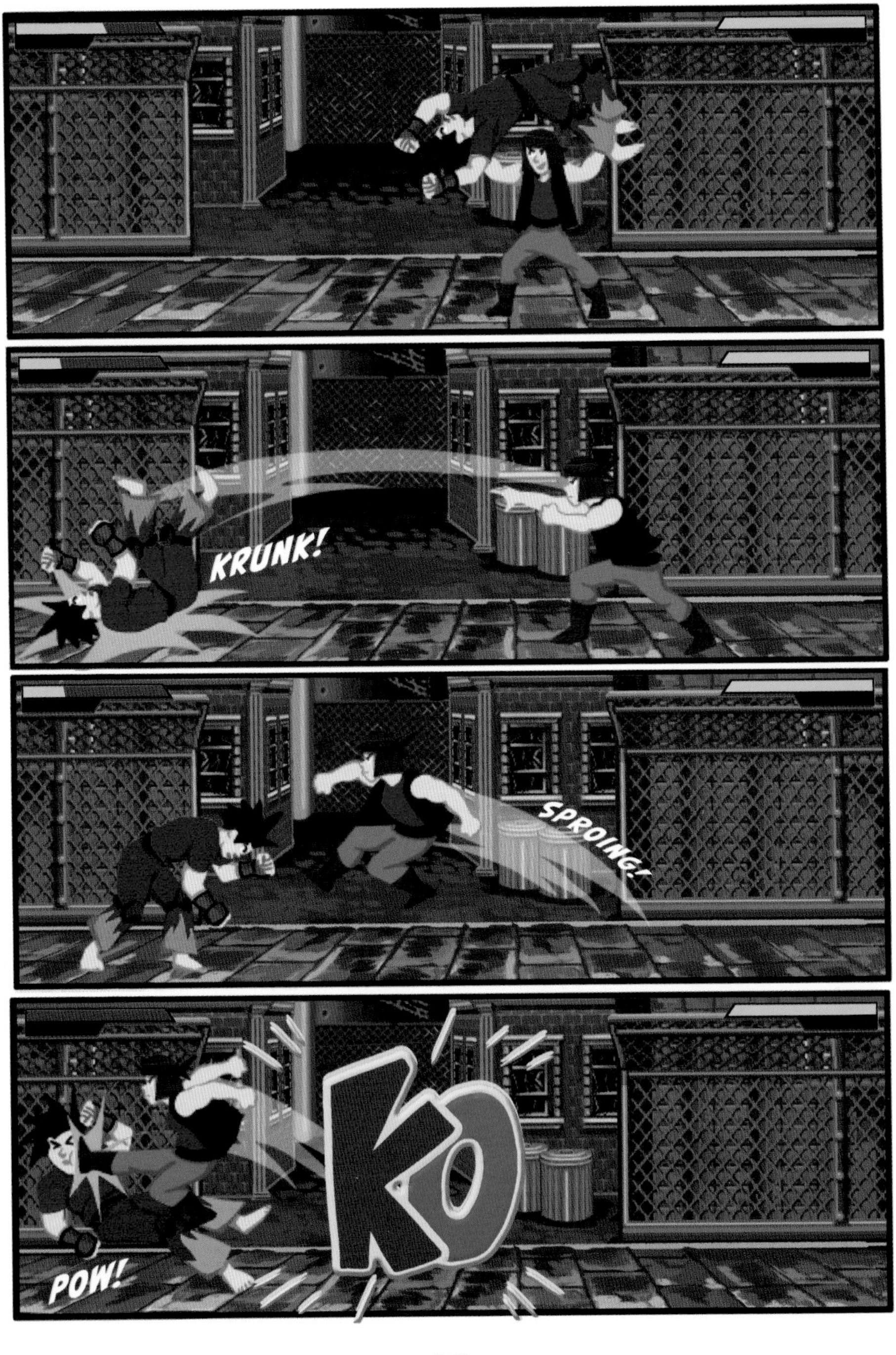
KRUNK!
SPROING!
KO
POW!

179

CHAPTER 11
DUO

181

182

183

186

187

188

189

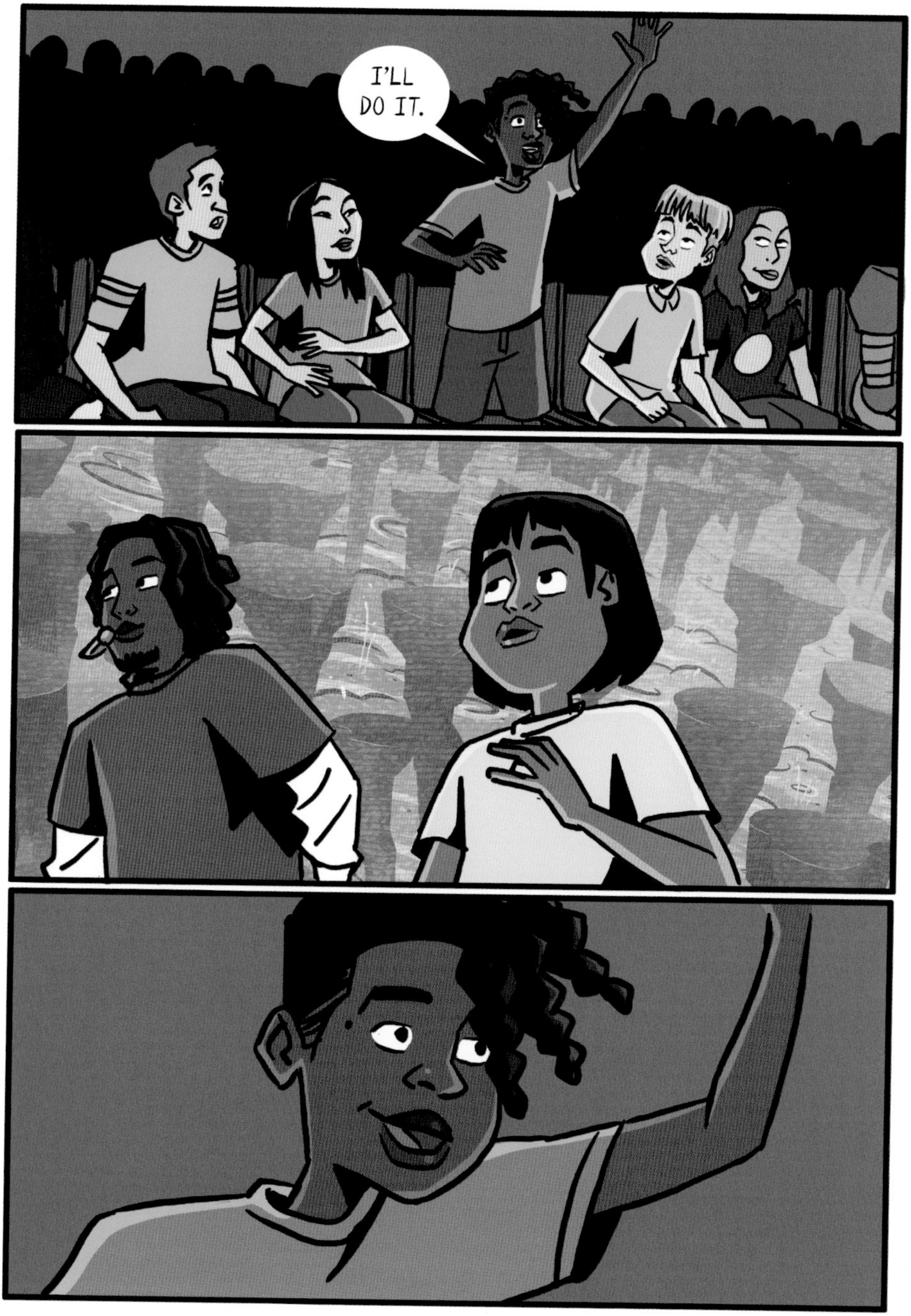
I'LL DO IT.

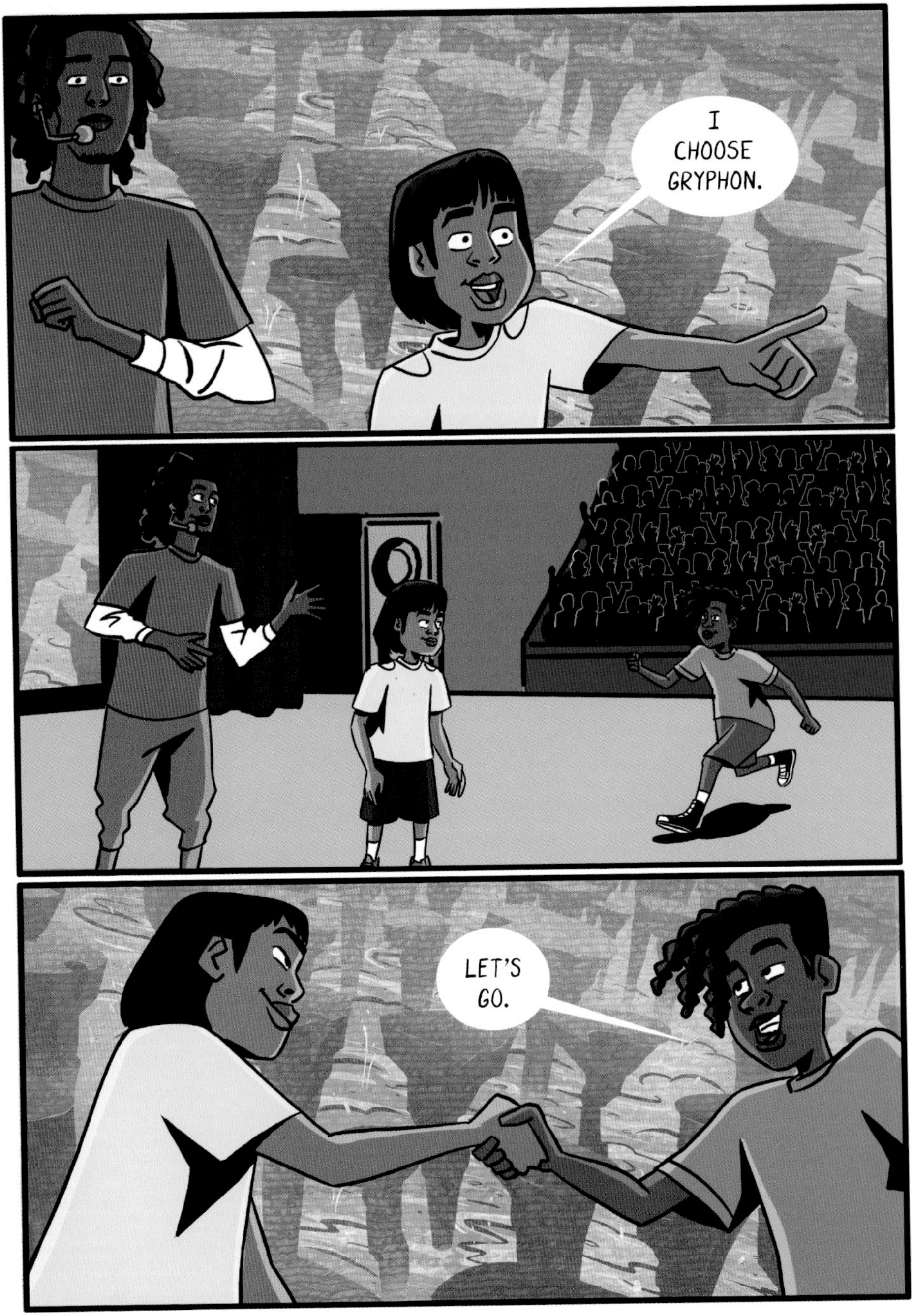
I CHOOSE GRYPHON.
LET'S GO.

193

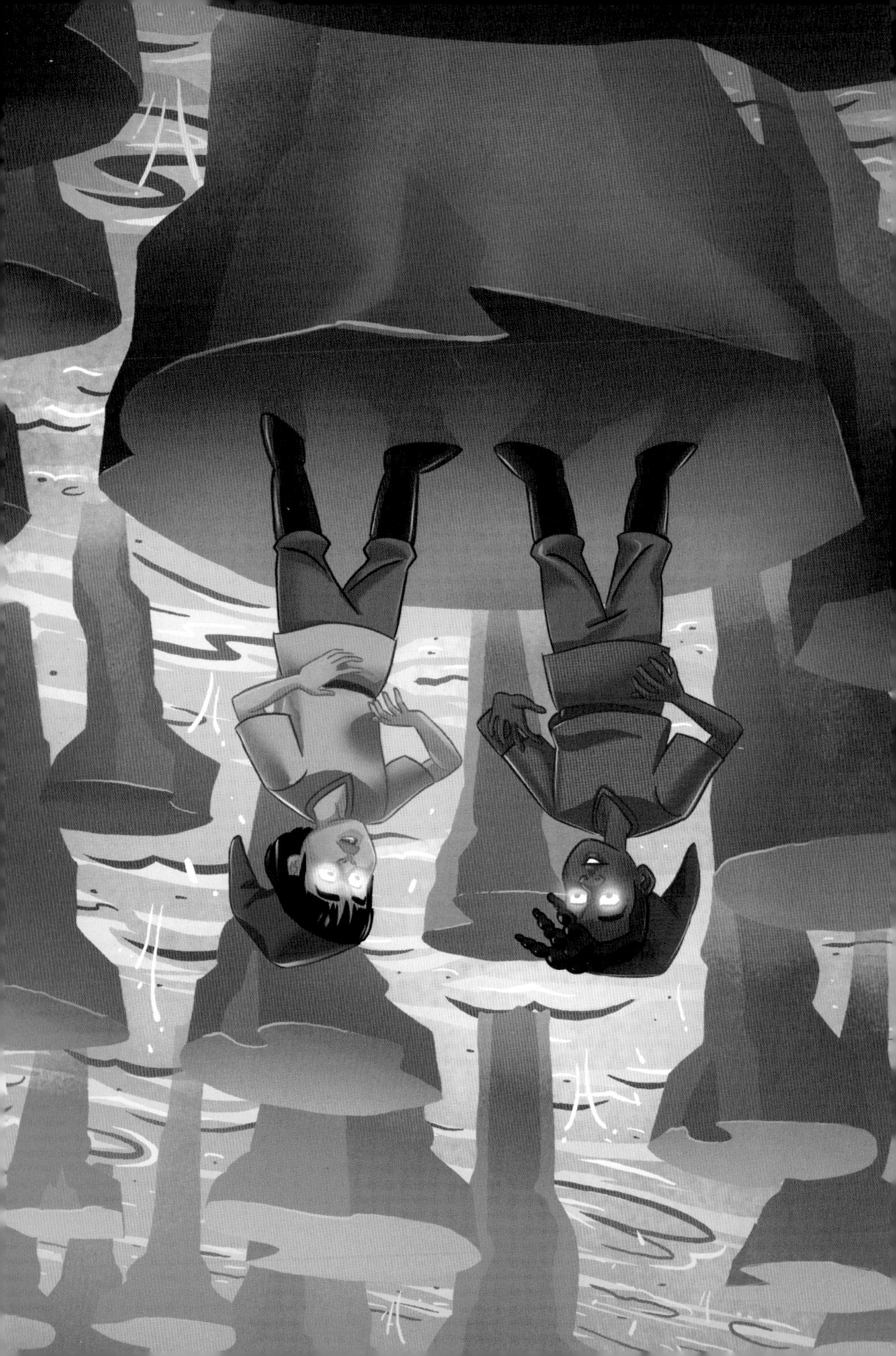

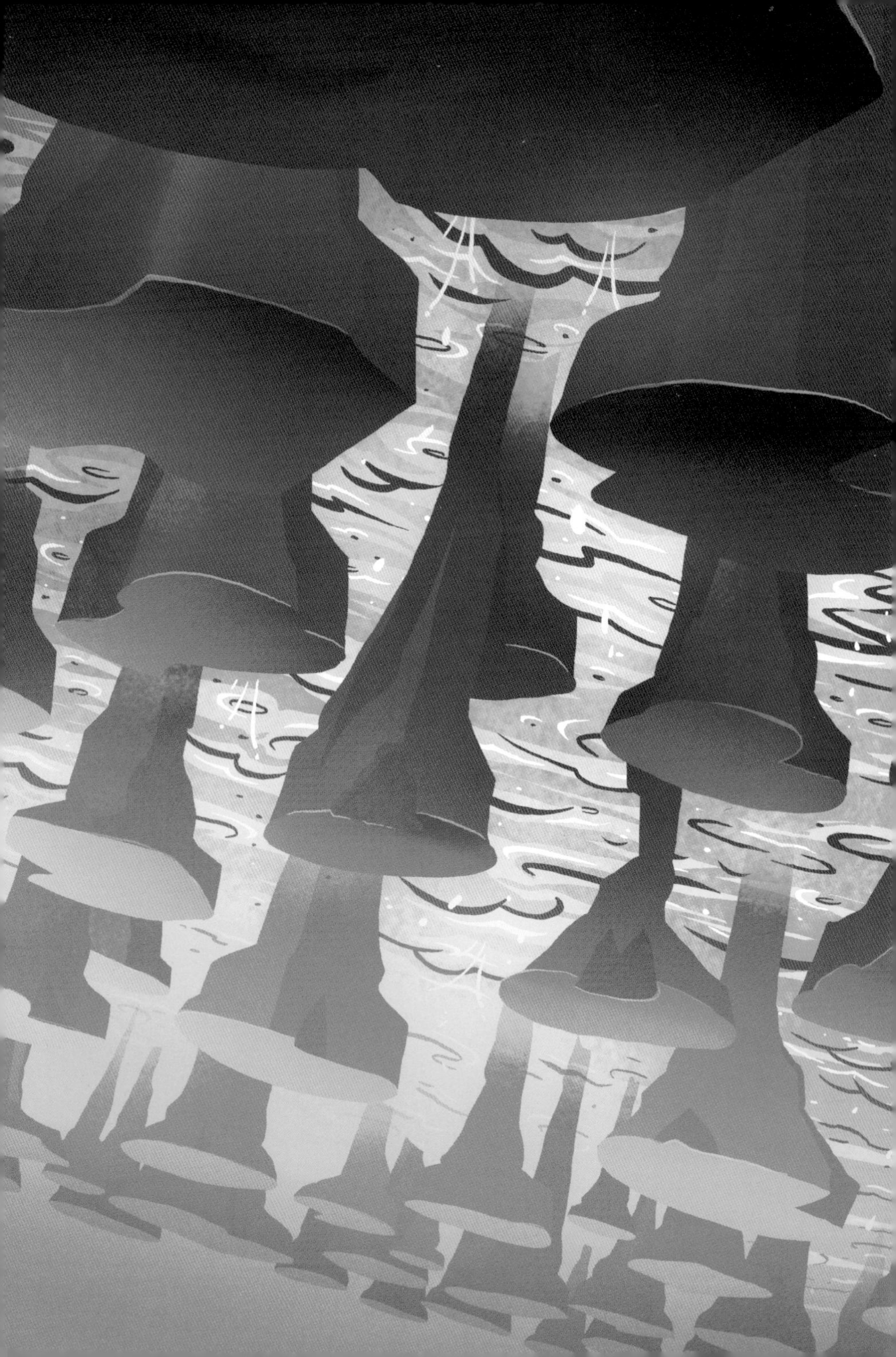

196

197

198

200

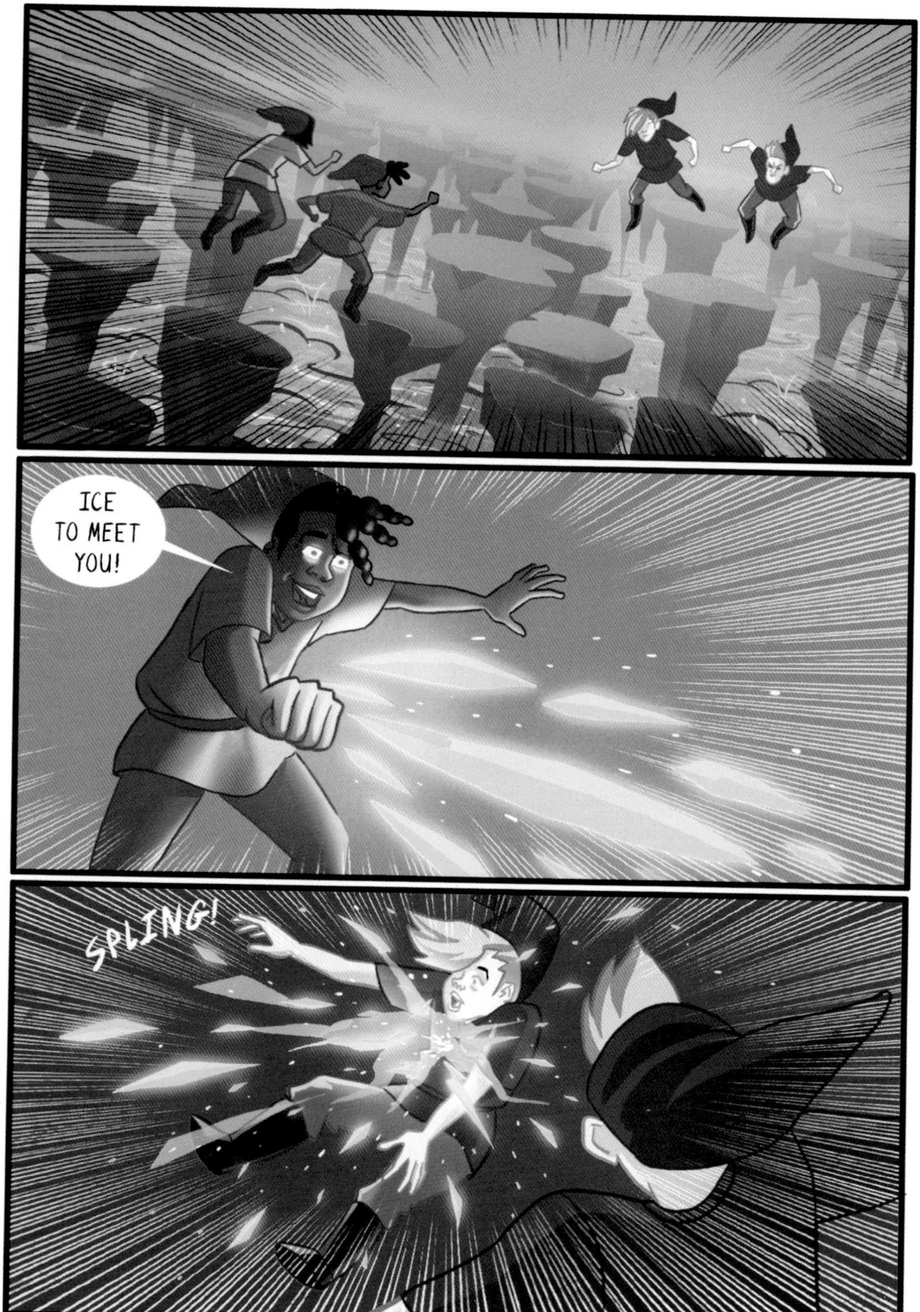
ICE TO MEET YOU!
SPLING!

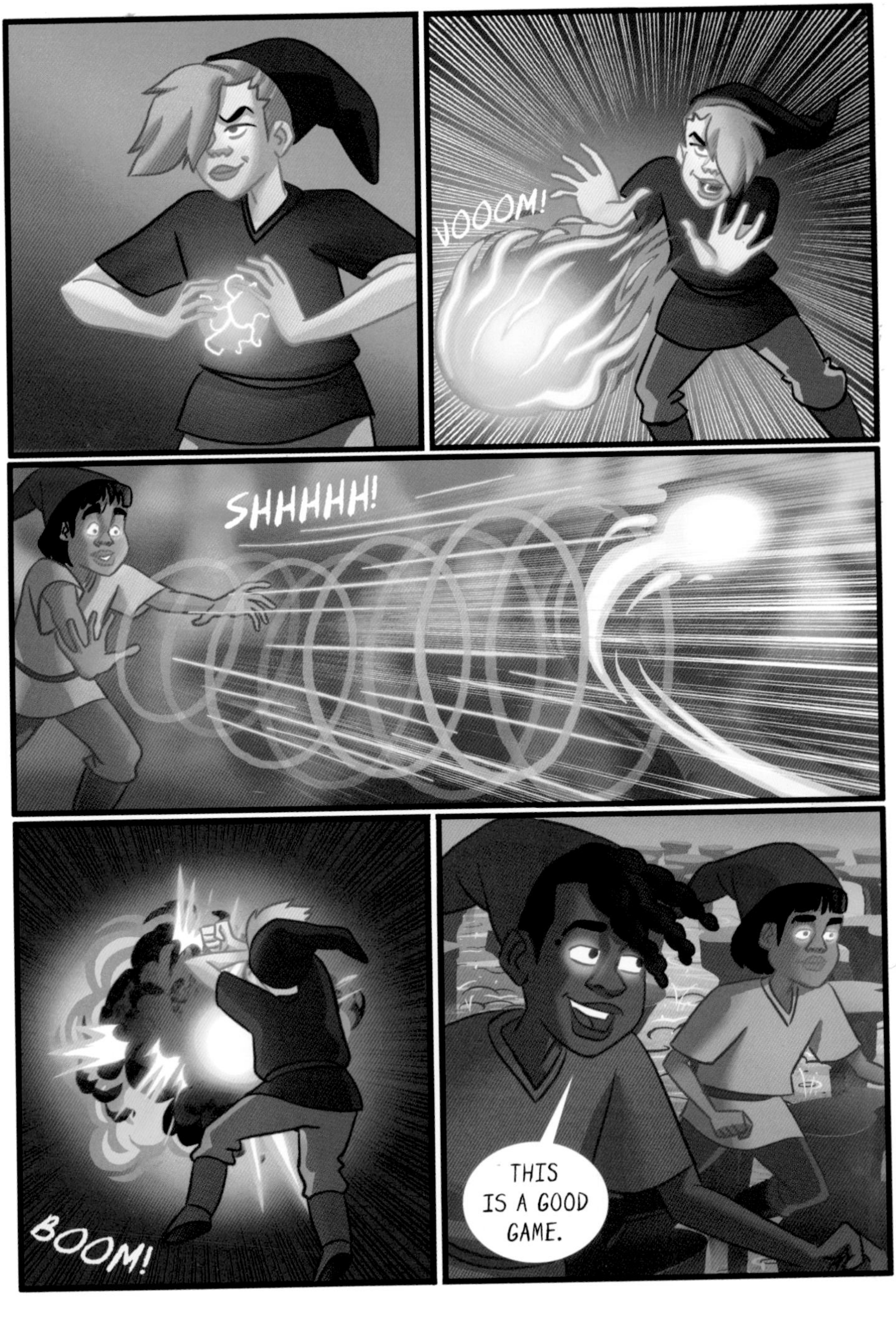
VOOOM!
SHHHHH!
BOOM!
THIS IS A GOOD GAME.

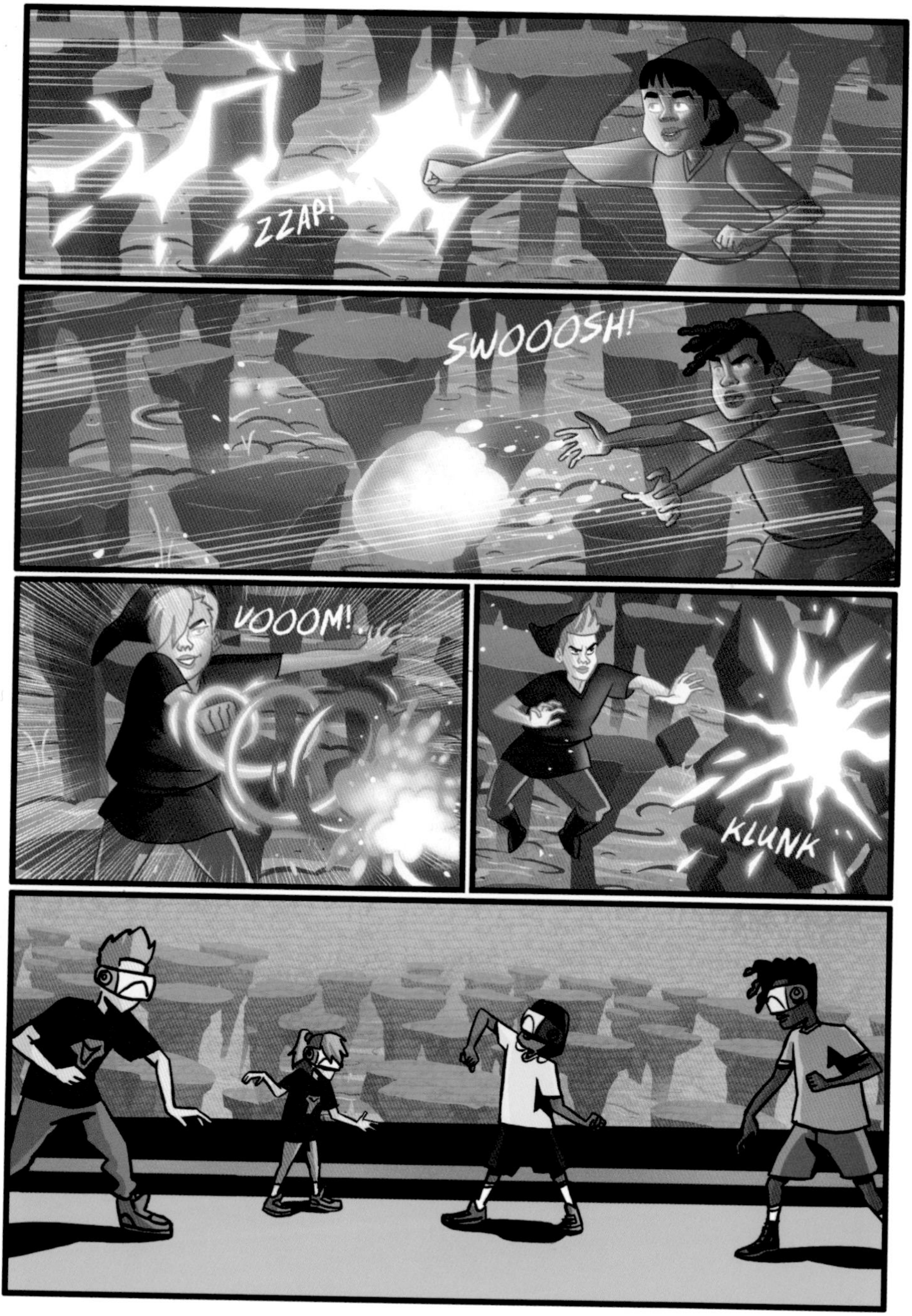
ZZAP!
SWOOOSH!
VOOOM!
KLUNK

205

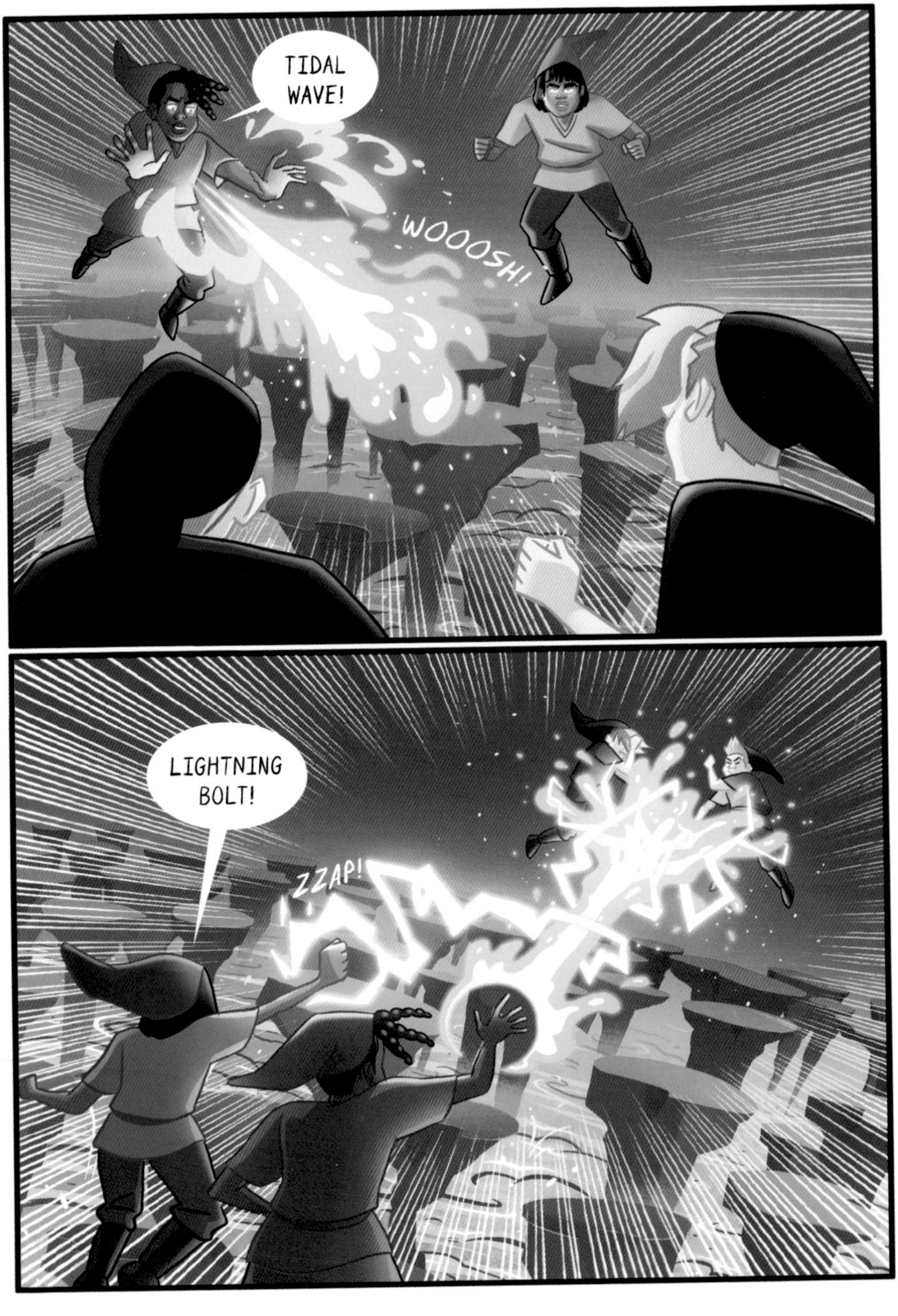
TIDAL WAVE!
WOOOSH!
LIGHTNING BOLT!
ZZAP!

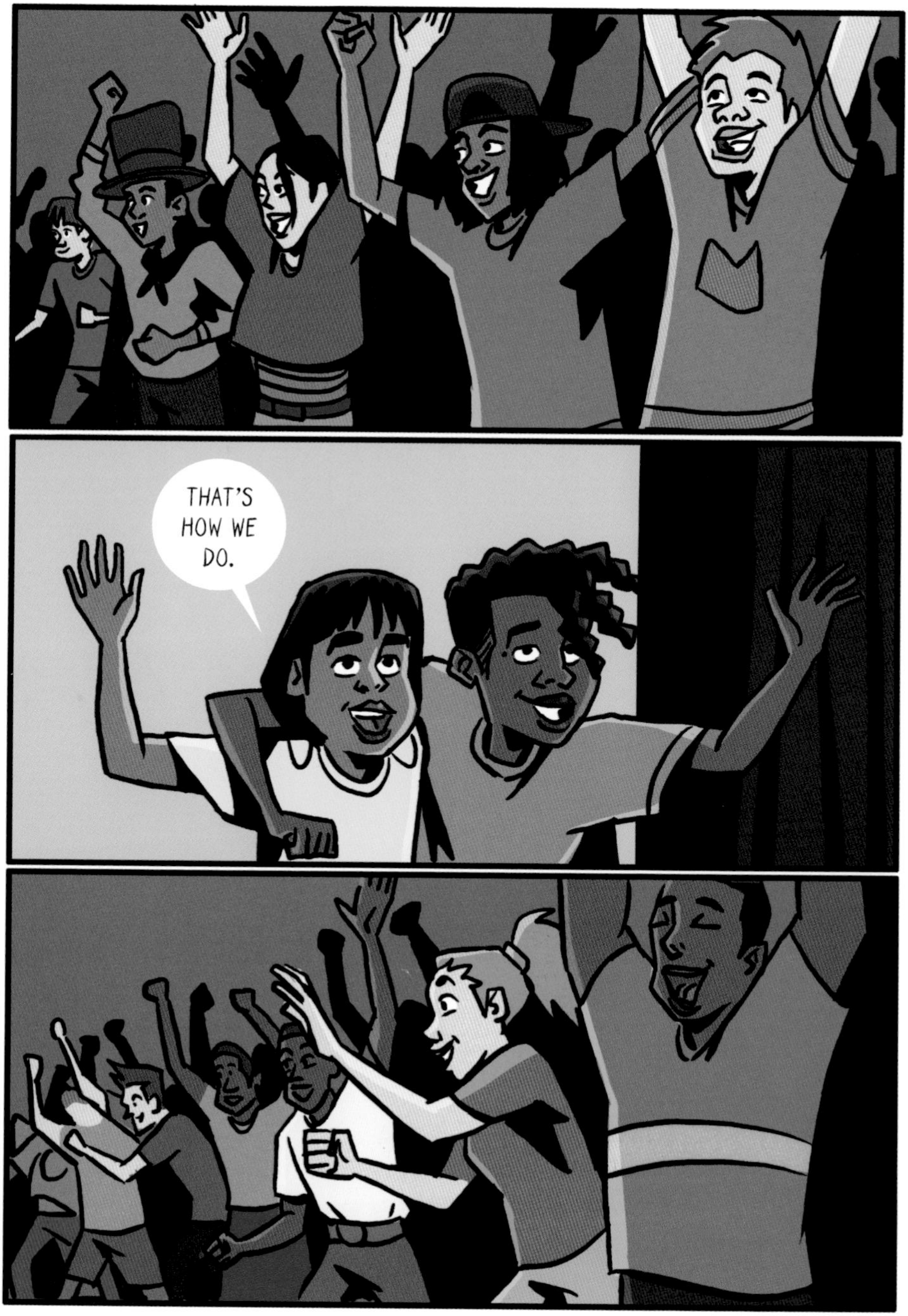
THAT'S HOW WE DO.

CHAPTER 12
NEW GAME

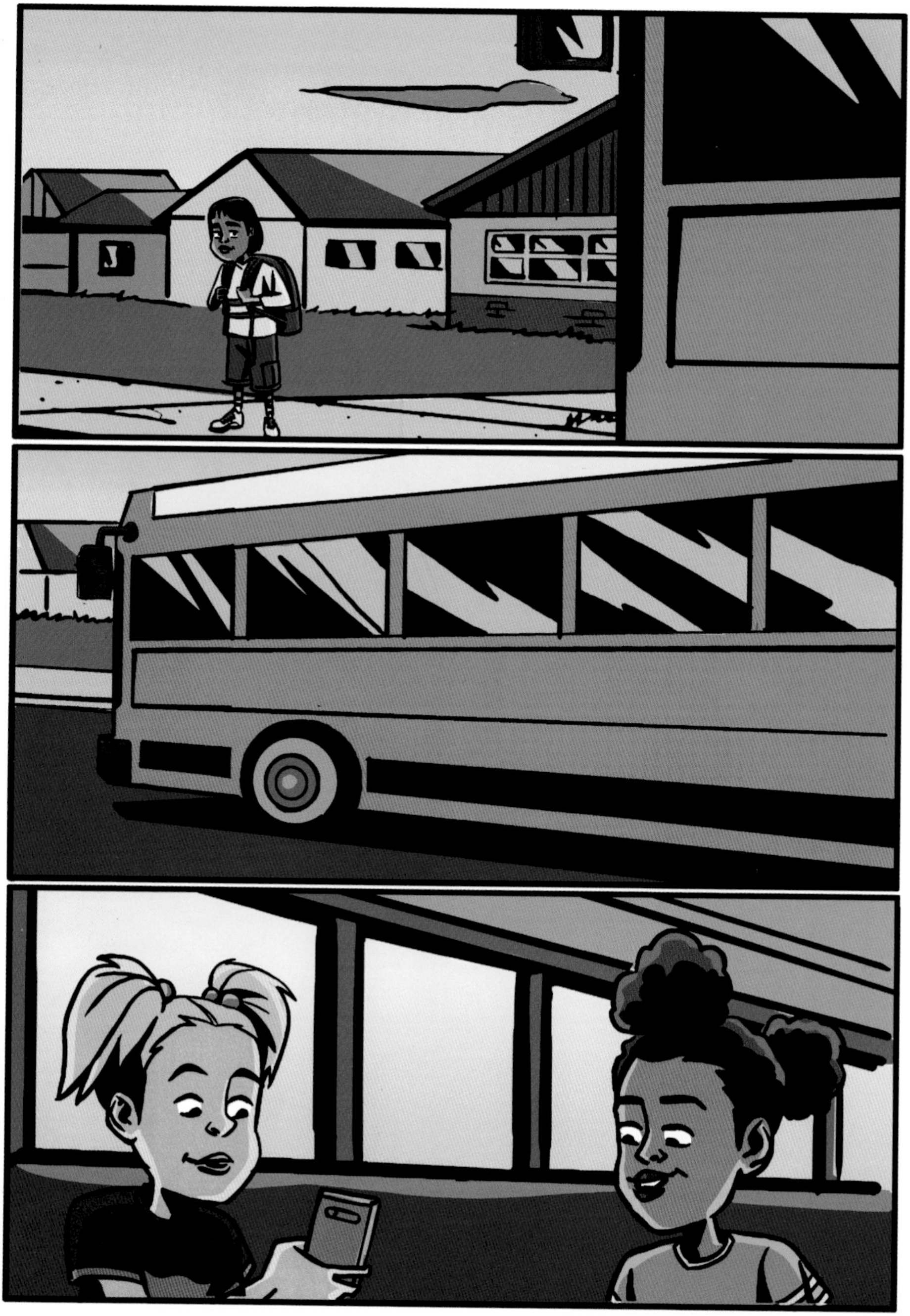

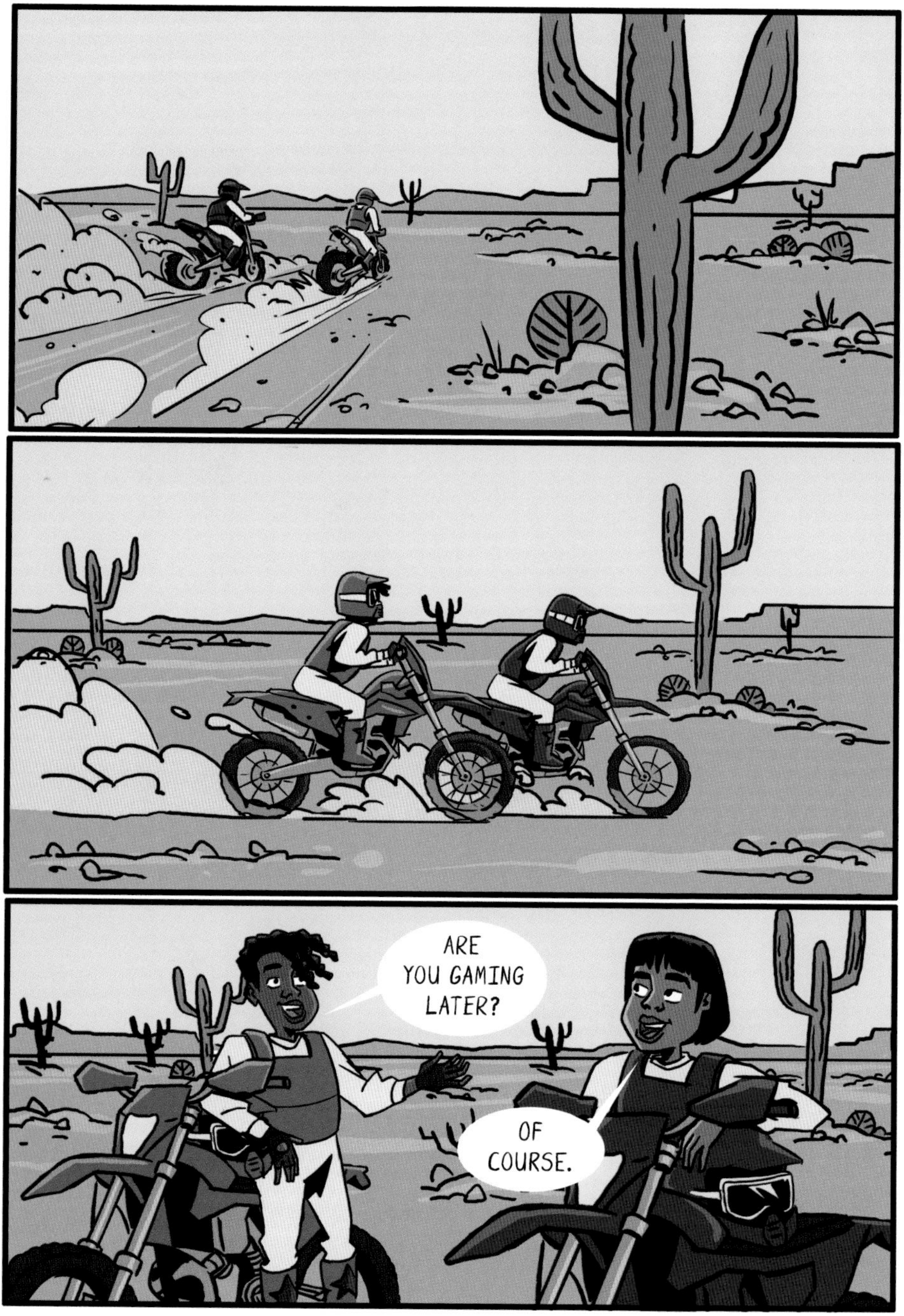
ARE YOU GAMING LATER?
OF COURSE.

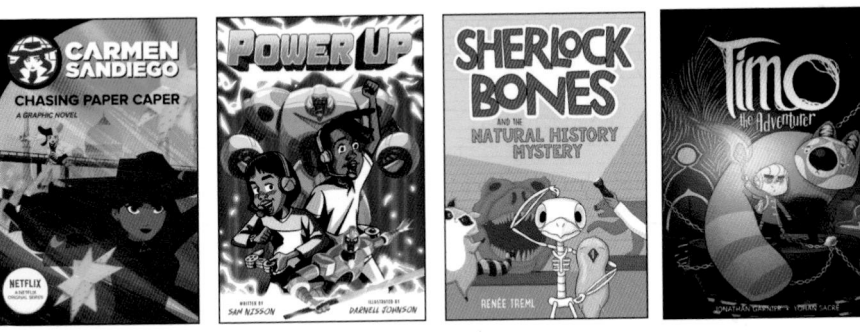

SQUAD UP

TO POWER UP:
LOOK FOR THE SEQUEL